THE FUTUR

In the center of t[...]u ever seen were two hu[...]wedge-shaped ships of gleaming metal. Kati's mouth hung open, and she stared.

"First Mother showed you the great ship in orbit around Shanji," said Huomeng. "That one brought our ancestors here. The ships you see here are the ones that brought us down to the surface of the planet. They have been waiting here for someone to use them again."

"They're so *large*," was all she could say.

"Magnetic lifters, and fusion drive. They each hold two hundred people. That's how many we were in the beginning, Kati; only four hundred people, and nobody was left on the mother ship in the end. She's been up there nearly two thousand years, quietly taking care of herself, waiting for our return."

On the surface, they fought with bows and swords. And she was the chosen one; she would lead them to their destiny.

THE FUTURE WAS YESTERDAY

In the center of the biggest cavern she'd ever seen were two huge wedge-shaped ships of gleaming metal. Kath's mouth hung open, and she stared.

"First Mother showed you, the great ship in orbit around Sheril," said Huommeg. "That one brought our ancestors here. The ships you see here are the ones that brought us down to the surface of the planet. They have been waiting here for someone to use them again."

"They're so large," was all she could say.

"Magnetic lifters, and fusion drive. They each hold two hundred people. That's how many we were in the beginning. Fath, only four hundred people, and nobody was left on the mother ship in the end. She's been up there nearly two thousand years, quietly taking care of herself, waiting for our return."

On the surface, they fought with bows and arrows. And she was the chosen one; she would lead them to their destiny.

SHANJI

JAMES C. GLASS

SHANJI

Copyright © 1999 by James C. Glass

A Baen Books Original

Baen Publishing Enterprises
P.O. Box 1403
Riverdale, NY 10471

ISBN: 0-671-57789-1

Cover art by Darrell K. Sweet

First printing, February 1999

Distributed by Simon & Schuster
1230 Avenue of the Americas
New York, NY 10020

Printed in the United States of America

FOR A.J., HONORED TEACHER

ACKNOWLEDGEMENTS

Special thanks go to John Dalmas for his valuable comments on the first draft of this book, and also to Mary Jane Engh for another reading. Thanks also to the Virginia Kidd Agency, the numerous editors and writer friends for their encouragement and support, and Algis Budrys for his teaching, especially during the WRITERS OF THE FUTURE workshop in 1991. Finally, love and thanks to my wife Gail, for putting up with all the quiet hours.

Notes On Character And Place Names

All names have meanings, and are drawn from either Mongol or Mandarin roots on Old Earth. The Tumatsin people are more closely related to Mongol, while the Hansui are ethnically pure Han. Names of the telepathic *Moshuguang* (Magic Light) elite are often compounded with *Meng* (dream) or *Moshu* (magic), and the reader should carefully note these names as they first appear, in order to avoid later confusion.

Key names are given in the following listing:

Gong-shi-jie (world of light), the source of light which fed the big bang, and formed our universe.

Huomeng (fire dream), Kati's teacher and confidant.

Juimoshu (old magic), Moshuguang woman, and the Emperor's seer.

Kati (pronounced Kahtee), short form of Katian.

Mandughai, Mongol name of the warrior-empress of Tengri-Nayon. Known as First Mother by the Hansui people.

Mei-lai-gong (ruler of light), super-being long sought by the Moshuguang to transfer energy and mass at infinite speed within the gong-shi-jie.

Mengmoshu (dream magic), the Chancellor of the Moshuguang.

Mengnu (dream daughter), the name given to Kati in the Emperor's city.

Mengyao (dream medicine), Mengmoshu's executive officer.

Moshuguang (magic light), a telepathic brotherhood of scientists and engineers working with First Mother to bring new rule to Shanji.

Shan-Lan (blue mountain), Crown Prince of Shanji.

Shanji, short form of *Shan-shi-jie* (mountain world).

Sheyue (musk), Kati's palace companion.

Shizi (lion), mountain cat of Shanji.

Tanchun (taste of spring), Weimeng's servant.

Tengri-Khan (sky ruler), Shanji's sun.

Tengri-Nayon (sky prince), neighboring star, from which the first people of Shanji fled a harsh rule.

Toregene (princess), Kati's mother.

Weimeng (dream feeling), Emperor's First Wife, and Kati's foster mother.

PART I
TUMATSIN

PART II
WARD

PART III
CHANGELING

PART IV
MEI-LAI-GONG

of drums, horns, and clashing cymbals of yellow metal

PROLOGUE

Toregene awoke to the turbine scream of a flyer, and discovered that her right leg was numb. She'd been crammed in the spider-trap like a cork in a bottle since dusk, and had somehow worked her right leg beneath her in sleep. No feeling there, clear up to her hip, and her neck and shoulders ached from the hours of hunching forward in the tiny space. For a moment she dared not move, and listened.

The flyer had passed right over her position, so low she could smell aromatics still raining from its wake. The engine whine diminished as the craft sped west towards the mountains, then steadied. The spider-trap was at the edge of a cliff overlooking Hulagu valley, a precariously placed strategic spot. Instinctively, Toregene opened her eyes and concentrated on the darkness, emptying her mind of any vision that might attract a Searcher. The patrols were daring and thorough, and there were always Searchers among them to invade the mind of an intruder.

Toregene listened for the snap of a twig, the crunch of a boot on needle-carpet, and heard only the caress of wind on the trees. The earth around her smelled of humus and damp roots. Something crawled across her cheek, and she flicked it off with a finger.

After some moments, she dared to move, pressing her back against dampness and straightening the pinned leg. Feeling returned; the pricks of a thousand knives, the

1

pain a Searcher's beacon if one were nearby. But now she was fully awake, and aware. This late at night, without even moonlight to guide their steps among the tangle of trees and brush, the ground troops would be confined to the valley, and rely on flyers to locate and report any pesky bands of Tumatsin who dared to interfere with the Emperor's occupation of their lands.

The flyer had made a great circle, and was now north of her, engine throbbing as the pilot cut back power for the return descent to the valley. Toregene sat up and pushed on the woven-needle roof of the spider-trap, raising it a half-meter on silent hinges, and staking it open on the side overlooking the valley. She got up on her knees, and looked out in time to see the flyer descending into the valley to a landing place behind a cluster of pre-fab buildings. Beyond the buildings stood great earthmovers at the edge of Tumatsin barley fields, now stubble, with even the gleanings gone to the Emperor's warehouses.

Two men got out of the bubble-canopied craft, and the orange of their auras was a good sign the patrol had been routine. The men entered one of the buildings there, and immediately the surrounding area was flooded with light from a dozen panels around the circumference of the encampment. A hundred or more troopers suddenly strolled there, all heavily armed. Toregene smiled, for there were no auras to be seen among the many men who magically appeared with the lights. They were merely projected images of some sort to give the illusion of a heavily guarded camp. Even so, Toregene scanned the area carefully, especially near the earthmovers poised for the destruction of Tumatsin fields, huge machines with tires the height of two men, and gleaming blades to level the earth for the Emperor's new living space.

She found two auras by the earthmovers, a third strolling the area around the metal buildings, a fourth walking the camp perimeter just outside of the light panels. Four troopers guarding the entire camp, at least two more inside the buildings, and how many more? Four, perhaps eight at most, she guessed. A single squad of Tumatsin warriors could take the camp and destroy it in a single night.

The thought frightened her, for Temujin would certainly vie for leadership of such an attack, and her marriage to him was but a week away. Her report could endanger the life of her chosen *bahadur* before their love could be formally confirmed or consummated, though they had been together many times.

And for what purpose? Destruction of the earthmovers was at best a delaying action, and retaliation was certain to follow, as it had against the tiny valley *ordu* of Dejmat; a dozen Tumatsin murdered by laser fire for simply refusing to leave the homes of their ancestors.

Tengri-Nayon glowed red near the zenith, the home star from which their ancestors had fled, the distant companion to yellow Tengri-Khan, which warmed this world of Shanji. The time of closest approach of the red star was within a generation, completing another two-hundred year cycle. Only once had it brought an attacking army daring enough to challenge the iron-fisted Emperor of two thousand years past. Two thousand years ago—a defeat so overwhelming it was alive, yet, in bitter Tumatsin tradition, in song, and story. In a few years, Tengri-Nayon would be the brightest star in the sky, and the cycle would be closed again. One more chance, but no more, for Toregene was certain that in another two hundred years there would be no Tumatsin left to greet their ancestors.

Toregene ducked instinctively as the door to the largest building below her opened, spilling out light. Four men came out in full battle-dress, carrying rifles, walking through the images of countless troopers to replace the real men guarding the encampment. Raucous laughter came from the open door, and music. Toregene quickly revised her estimate of troopers to sixteen, waited until the replaced guards had entered the building and closed the door again before she crawled out of her spider-trap. She pulled out her satchel and lowered the roof carefully, smoothing over the seams with a light covering of needles before slinking away from the edge of the cliff and onto the faint game trail leading away from it. Her leather-clad feet made no sound. Tengri-Khan would rise in a few hours, and it was a two hour walk to the temporary ordu Temujin had set up to keep watch on the valley.

She walked easily in the darkness, for the sky was clear, and starlight was sufficient for the eyes of a Tumatsin woman. But with the blessing of such sight there was danger, for the great cats who hunted the meadows and crags ahead could mistake her for one of their own, and become territorially aggressive.

The trail rose gradually to a rock fall at the base of a granitic spire, and along a narrow shelf to a skree field to the south. Toregene stopped there briefly to retrieve the goat-leather bag of fluorescent fungus from her satchel. The bag was half-filled from collecting along the way to her observing post, but she'd passed up three glowing clusters of the delicious seasoning under trees bordering the meadows on the way back to the *ordu*. She would take full advantage of her night travel.

She crossed the skree field, and the trail reappeared, heading down into thick stands of White Bark and shining Tysk. Above the tree tops loomed the sharp peaks of granite and schist extending tens of kilometers to the great sea west, hundreds of kilometers north and south. Shanji. The mountain world. Toregene navigated the trail by feel in the inky darkness of the forest, alert to the slightest sound. An owl passed over her, and she heard the whisper of its gliding flight. The cry of a *Shizi* from afar announced a new kill in the night, and brought a flutter to her heart. She came out onto a meadow and circled, quickly finding the first cluster of fungus she'd passed by, lacy strands glowing blue like magical spiderweb on needle-carpet beneath a young Tysk.

She brushed away the needles, and pulled the entire plant from soft soil, putting it carefully in her bag so as not to break any of its fragile tendrils and lessen full flavor. She picked a second clump at the end of the meadow, where a steep ridge began, then followed the trail upwards among stands of trees clinging tenaciously to weathered, crumbling rock.

At the summit of the ridge was a grand view both east and west: mountains as far as the eye could see in one direction, the yellow glow of the Emperor's domed city in the other. Toregene did not pause there, but hurried on, for the summit was barren and her silhouette visible for miles around. Exposed at the summit for only a moment, she now felt a prickling sensation at the back of her neck, a sudden sense of urgency in returning home to report what she'd seen.

She descended to a skree-covered saddle and looked west to see a flickering point of light set between two spires pinching at the night sky like a thumb and forefinger. The signal fire beckoned her home to the *ordu* placed in the canyon behind the spires, still an hour's walk away. She wondered if Temujin would be awake to greet her.

She traversed the second summit on the west flank, following the faint groove of a trail made by mountain goats, skree shifting and chattering beneath her feet. Ahead of her, a dark shape suddenly appeared, crouched on the trail, eyes glowing yellow in starlight. *Shizi*.

Toregene froze where she stood, withdrawing her blade from the sheath at her side, feeling the rush of blood and adrenaline bring The Change upon her.

Her vision brightened, and she saw the big cat clearly, hunched over the carcass of a small goat on the trail. She felt the ache of incisors thrusting forth in her mouth, the sudden tension around her eyes. The *shizi* crouched as if to spring at her, then sat upright with sudden recognition. Toregene growled softly, a low rattle coming from deep within her, then held out her single steel claw and waved it towards the west. "I will pass through here," she said. "Take your kill with you, and go."

The cat paused only an instant, then grasped the dead goat's neck in its mouth, dragging it easily off the trail and down the skree slope to a log which lay there. Only after it was settled watchfully did Toregene move again, treading softly past the pool of blood on the trail, the blade still in her hand.

As her enhanced vision began to fade, she looked back to see that the animal had begun to feed again. The throbbing of her pulse lessened, tension leaving her mouth and eyes as she squinted again at the trail, adjusting once more to her normal night vision. She returned her blade to its sheath, and hurried on.

She descended to a series of bluffs leading to the knife-ridge which made a great arc to where the signal fire had been placed. By the time she reached the second bluff, Toregene's fear had not totally disappeared, and she still had the feeling she was being watched. She tried to blank her mind, but failed. Now she was leg-weary, her feet sore from treading on sharp skree, and Temujin's face was suddenly in her mind, his wry smile, finely-arched nose and laughing eyes, the long braid of black hair that fell over his chest when they made love.

She held that vision, and plunged ahead down a grassy slope to the final bluff before the ridge. But the disquieting feeling still would not go away, as if there were a watchful presence nearby, and Toregene wondered briefly if the *shizi* had a mate which was now following her. She avoided the center of the bluff, and crossed near the trees lining its edge, picking up her pace with sudden apprehension.

A twig snapped, and she turned to see three dark shapes rushing towards her from the trees.

She turned to run, the final ridge only meters away, but she was tackled from behind, landing on her stomach with an explosion of breath and a terrible weight on top of her. Lights danced before her eyes as her arms were pulled roughly behind her, and she felt the bite of leather thongs on her wrists. Rough hands secured her ankles as well, then seized her shoulders and flipped her over on her back as she gasped for breath.

Toregene found herself looking up at the grinning faces of three soldiers of the Emperor. Two stood over her, the third kneeling at her feet and holding her blade in his hand. Young men, eyes glittering dangerously, yet amused. The one with the knife leaned over and dragged the flat of the blade across her throat.

"Look what we've found; a changeling bitch all alone, and far from home on such a cold night. I think we've caught ourselves a little spy."

"No, no," said Toregene, finding her breath at last. "I'm gathering herbs, and I'm close to home. This is Tumatsin land, so how am I a spy? I had a little sack with me when you attacked, but I dropped it."

One of the standing men held up the little leather sack. "And here it is," he said.

"Yes. The herbs are difficult to find in daylight, but glow in the night. I was collecting them."

The man opened the sack, withdrew a pinch of glowing lace and wrinkled his nose. "Smells like dung," he said.

"They add flavor to our soups. Please, let me up. I've done nothing wrong." Even as she said it, Toregene knew she was found out, for that presence was there again, probing her mind as she tried to blank it.

The man turned her sack upside-down and shook it, scattering the noctiluminescent fungus on the ground. "You will have no need of this, I think. The dead have no need for soup."

"No!" she cried, struggling. "I've done nothing!" Adrenaline surged in her body, and now it was as if she was seeing the grinning faces in daylight.

"Ohhh, see how her eyes glow. The light of passion is in her eyes, Shan. I think she wants you." The two standing men laughed.

The kneeling one reached over and poked her in the stomach with her own blade. "I will enter her with this after I'm satisfied. She's my captive, Majin, but I'm generous to my friends. Despite your jokes, you and Xiao will enjoy a moment with her before the end."

"Let me go!" growled Toregene, writhing and straining at her bonds. The pressure on her gums was now fierce, and she growled again.

The three men stared at her, and Shan was fumbling at his leather pants. "One should not pass by such an opportunity, but do put something in her mouth. I don't want to be bitten and infected with changeling diseases."

Toregene struggled furiously, writhing like a scalded snake, but suddenly her mind clouded, paralyzed by a terrible force that made her shiver. A deep voice came from the darkness among the trees.

"Enough of this. Stand back, all of you. Shan, quit fumbling with your pants. You look like a child giving himself pleasure."

The three men jumped back, auras changing to blue from being startled as another man came forth. The first thing Toregene saw was the huge arch of his nose, the distended, vein-lined dome of his frontal lobes. A Searcher, taller than the others by several centimeters, his eyes fathomless blackness in her enhanced vision.

"She is a spy, Mengmoshu," said Shan.

"Indeed she is, though she speaks the truth about using the night to gather her herbs. Mostly she has been observing our camp from a place I can now locate. We have been negligent in scanning the rim of the cliff overlooking the valley. She knows our strength there." The Searcher's aura was the red of Tengri-Nayon, with radiating streamers in gold. His mind clamped down on hers like a velvet claw, and now she lay motionless, unable to speak, screaming silently.

"Then she must die," said Shan. "It is a cold night, Mengmoshu, and we have been patrolling without women for two weeks. Certain pressures of our manhood could be relieved here before we kill her, and with all the *shizi* prowling about, the evidence of our feast will surely be gone by early morning."

Mengmoshu looked down somberly at Toregene, considering for a long moment, then said, "I understand, but the flyer will return within the hour, and we must walk to the rendezvous. There's no time for what you desire, Shan. I will act in behalf of all of us."

Shan snorted, and the other two men's eyes narrowed with displeasure. "You claim privilege of rank, Mengmoshu?"

Toregene felt a slight release of the force paralyzing her mind and body as the Searcher turned to face the smaller man. "Do you question my rank or authority here, Shan? Would you speak of this to others?"

Shan stumbled back a step, eyes wide, his aura flickering as if sucked from him. "No—no, of course not. We are in your service, Mengmoshu. You are the chosen of the Emperor here."

"Good, Shan. Humility leads to wisdom. Now, pack your things and leave. I will catch up with you shortly."

Mengmoshu leaned over, and pulled Toregene to a sitting position as the other men returned to the trees. She tried to cry out, but full paralysis had returned, and she could only grunt as he gagged her with a cloth taken from his pocket. He lifted her up like a child and carried her to the trees, setting her gently down on soft needle carpet, his face expressionless. "Shan, bring me the woman's blade. It must appear that she somehow fell on it."

Shan appeared, handing over the knife and looking down at her with barely controlled lust in his eyes.

"Now go, all of you. I do not wish an audience for this."

"Yes, Mengmoshu," said Shan. "We will walk slowly, so you can catch up. You cannot control the mind of a *shizi*,"

"I will follow," said Mengmoshu, and Toregene heard the crunch of footsteps going away from the trees. Mengmoshu turned his head to watch them leave, then knelt at her feet and stuck her knife into the ground there. He loosened the thong at her waist and pulled down her pants, but she felt no cold, no physical sensation of any kind, her body numb while her mind screamed in agony and shame. He untied her ankles, then removed her pants, and spread her legs to receive him, for she wore no undergarments.

Eyes fixed on hers, the Searcher loosened his own pants and pulled them down before leaning over her, face close. He raised her hips and thrust himself into her, but still she felt nothing.

"I feel your terror as if it is my own, but there is a purpose here," he whispered. "Now, listen to me." He began to rock rhythmically, and she heard his voice, yet now his lips did not move.

I do not follow any Gods, but obey the spoken will of my ancestors. If the Gods exist, then I pray they have brought you to me at the proper time in your cycle. What I do is a test of the Gods, and I risk damnation in shaming you, but there are those of us who hear the voice of our First Mother, those of us who work for one, undivided

*people on Shanji, united in purpose and in blood. I am
bred Moshuguang, the magic light, the chosen of the
Emperor. And I give my seed to the Tumatsin to create
those people, and perhaps . . . something greater. Now—
now—now!*

Mengmoshu rocked furiously, and grunted with sudden
release, sweat beading his forehead while she lay beneath
him, still feeling nothing. He withdrew from her, pulled
up his pants and sighed. He leaned over her closely, and
whispered, "In a moment I will be gone. You must—"

"Mengmoshu, aren't you finished yet? You should not
walk alone on a moonless night."

It was Shan's voice, a loud whisper, and not far away.

Mengmoshu was startled, his aura flashing blue. "I gave
you a simple order, and you have not obeyed it!" he
growled.

"I think of your safety. A *shizi* is prowling only ten
minutes from here, and I came back to accompany you.
Hurry!"

The Searcher sighed again. "A complication," he
whispered. "I will release you for an instant, and in that
instant you must scream as best you can. It is your death
if you do not."

He looked down at her, and suddenly her own knife
was in his hand, gleaming in starlight, coming up in a
high arc and down towards her heart in a single deathstroke,
and the scream that had started in her mind came out as
a horrible, muffled rattle ending as quickly as he'd released
and taken hold of her again. The knife struck the ground
only centimeters from her side.

Mengmoshu rolled her paralyzed body slightly to one
side, cut the bonds on her wrists, and lay the knife beside
her. He put a finger to her lips, then to his own and
stood up, giving her one last look before walking away.

"She's dead?" asked Shan.

"Yes. The *shizi* should do the rest. We need to hurry."

Toregene heard their footsteps grow fainter, and she was suddenly cold, sharp needles digging into her bare legs and buttocks. She lay there for several minutes, not daring to move, her vision still enhanced from fear—and anger. A foreign seed lay within her; she could feel its fluid excess oozing. She felt humiliated, dishonored, contaminated, unfit to be called Tumatsin. It seemed as if her vagina was suddenly on fire, and tears came to her eyes. She suppressed a sob, lest a *shizi* be near. In her present state, there would be no doubt which of them was the dominant animal.

When she was satisfied the men were gone she sat up shivering, removed the gag and pulled up her pants. She cradled the knife in one hand, and for one brief instant considered plunging it into her own heart. She was stopped by a single thought; her life had been spared, her humiliation a thing forced upon her by another. Of what was she guilty?

Her feeling of self-disgust returned in moments, but by then the knife was returned to its sheath. She breathed deeply and adjusted her clothing, crept out from the trees and sought a deeper calm by carefully picking up the scattered threads of glowing fungus on the ground. One delicate thread at a time, she refilled the sack, her normal night vision returning by the time she finished the simple task.

She began to walk, and her momentary self-control dissolved again. She was suddenly shaking, her knees giving way so that she fell twice before reaching the broad ridge trail. Her muffled sobs were of shame, and grief, the grief of a woman violated and despoiled by the Hansui seed burning within her. Her people would grieve with her, but Tumatsin law was clear. She would keep her status in society, but there would be no marriage to Temujin, no children of his body for her, a life without family, a maiden aunt to the children of others. Her hand went to the hilt of her knife, but again there was hesitation, an instant of anger, and her knees stiffened.

Now she was running the trail, knife in hand, and it was as if daylight had come early. She growled low, suddenly hoping a *shizi* would come after her, attacking within sight of the signal fire. She thought of plunging the knife into its open mouth, the claws tearing at her stomach and groin, the foreign seed spilling out with her blood as she stabbed again into an eye and through to the brain. Quite suddenly, Toregene did not want to die. She wanted to kill. And with that thought came resolution not to so easily give up her heart's desire, even if it meant giving up a virtue she'd been taught as a child. The virtue of honesty in all things.

The signal fire was less than a kilometer ahead, and a shadow moved before it. Temujin? Had he waited up for her? She was desperate for his embrace, his touch, that sweet breath in her ear as he held her. She ran harder, dislodging skree that tinkled like broken porcelain down the steep slopes on either side of the trail. More shadows around the fire, men standing up, watching her approach.

Three men—and Temujin was not one of them. She stumbled into the glowing circle of firelight, and fell to her knees, gasping for breath as the men clustered around her.

"*Shizi*—chased me—I fell," she gasped. "On the far ridge—two of them—and troopers—I don't know how many. They saw me—came after—I ran—then the *shizi*—I—" Her breath exploded in a burst of tears.

A man knelt before her to put a comforting hand on her shoulder. It was Kuchlug, Temujin's closest friend. He pulled the knife from her clenched fist, and put it back in her sheath. "You're safe, now. The cats have given up the chase. We saw the flyer over there a few moments ago. Temujin has gone down to report it, but he'll be back soon. Your hands are cut and bleeding! Ogadai, get some hot water for us! Uzbek, go down and tell Temujin that his bride has arrived safely!"

Uzbek sprinted from the circle of light as Kuchlug held Toregene's trembling hands in his, looking closely at her. "It's all right, now. Temujin will be here soon."

"The camp," gasped Toregene. "There are many soldiers guarding it. Too many—and now they watch us from over there. They will see every move we make. We can't—"

Kuchlug squeezed her hands. "Not now. Save your report for Temujin. For now, you rest, and clean your wounds in privacy. Your things are in the low tent behind me. Ah, here is hot water for you."

Ogadai had returned from the fire with a bulging, goatskin bag. Kuchlug helped her to her feet, and she took the bag. "My brown pack is in the tent?" she asked.

"Yes. Everything you left behind. Take your time, even sleep a little before Temujin returns. We will keep watch."

Toregene hugged him, and he grinned. "I'm filled with envy for my friend," he said. "Now go."

At the edge of the firelight, she found the tent and crawled inside, squinting in the gloom. She laced up the entrance flap halfway so there was still some light coming in, then rummaged in her pack for cup, cloth and the bag of special tea that was always with her since she'd been betrothed to Temujin. Laced with white root and jin-hua, the tea had thus far prevented the conception of a child by their frequent lovemaking before marriage. But Temujin was Tumatsin, and she was now dealing with the seed of a Hansui Searcher, her time of possible conception near or immediate. She made the tea strong, and gulped down a cupful, burning her mouth. She made a second cup, let it cool while she dabbed her hand wounds clean with the cloth, then drank the tea down. She soaked the cloth with tea and washed her genitals, flushing them twice with hot liquid, then again, wincing with pain.

She lay on her back, feeling the hot liquid working its way down inside her body. Hurry, she thought, but was consumed by fear.

PART I

TUMATSIN

CHAPTER ONE
KATI

Kati was four when she went to the Festival of Tengri and saw the eye of Tengri-Nayon.

The festival location was far beyond the mountains, and her mother had been cooking for two days, their *ger* filled with wonderful odors of mutton, cheese and *ayrog*. Other women of the *ordu* came and went, carrying bags of tea, and barley ground to a fine flour. Goats and sheep had been brought in from the high valleys, their bleating a constant din from the holding pen near the *ger*. They dined well on grainy gruel to fatten them after another long, hard winter, but Kati often wondered if they sensed their fate.

Today she was confined to a pile of hides to play with her little brother while the women worked, their faces glistening over a wood-fired stove, talk animated with laughter. Kati sensed excitement, a pleasure projected in amber eyes normally deep brown during the drudgery of ordinary days. There were quiet whispers, and sudden giggles as the women shared a secret story. She didn't mind being ignored, at least for the moment, for it was fun to play horses with Baber. They were separated in age by little more than a year, and Da had made four horses for each of them, stuffed with wool and painted by hand with the colorful trappings of their ancestors.

19

Warrior dolls clung to the flanks of the horses, faceless heads with black pigtails, images of bow and arrow quivers painted on their backs. Baber growled, thrusting forward two horses as they sat crossed-legged, knees touching. "Kati die," he snarled.

Kati met his charge with a single warrior on a black stallion. "Shanji!" she cried, twisting her horse to bite at the attackers, and all three riders toppled from their mounts at once.

"I win," she said. "Two to one."

Baber scowled. "You push too hard. You're bigger."

"I am an old, experienced warrior," said Kati. The women at the stove turned and smiled at her. One of them said, "Toregene, your little warrior-empress already does battle with the men. Surely she's old enough to begin riding. When will Temujin commence her lessons?"

Kati's mother shushed the woman, a finger on her lips. "Listen," she said, and the women bent close in whispers. Kati strained to hear them, and then the women giggled, snuck a look at her, amber eyes twinkling.

Kati wondered about their sudden pleasure from a secret whispered by Ma, but now Baber was charging again, this time with three horses, and she braced her remounted warrior for the attack.

The morning was crisp with cold when Kati was awakened by Ma. A single oil lamp flickered on the earthen floor of the *ger*, casting orange hues on tapestries and rugs covering the walls: scenes of warriors in battle dress, charging towards a great city of towers and pagodas spewing smoke and flame. In one, a tall woman in emerald green stood on a hill, arm outstretched, directing the charging warriors.

"Time for your first festival, Kati. Put on your leather tunic against the cold. We will ride two hours before it is light."

Kati rubbed her eyes. In the flickering light, the warrior figures seemed to move. Baber was already up and dressed, looking like a ball with legs in his layers of cotton, wool and leather. He stood by the doorway, watching the commotion outside: hooves stomping, horses snorting, the bleating of goats and sheep. Kati had slept naked in her blanket roll on a hide coverlet over the thick, straw mattress. She put on woolen undergarments, shirt and pants of puffy wool, then the double thickness pants and tunic to keep out the wind, grunting as she did so.

Ma smiled. "You grow so fast, it is time for new leathers. I will look for something at festival. Now I will braid your hair for the occasion."

"Do we have time, Ma?"

"We will make time. Now sit still."

Kati loved the feel of Ma's gentle hands on her long, black hair, combing it out, forming two braids and coiling them like snakes at her temples. The braiding rocked her head rhythmically, making her sleepy again, and she yawned. "Why do we leave so early?"

"It is best we be well along our way at dawn so the Emperor does not misunderstand our intention in banding together. He is aware of the festival, and its location. His flyers will see us headed in that direction, and leave us alone."

"Da says the Emperor fears us. He thinks we will attack him, like in the pictures." Kati pointed at the tapestry above her bed.

"He has little reason to fear us, dear. His weapons and machines are far more powerful than ours, and he is ruler of Shanji."

"So he can tell us what to do, and when to come home," said Kati.

Ma laughed. "Like your father and me? No, Kati, he is not a father to us. He has put us out of his city, and

leaves us to rule ourselves as long as we don't bother
him or his people."

"Why, Ma? Did we do something wrong? If I did a
bad thing, would you make me live by myself?"

"Of course not. You're my child, from my own body,
and I would never abandon you for any reason. But we
are Tumatsin, not children of the Emperor's people. They
call us changelings, and the people we came from went
away a long time ago. No more questions, now. You will
learn more at the Festival of Tengri, and see his eye that
watches over us until our ancestors return. There, I'm
done, and I have a little gift for you."

Ma put a loop of yellow metal over Kati's head and
around Kati's throat. A pendant hung from it, two pieces
of metal forming the outline of an ovoid shaped like
pursed lips. "So you will remember Tengri's eye after
you've seen it," she said.

"It's pretty," said Kati, fingering the pendant and smiling
at her new treasure. "Now I have jewelry like the other
women."

Ma hugged her from behind. "You are my little woman.
Now, eat some soup and have tea before we leave. Only
one cup of tea, though. We won't stop until mid-day. A
bowl and cup are on the stove for you."

Kati gobbled her food too quickly, and seared the roof
of her mouth with hot tea. Ma took Baber by the hand,
and led him outside, so Kati hurried to get her place.
She dumped bowl and cup into a bucket of cold water,
put on the little pack containing her horses and dolls,
and picked up the wooden dagger Da had carved for
her. She shoved the dagger beneath her waistband, as
would a man. Grabbing her cup, she rushed out the door
and nearly ran into Ma, returning to close up the *ger*.
She looked frantically for Baber. Horses were lined up
many paces in two directions, and she found him perched
on Ma's chestnut, dozing. She sprinted to the head of

the line where Da sat on black Kaidu, talking to other *bahadurn* of the Tumatsin. "Da!" she cried.

The men turned to look at her, and smiled as she rushed to the black flank of Kaidu. "Look at her belt," said Kuchlug. "It seems your flower has grown a thorn! Her eyes might yet turn green, Temujin!"

The men laughed, and Kati held up her arms to her mounted father. "Da, I ride with you. I ride like the wind on Kaidu!"

Temujin picked her up, hoisting her high to sit in front of him on Kaidu's hard back, and she squealed with glee. She was at the head of the line, ahead of all the other children, sitting on the fastest horse in the *ordu*, Da's warm chest at her back. She leaned back as he hugged her to him. He took her hands, and placed the reins of the great horse there.

"Just hold them still. I will tell Kaidu what to do, with my knees and legs. That is all a good horse needs."

Kati looked up at Da's face, breathing hard with excitement, her heart aching with joy. "He has a soft mouth," she said knowingly.

"Yes," said Da. He nuzzled her cheek, and she smelled *ayrog* on his breath. A bag of the strong brew was even now being passed from man to man at the head of the line, but it was forbidden to children.

Da twisted behind her, looking back at the line of horses, the small flock of sheep, a few goats and three yearling calves herded by boys on horseback. "We are assembled," he said, then shouted, "We go with the blessings of Tengri!"

People cheered, the women trilling, and Kati was thrilled by the sound of it. She felt only the slightest movement of Da's knees, and squeezed the reins in her hands as Kaidu stepped forward, tossing his great head and snorting fog. She wanted him to run, to feel the wind in her face, the hard muscles bunching beneath her, but

knew she must today be content with a leisurely pace
to match that of the older people and the herded animals
on the steep trail into the mountains. For the moment,
it was enough, but someday she would have her own
horse, and then she would fly with the wind.

Kati wrapped the slack reins around her hands so she
wouldn't drop them if she slept. She leaned back into
the warmth of her father, and sighed.

They had traveled for only two hours when the flyer
came to interrupt their journey.

Kati had dozed, rocked to sleep during the long ascent
on a rocky trail to the plateau at the base of the western
peaks. She was awakened by the flyer's whine as it passed
closely overhead, a silver craft shaped like a plate, an
open cockpit seating several men who looked down at
them.

"It's barely first light, and already they're out," growled
Kuchlug. "They grow bolder all the time, Temujin, and
we say nothing!"

The flyer proceeded to the plateau just ahead of them,
hovering, then descending until it was out of sight. "Think
of The Eye, my friend, and calm yourself, lest a Searcher
sense your hostility and make trouble for us. The eyes
of our women are more than enough betrayal of our
feelings. Ride back and ask Toregene to come up here.
I want her beside me to see anything important in their
auras if they stop us."

Kuchlug turned his mount, and sprinted away. Kati
was squeezing the reins so hard her fingers were numb.
"Are we doing something wrong, Da?"

"No, Kati. The Emperor knows about Festival, and
has always allowed it. I don't expect any trouble. Just
think of something nice. There's no need to be frightened."

Kati thought of what Da had told Kuchlug. "I will think
of my pendant Ma gave me this morning. See?"

Da hugged her gently. "Yes, it's pretty."

Ma rode up on her chestnut, and her eyes were tinged red. "Will we be stopped?" Baber leaned back against her, head lolled over, sound asleep.

"I think so," said Da. "Let me know if you see anything dangerous in their auras, and clear your throat if I start to say anything to cause suspicion."

Ma nodded, but the redness in her eyes was brighter now. Kati sensed a deep wariness in her mother. "I'm going to think about my pendant," she said seriously.

Ma didn't smile. "And I will think about the blackness of a cave," she said. "There is sure to be a Searcher with them." Ma sighed, and her eyes seemed to cloud over. While Kati watched, fascinated, her mother's eyes changed from red to yellow to their normal deep brown. Women could do things men couldn't do, and Kati looked forward to that time when, with the first budding of her breasts, her own eyes would reflect her feelings and she would be able to see the life force emanating from other people. It would mean she was no longer a child, but a woman, held in high esteem among her people.

They reached the plateau, the trail ahead faint in short, tuffy grass. Here and there, in the shade of large rocks, were the white splotches of rotting snow. The flyer had come down in the middle of the plateau, near the trail, and five men were standing there, a sixth still in the cockpit of the craft. Kati glanced at Ma, saw that her eyes were closed, her chest slowly rising and falling with deep breathing. She looked down at her pendant, stared at it, memorized the shape, two strips of golden metal, like the entrance to a cave, blackness inside. She held the image in her mind as they approached the waiting men. Behind her, people were chatting gaily about Festival as if nothing was happening.

One of the men held up a hand, ordering them to stop. Three men stood on the trail, two others off to one side,

all armed with weapons like the one Da kept wrapped
and hidden beneath the stove in their *ger*. She had once
watched it vaporize a tree limb, and knew its power.

Da reached around her, and tugged once on the reins,
bringing Kaidu to a halt. He raised a hand in greeting.
"We travel to the Festival of Tengri, across the mountains.
I have the written permission of the Emperor, if you
wish to see it."

Kati felt a sudden sensation, as if a day-dream had
passed through her mind like a wisp of smoke. There
was a presence, an awareness that was not hers. The three
men on the trail stepped forward until Kaidu snorted
and stomped a hoof. All were armored with bright, silver
metal, bareheaded, weapons held casually across their
chests, the round faces of the Hansui, except for one.
That one had a finely arched nose and chiseled face with
a protruding bulge laced with veins on the left side of
his forehead. *A Searcher*. It was the first one Kati had
ever seen, and she was amazed.

"We are aware of the Emperor's generosity in allowing
travel," said that man. "He respects all religions." The
man moved to Ma's chestnut, and looked up at her. Her
eyes were open, dark brown, and she regarded him calmly.

"Are you carrying any weapons?"

"We have no need for weapons. We have supplies with
us for travel, and food is provided at the Festival. There
is no need to hunt," said Da.

Kati thought of the wooden dagger in her belt, and
the man smiled, looked up at her, stepped to Kaidu's
flank and reached up to touch the hilt of her toy. "We
will not count this one," he said.

Kati looked at the man, without fear. "Can you really
tell what people are thinking?" she said, her eyes focused
on his forehead. "It must be very noisy, all those thoughts."

She felt Da tense, but the man laughed. "It can be
difficult, and yes, sometimes noisy."

"Will you detain us long?" asked Da. "We must be over the pass before it's dark."

"Only a moment, while we count the number of you traveling. When will you be returning?"

"In the evening four days from now," said Da, "and it might be late."

The man nodded, then looked again at Ma. "See that you keep to your schedule, and if others return with you, you can expect to be stopped for inspection. Young woman, is this curious little girl with the dagger your daughter?"

"Yes," said Ma, not looking at him.

"Such control. Have you no secrets to share with me?"

"None that are of importance to you," said Ma. "You can see that we're harmless. Can we go, now?"

Yes! I'm tired of sitting here! I want to go to Festival!

The man turned sharply to look at Kati, and his eyes widened. "Now *that* was a noisy thought," he said. "Another minute, and you can go to your festival. Lan, aren't you finished yet?" he shouted. The two men off the trail had been moving up and down the line of horses, counting people.

"Yes! We have their number!" came a shout from behind them.

The man stepped off the trail, his two companions following. "Then you may go. And have a safe journey."

I talked to him, thought Kati. *I talked to him with my mind!*

Da urged Kaidu forward, and as they passed the man with the veined forehead, Kati saw him looking straight at her, and he had a most curious look on his face. He waved, and she waved back. And when they had traveled in silence to the end of the plateau, she turned again to look at Ma, and saw that her mother's eyes were blazing red.

❖   ❖   ❖

Kati only vaguely remembered their high camp that night. She was lying on Kaidu's back, face pressed to his warm neck when Da had lifted her down and carried her to bed inside a shelter of hides where Baber was already sound asleep. She slept fully clothed, for it was very cold, and found that if she consciously breathed faster than usual, the suffocating feeling would go away. There was a fire outside, light flickering on the walls of the shelter, and once she was awakened by the sound of voices, men sitting around the fire, arguing about something. But then she slept soundly, clenching her pendant as she drifted off, her last waking thought that of a man with a strange head who could see into people's minds.

It was light when Ma awakened her, prodding with a foot. "I've let you sleep as long as I can. Hurry, now," she said, teasing, "or we'll wrap you up in the shelter." Kati was instantly wide awake. Baber still sat on his bed, eyes closed, while Ma attempted to roll it up. "Wake up your brother, and take him outside. I must hurry," said Ma.

Kati tickled him, and he giggled, hiding his chin from her. She pulled him from the shelter and held his hand to watch the commotion of camp-breaking. There was soup and bread at the campfire, people eating on the run. Kati served herself and Baber, and looked around. They were on a grassy plateau, the mountain peaks now behind them, and she could see the trail winding up to a saddle between two giant fingers of rock. Tengri-Khan was not yet high enough to peek over the summits, but colored the lower, western hills and valleys in orange and gold, and beyond them was a flat brilliance of reflected light that made her squint.

Baber pulled at her hand. "I pee, Kati. Now."

Kati sighed, led him to scrubby trees at the plateau's edge, and went through the ritual of removing his four

layers of clothing so he could relieve himself. She tried
to sit him down, but he shrugged her off.

"You sit down. Baber stand," he said.

She had to giggle, for his organ was like her thumb,
but he stood proudly, and played his stream back and
forth around the base of a tree while she watched.
"Already you are a little man," she said, and Baber nodded
his head curtly in agreement.

Kati bundled him up when he was finished, and then
took him by the hand again. They searched for Da, found
him mounted on Kaidu at the head of the line that had
formed while Baber was about his leisurely business. Ma
came up to take Baber back with her, but he complained.
"I ride with Da!" he cried.

"When you are older, Baber. You come with me, now,"
said Ma.

Baber pouted, tears in his eyes. "Kati always ride Kaidu,
not me. I ride with *Da*!"

Ma pulled him away with her, and now he was crying.
Kati felt his disappointment as if it were her own. But
Da held out his arms to her. "You are the eldest, and a
daughter. Until you have your own horse, you ride here
with me." Da hoisted her up, and Kaidu's reins were
again in her hands.

"When will I have my own horse, Da? When?" She
leaned back, looked straight up at his face.

"When you are ready," said Da.

The other men were all smiling at them, and then a
boy on a young, black stallion galloped past and reined
sharply to a halt at the head of the line. The hairless tail
of the stallion trailed a streamer of colorful ribbons, and
the boy carried a flag on a long staff, a sheet of cloth
striped vertically in yellow, red and brown.

Kati had never seen such a sight. "What is he carrying,
Da?"

Da whispered to her. "Abaka is fourteen, the youngest

of warrior age in our *ordu*. He carries a flag that identifies us so people will know where we come from, and he will lead us to festival. All *ordu*s have flags, in different designs but with the same colors. They are the primary colors of our women's eyes."

"Abaka looks very happy," said Kati. "He is lucky to be a boy."

Da hugged her hard. "To be a warrior, yes, but not a leader. Remember that the warriors go forth, while the leaders invoke strategy and watch from a safer place away from battle. Empress Mandughai watched from a hill when our ancestors did battle with the Hansui, made good their escape when the Emperor violated the terms of war by using his flying machines and weapons of light against them. It is the women who lead, Kati. Goldani and your mother ride behind us, but they are the two leaders of our *ordu*. I am their Captain in ceremony and war. Would you be warrior, or Empress?"

"Warrior," said Kati, giggling. Da hugged her again.

Abaka raised his standard proudly, turned his stallion and moved out at a stately walk. The column traversed a hill to a ridge and followed it west, dropping into a valley lush with trees and brush along a shallow stream of clear water, up another switch-back trail to another ridge, and so on until mid-day, pausing at another stream to water the horses and eat cheese and bread without dismounting. Tengri-Khan warmed them, but the air was still cold, and only a few of the men, including Abaka, dared to remove shirt and jacket to expose their bronzed skin to the light.

They climbed another hill and the trees were suddenly gone. Ahead of them was a maize of barren hills creviced with deep canyons, the land a lace of earth, and out towards the distant horizon there was a flat expanse of sparkling green. Da pointed over her shoulder, and said, "That is the great sea, which goes on without end. Most of our people live along its shore, and it's always warm there."

"Why don't *we* live there, Da?"

"Our *ordu* remains close to the land of our beginning. We are the watchdogs for our people, and when the time is right, the lands which the Emperor has stolen from us will be ours again. It is our obligation to keep watch on the Emperor, and we are honored to do it."

Kati said nothing, but wondered why the job couldn't be shared with others so that *everyone* could be warm some of the time. In her young life, she could not remember a day without cold.

The trail broadened and became visible far ahead, snaking across the barren hills towards the sea, criss-crossing trails from north and south. And as they came down onto a narrow plateau, Kati began to hear a distant sound: rhythmic pounding, deep, the clash of metal on metal, a tone for an instant, then again. Abaka was suddenly excited. He raised his standard high, waved it, and suddenly three boys rushed by, the tails and manes of their mounts festooned with ribbons, goat-skin drums in the laps of the riders. The boys began pounding on the drums, and Kati's heart raced with the breaking of the land's silence. Behind them, the women trilled, and several more riders, boys nearing manhood, rushed by to take a place behind Abaka and his drummers. Kati sat rigid on Kaidu's back, clenching the reins in her tiny fists, her heart pounding with excitement.

"It's good we're arriving with the others," said Da. "Now we can ride in together. See, Kati, how we all come together? I think this will be a fine festival."

Lines of horses were coming along the trails from all directions, north, south, several from the direction of the sea, convergent upon a broad valley sloping northward to a deep canyon dimly lit even at mid-day. The sound of drums, horns, and clashing cymbals of yellow metal grew louder as they neared each other, each line of horses preceded by a mounted youth with fluttering standard in red, yellow and brown, swirls of color in various geometrical designs. Da pointed out the standards of the Merkitis, the Naimansa, Kereits, Dorvodt, a blur of other *ordu* names, people of the sea and broad terraces west of the mountains, north and south. The trilling of the women was now continuous, and the beat of the drums pounded in Kati's ears.

People were waving to each other, and shouting names, but Kati was distracted by a curious sight. From the end of each line of horses, two mounted women were breaking ranks and converging on a slope above the plateau. Goldani rode by to join them, then Ma was suddenly there at Kati's side, thrusting Baber at her to hold. "Hold him tight," she said. "He's tired and wiggly." And then she rode off to join the other women on the hill.

Baber was thrilled. "I ride Kaidu!" he cried, and grabbed at the reins. Kati let him hold the reins, but gripped his hands tightly so that he couldn't pull on them, and after awhile he quit complaining, and was content just to hold them.

"Where is Ma going?" asked Kati.

"She'll follow us later," said Da. "Don't worry, just hold your brother still."

Baber was bouncing on Kaidu's neck, and the great horse shook his head. Kati shushed her brother, gave him a shake, and he was quiet again, pouting.

Lines of horses were three abreast as they walked down the slopes and into gloom of the canyon, Da exchanging pleasantries with a man from the Dorvodt *ordu*, a man named Altan. He too had a daughter perched in front of him on a white, broad-shouldered stallion with grey spots on its flanks, a hairless tail wound with ribbons of red, yellow and brown. The little girl's name was Edi; she was Kati's age, but shy, turning to smile occasionally, but saying nothing. Like Kati, she wore the pendant of Tengri's Eye, but its color was burnt-orange, not yellow.

The canyon was devoid of vegetation, high walls of soft stone, orange and red, wide seams of black rock glistening wetly and giving off the odor of burning oil lamps. The walls closed in on them until they were walking in single-file, and ahead was an overhang forming an arch which blocked Tengri-Khan's light as they passed under it, stone so close to their heads that Kati reached up to touch it and found her fingers stained orange.

The overhang went on for many paces, but ahead there was light again, and the sound of rushing water, a dull roar that echoed from the canyon walls. The drums had ceased to beat, all conversation halting as they went towards the light. Da's arms came around Kati and her brother; she heard him sigh, felt him relax, his chin on her head. "Now we come to Festival," he said softly.

They came out from beneath the overhang with a marvelous view of a suddenly wide canyon ending at a wall so high Kati looked nearly straight up to see its top. Water cascaded from the top of the wall into an emerald-green pool surrounded by fine sand, a few tumbled slabs of orange stone and a huge boulder at pool's edge, on top of which stood the oldest woman Kati had ever seen: a tall figure, her bronze face etched deep with age, dressed in a heavy, long robe of leather dyed in splotches of red, yellow and brown. The woman raised her arms in greeting, and the men ahead of Kati responded silently, raising their arms in unison. Da raised his arms also, murmuring, "We greet Manlee, the living presence of Mandughai, Kati. She is the leader of all our people, and has great powers, as you shall see."

The great beach of sand stretched hundreds of paces from them as they rode towards the pool, groups breaking off left and right under directions of a single man at water's edge, and it was then that Kati saw the standards marking

the place for each *ordu* to locate on the sand. Before
the pool, a pit had been dug and filled with logs and
splintered wood. Abaka stopped near it, jamming his
standard into the sand and dismounting there. Around
them was a tumble of horses and people as everyone
found their place, others still arriving, and more until
the crowd was crushed together, horses jostling for
position and whinnying nervously.

At that moment, the woman called Manlee looked up
to the top of the waterfall at a man suddenly there. She
waved an arm, and the man stepped back out of sight.

In an instant, the waterfall ceased to flow.

Hooves stomping sand, colliding bodies, a few muffled
curses, then all sound was gone—except for a dull roar
like the exhalations of a sleeping giant from the mouth
of a small canyon leading east from the beach and along
the wall.

Manlee held out her arms from the summit of the
great boulder, and her voice echoed from all around
them. "All are here! Unload your horses, and take them
past The Eye to the plateau for grazing, then return
immediately for the procession of Mandughai! Your *gert*s
are marked on the Festival fields! The rest of you remain
silent, and take ease at the sound of Tengri's breath!
We give him thanks for bringing us together again!"

Horses were unloaded and led away, Abaka taking
charge of Kaidu and two others, including his own black.
People placed their tents and belongings in piles, and
sat on them silently, listening to the sound from the canyon
mouth. Kati was awed. With the wave of her hand, Manlee
had made the waterfall stop! Surely this was magic! Still,
it seemed she was just an old woman, still standing on
the boulder, smiling down at them.

All waited patiently, some dozing, and the crush was
not so great now that the horses were gone, but the
expanse of sand was solid with clusters of people and

provisions, and Ma had still not arrived. Kati leaned against Da, Baber sound asleep in her lap. Her stomach growled. "When does Ma come?" she asked.

"Very soon," said Da, "and I think there will be a surprise for you then."

And there was, for when the boys came back from tethering the horses, two climbed the boulder to stand by Manlee, and they blew a long tone on bone horns, and all faces turned towards the narrow canyon through which they had come.

Twenty women rode sedately out of the canyon, colorful tapestries over the necks and rumps of their horses, long robes like Manlee's, pendants and huge earrings of bright metal sparkling as they came. In the hand of each woman, blade upright, was a long, curving sword, and across each back a short, re-curved bow, and quiver full of arrows.

Everyone stood up silently, and Kati's view was blocked. "Da!" she said, holding up her arms. Da smiled, hoisted her high over his head, and settled her down on his shoulders.

The procession neared her place by the pool, and suddenly Kati gasped in surprise, and fright. Some familiar faces, yes, yet horribly changed; now long, taut, cheekbones prominent, their partly open mouths displaying the curved teeth of a *shizi*. The eyes of all but one woman blazed red, the color of Tengri-Nayon, the color of wariness and alertness.

The lead rider was different. Her eyes were the color of the emerald pool.

"She is so beautiful," murmured Da.

The woman leading the procession was Ma.

CHAPTER TWO
EMERALD EYES

Manlee raised her arms at the top of the boulder, and shouted to the crowd before her.

"We are gathered in The Eye of Tengri-Nayon, and in the presence of the living Empress Mandughai, who watches over us! See that presence before you, and have faith in Her return. Tengri-Nayon comes nearer, and with it five thousand warriors such as you see before you.

"I have been told this in a dream, and have seen the emerald eyes of the Empress who will lead them in our liberation. She has heard the cries of Her people, and feels our pain. I have heard Her words in my mind, have seen the images of the Emperor's city in flames and a new beginning for the Tumatsin in the valleys taken from us.

"But you must believe. You must show your belief as you contemplate Tengri's Eye, and send forth a prayer to Mandughai for our liberation!"

The mounted women had reached the pool, turning their horses to face the crowd in a line along water's edge. Ma was in the center of the group, staring fixedly ahead like the rest of them. All eyes were on her, Kati realized. Everyone was looking at Ma! But Ma didn't seem to see them.

Kati was frightened, her little hands clenching at Da's

hair. "She doesn't see me, Da. She doesn't know I'm here. What is wrong with her?"

"Be still," said Da, reaching up to take her hands in his. "Your mother has gone within herself to make her appearance, and it is a difficult thing to do. She will be as you know her soon enough. Now watch, and listen."

"Now erect your tents, and put your possessions inside," shouted Manlee. "Tonight's meal is already being prepared on the Festival fields, and the procession will continue in only a few moments."

The mounted women turned, and went towards the mouth of the narrow canyon from which the dull roaring sound came like a breath. Manlee descended from her boulder, and walked along with them, one hand on the bridle of Ma's horse. They stopped at the canyon's mouth, and waited while chaos erupted on the sands around the pool. Tents were thrown up without care or ceremony, possessions tossed carelessly inside. Da put Kati down, and she awakened Baber, who'd been sleeping on their folded tent throughout all the din. She held him as their tent went up, his head lolling on her shoulder, eyes still closed. She shook him twice, and finally he was awake, complaining about being hungry.

"Soon we eat, but first we have to walk. Here, take my hand."

Baber was too tired to refuse. He took her hand as they lined up close to the mounted women. Da did not take her hand, but walked right behind her. That was good, for she was responsible for her brother. Ma had told her so.

The trail up the canyon was rocky and steep, and there was a sharp odor like burning oil that seared her nostrils. Baber was fully awake now, stepping high over the larger rocks without complaint, and without her pulling him. A breeze down the canyon brought a sudden draft of hot air, then was gone. And the noise was getting louder, a growling rumble that seemed to come from all around them. The canyon walls were closing in, and suddenly Kati was frightened. She squeezed Baber's hand tightly, and moved slightly in front of him. Ahead, the mounted women had stopped, looking to the right and holding out their swords in a salute. When they moved on, Manlee stayed behind, and held out her arms to those who followed.

"Remember to offer a prayer when you pass by. Tengri must hear from your hearts that Empress Mandughai's return is the will of all Tumatsin, not just a few. Offer your prayer, then move on quickly. There are many of us."

Those ahead of Kati stopped by Manlee, turned to their right and bowed their heads, eyes closed. The roar was now deafening, the air swirling and hot. When she came up to Manlee, the woman smiled at her, and Kati saw that her eyes were light green. The woman gestured, and Kati followed her hand.

And beheld The Eye of Tengri.

A depression in the rock wall, an opening to a cave, shaped like an oval, blackness beyond, and from it issued the roar and a stream of hot air smelling of burning oil. She held her breath, felt Baber pressing up against her, and closed her eyes in the face of the hot breath from the cave. And as she stood that way, for only a moment, it seemed that thoughts came to her that were not her own, but from those around her. Surely they were in her mind only, for the roar was too loud for conversation.

Hear their prayers, great one, and send your Empress to deliver them from the Emperor's injustice. Their faith grows weak, and there are those who plot war without your aid. We have been alone for so long. Why have you abandoned us? I ask this, as well as the people. Have we not—

Protect my children, and my wife, whose eyes mirror those of our Empress. Return to us this pass, and help

us to reclaim our lands. We feel alone, and forgotten—
I see a cave with a fire inside. Our prayers are
unanswered for a thousand years. What kind of God are
you?

People were pressing from behind, and they moved
again. Kati opened her eyes, saw Da walking with his
eyes still closed, his lips moving silently. Baber's eyes
were as large as a cup, his tiny fingernails digging into
her hand. The trail steepened, and then the horses ahead
suddenly disappeared on flat ground at the top of the
canyon. Kati hurried her steps, Baber running to keep
up, and they came out onto a grassy plain stretching north,
west and east.

It was the festival field, and Kati gasped in surprise
and delight.

There were tents as far as she could see, huge things
the size of a *ger*, but gaily colored and topped with golden
awnings from which long ribbons fluttered in the breeze.
The smell of meat cooking made her mouth water, and
there was the odor of *ayrog* and honey as well. The tents
surrounded a large, vacant area of grass bordered by
ribboned rope strung between standards bearing the flags
of the various *ordus*.

But the first thing she really saw were the ponies.

Seven were tethered at the near end of the big field.
Kati looked at Da, and squealed, "I want to see the little
horses!"

Da put a hand on her shoulder, and smiled. "In a little
while. First, we must eat, and then I'll take you to the
ponies. I think the little grey one with white spots is
looking at you."

Kati couldn't find the grey pony, because Da took her
hand and hurried her away towards the tents too fast.

They found the tent with their standard placed before
it, and waited for a long time until everyone had filed
onto the field and was settled. In the meantime, the

mounted women had appeared again and Kati watched Ma lead them round and around the big, grassy area in a line, swords upright, eyes fixed ahead. Ma had changed again, and her face was no longer fierce, her eyes their normal brown. How could she do that?

Cooking pits had been dug beyond the tents, and they feasted on strips of lamb and beef, onions cooked whole, breads and barley cakes, and cheese. There was tea, and *ayrog* for the men, in great supply, and finally *yijin*, the sticky cakes made from spun honey. Kati ate five of them.

As Tengri-Khan dipped near the horizon, some of the men were a little drunk, and even Da was talking louder than usual. Ma had not eaten, was still with the mounted women, now lined up at the far end of the field near the ponies. And then the most wonderful thing happened. Manlee suddenly appeared on the field, and shouted loudly, "Fathers, bring your daughters!"

Da had just put Baber in the tent for a nap. Now he took her hand, and said, "Do you still want to see the ponies?"

"Oh, yes!"

They ducked under the rope bordering the field, and walked towards the little horses. Other fathers were coming with their daughters, one of them Edi, the little girl Kati had met on the trail. They all converged on the ponies, and there was laughter in the crowd around them.

Da led her straight to a grey with white spots, a thick, black mane and tail. Kati knew where to look, and saw it was a girl horse. She was bridled, but without saddle, and looked down at her with velvety, brown eyes when Kati stroked her nose.

"This one has been watching you," said Da; he lifted Kati up astride the animal, and placed the reins in her hands. Kati could barely restrain her joy. She was going to *ride*!

"I will lead you around once," said Da, "and then you ride alone. Be gentle with her. She is a fine pony."

"I know, Da." Of *course* she knew what to do. Hadn't Da shown her that over the many hours on Kaidu?

Da led the pony, and they circled the field past hundreds of smiling faces, but as they completed the circle Da walked away from her, and she saw that Ma and the other mounted women were walking their horses on the circle ahead of her. She felt the pony's muscles tense, and pressed with her knees. The pony trotted behind the women without hesitation and followed their pace.

Kati was not aware of how many times they circled the field that day. She only remembered that each time the women ahead of her increased their speed until finally they were in a full gallop, Kati leaning forward, her hands clutching the mane of the pony, the wind whipping at her face and hair.

The day could not be more wonderful.

And then suddenly it was.

When they finally stopped, Da came to lift her down, and said, "is she a good horse?"

"Oh, Da, she's wonderful!"

"And what would you name this horse if she was yours?"

"I would call her Sushua, Da, like the little flowers in the rocks."

"Then the name of your pony is Sushua. She is your animal, Kati, and you must care for her. Your mother and I give her to you as your first horse."

"DA!" cried Kati. She jumped up and hugged her father hard, and around them there was laughter.

Ma and the other horsewomen had disappeared from the field. Da let Kati ride until dark, round and around the circle. Edi had named her pony Tani, and Kati learned the girl lived on a rocky shelf overlooking the great sea to the west. Her father was a fisherman, and Edi's favorite thing was collecting shells on the sandy beaches along the coast.

By nightfall, the two girls had become fast friends.

Kati left Sushua tethered on the field, and reluctantly joined the procession back to the pool. She was tired, and all the food and riding had produced a knot in her stomach that wouldn't go away. And she wondered where Ma had gone. Da carried a sleeping Baber, and Kati followed without having her hand held, feeling very independent. The line moved quickly down the canyon and past Tengri's Eye, for it seemed everyone was tired. When she neared the place where Manlee again stood, Kati saw orange glow on the canyon walls, and Manlee's hair was brilliant, like a transparent crown of light.

Again the hot blast of air in her face, but she held her eyes open, for the cave maw was no longer black, but a bright orange. Reflected light, she suddenly realized, coming from a hot fire deep within the cave. She stared at the brilliant oval of the maw, and thought of her pendant. Her eyes felt dry, and she briefly closed them. In the darkness, it seemed there was a pair of emerald eyes, looking at her. Kati could still see them in her mind when she reached their camp by the pool.

A bonfire had been lit, and flames were leaping up to twice the height of a man. Ma came out of their tent, dressed in her normal leathers, and was hugged by Da. Kati hesitated to come closer, until Ma held out her arms to her and then she was being swept up in an embrace.

"Thank you for my horse, Ma. I love her," she murmured into her mother's neck.

"I was watching you," said Ma. "You ride very well. But tomorrow you will see some real riding from the boys and the men in Mandughai's cavalry charge. I must dress up again for that, for I play the part of Mandughai."

"Because you can make your eyes turn to green, like today?"

"Only Manlee and your mother can do that," said Da. "Our family is honored because of such a gift."

"It says that the blood of our Empress Mandughai has been passed directly to our family, Kati," said Ma. "The blood of our ancestors is in all of us, but it is said that Mandughai herself left two sons behind when she returned to Tengri-Nayon. We have come from one of those sons, Kati. The blood of our Empress is in you, too."

Kati yawned. "I will have green eyes when I'm older?"

Ma smiled. "Perhaps you will. Are you sleepy?"

"Not too much. Can I watch the fire with you?"

"For a little while, and then you sleep. Tomorrow is a long and exciting day."

Da took Baber to the tent, and joined them near the bonfire pit. Many people were there, but few of them were children. They sat staring at the flames, and conversation was in whispers. Kati nestled in Ma's lap and Da sat behind, his arms around both of them. It was wonderful. Da pointed out Tengri-Nayon directly above them, the brightest star in the sky, and very red. But very soon Kati's eyelids were heavy, and her head was nodding. Ma lifted her up and took her to the tent.

The inside of the tent was orange in the glow of the fire outside. Ma undressed her and slid her beneath a blanket of wool. She leaned close, and Kati reached up to touch her face and lips. "Your face—the way it was for a while today—it scared me."

Ma smiled, stroked her cheek. "I am Tumatsin, and the Hansui call us changelings because our faces become fierce when we are frightened or very angry. It's just the way we are, Kati. It will be the way you are when you become a woman."

"Were you frightened or angry today?" Kati yawned again, eyelids drooping.

"No. Today was difficult. I had to think of something that made me angry a long time ago, and then hold that thought for hours. It was very tiring, but now it's over, and I can have fun the rest of festival."

Kati felt herself slipping away. "I will ride Sushua," she murmured, "and see the burning cave again, and hear all the things people ask for there."

"The people must be shouting their prayers," said Ma.

Kati's eyes were nearly closed. "No," she said, tapping her own forehead with a finger, "I hear them—here."

In the last instant before sleep, it seemed that Ma had suddenly leaned closer to her.

And that night, she dreamed a recurring dream of a night sky filled with purple stars.

Everyone was up at first light to cook their barley cakes over the embers of the bonfire and drink tea. There was no procession to the festival field, people climbing to it after their chores were finished and stopping only briefly at the burning cave. Kati heard no prayers this time and went straight to Sushua, who recognized and nuzzled her. She fed her grass, and a smuggled barley cake, and then Da lifted her up.

"You can only ride a little while. Today is for the boys and the men to show their riding skills. There will be many games for them."

Kati lived in the moment, first walking, trotting, then galloping Sushua round and around the circle. But it seemed such a short time before Da came to lift her off. She had to take Sushua away from the field to a little pasture beyond the tents, rubbing down her coat with bunches of grass and curry-combing her, and then leaving her there with the other horses.

The rest of the morning she ate bread, and cheese, and five pieces of *yijin* while the boys showed off on the field. Their hair was braided, and they went shirtless to show their muscles to the older girls who giggled and pointed from the sidelines. There were races: short sprints back and forth, one with many turns among tall poles stuck in the grass, another with the riders actually *standing* on the backs of their horses. Abaka, from her own *ordu*, was a fine rider, and made a great impression. Kati saw many girls pointing at him, and whispering among themselves.

After the boys were finished showing off, Kati got to ride Sushua again, then there was more eating and music: lutes and horns, drums and cymbals, a great crash of noise, and people began dancing to it, twirling and kicking, men picking up the nearest woman and spinning madly with her. Da and Ma did it too, Ma's arms around Da's neck as he twirled her round and round, and when they stopped they were kissing.

But after the dancing, things seemed to become more serious.

The men went out to the field with re-curved bows and quivers full of arrows, and shot at man-shaped straw dummies hanging from poles. The boys reappeared and did the same while the men were preparing their mounts, then drummers came to line the field. When the drums began pounding, everyone was suddenly silent, and the men charged onto the field on horseback, circling round and around and firing at the dummies from horseback. After each pass, the dummies bristled with stuck arrows.

Ma disappeared again, and soon Kati saw her mounted with the regalia of the previous day, but her face was normal. Her sword was in a scabbard at her side, and she was smiling. She and the other mounted women drew up in a line, and the men crowded in behind her, horses jostling together in excitement.

The drums pounded harder, and women in the crowd began trilling, a sound that always thrilled Kati. And then Ma drew her sword, pointing down the length of the field, and she uttered a shrill cry that raised the hair at the back of Kati's neck.

The horses leapt forward and charged down the field, Ma's sword outstretched, the men screaming, the women trilling, fanning out at the end of the field, and charging back again. Three times they did this, and each time the noise seemed to get louder, until Kati clapped her hands over her ears. Finally, it was over, the men reassembling in the center of the field, the mounted women unsheathing their swords one last time and saluting the crowd before putting their swords back in their scabbards with a metallic crash in unison.

And then, quite suddenly, everyone was laughing again and there was music. Ma dismounted before their tent, and pulled off the heavy, colorful robe, under which she wore her leathers. Her face glistened with sweat. She unbuckled her sword, handed it to Kati. "Hold this a moment."

The sword, in its scabbard, was heavy, longer than Kati's body. The blade was curved, hilt and pommel in brass. Kati held it as a precious thing, lifted it up to Ma when she asked for it. Ma put it in the tent with the robe. But Kati did not forget the feel of that sword in her hand.

The atmosphere was light again, and the weapons were put away in the tents. Kati rode Sushua for nearly two hours while the adults laid out blankets covered with trading goods from the various *ordu*s and spent a happy afternoon of trading and gossip. It would have been a purely wonderful day except for two things that happened.

The first occurred mid-afternoon, when someone first heard a distant whine and shouted for quiet. The whine grew louder, then a woman pointed east and cried, "Flyer!" Kati was trotting Sushua, and saw the silvery craft coming towards her at low altitude. She ignored it, and kept riding. People were scurrying around, picking up a few remaining bows and arrow quivers, and getting them into the tents. They looked up sullenly as the craft passed overhead, and some shook their fists. Kati watched their faces, and saw anger there. The craft passed over one more time, and again headed east, leaving the crowd muttering. Kati felt the tension of the people around her, and didn't like it. The festival was supposed to be fun, and adults could be so serious, she thought.

But it was the second incident that really bothered her, a confrontation with her mother that left her shocked and bewildered. One minute, Ma was happy and smiling, and the next she was dragging Kati painfully into the tent with her eyes blazing red.

Ma was talking to Manlee and two other women, and Kati was watching an older boy and girl nearby. The girl was smiling shyly, lowering her eyes as the boy leaned close to whisper in her ear. Kati was shocked at a sudden thought, and without thinking, tugged at her mother's leathers. Ma leaned down, and Kati whispered in her ear.

"That boy over there is so excited. He thinks the girl will go to the trees with him, and take off her clothes. Should he be thinking like—"

Ma's fingernails bit into her arm, and the tent was only steps away. Her little legs couldn't move fast enough to keep up, and Ma dragged her part of the way. Baber was in the tent, sound asleep. Ma dropped to her knees before Kati, grasped her arms hard, and her eyes were blazing red.

"How do you know such a thing? Are you making this up?"

Kati was stunned. "I—no, Ma, I could hear him. He likes the girl, and wants her to go with him."

"You could *not* hear him at that distance. Are you saying this for attention? I've told you about lying, Kati."

"I'm not lying," said Kati. I heard him thinking it, Ma. No, not really heard—" Kati paused, uncertain about her explanation. "I heard it here, Ma, but not words. I just knew what he wanted." She tapped her forehead. "Ma, you're hurting my arm! What's wrong?"

Ma's red eyes were inches from her face, her breath hot in a whisper. "You imagine you can hear a thought, but only a Searcher can do that, and you are not a Searcher. You are Tumatsin! To pry into a mind is an evil thing! To talk about it is even worse! If you imagine you hear a thought you will block it out as a false thing, and say nothing! Do you understand?"

Kati nodded, but her chest ached, and she felt tears welling up in her eyes, for she was now truly frightened.

"I'm not evil, Ma, but I do hear things. I *do!*"

Ma shook her roughly. "NO! It is your imagination! It was meeting the Searcher on the trail. They are evil people, Kati! You must not want to be like them in any way!"

Kati began to cry. "I'm not bad, Ma!" And then she was sobbing bitterly. "I'm not bad! I'm not!" she wailed.

Ma's eyes suddenly gushed tears. She pulled Kati to her, kissed her cheek, hugged her.

"Oh Kati, I don't want to hurt you! But promise me you will block out these thoughts you have, and never, *ever* talk about them. People won't understand. They will think you evil, like the Searchers. Please, Kati, do what I say."

"I will, Ma, I will, I promise." Kati sniffled, and put her arms around Ma's neck, and Ma rocked her back and forth silently for a long moment. And then they dried their eyes, and Ma took her outside again.

The festival continued gaily for the rest of the day, but Kati did not want to be near people. She went to the pasture and found Sushua and led her back to the field, where one of the boys helped her get mounted. She rode her horse, alone, round and around the circle until it was time to eat, but still she rode. Da finally came out with two barley cakes for her, thinking she was having too much fun to eat, and very happy she loved his gift so much. He did not say this, yet she heard it. Was hearing Da's nice thoughts also an evil thing?

Out on the field, away from people, there were no thoughts, only the wind in her face and Sushua's warm body beneath her. How could Ma think she would imagine such things and then talk out loud about it? The thoughts only came when people were close, like the Searcher on the trail. *He* hadn't been surprised—or had he? He'd looked at her curiously. The thoughts just came. How could she stop them?

At dark she had to stop riding. Da let her stay with Sushua in the pasture for a while, because she said she wanted to. The music was loud, and much *ayrog* was flowing. Away from people her mind was clear. Sushua had no thoughts; she just wanted to eat. Kati rubbed the little horse down while she was filling her belly, and hugged her often before Ma came to get her.

They were near the end of the line going back to camp, and Manlee was again standing by the burning cave, urging the prayers of the people. It made Kati angry that the woman didn't believe her own words. Tengri's Eye was just a fire deep inside a cave, and the old woman didn't believe the ancestors were *ever* coming back. Still, she looked again at the bright glow inside the maw of the cave, felt its hot breath, and closed her eyes.

The emerald green eyes were suddenly there again, slanted upwards, pupils black as night, and the sight of them seemed calming. The chatter inside her head was suddenly gone, and she felt warmed all over as if an arm had just gone around her shoulders, like when she was with Da. She felt a presence, a connection with something outside herself. Suddenly, she felt protected.

Kati stumbled on the trail, eyes tightly closed. Ma

squeezed her hand. *Please don't leave me!* Kati wanted
to say to the eyes. *Keep the thoughts away.* But she had
to open her eyes to avoid falling down, and she saw Ma,
whom she loved and tried to obey in all things.

She sat up for only a short time, and went to bed with
Baber, the tent's interior brightly lit by the glow of the
bonfire raging outside. She closed her eyes tightly, but
the image of the green eyes was gone. Exhausted from
the day, she quickly fell asleep.

And was awakened much later by a sound of sobbing
in the now darkened tent. Soft, and sad, it went on for a
long time, from where Ma and Da were sleeping.
Someone stirred.

"Toregene, what is the matter?"

A sniffle. "The strain of the day, I suppose. The children
are exhausted, and so am I. I'm ready to go home.
Temujin, do you love me?"

"Of course I do. You and the children are my life. What
a thing to ask!"

"Then hold me, Temujin. Hold me—love me."

From then on the sounds Kati heard were familiar ones,
the sounds Ma and Da made as they often pleasured
each other in their *ger* beyond the mountains. Suddenly,
Kati wanted to go home, to that place across the
mountains, where it would be quiet again.

People slept later the next morning, and some of the
men seemed grumpy when they arose. They cooked their
cakes over the coals in the great pit by the pool, and
then the tents were struck and people were talking and
sitting on the mounds of their possessions while the boys
went up to the fields to retrieve the horses. Gifts were
being exchanged among old and new friends, and Kati
was surprised when Edi came up to her and handed her
something wrapped in a piece of soft leather.

"I wish we could ride together, but your *ordu* is so far

from the sea," said Edi. "Here is something for you to remember the day we were given our horses, and when we rode together."

Kati unfolded the leather sheet, and saw a pendant made from a single shell that gave off every color in the rainbow. A single hole had been punched in it, and it hung on a leather thong with several smaller shells to either side of it. It was truly beautiful, and Kati said so.

Edi smiled shyly. "I wish we lived closer to each other. I won't see you until next Festival. That's five years." She hesitated. "All the other girls in my *ordu* are older than me. Or else they're just babies."

Kati was desperate for an idea about what to give in return. Suddenly, she thought of her dagger, and pulled it from her waistband. "Da made this for me, but he won't mind if I give it to a friend. Here, take it."

Edi took the dagger, ran her fingers along the blade. "I'll keep it always," she said, then stepped up to Kati and gave her a hug. "Goodbye." And then she ran away to her family.

Manlee came by to say goodbye to Ma and Da, and to remind them of their prayers. Kati saw Ma looking at her while the woman was talking, and looked away. Ma had hugged her awake in the morning, had braided her hair in silence. There was now a certain wariness about Ma, a tension between them. But this morning there were no thoughts in Kati's head, even with all the people so close, so perhaps it was a passing thing.

Abaka returned with the horses, with Sushua trailing behind. Da bridled her, and put a colorful blanket on her back for the long journey home. In short time the horses were loaded, Kati was mounted on Sushua, and Baber was grinning from his place before Da on Kaidu.

Manlee held up her arms, and there was silence. For many moments they listened to the roar coming from the canyon, and then Manlee shouted, "Now go with the protection of Tengri, and may he bring us all together again in this place five years from now. Have a safe journey!"

She waved an arm, and suddenly water was again cascading from the top of the cliff to splash with force into the pool. The great waterfall had been silent during their stay on the beach, only to suddenly reappear as they were leaving. Kati was again amazed.

Because they had camped close to the pool, Kati and her family were one of the last groups to reach the plateau. Kati looked for Edi, but never found her. Five years was a very long time. She would nearly be a woman before she saw Edi again. When they reached the plateau, she saw long lines of horses stretched along the trails headed towards the western sea, and wished she were going with them where it was always warm. But they turned east, and soon they were alone, headed towards their isolated *ordu* beyond the mountains to keep watch on the emperor.

Sushua trotted easily along with the others, but Ma made her stay near the rear of the column. Sushua seemed content with this, but Kati quickly became bored with the pace. When a flyer came over them at mid-day, she waved to it. When it made a second pass, at low level, she waved again, until Ma glared at her.

"Do not call attention to us," warned Ma.

Kati pouted. Ma was too serious about everything. Besides, she was sure one of the men in the flyer had waved back to her. What was the harm?

They camped that night in the place by the pass between the two fingers of rock, and it was cold again. The other *ordu*s were warm by the sea, and here she was again, back in the mountains and the cold. She fought for breath again before falling into a restless sleep that ended too soon.

They came down from the line of peaks above their *ordu* in mid-afternoon of the following day, and the column suddenly stopped. Kuchlug came back to get Ma, and she went forward to the head of the line. When she came back, her eyes were tinged red. "Mounted troops of the Emperor are near our *ordu*," she said to Kati. "We will wait until they are gone."

As they descended the final slope towards home, Kati looked north and saw a line of mounted people with the light of Tengri-Khan sparkling on their clothing until they disappeared beyond a thumb of rock. The column suddenly picked up speed, and Kati had a chance to gallop Sushua just as they were nearing the *ordu*. Adults leaped from their horses, rushed inside their *gerts*. As Kati pulled up with Ma before their *ger*, Da came out and said, "Everything has been searched, but they haven't disturbed anything I can see. Kuchlug, give me a hand here!"

Da and Kuchlug went inside the *ger* as Ma helped Kati dismount. She tethered Sushua to a post, and went inside. Da and Kuchlug had moved the stove aside and were pulling up boards beneath it. A leather-wrapped bundle was in a hole beneath the boards. It was the weapon Da kept hidden there. "Still here," said Da, "but we have to find a safer place to store these, away from the *ordu*. Tell the other men."

Kuchlug left after helping Da reposition the stove. Ma went to Da, hugged him. "This is not a good welcome," said Da. "We no longer have rights in the eyes of the Emperor. It is not safe here, Toregene. Maybe you should take the children and—"

"Our place is with you," said Ma. "This is our home." Her head on Da's chest, arms around him, Ma's eyes met Kati's.

A test of your imagination, my daughter. A Searcher will come, and when he does you must think of the blackness of a night sky. And if you listen to his thoughts, your face must betray no emotion at what you hear. You will show him you are only a little girl. Do you hear me, Kati?

Kati nodded her head slowly. *Not blackness, Ma. I will think of the green eyes that take all the thoughts away from me.*

Ma's hands clutched at Da's back, and her eyes turned bright red.

Kati suddenly felt a horrible fear, and knew it was not her own.

The fear was coming from Ma.

CHAPTER THREE
SEARCHERS

Sushua, like the wind, rushed down the scree-fall by the Emperor's Thumb with a great clatter, and out onto the plateau, trampling grass and scattering the petals of aging wildflowers fluttering in submission. Kati bent low over Sushua's neck, reins held lightly, knees squeezing rhythmically with the beat of the gallop. Cold air seared her face, but she was warmed by Tengri-Khan directly overhead, and the thick tunic of wool over her leathers.

Her boldness in riding had come in one great leap with the gift of a saddle from her parents on her sixth birthday, when they saw that her legs were suddenly longer, while Sushua had ceased to grow. The short, stubby saddle horn was enough for Kati to grab with a short jump, and mount with a push off from the stirrup. Now standing in those stirrups, it seemed she floated above the back of the little horse, yet they were one.

She held the charge for a kilometer on the level plateau, until they came to the westward trail and slowed. They climbed a hanging canyon to a rock peak that was really four pinnacles almost symmetrically spaced to enclose a small pasture with rich grass and the little flowers Sushua had been named after. The place commanded a fine view in all directions, including the Emperor's domed city and Edi's great ocean to the west.

Abaka had shown her the place only weeks before, when she'd first dared to ride with the older boys. The boys' conversation had been muffled, with some laughter at private secrets they shared, but Kati could see their memories of adventures they'd had with certain girls in the soft grass, and she'd held her tongue. Now she was here alone for the first time, and there were no thoughts to distract her, other than her own.

Kati dismounted, and rubbed Sushua down with a rough cloth until the horse groaned with pleasure. She combed out her mane and tail, tied ribbons to the long, black hair, then admired her work as Sushua looked back at her with a mouthful of grass and flowers. The wind moaned between the rock spires around her, and Kati was suddenly at peace with herself.

Ma had asked her out of the *ger* when the arguments among the men had become loud with accusations and denials. Two of the men had traveled far to deny knowledge of raids on the Emperor's new barley fields. They were liars, for Kati saw the images of two boys involved, even their horses, and knew that the boys were the men's' own sons. Da had even seen their lies, threatened to go to Manlee, and then the cursing had begun.

Now she was away from all of that. Now she was away from thoughts she should tell Da, but couldn't, because it was evil to do so. After that confrontation with Ma at festival, she'd hoped the thoughts would go away, but they hadn't. They'd just kept getting stronger, more numerous, and the green eyes that drove them away seemed to have abandoned her after that last night at festival.

There were no thoughts from Ma, her mind a carefully guarded thing since the day they'd returned from festival to have that one, brief conversation without words. Ma was wary in her presence, yet loved her still, with much touching: warm hugs at bedtime, bathing, the combing and braiding of her hair. She even let Kati sit with her at meditation before the little stone altar in their *ger* on those occasions when Da was outside and Baber asleep.

The altar was a flat slab of stone. On it was a bowl of grain, a cup of fresh tea, a bundle of dried, sweet grass and a candle. Ma would light a few stems of grass, which gave off a delicious odor, then the candle. She would stare at the flickering candle for several moments, then close her eyes and go deep within herself. There were no prayers, or thoughts, but when Ma emerged from those quiet moments, she seemed refreshed and serene, as if the troubles of her day had been washed from her. Kati had tried it several times, and twice fell sound asleep. And the green eyes had not been returned by her efforts.

But here, in her high place, Kati looked out towards the great sea, and felt a quiet peace within herself. She fingered her pendants: Tengri's Eye, Edi's colorful shell. She thought of Edi, and wished that she could live by the sea.

A flyer passed by to the south, turned, and came back across the plateau at an altitude lower than hers. The flyers were out four or five times a day now, and mounted patrols had come by their *ordu* several times this month alone. 'Just showing their presence,' Da had said. But that presence was on the increase, and the people resented it. In their thoughts, they cursed that presence, and the Emperor of Shanji.

Kati waited until the flyer had dropped into the valley of the Emperor's city, then mounted Sushua, and they picked their way carefully back down the canyon to the trail and the grassy plateau below. They walked the trail back to the *ordu*, arriving in time to see two men mounting their horses in front of Kati's *ger*. Da and Ma had come outside to see them off. Da's face was grim, Ma's eyes tinged red in warning as Kati came near.

"I cannot control the young hotheads in every *ordu*," said one man. "I can only talk to the parents, and remind them of their responsibilities in controlling older children, Temujin."

"Remind them also that any reprisals will come first to the *ordu* designated by Manlee to keep watch on the Emperor. And if they think they're safe from harm, they should remember that a flyer can reach them in two hours, and destroy all they possess in minutes. *Tell* them that, Bao," said Da.

"I will do what I can," said the man. Both men slapped their horses' flanks and rode away as Kati dismounted Sushua and tethered her.

Da stalked back inside the *ger*. Ma took Kati's hand, and whispered, "be careful with your father. This day has been very bad for him."

"I will be quiet," said Kati.

Bread and cheese had been put out on their low table in the center of the *ger*. Da sat cross-legged by it, and he was drinking *ayrog* very early in the day. Kati sat down beside him, Ma opposite them. Baber was missing, but Kati didn't ask why.

Da turned to Kati, and touched her cheek. "And where did you go to while all of us were yelling at each other today?"

Kati looked up at him, and smiled as sweetly as she could. "Sushua and I rode the plateau by The Thumb, and we went very fast."

Da smoothed her hair gently with his hand. "My little warrior. How quickly you've become such a fine rider. In a few years, only a horse like Kaidu will be good enough for you."

He took a long sip of *ayrog*, and wiped his mouth on his sleeve. "If the Emperor doesn't burn us out first, that is."

"*Temujin!*" said Ma.

Da sighed. "I'm sorry. But the other *ordus* are too far removed to understand how uncertain our safety is here. They make fun of the Emperor, and forget his power. Toregene, I can wait no longer. I must go to Manlee right away. I know she doesn't approve of what's going on, and she has influence with the women. The men see her as an old woman making promises that haven't been kept, but they will bend to the will of their wives."

Ma looked at him calmly. "I understand. When will you leave?"

"Tomorrow morning, early. I will ride through the night."

"Alone?"

"No. Kuchlug will ride with me, and—and I'd like to take Baber along, too."

"It will be difficult for him," said Ma quietly.

"I have a reason for taking him," said Da, smiling. He turned to Kati. "Now, this is a secret. Do not say anything to your brother."

Kati looked up at him with wide eyes.

"Festival is over two years away, and Baber is more than ready for riding. I will find a pony for him on the coast, and he can ride it home. We should be back in six or seven days."

Kati gasped, and whispered, "Baber will get his first horse! Oh, Ma! We can ride together!"

Ma smiled. "I'm outnumbered at this table. Very well, take Baber with you, but remember to feed him."

And at dinner that evening, after Baber had returned from playing with friends, Kati could barely restrain herself from giving away the secret, or from laughing when her brother made a mess of himself while eating his soup.

Da and Baber had already left by the time Kati was fully awake the following morning. She vaguely remembered the touch of Da's hand on her forehead when it was still dark, the sound of his soft voice in her ear. "May Tengri

care for my little Empress," he'd said, and then he was
gone.

Kati missed them both within hours, and wished she
could be there to see Baber's face when he was given
his horse. But in a few days, they would be riding together,
and she would be his teacher.

In the meantime, there were chores to do. She milked
three goats, swept out the *ger*, and carried feed for the
sheep in the holding pen. There were only three animals,
but within a week the pen would be full, for there was
now a bite in the morning air, and winter was only weeks
away. Kati did not like winter, with cold that froze her
nostrils shut in minutes and burned her face. The only
good day in winter was her birthday.

By noon her chores were finished, and Kati was bored.
So when Abaka came by and asked Ma if Kati would
like to join him and four other boys in chasing down
strays, she was immediately excited and pleading with
Ma to let her go. Ma relented, for Abaka had become
fond of Kati, and with two younger brothers in his family
treated her like the little sister he would never have. So
Kati rushed to saddle Sushua, and caught up to them
by the time they'd reached the Emperor's Thumb.

In two hours they found one group of four stray sheep,
herded them back to the holding pen near the Thumb,
then went out again, this time searching the many hanging
canyons and gullies dropping down from the pinnacles.
There was nothing to find, and Kati was suddenly bored
again. She traversed a slope, saw the boys below her,
heading down, but Abaka had remained on a ridge not
far from her. He had a hand up to shade his eyes, and
was looking south towards the Emperor's valley. She rode
up to him, and he turned, startled.

"What is it?" she asked.

"Nothing. I thought I saw some riders down there, near
the trees. Probably another one of the Emperor's patrols.

They're all over the place, now. I wish they'd leave us alone." He turned his horse. "We'd better go. There are no more strays, and your mother will worry if we're late."

Abaka started down the slope, Kati right behind him. But Sushua's nose banged into the rump of Abaka's horse when he suddenly stopped and pointed below. Five mounted troopers had suddenly come from nowhere, and were surrounding the boys waiting on the trail below. They trotted quickly down the slope to join them, and Kati saw that one of the troopers was a Searcher.

We waste our time. There is no problem here.

A thought clear and loud, in her head. Kati pulled up beside Abaka and gazed at the Searcher, a young man with the characteristic, lightly veined bulge on his forehead, the finely arched nose.

"Ah," said the man, "there are more of you. I'm told you search for strays before winter arrives."

"That is true," said Abaka.

"We found four," said Kati, brightly.

The Searcher smiled faintly at her, then looked at Abaka. "You have seen something from the ridge. Some riders, down near the valley, correct?"

Abaka swallowed hard. "Yes."

"How many?"

"I didn't have time to count. They disappeared in the trees."

The Searcher paused. "Also correct. You would be wise to return home now. We're searching for some troublemakers, and you wouldn't want to be mistaken for them."

We just want to be left alone. The troublemakers come from the west, not our ordu.

The Searchers eyes widened, darted from person to person, but Kati just sat there, a passive look on her face.

How useful. Reveal yourself, and I will thank you personally.

Kati felt his mental probe sweep over her, but she was alone, in the darkness of a cave.

No.

The Searcher chuckled, turned to his comrades. "There is nothing here. We ride west." He turned his horse, and the rest of the troopers followed him away without a word. Kati and the boys followed the troopers for several minutes before the men turned off onto another trail heading along a ridge towards the west, and then they quickened their pace.

When they reached the *ordu*, Abaka told Ma about seeing the riders, and then the questioning by the troopers. "There could be more trouble soon," said Ma. "Go to your *gerts*, and stay there. And tether your horses where they can be seen from the air. Kati, get inside."

Kati helped her mother make the barley cakes, and swept the floor while Ma cooked. They ate in silence, Ma deep within herself, and Kati could see nothing there. And their meal was only half finished when there was a commotion outside: the trampling of horses' hooves, and a shout.

"Hello! We need help here!"

Ma got up from table, pulled the door flap aside, and peered cautiously outside. "What do you want?" she said.

"We've lost a horse, and have a long ride ahead. Do you have an animal we could borrow? I'll sign a note for it."

A boy's voice. Kati went to the doorway, peered out around her mother. There were six boys, Tumatsin, all around Abaka's age, and they looked frightened. Two of them were doubled up on one horse. All the animals were glistening with sweat, their breath great puffs of fog. They looked exhausted.

"What is your *ordu*?" asked Ma.

"We come from the coast," said the oldest boy, thin faced, with hard eyes.

"I asked the name of your *ordu*," said Ma.

"It's enough that we're Tumatsin," the boy said angrily. "You are a living presence of our Empress, and our parents honor you. Do you refuse to aid us? Please, we have little time to wait."

He is from the Merkit ordu, and the boys have done mischief to the Emperor's machines. They flee from his troopers.

Ma sucked in her breath, and cast a glance at Kati, who looked at her calmly. "Never mind," she said. "Your *ordu* has been revealed to me, and we have no horse for you. Now leave us, before the Emperor's troopers come and think we are responsible for your thoughtless actions. Go!"

The older boy looked at her with wide eyes, frightened by her knowledge. He said nothing, but jerked hard on the reins to turn his horse, and galloped away, the others close behind him.

Faces appeared from the doorway flaps of other *gerts*. "Stay inside!" shouted Ma. "Troopers will be coming!"

Ma brushed past Kati and went inside. Kati followed her, and they sat down again at the table. Ma's eyes were suddenly red. "I fear I've sent them to their deaths," she said. "The children of my own people." She looked at Kati, and tears were in her eyes. "Your powers have grown."

"Yes," said Kati. "But I have learned how to hide it. I even talked to the Searcher on the trail today, but he didn't know it was me. They don't expect such a thing from a little girl. Why am I different, Ma? Why is it I can do things even you cannot do?"

Ma reached across the table, and clutched Kati's hand. "There are so many things I want to tell you, but I cannot. Perhaps when you are older. The blood of our Empress is in you, and your life must be preserved at any cost. I fear for you. I fear for us all, because we are now in great danger. If troopers come, I want you to remain inside. Do not show yourself to them. And do not think you are clever in the presence of a Searcher. They see deeper than you think, and being a child will not fool them. Please, Kati, believe what I say!"

"I do, Ma. I promise I'll be careful."

Ma sighed. "I wish your father were here, but maybe it's best he isn't. He should have reached Manlee by now."

They were startled by the sound of many screaming turbines. The *ger* walls shook as several flyers passed overhead at low altitude, heading west. Ma looked at Kati with eyes blazing red.

"They have seen the boys. They will kill them," she said.

And just before dusk, Kati saw their bodies.

A line of troopers came down the trail from the Emperor's Thumb and into the *ordu*. At the end of the line were three horses led by a trooper, and draped across the saddle of each horse were two bodies blackened beyond recognition. The leader of the troopers was an older man with grey streaks in his hair, and on the horse next to his was a Searcher. They stopped before Kati's *ger*, and the leader called out so all could hear.

"Come out here, all of you! I want you to see what treachery can bring to you! Everyone out! NOW!"

Ma went outside with the others, while Kati peeped through a slit between tent flap and wall. At the sight of the blackened bodies, some of the women began sobbing. The horses carrying the bodies were brought before Kati's *ger*, so all could see, and she could smell the stench of burned meat.

"These young boys have committed sabotage against property of the Emperor. They have paid for it with their lives! Our Emperor grieves with you, for he knows personally the hurt of losing a child. But your people have left him no choice. Sabotage, and destruction of property, is an act the Emperor does not tolerate among his own people. Hansui criminals are executed for such acts, and though you are not the Emperor's people, you are not exempt from his justice!"

"The boys are not from our *ordu*," said Ma. "They are from the west, and when they came here to obtain a new horse we refused them. We are not responsible for what they've done."

"We are aware of that," said the Emperor's soldier. "But your presence here encourages their foolishness, or else they would not have come to you for help. I will be blunt with you, woman. There is talk that the Emperor does not desire your presence here, that he would have you move to the west with the rest of your kind. Why do you remain here? The weather is harsh, and life would be more comfortable for you by the sea. Do you remain here to spy on the Emperor's city and lands?

"NO!" cried Ma. "This is our home! We have been here for generations! The land on which you grow your barley was once ours!"

Kati was watching the young Searcher. He was frowning, his hands clenching hard on the reins of his horse. Now he looked at Ma. "But there was a time when you *did* spy on what was happening in the valley."

Ma was suddenly rigid. "Yes, but that was years ago, when the land was being taken from us. We are resigned to that loss, now, and we want no trouble. My husband is meeting at this moment with our leader Manlee and others from the western *ordus* to stop the troublemakers. We can do no more than that."

Kati had felt nothing. The Searcher must be concentrating on Ma, and she was opening herself to him.

"She speaks the truth, Quan," said the Searcher.

"I sympathize," said the soldier, "but we follow the Emperor's will, and this latest incident may very well trigger a final judgment regarding this *ordu*. You would be well advised to begin packing your things, and to be ready to move quickly."

"But we are *innocent!*" cried Ma.

"I will speak to that innocence with my superiors," said the Searcher. "They have some influence with the Emperor." He looked directly at Ma, and she stiffened.

"I understand," she said. "Thank you."

Something was going on between Ma and the Searcher. But Kati could hear nothing passing between them. Perhaps it was drowned out by the hostile feelings of the Emperor's soldier, who now glanced darkly at the Searcher, then looked back at Ma.

"Influence, or not, I know what I've heard, and I'm generous to give you this warning. Pack your things, and be prepared to move. The Emperor has had enough with this trouble."

"We will follow your advice," said Ma, "and we do appreciate the warning." Her voice was calm, and she pleaded no further. The Searcher had told her something, and Kati had not sensed it. How could that be, when the soldier's desire to burn down her *ordu* was so clear in her head? For only one instant, she had felt something pass through her without dwelling there. And she had been concentrating so hard!

Ma shouted to the other people gathered near the doorways to their *gerts*. "You've heard the warning! Now saddle your horses, and pack only what you need for travel. We need to be ready to leave at a moment's notice."

Some of the women broke into open sobbing. Ma looked back at the soldier, and said, "Though we are innocent of wrongdoing, we will await final judgment of the Emperor, and have trust in his wisdom."

The soldier put his hand on his hip, and struck an arrogant pose. "You are wise, woman. I, myself, will speak to your likely innocence, and also your cooperative nature. This could go well for your *ordu*. But even if you remain here, remember what you've seen today, and tell it to *all* your people. Tell them that opposition to the Emperor is futile, and that they live on their lands only by his grace. He is the ruler over all the lands, the mountains, the sea, and beyond the sea. He is the ruler of Shanji!"

The soldier waved his hand, and the column of men moved out, leading the three horses with their horrible burden. As soon as they were out of sight, the people came over to Ma and clustered around her, the women crying, the men cursing and mouthing useless threats against the soldiers.

"The most important thing is our lives. And I tell you we are in great danger here. Be ready to move! We cannot fight if we are dead. Now get to your packing, and get your horses saddled and tethered by your *gerts*."

Ma turned, and Kati saw her eyes were blazing red, and in her mouth were the sharp, pointed teeth of a *shizi*. No wonder the people had moved so quickly, though they were grumbling. Ma brushed past her into the *ger*. "You heard?" she growled.

"No. I heard nothing, but I was trying very hard. I think the Searcher was talking to you without words."

"He was," said Ma. She began stuffing travel woolins into a bag. "I don't know why, but he seems to be a friend. He said the Emperor wishes us destroyed, but the Searchers who advise him say we should be moved instead. They say no Tumatsin life should be taken, but now the flyers have done it, and it will be easy for them to do it again. He seemed fearful for us, and I have no idea why. The Searchers are certainly not our friends. Kati, pack your little bag with extra shirt and socks, and your tunic with the hood. You can take one doll, but no more."

"Where will we go?"

Ma worked furiously, filling one bag, and opening another. "We will go to Manlee in the Dorvodt *ordu*. It sits on the edge of a cliff overlooking the sea, and there are many children your age there. Your father was going there first, and Manlee will know where to find him. We must be prepared to ride through the night."

Kati opened her little bag, and began to pack it. "Maybe I can find Edi again, and we can hunt for shells on the beach. I would like to live by the sea, Ma."

"I know. Life is hard here, with the cold. We have only stayed because our people needed an outpost for watching the Emperor, and we have served that purpose. But I think the Emperor's next step will be to drive us into the sea. If our Empress Mandughai is watching, then she'd better do something soon. We have waited for a thousand years, and our time is running out."

"The lady with the green eyes," said Kati, looking at the tapestry over her bed. "When I was at festival I saw green eyes, and they made the thoughts go away for awhile, but then the eyes were gone, and haven't come back. I think it was all my imagination."

Ma dropped the bag she was stuffing, and rushed to Kati, kneeling down in front of her and grasping her arms. "No!" she said. "It was not your imagination! It was a sign! A sign of recognition by the Empress. She watches you from afar, even now. She watches your powers grow, powers that no other Tumatsin woman has. You are different, Kati, something new. I wish I could tell you why you are this way, but I cannot do this until you are a woman. You will be able to understand it then."

Ma's face was still fierce, with the sharp teeth and blazing eyes, a sight Kati hadn't seen since festival. Kati touched her mother's teeth with a finger, and scowled. "I don't want to be different. I want to be like you."

Ma hugged her. "You will be like me, and much more. But you must grow to womanhood, and be safe. Kati, it's not just the Empress who has seen you, but the Searchers themselves. They know about you. They want you safe. The last thing the Searcher said to me without words was 'whatever happens here, you must do all within your power to protect the child. She must not be harmed.' The child is you, Kati, and he didn't even see you. But he knew you were there. For reasons I do not understand, the Searchers want you safe. It's the main reason I have for moving, and fast! Get your bag packed quickly, now, and see to Sushua while I fix us something to eat.

Kati did as she was told. She topped off her bag with a single doll, a warrior mounted on a black horse like Kaidu, then went outside and brushed down Sushua, combed her tail and mane while the little horse nuzzled, then ate the treat of flowers she'd hidden in the pocket of her tunic. Sushua nickered when Kati moved away, so she came back and gave her a hug before going inside to eat.

That night, long after it was dark and she was in her bed, her thoughts whirled with confusion. She *was* different from Ma, because she could hear *everyone*'s thoughts, not just Searchers'. Was that why the Searchers were interested in her? Because she was like them? And *why* was she like them, and not other Tumatsin women? Ma said she would tell her when she was older. Why couldn't she tell her *now*?

When Ma had been telling her about what the Searcher had said, she'd seemed excited, almost happy, and yet they were in danger. The green eyes were a sign of the Empress watching her, but Kati hadn't seen those eyes in nearly three years. Had Ma left something out, something else the Searcher had said without words?

It's all imagination: the eyes, the Empress coming, that cave at festival that is nothing but a fire burning deep within a hole in the ground. Nobody is watching us except the Emperor, and he doesn't want us here.

Ma came over to her bed when Kati's eyes were already heavy, and pulled up the wool blanket to her chin. She leaned over to kiss her cheek, and put a cool hand on her forehead. "Sleep well, my little Empress. I love you with all my heart, and I will watch over you as long as there is life in me."

Da had called her his little Empress many times.

But it was the first time that Ma had called her that.

PART II

WARD

PART II

WARD

CHAPTER FOUR
TRAGEDY

The flyers came at dawn.

Ma woke Kati when it was still dark. She loaded four bags of clothing, food and utensils over the rump of her chestnut while Kati was dressing. Kati came outside to hang her single little bag from the horn of her saddle and say good morning to Sushua. They went back inside to roll up the wall tapestries and wrap them in hides for burial. The tapestries were too bulky to carry along, but they had been with the family for several generations and could not be left to the scavenging of the Emperor's troops. Ma seemed certain they would have to leave, and so they wrapped up the tapestries and Ma broke down her altar, placing the elements of it in a coarse woolen bag. They took these things to a grove of trees a hundred meters from the *ger*, and Ma used her hands to sweep aside the carpet of needles covering wood slats that were the roof of a stone-lined cairn set into the ground. Four of the Emperor's rifles lay within the cairn, wrapped in oiled leather. They put the tapestries and bag in with the rifles and covered it all up again.

The *ger* looked barren without the altar or the colorful pictures on the walls. There was only the stove and the low table, with a few water bags, plates, bowls, utensils remaining. Kati was suddenly aware of how few possessions

73

they actually had. Ma moved silently in flickering lamp-light, firing up the stove, and cooking their barleycakes and tea.

Kati felt her mother's sadness. This *ger*, this *ordu*, had been home for most of a generation. The old people had been children here. Still, Kati felt excitement about moving west to the sea where it would be warm all the time. And Edi was there. She could not feel sadness for herself, but only for Ma.

They ate their cakes, and drank tea, and the hot fire within the stove warmed them. The first light of Tengri-Khan streamed in between the door-flap and the walls.

And then the flyers came.

The whine of turbines came from east, north and south, and was suddenly right over them. Someone screamed outside. Ma's eyes were wide and yellow in an instant. "Stay here," she said, then jumped up and ran outside while Kati sat at the table, stunned. She heard Ma call out.

"Get the horses to the trees!"

The whine was deafening, and Kati clapped her hands over her ears, and then there was a bright flash lighting up the walls of the *ger* from outside. People and horses screamed, and Ma called out, her voice a shriek.

"Kati! Get under the table!"

Kati's breath was sucked away, and she was filled with fear at the sound of her mother's voice. Cups and cakes on a plate spilled to the earthen floor as she squirmed to get under the table, but it was too low to accommodate her with her bulky tunic and all she did was push it up at an angle. Bright light flashed again and again before her eyes, and her hands clawed at the floor, trying to dig a space. The screams outside were high-pitched and horrible, especially from the animals, screams of pain, and agony. Kati gasped a breath, her chest aching, and sobbed as tears gushed from her. The table was pressing on her back, and she burrowed into the dirt beneath it.

And then there was a terrible flash, very near, lighting up her darkness beneath the table. There was a loud cracking sound, and the walls around her creaked, then moaned, then gave way. The roof of the *ger* came crashing down all around her and on top of the table, pressing down on her and pushing her face into the dirt in sudden pitch-blackness. Dirt was in her mouth and nose. She jerked her face to one side, spit the dirt out, and snorted. The weight on her back was horrible, and she struggled for a breath, scrabbling with her feet to push forward until her head was pressed against the table. She got her knees beneath her and pushed up, and suddenly she could take a breath. She sucked it in, and then she was crying. "Ma!" she screamed. "Ma, I can't move!"

There was no answer. A horrible silence just outside the *ger*, yet Kati could hear shouting from a distance before another flyer came over to drown the sound out. Everyone had run away, and she was trapped here beneath the heavy canvas and hides of her collapsed *ger*. The weight was too much for her. Her back and legs hurt, and there was sharp pain in her knees. If she relaxed even a little, the weight pushed her down in the darkness, her face so close to the dirt she could smell it. "Ma! Help me!" she shrieked.

And then she smelled smoke. At first it was just an odor: wood smoke, mixed with the smell of smouldering wool. She sucked in a breath with shock. The stove. It had been filled with wood, burning hotly to warm them while they were eating, and now it was covered with canvas and hides. It was burning the *ger*! "Ma! Someone! There's fire, and I can't get out. Someone *help* me!" she cried.

The smoke was getting denser in the pitch-blackness before her face, and it burned her eyes and nose. She closed her eyes, and took quick, shallow breaths. The agony in her legs and knees was now awful, but she was locked into position by the great weight above her, and she could only move her arms. She took a deep breath of choking smoke to summon up another scream, when suddenly she heard something: horses' hooves on hard rock, a clattering, metallic sound, first a trot, now a gallop, drawing nearer. Someone had come back! She waited until the horses were right by the *ger*, took a deep breath to cry out, then stifled herself with a muffled choking sound.

Something had passed through her mind for just an instant, a presence she had felt before. And then she heard his voice.

"Well, they were certainly thorough about it. How brave they are. Tell them we've arrived, so they don't select us as new targets."

"Yes, Chosen One. I've done that."

"Tell them also not to fire on those who flee. If they do so, I will know, and I will have their heads for it! They are in enough trouble as it is with the Brotherhood. They were supposed to attack only if the people refused our demands to leave, and they didn't even wait. We could have been killed by their fire, as close as we were. Tell them that, Hung!"

"Yessir."

The sound of a horse galloping away, but others trotting nearer. Kati was choking from the smoke she'd inhaled. She tried to take a breath, but it was smoke, not air. Stars danced brightly before her eyes, and her chest hurt.

I'm trapped here, and there is fire, and I can't breathe. Please help me. Someone help me!

"There is someone here," said the man outside.

"There—smoke coming from the rubble. Something is burning there. Put it out."

"We have no implements for that, sir."

"Then use your hands. Throw dirt on it, but put the fire *out!* Use your rifle to cut away the canvas."

I'm in here. Please don't kill me. The fire is close, and I CAN'T BREATHE! The stars were colorful now, and

Kati felt herself slipping away. But now she heard the sound of feet trampling the pile of canvas above her, then a long hiss. A sharp odor brought her near consciousness, and then the men were shouting.

"Here. A burning stove. Bring dirt!"

Feet were trampling all around her. *You're stepping on me. I'm here, beneath a table. Please hurry. Please don't hurt me!*

There was the sound of ripping canvas, and another hiss, and then light flooded her place, and the weight pressing down on her was suddenly gone. The table above her was ripped away, and she fell forward on her face, moaning. Rough hands gripped her beneath her arms, lifting her up, and there was a gentle voice softly in her ear.

"By the eyes of First Mother, it is you, and you're alive. Come to me, child."

You are safe, but there is a terrible thing to see here. You must keep your eyes closed.

NO! The light was bright, and Kati's eyes still burned from the smoke. She blinked rapidly as the man swept her up into his arms. She clutched at the leather armor on his chest, and his face was near, but it was only a blur at first. "Put me down!"

"Bring my horse," said the man. "I have what we came for, and we must leave quickly!"

Kati struggled in his arms, reached for his face, but he grasped her hands hard and held them. "Ma!" she cried. She blinked again, and her vision was clearing. He was walking away from her *ger*; she looked over his shoulder and saw the ruins of her home still spewing smoke, and a body lay near it. The body of a boy, groin and stomach scorched black. He lay on his back, eyes open. It was Abaka. Beyond him lay several sheep, and a horse, their bodies burned horribly.

Kati moaned, and writhed in the man's arms. The gush

of tears stung her eyes, but cleared them. She twisted herself, trying to look over his other shoulder, but he turned, handed her to a soldier who took her beneath her arms and held her at arm's length away from him as the Searcher mounted his horse. The soldier lifted her up, as the Searcher growled, "Careful, fool!"

She was facing the Searcher, and he was an older man, much older than Da. The huge bulge in his forehead was purple with veins, and his hair was grey. He lifted her, trying to turn her around in front of him, but she grabbed his armor at the collar and hung on grimly, for now she knew what he didn't want her to see.

Only paces behind him, a woman was stretched out on the ground, arms flung to either side of her, a terrible hole burned in her chest. Even in death, her eyes were open and blazing red. One arm of the woman was draped over the flank of a little horse, grey with white spots and black mane. The stomach of the horse had been exploded by a burst of fire, and its entrails had spilled forth, still steaming in the morning cold.

Kati screamed, and held out her arms, kicking at the saddle, and into the Searcher's groin. He grunted, then firmly yet gently twisted her around and seated her in front of him. Still she struggled, trying for one more glimpse of what they had done to Ma and Sushua, but the Searcher wrapped his arms around her tightly and began walking his horse away from the scene.

You should not have seen that. I cannot change what has been done to you, but you are safe with me.

Kati struggled for breath. It seemed as if a hand had clutched her heart, and was squeezing it. Her sobs came in spasms, tears streaming down her cheeks. That one brief glimpse of what they had done burned bright in her mind. She was vaguely aware of the sight of other bodies along the way, and other collapsed *gerts*, but they were forgotten in a moment.

Kati writhed in the man's arms and screamed her agony, but it came out a muffled choke. The hurt inside had reached her throat, constricting it, and the force gripping her insides was increasing, bringing numbness to her chest.

First Mother, what can I do? We have made a mess of this, and I don't want to hurt her. The strength of her pain is awful. It tears at me.

Kati moaned, leaned back against the Searcher's leathered chest, and looked straight up at him. His eyes were fixed straight ahead, and tears glistened on his cheeks.

You have killed Ma, and I have done nothing to you. And now I will die.

The fist in her heart squeezed harder and harder, and she gasped for breath, unable to cry further. Her forehead was suddenly icy cold, yet sweaty, and her vision clouded.

Perhaps this was death coming, and she would be with Ma and Sushua soon.

First Mother! I cannot deal with this! Show me what to do!

The Searcher squeezed her, then shook her gently, but she closed her eyes and wished for blackness to come. And suddenly there was a new voice in her head—the voice of a woman.

Kati. Kati—my child.

Kati stirred within her darkness. This was not the Searcher, but someone new. Never had she felt such a powerful presence, and it seemed she was warmed from the inside, from where her heart was. Her skin tingled powerfully, the sound of horses hooves and wind in the trees suddenly gone, and in her mind the blackness was now filled with purple spots of light like distant stars at night. "Ma?" she said out loud, her eyes still closed.

No, my dear. Your mother is gone, and I can do nothing to change that. But you must trust the one whose arms

*hold you now, and believe that he will keep you safe. He
and his brothers are my children, and I place you in
their care, for there are things I would have you do for
me when you are a woman.*

"Who are you?" whispered Kati, and it seemed the
Searcher's arms were suddenly tighter around her. And
then she gasped, for out of the night sky of her mind
there suddenly appeared a thing she had seen before—
two slanted eyes, blazing emerald green, opening up
before her with incredible brightness to fill the void.

*I am Mandughai, Kati. I am First Mother, Empress of
Tumatsin and Hansui. I am Empress over all the peoples
of Shanji. I was with your grandmother, and your mother,
and I will be with you.*

You take the thoughts away, thought Kati.

*Only for a little while. Your grief must run its course,
but now you must rest. Sleep, now, and know that I am
with you, always.*

The eyes closed, and for a moment the purple stars
were back, flickering together, a slow, rhythmic pulsation
in Kati's mind. Then only blackness.

The Searcher's horse stumbled on a stone and Kati
was jerked awake. For one brief instant she thought it
had all been a bad dream. She would open her eyes,
and there would be flickering lamplight in the *ger*, Ma
busy cooking cakes on the stove. But what she saw was
the neck of a horse, and they were coming down into a
broad valley on a narrow trail, a steep dropoff to one
side. The Emperor's great city loomed ahead, jutting out
of a sheer cliff, covered with a transparent spherical tent
glistening like ice in Tengri-Khan's afternoon light.

The Searcher's arms were loosely around her, but warm.
He leaned over, and whispered to her, "At last you're
awake, just in time to see your new home. It's very large,
and further away than it seems. Are you hungry?"

No. I will not eat your food. I will not eat anything again.

The Searcher squeezed her gently. "Very well, but I think you will change your mind. Let me know if you want something."

I want to go home. I want to find Da and my brother, and be with my own kind.

The Searcher squeezed her again, but said nothing.

They rode slowly, for the trail was dangerous. The huge valley below had been harvested, only stubble remaining. Three large machines sat at the edge of a plowed area, and man were swarming over them, making repairs. Closer to the city there were fields of dry grass, and cattle eating from bales of feed scattered there. There were no goats, or sheep, only cattle to be seen. No people, or *gerts*, no dwellings of any kind. Everyone must be living in the city.

And it was the city that held her attention as they drew closer. She had only seen it before from a great distance from her place within the pinnacles, and there it had seemed to sparkle like a jewel. Now she could see why. The transparent tent was not one piece, nor was it a true sphere. It was made up of many flat squares connected together by a network of beams like the web of a spider. Not all of the squares were clear, but colored in hues of blue, red and green, and beneath them the city rose in curved terraces, with tall buildings having every color in a rainbow. The terraces slanted upwards towards a summit, where there was a building with a golden dome glistening in the light of Tengri-Khan.

Closer still, Kati could see lines of open space between the tightly packed buildings, lines radiating downwards from the one with the golden dome, and patches of green spilling over the terraces like waterfalls. And ahead of them was an enormous gate of what looked liked polished wood, black and glistening, set into the base of the all-encompassing tent, and it was opening to receive them.

The Searcher leaned over and again whispered in her ear, "This is only a small part of what there is to see. The rest is beyond the mountain. You see the gold dome up there? That is the Emperor's palace."

Kati craned her neck to see the dome as they approached the gate on a wide, dirt road lined with unlit torches and sparkling rocks. Several troopers were at the gate, and more to either side of it, watching their approach. The troopers at the gate bowed respectfully, and waved them through the gate while Kati gawked at the colorful buildings packed together on the steep slope before them. She heard a flyer's whine, and looked straight up to see it hovering far off, above the city's tent. A blue panel, twice the size of the flyer, slid aside; the flyer descended through the opening, and drifted until it was out of sight beyond the gold dome at the summit of the terraces.

Inside the tent it was suddenly warm, and there was no breeze on her face. There were odors of animals, food cooking, and human sweat, a sudden closed-in feeling that bothered her. Sound filled her ears, a dull roar like rushing wind coming from every direction.

They crossed an open space paved with white, flat stones fitted tightly together, to a pagoda shading several benches, now empty. Beyond the pagoda, pairs of metal columns connected by rails rose up the steep slope towards the golden dome, the rails seeming to come together in the far distance. And hanging from those rails, sliding down towards them, was a box, painted red, surrounded by windows. The machine drew near and Kati saw one man standing inside, looking out at her.

The Searcher stopped his horse in the shade of the pagoda, dismounted, and lifted Kati down from the saddle. Only one trooper remained with them; he took the Searcher's horse, and rode back towards the gate without a word. The red box came down soundlessly, stopped before them, and a door slid aside.

Kati's hands were clenched at her sides. The Searcher took one fist in his hand, squeezed it gently and said, "We will ride this car to the Hall of Ministers at the top of the city, then you will rest, and have something to eat if you wish. There is a fine view of the city while we ride."

She followed him inside where there were many empty benches, one man standing before a panel of lights. The man's fingers moved over the panel; the door slid shut, and the car began to move as Kati's heart thumped hard. The Searcher stood her on a bench, so she could see outside in all directions, and they rose at a steep angle, the gate quickly dropping away from them and beyond it the fields, the great wall of rock, the first mountain peaks showing clearly above its edge, and then, in the far distance, a summit she recognized. The pinnacles, the place where she had seen the Emperor's city—with Sushua. She looked out at the mountains, and the horror returned. She began to cry softly, and the tears were hot on her face.

I feel your pain, child, but it will pass in time. Your life out there has ended, but a new one is about to begin.

The rest of the ride was blurred by tears. She was oblivious to all the buildings, and the people in the streets below her, even the beautiful hanging garden with its waterfall and pool, which she only glimpsed. Kati saw only the mountains, thinking of Ma and Sushua, Da and Baber, those she loved and would never see again. By the time the car stopped, her sobs were like hiccups, and her chest ached from it.

The Searcher had remained silent. Now he took her hand as the door opened. Another Searcher was waiting there, a boy no older than Abaka had been when they'd murdered him. He was dressed in white, tight-fitting clothing from high-collar to feet. Like all the other Searchers she'd seen, his face was longer and narrower than that of the typical Hansui, and he had a finely arched nose. The bulge on his forehead did not detract her eye, for it was small, a delicate web of blue veins showing there.

Kati decided he was really quite handsome—for a Searcher.

He stepped forward, and bowed. "Mengyao, Chosen One, I came to tell you that Mengmoshu wishes to see you immediately after your return. There is a horrible flap brewing over this incident. Is this the child?"

"Yes. I must first find a comfortable place for her, and see that's she's fed. We've been riding all day."

"I will take charge of her, Chosen One. It will be an honor. Mengmoshu was most insistent. He wants to see you immediately in his offices."

"Then I must go," said Mengyao. "See to her needs, and make her comfortable for the night. This will likely be a long meeting." Mengyao's hand pressed on Kati's shoulder. "This student will take care of you for now, but I will see you again soon."

And he walked away.

The student knelt before her, and she gave him a stony look. In return, he smiled, so that there were little lines around his deep brown eyes.

"I praise First Mother for your safety. My name is Huomeng, which means 'dream of fire.' What is your name, child?"

If I'm a child, you are little more than that.

"Ha!" said Huomeng. "What is said about you is true, and so we will speak without words."

I am thirteen, and began my studies for the Brotherhood only a year ago. Mengyao does me honor in seeing to you. Now, what is your name?

I am Kati.

"Kati," said the boy, as if tasting the word. His black hair was cut short, and combed straight back from his forehead to form a short tail at the nape of his neck, held there by a golden ring. He smoothed his hair with a sweep of his hand, looking reflectively at her. "I don't know the meaning of that, but it's a nice name. We need to get some food for you, Kati. Will you take my hand?"

Kati put her hands behind her, and glared at him.

I understand, but now come with me.

He rested a hand lightly on her shoulder to guide her, for he was several heads taller than she. They walked beneath a red awning towards a door guarded by two great *shizi* made from black stone. The door opened as they approached, closed behind them, and suddenly there were people everywhere, rushing to and fro in a great, golden hall lined with balconies, and a ceiling higher than the tallest tree Kati could remember. All the people, men and women, were dressed in the white, tight-fitting clothes worn by Huomeng. They looked at her curiously, but did not smile, and went their way.

Huomeng took her to a woman seated behind a huge table in the center of the hall, and talked to her in hushed tones while Kati stared about her at her surroundings. The woman picked up a slender instrument, and spoke into it, and then Huomeng put his hand on Kati's shoulder and guided her to another door leading to stairs. "All our guest rooms have been taken, so it's not the best," said Huomeng, "but it will do for a short time. Food is being brought down for you."

They descended three flights of narrow stairs in the glow of yellow, odorless lamps overhead, and came out in a room with a single table, on which slouched a trooper with full armor, a short stick of gleaming metal at his side. The trooper stood up as they entered, and gave Kati a look that chilled her.

"This child is to be kept safely overnight for Mengyao, and food will arrive for her shortly," Huomeng said curtly. "I was told we can use room two."

The trooper said nothing, but went to a gate of metal bars, beyond which was a hallway with solid, closed doors on one side, the other side a lattice of metal bars. "Second door," mumbled the trooper, and he unlocked the gate.

He doesn't like orders from a boy.

He will take them anyway, Kati, because the boy becomes a man, and remembers things.

The trooper closed the gate behind them, then went to a closed door and began unlocking it. The left hallway was all cages, and a few steps away Kati saw a pair of hands grasping the bars, a frightening face dimly illuminated there. The trooper fumbled with the door, started to open it.

"There is space for her with me, Te! Bring her here! I've been without a woman for many nights!"

"Shut up!" snarled the trooper, "or I'll give you a taste of my whip!" He looked at Huomeng, made a circular motion at his own temple with a finger, then opened the door and said, "she should be comfortable in here."

The room was a box, half the size of a *ger*. Bare walls, a lamp in the ceiling, table, chair and cot, a ceramic seat in one corner that caught Kati's eye. It had a hole in it, and there was water in the bottom of the seat. A fancy toilet, little better than a pot.

The trooper left, but Huomeng stayed with her until a woman dressed in white arrived with a tray heaped with covered dishes, a cup, and a pot of tea. She placed the tray on the table, nodded politely to Huomeng, and left without a word.

Kati's stomach growled at the smell of food, for she had been hungry for hours. Huomeng sat her down at the table, and uncovered the dishes one by one. "Rice, with beef strips, vegetables from our farms beyond the mountain, tea, and some sweet grapes to finish the meal."

The food odors were wonderful, but Kati clenched her hands in her lap and shook her head.

"It's your choice, Kati. I will not force you to eat, but you accomplish nothing by starving yourself. Your life is more precious than you realize, but you must first want to live it."

Huomeng went to the open door, pointed to a thing on the wall. "There's a blanket on the cot. When you want to sleep, you can turn off the light here." He wiggled the little lever on the wall; the light went off, then came on again. Kati blinked in surprise.

Huomeng smiled again. "Please eat, and rest. Either I, or someone else, will be back to get you in the morning. If you need anything else, ask the guard. He is now responsible for you."

Kati glared at the food, mouth watering, but pressed her lips tightly together.

Goodbye, Kati. I hope to see you again.

She turned to look at him, but he was gone. Suddenly, she was alone, in a strange place far from home, with strange foods before her. The odors made her head spin, and her stomach felt like it was eating itself.

Kati sat there for a long time, looking at the steaming dishes, and rubbing her tortured stomach.

If I don't eat, they will force it on me. I cannot hurt them by not eating. I only hurt myself, and I've done nothing wrong. Why am I so important to them? Why am I still alive?

Finally, she could stand it no longer. She looked around furtively, then picked up the wooden utensils on the tray and began to eat.

In half an hour, she'd finished everything.

She lay down on the cot, and tried to sleep. The light was on, the door still open, but she left them that way. The occasional grumblings and clanking of the guard up the hallway told her she was not truly alone, and she did not want to be in darkness.

But even with the lights on and her eyes closed, her mind began replaying the events of the day. She saw Ma and Sushua lying there, Abaka's burned body, his eyes staring. She thought of Da, holding her, Ma's gentle hands in her hair, and Baber getting his horse at the great sea. The memories rushed through her like a wind, and then she began to cry.

She buried her face in the cot, and her body shook with sobs, tears soaking the canvas beneath her face. And suddenly there was a voice from down the hallway outside.

"Little girl! I hear you in there! Are you lonely, little girl? Come down here! I have something that will make you happy!" And then the man was grunting in little gasps.

The guard came by her doorway like a storm, the metal stick in his hand. "If you wish to waggle your limp organ in public, then I will do something to stimulate you!" he shouted.

Instantly, there was the sound of sizzling meat, and a horrible shriek from down the hallway, followed by moans, and retching.

The guard appeared at her doorway, his face an angry mask. "Sorry. He won't bother you again. Now, get some sleep before they come for you." He reached inside to the wall, and the light went off. Then he closed the door.

Kati fell back on the cot, shaking all over. She clenched her hands over her heaving chest and bit her lip, tasting blood. Her fingers found the pendants: the pretty shell, the Eye of Tengri. The remnants of a past life. She clutched at them like a dying person with a precious object, a last touch with life. And far into the night, before sleep finally took her, she keened her grief into the darkness, for all that she had lost that day.

CHAPTER FIVE
WEIMENG

Lady Weimeng suffered a dream about her dead child.
The first wife of Wang Shan-shi-jie, The Son of Heaven,
tossed restlessly in sleep and moaned. In her dream the
girl-child Mengnu was now five, and they were in the upper
garden with a fine view of the western mountains. Mengnu
was wading in the gravel-bottomed pool there and giggling
with delight when the carp tickled her tiny feet. Her dark
eyes twinkled with merriment in a round symmetrical face,
and she clapped her hands in glee, dropping the hems of
her golden robe and soaking it. Her box-cut black hair,
coming down to her eyebrows, gave her the appearance
of a fine, porcelain doll made by the ancestors.

Weimeng watched her daughter try to catch the carp
with her hands, heard her squeals of excitement when
a big one slid from her grasp. She turned her attention
again to ink and brushes, the drawing pad in her lap
where she sat on a carpet of moss at the edge of the
pool. She dipped a brush and resumed her drawing of
the mountains, placing a pagoda at the summit of a sharp
peak before feeling a hand on her shoulder and looking
up to see The Son of Heaven standing there, smiling
down at her.

"My husband," she said, lowering her eyes before him.
"Da!" cried Mengnu. "I will catch a fish for you!" She

plunged her little hands deep into the water, splashing herself, coming up sputtering and empty-handed. "They are very fast, Da!" she said, grinning.

"They will not be so fast when you're older," said the Emperor of Shanji. He sat down by Weimeng, slid an arm around her waist and rested his chin on her shoulder to look at her painting.

"Ah, there is a new structure on the three peaks that are one," he said, and Weimeng smelled cinnamon on his breath.

"It overlooks the great plateau. I would have it there to commemorate the first landing on Shanji," she said.

He kissed her neck. "Then I will build it for you, and when Mengnu is Empress she will burn incense there in memory of us."

His face was smooth, lips soft when she touched them. They were young again, and in love, and the heiress to their throne splashed merrily in the pool beside them.

But then it seemed that a dark cloud had suddenly passed over them and the light of Tengri-Khan was blocked off. Weimeng looked up and saw two monstrous storks descending upon them, black as night, beaks like swords, claws outstretched. She was seized with paralysis, unable to move a muscle as the great birds descended to the pool and grasped her daughter by the shoulders, lifting her from the water.

Mengnu screamed, "Ma! Da! Don't let them take me!" But Weimeng could not move, nor could she utter a word, and her husband was suddenly gone. She could only watch helplessly as the great black birds carried her shrieking, struggling daughter away from her towards the mountains until they were out of sight and she was alone by the pool, and the tears raining from her face had ruined the painting in her lap.

She found her voice, and cried out, "Mengnu! We will search for you, my darling! We will find you!"

And she was awake, surrounded by the golden curtain of her bed, the pillow-surface at her cheek saturated with tears. She must have cried out in sleep, for there was movement beyond the curtain, a silhouette there in the dim light, then a soft, feminine voice.

"Are you ill, My Lady? I came as quickly as I could when I heard your call."

It was Tanchun, her First Servant, ever watchful.

Weimeng sat up to catch her breath, for it seemed like her heart was skipping beats. "I've had a dream. Please get Juimoshu for me at once."

"It is very late, My Lady. I must disturb her sleep."

"Tell her I've had a dream about my child and would know the meaning of it immediately. Go quickly!"

"Yes, My Lady." And Tanchun was quickly gone from the palace suite.

There *was* meaning to the dream; of this, Weimeng was certain. There was significance in black storks taking back the blessing of a child and flying westward to the mountains. And the pagoda. Why had she drawn that? Only Juimoshu had the power to penetrate such womanly dreams and see the meaning behind them, for she was the only living female among The Chosen Ones, and claimed direct contact with First Mother. She would come to Weimeng because it was her responsibility to interpret such dreams for the royal family. But mostly, she would come because Weimeng was the artificially inseminated child of her own body.

Weimeng arose, and put on a red robe embroidered with golden *shizi*. The entire suite was in red and gold: thick carpets of wool, lamps of brass, wall hangings of scenes from the western sea to the mountains to the farming plains and villages east of the city. Scenes of everyday life among her people. Scenes of families— with children. With consciousness fully returned, Weimeng's heart ached again over Mengnu, the only child she'd ever been able to carry to full term. But Mengnu was stillborn, and buried without ceremony because it was her husband's will.

And then he had taken a second wife, a girl forty years his junior, and she had given him a son.

Weimeng sat down at the ebony desk in the center of the suite, facing the great double-door entrance to the suite, now closed. Two chairs sat before the desk; in one corner opposite her canopied and shrouded bed was a conversational corner of two couches and matching chairs that hadn't been used in five years. Her husband had been in the suite only a few times during those years, and then only to ask her advice on various political matters. They had not slept together since the death of Mengnu, and now his bed was shared only by Yang Xifeng, the mother of his son.

The top of the desk was littered with sketches and paintings in inks and watercolors which occupied her days and long evenings with only servants as companions. The odors of incense and cinnamon tea lingered there from the previous evening, but now the tea was cold and strong to the taste, making her grimace when she tried a sip.

Years ago, her days had been spent in court at her husband's side, asking questions, giving advice which softened his natural tendency for harshness, relaying subtle, long-term desires of The Brotherhood which came to her through her mother. But those days were now past, the rule of Wang Shan-shi-jie growing harsher each year, his connection with The Chosen Ones more tenuous and with it his belief in and respect for First Mother, for whose children he was responsible.

Weimeng feared for the stability of her husband's throne, for he both underestimated and disregarded the power and influence of The Brotherhood, despite her mother's repeated warnings. First, the Tumatsin lands had been taken away to grow crops that were only excess, and now there had been an attack on a village. Children had been killed, and The Chosen were furious over it for reasons unknown to her. Was it the death of children that had triggered her dream?

There was a soft rap on the suite's door. "Enter!" she said.

The door opened slightly, and Tanchun peered around it. "Lady Juimoshu has arrived, My Lady."

"Show her in, and bring hot tea, please." Weimeng shuffled her drawings together in a neat stack, and placed it to one side as her mother entered the room.

Her mother squeezed past Tanchun, and stopped as the door closed behind her. "I've been awakened from a sound sleep, my dear, so I presume this is very important to you."

"It is, mother. I think First Mother has spoken to me in a dream about Mengnu."

Juimoshu's eyes narrowed for a brief instant. She walked forward slowly, body proudly erect for a small woman in her sixties, and sat down in a chair before her daughter's desk. She wore a plain robe of natural black wool, and her grey hair hung to her waist in a great mass spilling down over her back. Her small black eyes were set close together on either side of a finely arched nose, her intense gaze always giving her a searching look that gave people pause for thought when dealing with her.

Juimoshu folded her tiny hands in her lap. "Well, what is it? I thought the dreams about your dead child had finally ended, and you were resigned to your fate at last. Tell me, daughter."

Weimeng leaned back in her chair, hands in her lap. "What you say is true, though I've continued to wonder why First Mother has abandoned me in such a cruel way."

"You have been in my prayers to Her, child. I can do nothing more than that."

"And perhaps those prayers have been fruitful, mother. This dream of Mengnu is the first in over a year, and there is symbolism in it I need to understand. Here is what I saw in that dream."

Weimeng told her mother about the dream in complete detail, for it was yet fresh in her mind and her heart still ached with the memory of it. She was interrupted once by Tanchun, who returned with two cups of hot tea for them and quickly left the room. But the tea remained untouched during their conversation.

Juimoshu steepled her hands before her face and closed her eyes as she listened, remaining that way for several moments after Weimeng had finished telling her story.

Now, her eyes opened. "You've not had this dream before tonight?"

"No, mother. It is something new, and quite intense."

Juimoshu again folded her hands loosely in her lap and sat there for a long moment, looking down at them, deep in thought while Weimeng waited patiently.

"There *is* significance in this dream," she finally said, "but I hesitate to say what I think because I do not want to give you false hope."

Weimeng stiffened. "What *is* it, mother?"

Juimoshu sighed. "The black storks are a symbol given to young women who have lost a child, but who will conceive again. Because of the damage done to you during the still-birth of your daughter, that is clearly not possible for you and yet there is the inference of another child to come. And there are other peculiarities here. An imperfect child is taken to Tengri-Khan for recasting into a more perfect form to follow, yet in your dream the storks flew towards the mountains in the west with a child still alive and struggling. A direct interpretation of this infers a new child will come to you from the west, not from the source of all life, and that child will be the reincarnation of your little lost one."

Weimeng caught her breath, and leaned forward, putting her hands flat on the desk, her eyes stinging. "Mengnu? She will be returned to me? Oh, mother, can it be true?" Tears ran down her cheeks and she stifled a sob.

Juimoshu waved a hand in warning. "Take care, daughter. I tell you only what the dream says to me, and I cannot be certain about its meaning. To give you false hope would be a terrible cruelty I could not endure."

Now it was Juimoshu who leaned forward, gaze intense, clenching her hands together in her lap. Her voice was nearly a whisper. "Even so, I have also dreamed this night, but it was a dream without vision, only words. The voice of a child, crying out in the darkness, and I felt a horrible sadness that left my body aching when your servant came to wake me. And the words were 'Da,' and 'Ma', said over and over again, words as in your dream. Not 'mama', or 'baba'. Did you not notice that in your dream?"

"No. I have heard these words used by children before. They are from the old dialect, before the coming of First Mother."

"A dialect still used by the outcast peoples to the west, the people your husband would have long ago driven into the sea if it hadn't been for your humane intervention."

"A Tumatsin child?" asked Weimeng, wondering how that could be. "A Changeling?"

Juimoshu nodded her head. "A Tumatsin child is lost, and seeks its parents. Boy, or girl, it is near, for I have felt its sorrow since being awakened and I feel it even now. There is a terrible pain of loss—here." Juimoshu placed her hand over her heart, and nodded again.

Weimeng stood up, excited, and leaned over the desk. "There was an attack on a Tumatsin village this morning, and several people were killed! Could there have been prisoners taken? Children?"

Juimoshu stood up, took Weimeng's hands in hers. The

wrinkles around her eyes had suddenly deepened and her face was drawn, as if she were experiencing physical pain. "I hear your thoughts, daughter, and I will make inquiries. But now I must rest. The feelings inside me have grown steadily in intensity since my coming to you, and I must pray to First Mother for relief before attempting sleep again." She squeezed Weimeng's hands, then turned to leave.

Weimeng felt a lightness in her chest, an euphoria that swept over her, bringing a flush to her cheeks. "You must find the child, mother! And I will also listen for its call!"

Juimoshu waved a hand to one side, shuffling slowly towards the door. "You've inherited few of my abilities, daughter, and once that was a disappointment for me. But at this moment, I think you have been blessed."

Juimoshu reached the door, opened it, and shook her head. "Such *power!*" she said, and then she left the room.

Weimeng was too excited to sleep. She drank both cups of tea, now cold, and paced the circumference of her suite many times before weariness returned. She turned down the lights, and returned to her bed, where she offered up a fervent prayer to First Mother for the gift of a child, hoping there would be a sign, a vision, a voice crying out for her. There was nothing there, and finally she drifted away to a quiet place beyond consciousness.

But in the morning, she arose with the uneasy feeling that someone had called out to her shortly before she'd awakened.

Mengyao took the lift up to the seventh floor of the palace, which housed the offices of the Moshuguang, The Magic Light, The Brotherhood of The Searchers. Mengmoshu's office was centrally located along a long, stark hallway painted white and softly illuminated by ceiling panels. Each door was numbered, without titles to identify the occupants. He stopped at number ten, and knocked softly three times.

"Come!"

Mengyao entered, closed the door behind him, and seated himself in a plush, white chair before a plain table in the center of the room, behind which the Chancellor of the Moshuguang sat pecking away at a workstation. The office was large, ten meters on a side, but sparsely furnished: workstation, table, two chairs for visitors, a plush couch and chair in one corner. There was a thick, red carpet, but no windows, greenish light coming from three ceiling panels. One wall was entirely filled with video monitors, all dark at the moment, another lined with shelves of books and cassettes and the diskettes of the past hundred years of Moshuguang science and politics.

Mengmoshu nodded a greeting, but continued working for several minutes while Mengyao sat in silence. Finally he leaned back in his chair and brushed an errant lock of gray hair from his forehead. "I've checked every report for the last five years, and there is only one Tumatsin woman who has even traces of green in her eyes. Her name is Manlee, and her children are grown to adulthood with no unusual characteristics. All of them live by the sea. Are you certain we have the right child?"

"There can be no doubt," said Mengyao. "We found her beneath a collapsed *ger*, nearly unconscious, yet her mental call was so strong even some of the men sensed something at a distance. Her mother was killed in the attack, and apparently also her little horse. I tried to shield her from the sight of bodies, but she saw them, and her grief was so severe I could barely stand up under it. When I tried to control her, it was like grasping a bar of steel, yet her emotions flowed like water. I prayed, Mengmoshu. I prayed to First Mother for relief, and she came not to me, but to the child."

Mengmoshu's eyes widened. "She spoke to the *child*?"

"Yes. She offered words of comfort, endearments, and said the child must do something for Her when she is a woman. The words were meant to be heard by me; She made no effort to shield them. First Mother has claimed her, Mengmoshu. She is The One."

Mengmoshu blew softly through pursed lips. "So it seems," he said. "She is somehow connected to Manlee's line, then. Her *ordu* was formed only eighty years ago, according to our records, and several families have moved in from the west since then. Was her father killed?"

"There is a father, and a younger brother. A report from yesterday says they had gone west to Manlee to try and stop the provocations that have inflamed The Son Of Heaven. As far as I know, they are safe for the moment."

"Unless Wang decides to attack the coastal *ordus*. We must lobby strongly against that when we have our audience. That is in half an hour."

"We see the Emperor *today*?"

Mengmoshu waved his hand, unconcerned. "It is posturing. I will do the talking, but He might ask you for details of what you saw after the attack. The will of the Moshuguang has been clearly overruled in this case. We must handle Wang delicately, yet let him know of our displeasure, and convince Him again of the importance of the Tumatsin people in our biological programs. He still thinks Juimoshu came from that effort, and I don't intend to tell him otherwise. Where is the child now?"

"In order to quickly meet you, I turned her over to novice Huomeng when he met us at the monorail. I would guess he's taken her to the Hall of Ministers, where there are usually spare rooms for guests."

"A fine youngster," said Mengmoshu. "His memory is prodigious, and his nature gentle. Some find him a bit precocious, but that is to be expected with his intelligence.

He shows great promise; his psi abilities appeared at age ten, quite young, yet this girl you've returned with is younger still. I must question her in the morning."

"Go gently with her, Mengmoshu. She's been horribly traumatized by the attack, and soon her sorrow will turn to hate. She must see us as friends. She must see us as her new family. If she is The One, there must be devotion between us, or we will be destroyed."

"I understand that, Mengyao, and you know my methods are not harsh. Perhaps it would be good to have Juimoshu present for the questioning. A woman's presence could be comforting to the child. What's her name?"

"Kati."

"Yes, Kati might find reassurance in a grandmotherly presence. I will see to that."

Mengmoshu stood up. "I know you've had a long and difficult day, Mengyao, but now I must ask you to join me in an audience with The Son Of Heaven. It should not take long, but it is necessary."

"I'm at your service, Mengmoshu," said Mengyao, rising. There was no thing he would not do for the man who stood before him.

They left the office and walked to the end of the hallway, where elevator doors of brass were guarded by two troopers with laser rifles and sidearms. The elevator took them down five floors, opening to a reception hall adjacent to the throne room. Panels glowed from a gilded, low ceiling, and lining the room on three sides, set on pedestals, were the bronze busts of all fifty-five past Emperors of Shanji. Tapestries of silk, in paints, inks and embroidery hung on the walls: mountains, village scenes, fields of grain, and various views of the Emperor's city from centuries past.

Mengmoshu went to the reception desk while Mengyao

admired the tapestries. All showed scenes of a feudal society as founded by Wang Chen-Ma, the first Emperor, the one who had fled Tengri-Nayon with his traditionalist followers. Several were portraits of royal courts: a Son of Heaven surrounded by family, those nobles and merchants most influential at the time, heads of craft and trade guilds most adept at bribery and flattery. Only tranquil village scenes commemorated the peasants who made profits for their masters. And there was nothing related to the great agricultural expansion to the east.

Other tapestries had been on these walls, but removed years ago, stored or destroyed. Mengyao remembered the scene of shuttles dropping from the mother ship that had brought the people from the red star to Shanji, the burning city from the time when the Emerald Empress of Tengri sought to reclaim the errant people who had fled her harsh rule. History was selective on the walls of the Emperor's palace.

Mengmoshu soon rejoined Mengyao by the tapestries, looking displeased.

"We are scheduled for this time, but everything is running behind because of the transportation guild's lobbying for a new tunnel to the east. She said it would be less than an hour, and we should sit near the door to be called."

They went to a pair of ebony benches on either side of the throne room door, and found places to sit there with six other people.

Over an hour later, three men came out of the room, angry and grumbling to themselves about short-term thinking.

The other six people were called one-by-one: two merchants, three farm managers and a man with a wrapped gift from the Arts Guild.

Mengmoshu's face slowly turned into an angry mask, and he shifted his position on the bench with increasing frequency. "Let him posture all he wishes. We will remain here until he sees us."

The others came out one by one, all grim, except for the Arts Guild representative, who looked rather pleased with himself.

They would be next, after a wait of over three hours. Mengyao's buttocks were numb, and his stomach was grumbling, for he hadn't eaten all day.

The door opened again, and they arose in anticipation of the audience, but a young woman came out, leading a little boy by the hand. Both men bowed courteously, for it was the Emperor's second wife and his son. The woman, Yang Xifeng, was in her early twenties, and lovely to behold: small face and features, a long, graceful neck and slender body, tall for a Hansui yet proudly erect and seeming to float as she walked. She nodded to acknowledge their greeting as she passed by, the little boy Shan-lan looking up at them shyly. Both men sensed his fear of them, but from Yang Xifeng there was nothing. Both wore the golden robes of the Emperor's court. They crossed the reception hall, and disappeared into the elevator taking them to their living quarters below.

"The boy is too thin for a five-year-old. He does not look healthy," said Mengyao, as they sat down again.

"I hear he's a delicate child," said Mengmoshu, "but even now his presence is required at court, and he likely hasn't eaten for hours. The Emperor begins the training of his heir at childhood, and has a difficult task ahead of him."

"There will be other children, I suppose."

"That I doubt, considering the age of The Son Of Heaven. Shan-lan is marvel enough. You felt his fear?"

"Yes."

"Then we will soon be called."

And ten minutes later they were finally ushered into the throne room of Wang-Shan-shi-jie to find the

Emperor sitting on his throne—alone. The man who had ushered them in quickly left, closing the doors behind them.

Compared to the reception hall, the room was small, twenty meters on a side. All was in red, except for the throne in white stone. Thick carpeting, painted walls and ceiling, six rows of pews for group audiences, with an aisle down the center leading to the throne, behind which hung thick curtains. Juimoshu often hid herself behind those curtains, probing the minds of plaintiffs during delicate hearings, but she would not be there now. The Emperor trusted her judgment in all matters, except when dealing with the Moshuguang, for she was one of them.

Wang-Shan-shi-jie beckoned for them to come forth. "Please excuse me for the long delay, but I presumed you would wish to speak in private."

Let no other ears hear our displeasure.

Of course. And no witnesses to any promises. Remember that.

They walked forward to the throne and bowed deeply before it. The Emperor smiled down on them, elbow on one arm of the throne, a fist against his chin. Now in his mid-sixties, his hair was white, braided into two pigtails hanging down across his chest. His robe was gold, but on his feet were the soft, black slippers of a peasant, and he wore no jewelry. A myriad of lines creased his face, but his eyes were wide and alert and focused on their faces, never moving from them.

"You've had a long day, and I will try to be brief," said Mengmoshu, then smiling, "It has been months since I've seen your son. He's a handsome boy."

"He is my joy in times of difficult decisions," said the Emperor. "And pleasantries aside, I believe you are here to discuss one of those decisions."

Careful. He takes responsibility for it.

"The decisions are yours to make, Son Of Heaven. I'm

here only to clarify an understanding I thought we had with you. Perhaps I have not remembered it correctly," said Mengmoshu in a respectful tone.

"And how do you remember it, Chancellor?" The Emperor's fist had not moved from his chin.

"We discussed the discovery of a gifted Tumatsin child we'd traced to an *ordu* just west of here, an *ordu* you felt was the source of all our recent sabotage. Whatever happened, it was our wish that child would not be harmed, and we could bring her here for study and possible training."

"Yes, I remember. And I hear this has been accomplished. The child is now resting comfortably within the Hall of Ministers. Is there a problem with this?"

"It is only good fortune that has saved the child. My understanding was that we would be allowed to retrieve her before any military action was taken against the *ordu*. But your flyers did not wait for that. We had nearly reached the *ordu* when the attack took place; Mengyao here was nearly cut down by laser fire as he tried to approach. Your people nearly killed a senior member of the Moshuguang, and the child was near death when we found her!"

The Emperor blinked once. "I do admit to a military error in timing, and the flight commander has been admonished for it, but he was following my orders to destroy that *ordu* and anyone in it. When Mengyao voiced protest from the ground, the attack was broken off, and I showed considerable mercy in not pursuing the survivors in case the child was among them. What else would you have had me do? I went against my own orders to appease your wishes and save a child I have no interest in. Be reasonable, Mengmoshu." He smiled, as if talking to a small child.

"The child's mother was killed, and she has been traumatized by it. If she has the abilities we seek, I fear it will affect her training."

"That is tragic, of course, and you have my full support in making her comfortable in her new home. But tell me, Mengmoshu, would it have been less traumatic if you'd simply taken her away from her family?"

"Yes, I think so. Her mother is dead, and the child's abilities likely come through her, though it could be by the father. We're not sure. The father and brother had traveled west, and have fortunately survived. We must know the complete lineage and want them kept safe. We urge you not to attack any *ordus* on the coast."

The Emperor chuckled. "Such concern for the Changelings is most humane, Mengmoshu. I hear the words of my first wife, and respect them. But *I* rule Shanji, and the sabotage had to stop. I have taken action to assure that, yet I am also humane, even with the Tumatsin.

"So put your mind at ease, Mengmoshu. The Tumatsin have a sacred place, a canyon and fields far to the west. I have today sent them a decree giving them this place, and all lands west to the sea, as their own. I will not violate this territory I have deeded to them, but any Tumatsin who ventures outside of it will be shot on sight. And I maintain the right of inspection, by air or ground. They are forbidden to build an army, for they have no need of one. I will protect them against any foreign aggressors. It's all in the decree, Mengmoshu. I will send you a copy of it."

It is better than we'd hoped for, Mengmoshu.

"Your judgment is most generous, Son Of Heaven, and we appreciate it. If we wish to search out relatives of the child, may we enter the Tumatsin territory?"

"Of course. You need only ask, so I may provide you with an escort." Now the Emperor seemed to relax, taking the fist from his chin, and leaning back, his piercing gaze suddenly softened.

"I have sorrow for the child, for I know the feeling of

losing a loved one, Mengmoshu. I have had these feelings
in my life in several ways."

*An infant child dead, then putting aside a loved, but
barren wife, and now my own inability to conceive again.*

"Please let me know what you require for the child,
and I will honor it. Now, is there anything else? Even
an Emperor must eat, and my family is waiting."

"In your wisdom you have anticipated all our concerns,
Son Of Heaven. We will work with the child, and hope
to use her in your service," said Mengmoshu, bowing.

"Another Juimoshu, perhaps," said the Emperor,
standing up. "She has been very helpful to me, but now
we both grow older by the day." He took the two steps
down from the throne's platform, and put a hand on
Mengmoshu's shoulder. "Walk with me, Chancellor."

They walked towards the door, Mengyao following
respectfully behind by a step. "I wish to continue working
with the Moshuguang in an amiable way, Mengmoshu,
and will do so as long as its activities are confined to the
sciences of the body and mind," said the Emperor. "But
those sciences must be used in my service, and I remain
a traditionalist like those men who have ruled before
me. I know that your breeding program goes beyond
producing your own kind, that your true purpose is the
creation of a super-being capable of transferring great
energies from afar with only the use of the mind. I think
you would best put your efforts in other directions."

"It is a task put to us by First Mother, from whom we
are descended," said Mengmoshu.

Careful. He fears this.

"Ah, yes, your ancestral Empress of Tengri-Nayon.
I, too, honor my ancestors, but I do not pray to them,
nor do they speak to me. I live only in the moment,
Mengmoshu, and perform the tasks at hand. My advice
to the Moshuguang is to do the same, advancing the
sciences useful to us, while keeping the traditionalists'

values. You might show me, for example, an economical
way to dig a six kilometer tunnel through the mountain
for commercial access to our eastern farms. That is
something real, Mengmoshu. Not mythical."

They left the throne room, and accompanied the
Emperor to his elevator in silence for a moment.

*It is a genuine request, Mengmoshu, though he wishes
to divert our interests.*

"There is wisdom in what you say," said Mengmoshu.
"If you will send us specifications for the tunnel, we'll
begin work on the problem immediately."

The elevator doors opened; the Emperor stepped
inside, and smiled. "Good. We will work together, then,
for the betterment of Shanji." The doors closed, and he
was gone.

They waited for the elevator to return, and went back
to Mengmoshu's office, where they were served tea.

"He was remarkably controlled today," said Mengyao,
"but his fear of our biological work is real."

"Needlessly, I think. We emulate nature, and six
generations of laboratory work have given us nothing.
We can only continue our present course. Have you been
experiencing discomfort, Mengyao?"

"Yes, for the past hour. A kind of anxiety."

"It comes from the child, Mengyao. It comes in waves,
and is very strong at such a distance from her. I am eager
to meet this child, and you are familiar to her. Would
you have breakfast with me here at seven tomorrow?
Her interview will begin after that."

"I will be here," said Mengyao.

That night, in his living quarters on the fourth floor
of the Hall of Ministers, Mengmoshu slept a troubled
sleep.

He was awakened three times with a feeling of sorrow,
flashing visions of dead bodies, the face of a woman that

vaguely disturbed him. The third time he was left wide awake, and suddenly there was a voice.

Mengmoshu, I cannot sleep with this racket. Is this the child brought back from the Tumatsin?

It was Juimoshu.

Yes. I've never felt such power from a young one, but her grief is terrible and we must handle her carefully. We have the support of the Emperor in treating her well.

Then there is something you must know, said Juimoshu.

They spoke without words for an hour, and formed a plan for the coming day.

CHAPTER SIX
MENGNU

When the guard came, Kati was instantly awake.

Her head ached and she felt as if she'd not slept at all, yet apparently she had, for she was on the cot, a light blanket over her. The guard came in with a tray of food and put it on the table when he saw she was awake. "Someone is coming for you," he said, then left the room and closed the door again.

She was ravenous. There was bread and cheese, a hot, grainy cereal with milk added to it, a small pot of tea. She wolfed it down greedily, drank all the tea, then relieved herself on the fancy toilet in the corner.

She waited on the cot only a few minutes before there was a soft knock on the door and it opened slightly. A small face peered around the edge of it. A woman. An old woman.

"Kati?"

She nodded, and the woman came in, and instantly there was a presence in Kati's mind. *She is a Searcher*, thought Kati, amazed.

You are surprised, I see. The woman was tiny, dressed in black. There was no bulge on her forehead, or prominent veins, yet the forehead was unusual, not flat but domed, extending to the temples.

It's possible for a woman to be a Searcher, Kati, but

there have been few of us. I am Juimoshu. Some people would like to talk to you, and I will take you to them.

I have nothing to say to them.

The old woman walked forward, knelt before her, their eyes meeting. *But you will. They are like us, Kati. You have much in common with them.*

I am not a Searcher. I am Tumatsin, and I want to be with my people.

Juimoshu reached out to take Kati's hands and Kati balled them into fists in her lap. Juimoshu took them anyway, and her touch was warm, her eyes soft. Kati felt calmness, a sense of protection in those eyes.

You have a gift, Kati, and we want to find out about it. We want to know how you received it, for no other Tumatsin has received such a gift before. We think First Mother has blessed you.

"You mean the lady with the green eyes?" said Kati.

Juimoshu smiled, and squeezed Kati's hands. Her voice was husky, yet somehow melodic. "Yes, Kati, the lady who spoke to you from very far away. She is our ancestor and yours, too. She wants us to take care of you for Her. You've been in those clothes all night. Let's get you bathed, and then I'll find a nice robe for you to wear when we meet the people. Will you do that for me?"

She could detect no threat and nodded, even let the old woman take her hand to lead her out of the room and back to the barred gate. The short bow of the guard did not escape her, nor did the blankness of his mind. The woman leading her was someone he feared, a person with authority over him.

They climbed three flights of interior stairs to a hallway in white, and went in the first door there. The room was a marvel in porcelain, brightly lit. There was a row of fancy toilets, cubicles with transparent doors, and a huge, sunken tub, filled with steaming water. There was room for several people in that tub, and the water smelled

like herbs. Juimoshu handed her a bar of soap, fragrant
and smooth, not like the coarse soap of the Tumatsin,
and said, "Bathe yourself, and I will wait outside."

Kati climbed into the tub, wearing only her pendants,
and it was the most wonderful bath she'd ever had. The
odors of herbs and flowers filled her, anxiety draining
away with the heat. She rubbed the soap all over her
body and into her hair, again and again, until finally
Juimoshu called, "Hurry, now. Dry yourself with the towel
by the tub and I will bring in your robe."

The towel was thick, and soft. Kati rubbed herself until
her skin tingled, then held the towel in front of her as
Juimoshu entered with a black robe and a pair of matching
slippers.

How different you look. Lovely.

Kati put on the robe, felt Juimoshu's hands, then a brush,
on her hair. The woman brushed her hair down slowly,
gently, her tiny hands occasionally smoothing it. "We'll
let it fall naturally, so it will dry faster," she murmured.

Kati felt relaxed, nearly sleepy from the heat of the
bath, but it was not for long. Her anxiety grew as they
climbed another flight of stairs to walk a long hallway
surrounded by transparent material like clear ice with a
view to the outside: clustered buildings to the right, to
the left a panorama of the city sprawling below, down
to the valley and the mountains beyond, and before them,
a great, golden dome dazzling in the light of Tengri-Khan.
They came out into another hallway in white, with closed,
numbered doors on either side.

Kati's heart was pounding again. She felt a gentle
squeeze on her hand. Juimoshu knocked softly on a door,
opened it slightly. "I have Kati here," she said.

"Come, dear. These men are your friends."

They entered a room all in white except for a large,
ebony table with matching chairs. The walls were barren
of decorations, and light came from the ceiling. In one

corner were a couch, a low, small ebony table before it, and two chairs. Two men had been sitting there and they stood as she entered. Both were Searchers, but now dressed in white, not their usual military garb. Older men, but not so old as Juimoshu, looking similar to each other, like brothers, one slightly larger. The smaller one she recognized as the man who had brought her back from the *ordu*.

Greetings, Kati. I am Mengyao, and the man beside me is Mengmoshu, my superior. Please sit here, and let us get to know you. Juimoshu will also join us.

Juimoshu led Kati to the couch, and sat down next to her, facing the men. Kati was enveloped by soft fabric, feeling small. She twisted her fingers together, and looked at Mengyao.

I know you from yesterday. Why am I here? My mother! You killed her! Kati's cheeks were suddenly flushed with anger.

The men stiffened, seeming startled.

Gently, child. We, the Moshuguang, tried to prevent that, but there was an error by the military people. Our Emperor sends his regrets to you for what happened, but we cannot undo it. We're sorry about your loss, and intend to devote ourselves to your care.

I WANT TO GO HOME! It was the other man who'd spoken to her, not Mengyao.

Both men blinked hard, and Kati felt Juimoshu flinch beside her.

"I think we will speak with words," said the man Mengmoshu. "It will be easier for all of us, and less painful."

"I want to go home," said Kati sorrowfully.

"I know. I know," said Mengmoshu, "but you are with us, now. You are with people like you."

"I'm *not* like you! The Searchers are evil! They go into people's minds, and steal their private thoughts. You are the Emperor's spies. Ma has told me this." Kati clenched her hands, and felt sudden hatred for these people who held her captive.

Kati felt Juimoshu's hand brush her cheek. "We are not evil, dear, but we do serve the Emperor in searching for lies people tell him. Tell me, Kati, did your mother know you could speak without words?"

"Yes, she knew, and it frightened her. She was always afraid for me after she found out."

She was careful of what she thought when I was near. Oh, you heard that!

Both men smiled.

"In time you will learn how to mask the things you wish hidden," said Mengmoshu. "Tell me, Kati, what am I thinking about?"

It was as clear as if he'd held up a painting for her to see: a waterfall splashing over smooth, moss-covered rocks into a little pool, and there were colorful fish swimming there. Kati told him what she saw, and he smiled, but his vision had triggered a torrent of memories that flashed through her in an instant: the waterfall at Festival, the Eye of Tengri, Ma on her horse, the sword in her hand.

All gone. All gone.

"I know the place of worship for the Tumatsin," said Mengmoshu, frowning. "I have been there, and felt the heat from what you call 'The Eye.' Your memories will always be with you, Kati. At first they will be painful, but later you will see they relate to only a part of your life. Now you are moving on to something else. That woman was your mother?"

"Yes," said Kati, her voice cracking.

"You must always hold your mother dear in your heart, and honor her memory. She has made an exceptional child. How would you best remember her, Kati? Show me."

The quiet time, the moments before sleep, Ma leaning over her in dim light, stroking her cheek. Kati felt a tear run down her own cheek, and blinked, but the vision did not go away. She looked at Mengmoshu, and the vision was suddenly stronger. The vision was no longer only in her mind, but in his, and she was seeing it there.

"I miss her voice, her touch. She was my *mother!*" she sobbed, and the vision was gone. Mengmoshu scowled, shifted uneasily in his chair, and Mengyao glanced at him. His mind was now dark as a cave. Hiding something from her. Kati sobbed again, and felt Juimoshu's arm go around her shoulders. Mengmoshu seemed deep in thought, saying nothing. Mengyao glanced at him again, then at Juimoshu, raising an eyebrow.

"I will continue," said Juimoshu, "with a question for Kati." She hugged Kati gently, and spoke close to her ear.

"Have you ever seen the colors of people, dear, the kind of glow that surrounds them? I know that Tumatsin women can do this, and it's an ability we do not share with them."

Kati breathed deeply, calming herself, and wiped her face dry with one hand. Mengmoshu was still a darkness to her, his eyes focused at a point above her head without expression. Why had he suddenly become so quiet?

"I'm too young for that. Ma said I would see the life auras of people when I was ready to be a woman. She could do it, but I don't know what she saw. Ma could tell what people were feeling, though, and whether or not they were dangerous to us. She said it took practice."

"And how did she practice this?" asked Juimoshu.

Kati told them about her mother's shrine, her meditation with a flickering candle. Talking about Ma made her feel better. "I tried what Ma did, but it only put me to sleep," she said.

Even Mengmoshu smiled slightly. Kati's eyes hadn't moved from him. *What are you hiding?*

Mengyao suddenly leaned forward and said, "Kati, we'd like you to play a little candle game with us. It's important that you be relaxed when you play, and you might even learn something new about yourself. Would you like to try it?"

Kati shrugged her shoulders, but looked at him, away from the other man.

Mengyao got up, went to the big table, and returned with a stub of white candle, placing it on the table before her. He held out a metal tube, there was a click, and flame shot out of the tube, lighting the candle. He leaned over the table, looked closely at her, smiling.

"You see how steady the flame of the candle is because the air in this room isn't moving? See the tiny blue flame? So tiny. It's very hot there, and then there's yellow and orange. Watch the flame, Kati. Try to see the blue flame."

She saw only yellow and orange, but her eyes were now focused on the flame. Juimoshu's hand rubbed her shoulder gently, then rested warmly there.

"Watch the flame, Kati, and relax. Relax. Do you feel its heat?"

"No. It's too far away," Kati murmured.

"Then put out your hand, but not too close or too fast. We want the flame to be quiet. Sneak up to it, slowly."

Kati struggled briefly to escape the soft embrace of the couch, and sat on its edge, leaning forward so her fingers were a hand's length from the flame when Mengyao stopped her.

"Close enough. Now do you feel the heat?"

"No."

"Good. Now we will play the game, Kati. I want you to imagine that little points of light, like stars, are coming out of your fingertips. There are only a few at first, then many more, and the stars are making a bridge between your fingers and the flame, a little curved bridge that's reaching out to find the heat. Imagine it, Kati. See it in your mind, not your eyes. Reach for the flame without moving your hand."

Kati stared at the flame, relaxed again, and her eyes

seemed to lose their focus. She still saw the flame, but her fingers were a blur. She tried to slowly shift focus to her fingers, but as she did so it seemed that a piece of the flame moved with her, a tiny, yellow tongue snaking out and fluttering there, seeking a direction. *Come here*, she thought, and the yellow tongue moved, growing longer. Suddenly there was an orange glow at the ends of her blurred fingers, and the yellow tongue moved with blinding speed, attaching itself there.

And Kati felt heat.

Surprised, she jerked her hand, and the yellow tongue snapped off, wavering wildly, but seeking her again, reattaching itself, and this time she held still. Warmth flowed into her fingers.

"Draw heat from the candle, Kati. Let it flow to your hand, and through your whole body, warming you all over. And look for the blue flame. Make it bigger. As you draw heat from the candle, the blue flame will grow."

And there *was* a blue flame now, a tiny thing the size of the candle's wick. Kati imagined heat flowing like liquid, issuing from the burning wax and pulling the blue flame with it. And it grew.

Her fingertips were now warm, and she could feel heat in her hand, moving slowly. But the blue flame grew rapidly, and with it the heat, and the heat was not moving fast enough beyond her fingers. Her fingertips were growing hotter and hotter, and she wanted to move her hand.

"It's hurting," she whispered. "It's *burning* me."

The candle flame wavered for an instant as her hand shook once, then again. Her arm was tired and her fingertips fiery hot. It was her imagination, the flame not touching her, and yet there was *pain*. She willed her hand to be still, but it wouldn't obey. She started to jerk it away—

And Mengyao grabbed her hand, putting her fingers briefly on his cheek, then pushing her hand back to her.

"Place your fingertips on your lips, and see what you have done," he said quietly.

She did so, and her fingertips *were* hot! She placed them on her lips, her cheeks, and felt the heat drain into her. Very quickly, they were cool again. She looked up at Juimoshu, but the woman was looking at the men, smiling. Mengyao leaned back, grinning, but Mengmoshu had a stony look, his fingers steepled before his face.

"You have not imagined it, Kati," Mengyao said. "You feel the energy that came to you from the candle, crossing a space to reach your fingers. You did that, Kati. You did it with your mind."

"How?" she asked, rubbing her fingers together.

"Perhaps we'll discover that during your training," said Mengyao. "This will be your first exercise, Kati, to work with the candle each night before sleep. We do not want you hurt, so if it gets too hot, you should increase the distance between your fingers and the flame. We will work with you."

Finally, Mengmoshu spoke again. "*All* of us will work with you. Kati, you are a special child with great gifts from First Mother. We will discover those gifts, and develop them with you. First Mother has commanded this of us, and we obey Her will."

Kati felt sudden concern coming from this man, a keen interest in her welfare, yet he showed her no visions of thoughts he had. There was only a warm feeling that hadn't been there when she'd first met him only minutes ago. All three people seemed to genuinely care about her, yet they had taken her mother away in death, and brought her to this foreign place. She was suddenly confused.

"I think we've done enough for now," said Mengmoshu. "Juimoshu will take you to your quarters. You'll be living right here in the palace, Kati. Life will not be as harsh as it was in the mountains, and you will live like a child of nobility here."

"I cannot go outside?" Kati asked.

"Oh, yes. That will come, in time. A flower needs the light of Tengri-Khan. We will not let you wither."

Juimoshu put an arm around her. "There is a very nice lady who is anxious to meet you. I think you will like her, Kati, and she wants very much to take care of you. Her baby died, you see, and she is quite lonely. She has lost someone just like you have. Shall we go now?"

Everything was happening so fast. Kati nodded her head numbly, for it seemed all was decided for her. She stood up with Juimoshu, who again took her by the hand. They walked towards the door, and then Mengmoshu called out, "Wait a moment."

The man knelt before her, close, and looked straight into her eyes.

The three of us will be your teachers, but only in matters of the mind. There will be other teachers as well. We are all your friends, Kati, and in time you will have many friends here. Although we keep you here, do not think of yourself as a captive. The day will come when you will determine your own course of life. In the meantime, we will teach you, and if there is something you wish for, you only need to ask for it.

But I wish to go HOME! I want to be with Da and Baber!

I understand. In time, I will help you find them again. And when you're a woman, if you wish to live with the Tumatsin, it will be so. In the end, we are all one people. Remember that. All one people. But you are in the hands of First Mother now, and your destiny will be decided by Her. We are only servants, Kati. Believe in First Mother, who has spoken to you. Listen to Her carefully when she speaks to you again.

I will. Then I will ask her why my mother is dead.
Kati met his gaze solidly and he blinked, but then he reached up and touched her cheek.

You can talk to me anytime you wish, child.

He stood up, made a motion with his hand, and Juimoshu led her away.

The feeling of great warmth had been there again. Suddenly, the man had affection for her, but why? He was the leader of the trio; she had sensed the other two pausing for his questions, deferring to him. That vision of Ma, in *his* head, not hers, something about it had changed his feelings, had made a connection between them. Again, she was confused.

Juimoshu led her to two brass doors at the end of the hallway and pressed something on the wall. A trooper was standing there, fully armed and armored, his gaze fixed straight ahead. The doors slid open, revealing a cubicle in brass and they stepped inside, the doors closing them in. Juimoshu took a piece of metal, poked it in one of several slots by the door and turned it with a click. Kati's stomach suddenly seemed to rise, and she gasped, involuntarily squeezing Juimoshu's hand. Just as quickly, her stomach settled again and the doors opened.

Two guards faced them, rifles across their chests, faces tense and alert. They nodded, Juimoshu pausing briefly before they stepped out into a hallway curving left and right along the arc of a great circle. The walls were painted in gold, the carpet thick, and red. They turned left, walking past painted portraits of men and women in regal dress, tapestries showing gardens and mountain scenes and villages that were surely not Tumatsin. There were no *gerts*, but white huts clustered around central squares with pools in their centers and fields of grain stretching to the far distance.

It seemed they walked far before coming to a huge door out of black wood, and Juimoshu knocked softly on it. The door was opened by a young woman wearing a yellow robe, hair rolled into buns on both sides of her face. Kati thought she was pretty. Was this the woman?

"We are expected," said Juimoshu.

"I know," said the woman. "She was too excited to sleep after you came back again last night. And this must be Kati." The woman gave Kati a beautiful smile, and beckoned for them to enter.

"This is Tanchun," said Juimoshu, "First-Servant of Lady Weimeng, with whom you'll be staying."

Tanchun bowed low, hands folded, a gesture that surprised Kati and made her feel uncomfortable. So she nodded her head, and managed a faint smile.

"This way," said Tanchun, and she walked gracefully ahead of them, as if floating.

The place was not one room, but many, and Kati had never dreamed of such beauty and luxury existing. The first room had a floor of black polished stone, a low table in its center surrounded by cushions, couches and chairs along three walls beneath mirrors with gilded frames. They walked left under an arch to a second room, walls painted yellow, three women sitting behind desks, working at machines with illuminated screens. They were filled with a script Kati had seen on wall hangings in her own *ger*, but could not yet read, for education of a Tumatsin girl began in her seventh year. Everywhere they walked, the floors were black stone.

There was a third room like the first, then one with a closed door, then another set of double doors, high and black. Tanchun went to those doors, and knocked three times.

"Enter!" said someone, quite loudly. Kati was feeling an excitement, and it was not her own, though she was nervous.

Tanchun opened the door. "They are here, Madam."

"Please bring them in!" said a woman.

Kati squeezed Juimoshu's hand hard, and gasped at the sight of the opulence before her: the red carpet, the colors of the wall hangings, the huge, golden, canopied bed on one side of a huge room with high ceiling. A woman stood up from behind a black table in the center of the room. Tall and slender, she wore a yellow robe that showed the curves in her body. She was not young, or old. Certainly older than Ma. Her hair showed no grey, and was in side buns like the style of her servant, but her face was not so round as Tanchun's. She had a beautiful smile, and stretched out her arms as she walked towards them.

"You have finally brought her, mother. It seems I've been waiting forever." She put her arms around Juimoshu, and hugged her fiercely.

Mother? This is your daughter?

Yes. She is a good woman, Kati, and she has lost a child. She wants to take care of you, and I want it, too. I want it for both of you.

The woman knelt before Kati, and grasped her hands.

"This is Kati," said Juimoshu.

"I am Weimeng," said the woman, her eyes moist and sparkling. Emotions poured from this woman: joy, love, sorrow, elation, a jumble of feelings that were overwhelming yet somehow comforting, so much so that Kati felt herself smiling.

"Oh, mother, she's beautiful! Has The Son of Heaven been consulted about this? Does he know?"

"I have spoken to him early this morning and he has given his approval," said Juimoshu.

"Then it's not a dream, and she is really here. My little girl is really here."

The joy of the woman was coming in waves, but there was something else. Something about a dead child—

"She is called Kati, daughter. That is her name," said Juimoshu.

"I know. I know. Kati, they say I can take care of you while you're here, and it's something I want badly. Would you stay with me, live with me here? I have a room just for you, a place for your privacy when you want it. I know you can be very happy here. Will you stay?"

What could she say? Everything seemed planned and decided for her. "If you wish it," she said.

"Oh, I do! I do! Weimeng embraced her tightly, Kati's arms at her sides, stiff at first, then relaxing. The woman's cheek was smooth against hers, and wet with tears. There was a sweet fragrance in her hair.

Weimeng released her and wiped the tears from her own cheek. "Come now. I will show you your room." She took Kati's hand, and they went to the closed door, Juimoshu following silently behind.

They went to the door near the entrance to Weimeng's suite, "This is *your* place," said Weimeng, and opened the door dramatically.

It was not one room, but three, and Kati was stunned by the sight. A room with plush, golden carpet, couch, three chairs and table, walls red, light from globes hanging from a brass chandelier, two mirrors with gilded frames making it seem even larger than it was. The mirrors were colorless, unlike the ones of polished brass she was used to. Through an arch there was a bedroom with drawers in plain walls, a porcelain receptacle and shelf with running water before a large mirror opposite a canopied bed shrouded in fine, gold net. Adjacent to it was a room in porcelain, with black stone flooring, glassed-in cubicle, with a fancy toilet and a huge, sunken tub. Colorful bottles sat on a shelf surrounding the tub, and the air was filled with sweet odors of herbs and other things she didn't recognize.

Kati looked at it all in a daze as Weimeng led her back excitedly to the first room. "Now, I will show you the best thing," she said, smiling.

In each room, one wall was curved outward, like the surface of a sphere. Weimeng pressed a button of metal on one wall, there was a buzzing sound and the light of Tengri-Khan flooded the room. The wall opened up like a mouth, and there was a clear panel there, like a piece of the city's tent. She looked outside, and saw the entire city sprawling below her, the tent still high above her position. She could see the valley and the great cliffs and the mountains far beyond. She could see the three peaks that were one.

"I have kept these rooms for guests, and you are the first to use them. Now these rooms are yours."

But Kati, clutching at the window sill, was lost in the sight of the mountains.

"Tanchun!" called Weimeng. "Have the fitters arrived?"

"Yes, Madam. Two are here, waiting," came a distant voice.

Tanchun arrived, Kati's leathers stacked neatly in her hands. "These have been washed, Madam," she said, and put the leathers in a drawer, opened a sliding panel on one wall as they followed her into the bedroom. Two women appeared at the archway, carrying heavy books and a metal case. They bowed deeply, and waited.

Juimoshu touched Kati's shoulder and the girl looked up at her. "Now is the time for me to leave," Juimoshu said gently. "We will give you some days to get used to your new surroundings, but then there is work for you to do. One of us will come for you. In the meantime, remember to practice each night with this, as we instructed." She gave Kati a small, fat candle, and the metal fire-tube, and showed her how to use the tube.

Then she left.

Weimeng was issuing a stream of orders to Tanchun and the other women, and everyone was hurrying. They took off Kati's robe, and the women measured every part of her body, writing things down, and then they showed her a thousand pictures of robes and suits, gowns and shoes, all manner of colorful clothing in the thick books they'd brought. Weimeng sat on the floor with Kati, arm around her, and pointed to the pictures.

"Do you like that?"

"It's pretty," said Kati.

Weimeng tapped the picture, and the women wrote something down.

Over and over again. So many clothes, all beautiful. The process seemed to go on forever, and when the women finally left they bowed deeply, broad smiles on their faces, seeming quite pleased with themselves. It suddenly occurred to Kati that everything she had liked in those pictures would soon be hers.

Tanchun served them lunch back in Weimeng's suite. There was bread and cheese, strips of meat mixed with vegetables and ropy starch that filled Kati to bursting. And they talked as they ate, about everything, including the sad things, but for the moment, at least, it was hard for Kati to be sad. The joy and feelings of love coming from Weimeng seemed to drown it all out.

But there was a point, when Kati talked about Ma, that she began to cry. She was surprised when Weimeng cried with her, tears flowing freely. The woman reached across the table, held Kati's hands in hers and said, "You cry for your mother, I cry for another, but now we have found each other, and neither of us need ever be lonely again."

And Kati knew it was true. Ma and Sushua were gone forever, but she was still alive, and Da and Baber were still out there, perhaps searching for her even now. Hadn't Mengmoshu said he would help her find them someday? Her presence was bringing joy to Weimeng, and that was a good thing. And there were things to learn about this place, things to learn about herself.

She remembered the emerald eyes of Mandughai, the voice in her head, saying, 'There are things I would have you do when you're a woman.' Had Mandughai brought her to this place? Was there a purpose in all that had happened to her?

That night she was exhausted, and Weimeng had allowed her some private time before she would come to prepare her for sleep. Kati got out her candle, lit it, and stared at the steady flame for sometime, but it did not make her drowsy. She put out her hand and imagined the bridge of light. The yellow tongue of flame was instantly there. She felt its heat, but kept it constant by slowly drawing back her hand to an arm's length. The blue flame grew until the candle was hissing, dissolving before her eyes, and then she jerked her hand away. The candle had burned down to a stub in minutes.

The exercise was easy, and perhaps they would be able to find something more interesting for her to do.

Weimeng came to tuck her into bed, and Kati felt as if she were floating on a cloud. The woman's hand stroked her forehead as her eyes closed, and as she drifted off she heard a whisper close to her ear.

"Sleep well, my baby. My darling Mengnu. Mother is here."

Mengmoshu spent the entire afternoon and evening correlating all reported Tumatsin births over the past seven years. It was late when he found what he was looking for: a daughter Kati, born to Temujin and Toregene in the unnamed *ordu* near the three peaks, the *ordu* that had served as a Tumatsin reconnaissance outpost for several years. Born in the season of last frost—seven years ago. His apprehension grew as he searched further.

He found that Toregene shared the lineage of Manlee, the woman whose eyes could be green when she desired it, the woman who led the spiritual life of the Tumatsin.

Toregene. Her smiling face above a loved child. Her twisted face beneath a man who forced his seed into her.

And now a child, only seven, with the powers of a mature Searcher, and something far beyond that. A child now placed in his care.

He could not eat, and went to bed early.

He prayed for hours, perspiration pouring from him.

Finally, the matrix of light appeared, the pattern of sparkling stars that signified Her presence. And then the emerald eyes, without a face, opening up to gaze at him.

I feel your agony, Mengmoshu. Let it flow from you, for there is much to do.

First Mother, in my zeal to do your work, I violated your principles. I forced a woman, and now there is a child from it.

I do not condone your method, Mengmoshu, but you saved the woman's life and the child is something entirely new. She gives us hope for moving to the next step.

Then I am the father?

Of course. There can be no doubt of that. She is the child of your body, but she must not know this now. You must keep it from her, and that will be difficult. She already sees deeply, and I will begin work with her soon. I feel her even now. She is exciting, Mengmoshu. You have served me well.

I feel remorse, and guilt about her mother.

Then feel it, and let it pass. Love your child, and teach her all you can. I will do the rest. You are her father, Mengmoshu. Now you must act the part.

The eyes closed, the stars flickering, and then there was darkness again. Mengmoshu lay still for a moment, his mind raging. He willed calm, bringing himself to a state near sleep, then reached out to a place nearby.

Kati, are you there? Can you hear me?

There were no thoughts, only a vision of the mountains as seen from a window in the palace dome.

And there were no sorrowful cries that night.

CHAPTER SEVEN
PURPLE LIGHT

Weimeng could not understand why Kati wished to ride a horse, and she was horrified by the idea of it.

"That is a thing for men and older boys, dear, certainly not for little girls. And if you were hurt, I would never forgive myself."

"I love horses," protested Kati. "I was riding them by myself when I was four, and I want to ride again. Please, Madam. Please."

There was purpose in her protest and her pleadings. First of all, her eighth birthday was only a week away, and Weimeng was particularly generous on such occasions. Kati wanted a horse, but how could she obtain one if people around her felt she could not, or should not ride?

Second of all, Kati was bored.

"The troopers' sons ride all the time; I can see them from my window. You could get someone to watch me, to be sure I don't hurt myself, and *then* you'll see how well I can ride. You can ask *anyone* to do it; you are First Wife!"

This ploy usually worked, and today was no exception, when she saw Weimeng stiffen.

"I will make inquiries," said Weimeng, "but it must be a small horse. The big ones are far too dangerous for a child." Her brows were knitted with concern.

"Oh, *thank* you!" Kati hugged Weimeng fiercely, looked up at her. "It's only that I'm bored. I want to be outside more. I want to feel the wind and smell the trees. I don't want to be inside all the time, working with the teachers. There are no children for me to play with here."

Weimeng stroked her hair, held her close. "It is so easy to forget you're not a palace child, Kati. First Lady brought you to me from the mountains, and your life was different there. Go back to your studies, now, and I will see what I can do to solve these problems of yours."

Kati went back to her rooms with a reasonable expectation of receiving a horse for her birthday, because Weimeng *would* find someone to ride with her. Weimeng was a gentle woman. Too gentle. She was first wife of the Emperor, but had surrendered to her own shame. She did not take advantage of her status, or the deep respect the Moshuguang and members of the palace staff had for her. She accepted the rejection of a husband, and did nothing to oppose it.

If I were first wife, he would have reason to fear me.

It had been a shock when Kati had learned who Weimeng really was. It was only two weeks after she'd come here, and they were eating lunch in Weimeng's suite. The doors opened, without a knock, and The Son of Heaven marched in rudely, interrupting their meal.

"So this is the child," he'd said, looking Kati up and down, hands on hips, an arrogant posture.

And how did Weimeng react? Angrily? No, she dropped to her knees before him, kissing his hand, and saying, "Oh, Son of Heaven, I thank you for allowing me the gift of this child."

Son of Heaven. The Emperor of Shanji. Kati could only stand stiffly before him. At that moment, she had wished only pain and slow death for the man.

"I am pleased if she brightens your life, woman," he'd said, "but let there be no misunderstandings here. She is only a foster child, and there will be no adoption. There is only one heir to the throne."

And then he'd paraded haughtily from the suite, a guard on either side of him.

Weimeng had then explained who she really was, and how she'd arrived at her lonely existence before Kati came. And Kati had a new reason to hate the Emperor of Shanji.

Now she went back to her learning machine, and the drudgery of memorizing her characters, one by one.

Huomeng arrived in the early afternoon to check her progress. Mengmoshu had assigned the boy to tutor her as a part of his own training. His purpose within the Moshuguang was to be a scientist and educator. He arrived on time, as usual, and checked the extent of her work.

"Your progress is far greater than I expected," he said, with the condescending tone of voice he used with her. "Your memory is nearly as good as mine."

But much faster.

"Perhaps. But your real learning is about to begin. I brought these for you."

He handed her two disks, and without asking his permission, she immediately inserted one into the machine.

"This one is the geography of Shanji. The other is more about astronomy, and it describes the Tengri-Nayon system that was the home of our ancestors. I think you will find that one more interesting."

He clearly wanted to talk about the second disk, so she booted up the first one instead.

The new lesson appeared on her screen, showing a blue planet with two large continents, one straddling the equator, the other peeking from beneath the edge of a mass of ice frozen at the south pole. Huomeng pointed at the city's location near the southwestern shore of the equatorial continent. "There are fertile valleys here, and to east and north of the mountains, but then the land becomes arid, nearly a desert. It goes all the way to the northeast quarter, where there is heavy rainforest we haven't even explored yet. First landing was here, on the plateau next to what you call the Three Peaks."

I used to ride Sushua there, and the peaks were my favorite place.

Huomeng smiled. "As you can see, we haven't moved far from the original landing site, but that is the way of the traditionalists. Our population has grown slowly under the dictates of our Emperors, but his influence has not been so visible in the eastern plains. The population there is growing rapidly, and all the fertile lands are now being used. The Emperor doesn't know this yet, because he hasn't cared enough to visit the people there. And we have not told him. Soon, we will have to move people to the northeast, along the coast, even the forest interior. That is over three thousand kilometers from here, Kati. I think the days of a small, feudal kingdom governed by one man will soon be coming to an end."

"He will not allow it," she said.

"He will have no choice," said Huomeng. "It will be a matter of survival."

"But the Moshuguang does not tell the Emperor what he should hear. You are supposed to serve him."

"We serve First Mother, and are in her hands. The Emperor is not."

There was hardness and finality in the sound of Huomeng's voice. For the first time, Kati saw the huge gap, both political and philosophical, between the Moshuguang and the man who sat on the throne.

There was not one ruler of Shanji, but two. And one of them lived far away from this world, appearing to chosen people only in their minds.

"Now you will read to me," said Huomeng.

She read to him from the text on the screen, pausing only twice for his explanation of a character she hadn't seen before. It was all boring. She yawned.

"My hour is finished," said Huomeng, looking displeased. "Be ready to read the other disk to me in two days. And get more sleep."

"I get too much sleep. I'm like the rodents that burrow into the ground."

"Then get outside more."

"I'm *trying* to."

"Oh. Have you said anything to Mengmoshu?"

"No."

"Do it. They will find an excuse for you. I must go."

She glared at him, then deliberately yawned again as he left. Her meeting with the teachers of the mind was three days off. Too long.

Mengmoshu, I have a problem.

I'm busy, Kati. Can it wait?

No. You're always busy. I feel trapped in this room. I cannot go on learning this way. I need to get outside, but Madam fears I will be burned by Tengri-Khan, or breathe a dust mote, or scuff my knee. I want to ride a horse! You said I'm not a captive. I want to get outside more.

Weimeng means well. She is a cautious mother, and we will speak to her. Be patient another day.

One day?

That's what I said. Do your work, now, and I'll do mine. Be patient, and trust me.

Kati felt that peculiar fuzziness in her head, indicating he had tuned her out for the moment, and likely for the rest of the day. Mengmoshu did not like her interruptions, but it was always him she sought out when there was a problem. She was somehow comforted by the knowledge that day, or night, the mind of Mengmoshu hovered just beyond the edge of her consciousness.

She went back to work, inserted the second disk into her machine and discovered that Huomeng had been correct. This was more interesting to her, a short program with many colored pictures of two planetary systems. The first picture showed Tengri-Khan, a yellow star with dark spots, and small tongues of flame issuing from its surface. Eight planets, five of them close in, barren and pocked-marked, lifeless places. Further out was the blue world of Shanji, a planet without a moon, like the other little ones. But much further out were two giant balls of gas, with swirling storms and many moons of ice and frozen gases.

The second system was most interesting. Tengri-Nayon, the red star of Empress Mandughai; seen up-close, it was really more orange than red. A very young star, the text said, only recently born, with a planetary system not yet fully formed. It was a violent looking place, jets of matter streaming from the poles of a sphere whose surface boiled with protuberances, fans, and great bridges of fire. Of the inner four planets, two were inhabited, one covered with streams of white clouds. The other, an orange ball with wisps of clouds, and large patches of green on its surface was called Meng-shi-jie. The home of Mandughai.

She had not always lived there, the text said. The first palace had been a city floating in the atmosphere of the hot, gaseous giant Lan-Sui, a planet that had nearly become a star. People still lived in those floating cities, but a gradual, inward migration was taking place as Lan-Sui cooled. Each year there were fewer and fewer people to mine the nine moons for water-ice and metals, and to scoop gases from Lan-Sui for use in the Empress's new technologies, whatever they were. The text did not describe them.

A new question arose in Kati's mind. The time for light to travel between Tengri-Nayon and Tengri-Khan ranged from four years to six months as the two stars followed wobbly, parallel courses, the younger star strongly influenced by some massive, unseen companion. Huomeng had already informed her that nothing could travel faster than light. So then how could Mandughai communicate as if she were quite near, with no time taken between a question and an answer? Was a part of her always in their minds? Or was she, in fact, living nearby, hiding herself?

A new question for Huomeng, but when she asked it, the following day, he told her that Mengmoshu must answer the question for her.

She decided she had found a question he could not answer, and was pleased with herself.

There was only testing again. Mengmoshu put the helmet over her head. At first there was darkness, then a matrix of stars before her eyes, flickering, then strobing slowly, and a tone in her ear.

"Relax," said Mengyao, "and watch the lights. Try to make them brighter. Imagine each point becoming larger, and focus on one of them. Let yourself move towards it."

The tone was meant to soothe her, but didn't. She felt apprehensive, unusually alert, the strobing lights not getting brighter, but closing in on her.

"You're not relaxing, Kati," said Mengyao.

"I'm trying," she said petulantly. "Nothing's happening."

"Pick one light. Focus on it."

"I am. It doesn't work. I'm tired. I don't want to do this today." Kati felt agitated, even angry. She began to squirm in the soft chair where they'd placed her.

"Kati, you have to concentrate," said Mengmoshu softly.

I don't want to do this today! Let me up! NOW!

She scrabbled at the helmet with her hands, pulling at it. She touched something sharp, and the lights flicked off, leaving only darkness.

"This is hopeless," said Juimoshu. "She's too agitated today."

Mengmoshu pulled off the helmet, and looked at her closely.

"What is *wrong* with you today? You're behaving very badly."

Kati glared at him. "I'm tired of tests, and tricks. That's all we do. You said I could go outside. You said you'd talk to someone. We work and work, and at night I work more with the learning machine. I'm BORED! I want to do something ELSE!"

"You are becoming quite demanding, child," said Mengmoshu, returning her hard look with one of his own. "I asked you to be patient. You are here for work, not play, and you can wait a while for—"

"Enough, Mengmoshu; we waste our time," said Juimoshu. "Tell Kati what you've arranged, then take her there. Allow her some fun, and then we can do something useful here."

"*What* have you arranged?" asked Kati.

Mengmoshu was scowling at all of them.

You've lost control of the situation here. Say something! I will not be forced by her.

"Forced? No. Look, I will do a trick for you," said Kati. She picked up a metal fire-tube from the low table before her. A little flame appeared. She only glanced at it, and the flame shot upwards by a meter, roaring, then sputtering and going out, the fuel in the tube spent.

"I've done my trick. What have you arranged?"

Mengmoshu sighed. "Not now. We have work to do."

"This is silly, both of you," said Juimoshu. "He has found someone to ride with you, Kati. It was to be right after we were finished here."

"She must learn patience first," said Mengmoshu.

Mengyao shook his head. "If she goes riding now, perhaps we can get something done."

"I agree," said Juimoshu. "A child must have fun, as well as work."

"I can go riding?" said Kati, suddenly excited. "You found a horse for me! Oh, *thank* you, Mengmoshu. You *did* keep your promise!" She slid off the chair, hugged his legs, looked up at him. "Can we go now? I promise to be good. When we come back, I will work very hard for you. Please?"

His hand rested lightly on her head, and his face was soft again. "Very well, but then we work."

Juimoshu and Mengyao were smiling at her, and suddenly Mengmoshu took her by the hand, softly, in a new way for him. He led her back to her rooms, where there was another surprise. A new set of riding leathers had been laid out on her bed, leathers identical to the old ones which no longer fit her.

Weimeng came in with Tanchun, and they helped her dress, while Mengmoshu waited outside in the hall. Weimeng was very frightened for her, and said so.

"I'm a good rider," said Kati. "Come and watch me."

"I cannot," said Weimeng, wringing her hands together. "I would be too terrified to open my eyes. But they tell me you must do this, that it's a part of your training. Oh, *do* be careful, darling." Weimeng hugged her hard.

It was only the second time Kati had been outside the palace dome in nearly a year. The first time had been when Weimeng took her to a beautiful garden just below the golden dome, a place with flowers and a waterfall splashing into a little pool. Kati had waded in the pool, and the little carp there had nibbled on her toes. She'd laughed, and said "they're tickling me," and suddenly Weimeng had burst into tears. Weimeng had soaked her own, beautiful robe wading in to grab Kati, had carried her away from the garden and back to her rooms, crying all the way.

Kati had not been outside since that day—until now. And she was thrilled.

Mengmoshu himself was suddenly not so serious, even seemed to share her delight. She ran ahead of him to the rail car taking them to the lower edge of the city. A few people in their white uniforms looked at her curiously in her leathers, but said nothing. There was a wariness about them when they saw her escort.

Only the two of them rode the car down with the driver, Kati's nosed pressed to the window.

The people fear you.

No. They are cautious, so I won't hear a bad thought about the Emperor.

But they live in his city! Don't they like him?

There are many new things they wish to do, but the Emperor will not allow it. He keeps to the traditional ways. He is not progressive in using the technology we've developed. I will show you these things, Kati. There's much you haven't seen yet.

They reached the station near the dome's gate, and walked to it past buildings in green and yellow. Faces peered from the windows there, and some were those of children. There was a cluster of troopers by the gate, and several horses. Kati squealed, and pulled on Mengmoshu's hand when she saw them. He let her lead him, and even smiled.

Will you ride with me?

No, not today. There is someone else, closer to your age. I will watch, this time. Be careful what you say, now. You are known by another name among these people, and it is Weimeng's wish. Please honor it, so she won't be disgraced. I will explain later. Remember, you are the foster child of Lady Weimeng, First Wife of the Son of Heaven.

And very quickly, Kati heard the name the people would call her. They came up to the troopers, and the men turned, bowing first to Mengmoshu, then to Kati. She was astonished, and could only smile in return.

"Chosen One," said an armored man, "you are early.

We hadn't expected you for at least an hour." He turned to a shorter man. "Fetch Lui-Pang right away, and tell him to saddle the black mare for Mengnu."

The shorter man hurried away.

So her name was Mengnu, among the people. The name of Weimeng's dead child, but Kati was in a happy mood, and the false name didn't bother her. Kati had replaced Mengnu, bringing joy to Weimeng, and she knew the woman loved her as her own. What was the harm in using a name given by the woman who tried so hard to be a mother to her?

Minutes later, a boy appeared; a very handsome boy, tall and slender in the saddle. He rode a white stallion with patches of grey, like handprints, and a little black mountain horse followed closely behind. Kati could not restrain herself. She ran to the boy, and he smiled down at her.

He was *very* handsome, she decided. "Is that my horse?" she asked.

"It is if you're Mengnu," he said.

"I am." She went to the little horse, stroked its muzzle, hugged it.

"I will help you up," said the boy, beginning to dismount.

Kati jerked the tether rope from his hand, saw the reins wrapped around the saddle horn. "I can do it myself," she said. Before he could dismount, she stretched to reach the horn, hopped to snap one foot in a stirrup, and swung smoothly upwards to seat herself.

"Check her stirrups, Lui-Pang," said someone. The men were grinning at her, looking pleased. Even Mengmoshu gave her a little nod of approval.

Lui-Pang adjusted her stirrups, initially too short, and she directed him, standing to check the fit. The animal tensed beneath her, and she felt its excitement. She trotted her horse to the gate, and waited there while the boy mounted up on his stallion and joined her.

"We have one hour," he said. "I've been told we should stay on flat ground in the valley. Let's go slowly, at first. I'm responsible for your safety."

"I want to go fast, and so does this horse."

"She's a good horse," said Lui-Pang, "as long as you're good to her. But I think you know what to do."

He looked down from several hands above her. They walked the dirt road lined with unlit torches and turned left, away from the mountain trail, a broad plain of short grass sloping downwards ahead of them. "We are far enough," he said, and surged ahead at a trot. Kati was instantly beside him, the little mare quick to respond to the touch of her knees. The boy Lui-Pang smiled, and increased his speed. Kati went right with him.

A minute later they were side-by-side in a full gallop across fields of grass, and the wind was whipping Kati's face, the little mare straining beneath her, its neck stretching out as Kati floated above the saddle, exhilarated by the pounding thrust in her legs. They held that pace for several minutes, until Lui-Pang veered right to a trail leading to the summit of a hillock, where he slowed to a trot, Kati right behind him. They stopped at the summit, and Lui-Pang pointed back to the city, a small, sparkling ball, then south to where the grass fields seemed to go on forever.

"There's a desert out there, somewhere," he said.

"Will we see it?" said Kati.

"No, it's too far. But I will go there someday, when I'm a trooper. My father says people will eventually be living there to work in the factories. There is no more space in the mountain for making tools, flyers or weapons, even things for the homes of the nobles."

"Is your father a trooper?"

"Yes. He was with Mengyao when you were brought back from the mountains. I know who you really are, and I'm not surprised at how well you ride. Among the

Hansui, girls don't ride at all. They are taught manners and fashion, and little else among the nobles."

"I'm not a noble," said Kati.

"I know, but you are kept by the Emperor's First Wife and your teachers are Moshuguang. I hear that you have special powers."

He was frankly staring at her in an appraising, yet friendly way. "Can you actually change the color of your eyes?"

Kati could sense only curiosity in his mind, and admiration for the way she rode a horse. His dark, closely-spaced eyes twinkled with a kind of amusement. He had the round, Hansui face, but a narrow nose that, together with the eyes, gave him an intense, almost dangerous look. Barely older than she, he was still thin, but his shoulders were broad, and square.

Kati suddenly felt shy, and couldn't keep herself from smiling. Lui-Pang returned the smile, and said, "You are young to be a student of the Moshuguang."

"I'm eight," she said.

"And I am twelve. I've been riding for six years, and now I work with sword and bow. When I am sixteen, I will receive my rifle and become a trooper. I follow in the way of my father, and his father."

"You are lucky to have a father," said Kati. "I have lost mine."

"I know. But maybe you'll find him again, someday. Your life in the palace must be good, though."

"I'm comfortable with it, and Lady Weimeng is good to me, but being here is nicer than in the palace. This is where I really want to be—outside, and in the mountains, maybe by the big sea in the west. Can we go farther? I can still see the city."

This time they went at a leisurely trot, down the hillock and out onto sloping fields of grass. After a while, the scenery was all the same, and then Lui-Pang stopped.

"We have to return, now. If we hurry, we can be back on time."

"I don't want it to be over," said Kati.

"Neither do I. If you ask for it, I will be assigned to you again as an escort."

Kati smiled. "I will ask it. Are you ready?"

"Yes."

Both horses jumped together, and Lui Pang was fair. He held back his stallion just enough so that Kati's little animal was still nose to nose with it when they charged down the dirt road towards the gate, scattering people before them. They reined in, making a cloud of dust, Kati dropping expertly to the ground before they were even stopped. The waiting troopers clapped their hands with approval of the performance, and Mengmoshu was puffed up like a proud father, smiling as she rushed to hug him without shame, without inhibition. It was what she felt like doing, without knowing why.

You did well, and I shouldn't be surprised.

But can I do it again? Lui Pang is very nice, and he rides fast when I want to. He does not treat me like a little child.

I will arrange it, but only two days a week. Your work must be done.

Thank you, Mengmoshu. Thank you for hearing me. She hugged him again, while the other men looked on, curious about them.

Lui Pang led her horse away, but she saw him again a few minutes later, while Mengmoshu was talking to a trooper she suspected was the boy's father. Lui-Pang was with five other boys his age, and they were carrying long swords made from a plastic material, holding them casually by the curved blades. When they passed by, Kati nodded sharply to Lui-Pang, and smiled brightly. He seemed to understand her unspoken message. They would ride together again.

When Mengmoshu joined her, she pointed to the boys, and asked, "What are they doing?"

"They study the art of the sword with Master Yung, who teaches the traditional ways. The swords they use are made from flexible tubing wrapped with polymer fabric. They have the proper weight, but are safe to use in practice. They aren't real swords, Kati. The boys don't practice with steel blades until they're fourteen."

"I want to learn that," said Kati. "And I want to learn how to shoot arrows with the bow."

"This is not traditional for girls, even among the Tumatsin," said Mengmoshu, guiding her back to the monorail car.

"But I want to learn *everything*!" she said, excited again.

Mengmoshu's hand stroked her hair once, then rested on her shoulder. "Then we will find time for it in the future. Are you ready to work now?"

"Oh *yes*! I promised you that."

But Kati was disappointed by the rest of the day. They returned to the palace, and the room where Juimoshu and Mengyao waited patiently. They put the helmet on her, and the twinkling stars were there. Kati worked hard, focusing on the lights, trying to make them bigger, seeing herself as a moth attracted to a flame, but the lights remained as they were, just flickering spots.

"I'm sorry," she said, as they removed the helmet. "I'm trying hard, but it isn't working." She had badly wanted to please them, and had failed to do so for the first time.

"It might be the test itself," said Mengyao. "Don't blame yourself, Kati. We're not sure what we're looking for here, and our procedure might be wrong."

But Kati was near tears when Juimoshu returned her to her rooms. Her mood lightened when she ate with Weimeng that evening, telling her about the ride with

Lui-Pang. Weimeng acted as if it had been an adventure of terror, gasping as Kati told her story.

She grew serious again as Weimeng was tucking her into bed, and they were having their nightly, quiet moments together before sleep. She looked up at Weimeng, and said, "Among the people, I am called Mengnu."

Weimeng blushed, averted her eyes from Kati's. "I should have warned you. One day, I said it to someone, and then I could not take it back. The name is dear to me."

"The name of your baby who died," said Kati.

"Yes," said Weimeng, and there were tears in her eyes. Her fingers brushed Kati's cheeks and forehead. "But now I have you, and often I think of you as my own child, returned to me by First Mother. Perhaps it's a fantasy."

Kati took the woman's hand in hers. "I know who I am, and a name is just a name. I have not corrected what the people call me, and you are like my mother, now. If you wish to call me Mengnu, I don't mind. It is your privilege."

Weimeng burst into tears. She embraced Kati, and cried into her shoulder, murmuring, "My darling child, how much I love you. The joy you've brought into my life is something I don't deserve, but you are here. And perhaps, in time, you will come to call me mother."

Later, as Kati neared sleep, she felt warm and content about bringing happiness to Weimeng. She drifted off peacefully, but it seemed she'd slept only a little while before being awakened again. There was a presence in her mind, hovering there without identity.

Hello? Who's there?

No answer, but the presence was still there, and she kept her eyes closed.

The matrix of twinkling stars appeared suddenly, and she was nearly awake, for she had seen the sight before when, like now, Mengmoshu's helmet was not on her head.

Mengmoshu? Are you there?

And then there was that beautiful voice, as if murmuring into her ear.

No, dear. It is I.

Mandughai! It has been a long time!

I know it seems that way, but I've never left you.

The emerald eyes of Mandughai had not appeared. There was only darkness, with the matrix of twinkling lights.

Kati, I want you to look beyond the stars. Look closely, and tell me what you see there.

Kati looked, and at first there was only blackness, but as she relaxed again it seemed there *was* something vaguely familiar there: a faint, shimmering curtain, deep purple, filling the void.

I see a faint, purple light everywhere.

Look at that light, Kati. Let the stars rush by you, and go to the purple light.

It seemed to happen without effort. The stars grew, and rushed past her, and the purple light grew brighter, only it was not one, continuous thing, but a myriad of tiny points, close together. She rushed on, and the points were further apart, each one steady, not flickering.

Pick one light, Kati, any light. I'm here, waiting for you.

Kati plunged on towards a spot in the center of her mental field of view, the spot of light there growing, and growing, filling her vision, and then she was there, diving into it, and beyond—

To a place nearly dark, but filled with a shimmering curtain of the deepest purple she'd ever seen, and suddenly the emerald eyes of Mandughai were there, blazing before her.

Welcome to my world, Kati, for I have not come to

*you. You have come to me, and I have long awaited a
visitor to this place of mine. You are beyond the stars,
Kati. There is no time, or space here. This is the place
from which all the known universe came in the very
beginning. It is a place of light, of great energy. It is the
place of creation for our universe, and many more. As
you grow in strength, I will show you how to travel here,
and how to re-enter the universe at any point you choose,
for this place of light is everywhere within it. And you
will travel at infinite speed.*

The eyes of Mandughai were bright against the deep,
swirling purple of her world, and Kati was mesmerized
by the sight. So the question that came to her mind,
somehow, seemed childish.

Will I ever see your face?

The time for that will come. Now I will guide you back.

A purple flash, and then the twinkling stars were back,
Mandughai's beautiful eyes with them.

*We've had a nice visit, Mengmoshu. You should be
proud.*

I am, First Mother.

Mengmoshu! You're here with us!

*I waited for you, Kati. You've gone beyond where I
can go. But I'm always here.*

I know that.

*Mengmoshu will care for you as a father would, Kati.
In a way, you are our daughter. You will learn from us,
and grow, and at times it will be difficult. But you will
never be alone. Come to me anytime, Kati. Practice what
you have just learned. I will be waiting.*

The eyes vanished, along with the stars, but Mengmoshu
remained.

Sleep, child. This is just the beginning.

He was still with her when she drifted off.

CHAPTER EIGHT
SHEYUE

Kati did not get a horse for either her eighth or ninth birthday, but for her tenth the gift from Weimeng was a person.

Her name was Sheyue, which means musk, and she was twelve years old.

Weimeng gave a party in her suite, and all of Kati's teachers were there, including Huomeng. It was the first time she'd ever seen him in the black formal robe of the Moshuguang. He filled it out nicely and looked quite distinguished, she thought. But she missed the presence of Lui Pang, who was not from a noble family, and had not been invited. She thought about him a great deal these days.

The atmosphere was festive and there were many gifts to open. Most of them were clothing, including a new set of riding leathers, for her legs were suddenly growing longer and sometimes she felt as if she were walking on the stilts worn by the comic who provided their entertainment at the party.

He was a small man, dressed in a lady's red robe, and he wore a black wig with the double buns of a noblewoman's coiffure. His face was painted and rouged, with huge, black eyelashes which he batted and fluttered throughout his act. In one hand he carried a delicate fan, behind which he flirted with the men as he minced around the room on those long stilts. At first the men were embarrassed, but soon they joined the women in laughter at the man's antics.

Juimoshu gave Kati a pendant: a disk of gold on a long chain, and in the center of the disk was a single emerald, dark green. Kati put it on to join the other two pendants she'd worn continuously since coming to the Emperor's city.

Huomeng, always the teacher, gave her two disks for her learning machine. There was a pair of riding boots from Mengyao, and then Mengmoshu presented her with a long, curved sword of flexible polymer and informed her that private lessons with Master Yung would begin the following day.

Kati was thrilled. It was the most wonderful birthday ever. She hugged everyone, but when she got to Huomeng his eyes got very large and so she shook his hand in thanks.

"There is one more gift," said Weimeng, just as Kati thought it was all finished.

Tanchun came in, leading a tall, lovely girl by the hand. The girl had a long, graceful neck and skin like white porcelain. The buns of her hair were decorated with sparkling combs, and she seemed to float across the carpet, her body held proudly erect. As she came up to Weimeng, she bowed, lowering her eyes first, tiny, painted lips curving into a serene smile. The blue robe she wore seemed to enhance her calm presence.

Everyone seemed startled by the appearance of this girl. Huomeng's mouth hung open, and he was gawking stupidly at her.

Weimeng gestured to Kati, and said, "This is Mengnu."

The girl turned to Kati and bowed again. Her voice was clear, but soft, almost a whisper. "My name is Sheyue," she said, "and I am honored to be of service to you."

"Sheyue comes to us from one of our finest families," said Weimeng. "She will be your companion when you wish it, and will instruct you in the ways of fashion and etiquette as practiced in palace society. Her rooms will be near this suite, and you can be together as often as you like."

Kati was surprised, momentarily at a loss for words, but she felt a terrible fear coming from behind that serene face, and it was the fear of rejection. There were no thoughts in Kati's mind, no advice coming from anyone, but Sheyue's fear was like waves crashing against a cliff-face. Her family was highly honored by Weimeng's choice. To return this girl to her family would be an unbearable disgrace for her.

Kati smiled, and held out her hands. "Welcome, Sheyue. My rooms are also yours, and I hope we will be like sisters. I've always wished for a girl I could talk to and share secrets with."

She clasped Sheyue's hands, then embraced her. Her hair smelled like sweet grass, her relief so strong it nearly brought tears to Kati's eyes.

Kati looked at Weimeng, and said, "Thank you for the gift of a friend. It is more than I could wish for."

Weimeng looked pleased, and everyone was smiling, even Huomeng, who had lost that stupid look on his face. There had been tension in the room, but now it was gone. Everyone began talking again and the comic came back to resume his flirtations. Sheyue laughed at him, but hid her laugh in a secretive way behind one hand.

Kati took Sheyue's hand in hers, and led her around the room, introducing her teachers to the girl. She saved Huomeng for last, because he hadn't thought to mask the terror building in him and she was relishing every moment of it. When they reached him, his eyes were wide again, and he stood stiffly, making a curt bow when Kati introduced him.

"Welcome," he croaked, then seemed to recover his senses. "I come here to tutor Mengnu, so perhaps I will see you again."

His mind was suddenly a blank, and Kati knew he had sensed her peering at him. But he was clearly awed by Sheyue, a girl he thought his age, or even older. When meeting him, she'd looked straight into his eyes, then lowered her long eyelashes as she began her bow. "Honored teacher," was all she'd said.

This girl would not just be a companion, thought Kati. There was much to be learned from her.

The adults were now talking to each other, and Kati went to Weimeng. "May I show Sheyue my rooms?"

"Yes, dear, but come back within an hour. We will have a meal to end your party."

Kati fetched her new leathers, boots and sword, and led Sheyue to the rooms adjacent to Weimeng's suite. She showed her the rooms, the view from her sitting room window, the canopied bed. Sheyue nodded pleasantly at each sight, but did not seem impressed at all, so perhaps she was used to such luxury. But she asked about Kati's leathers, intrigued by them.

"They are for riding," said Kati. "The leather breaks the wind, and keeps me from being scraped or chaffed."

"You ride a *horse*?"

"Twice each week. One of the troopers' sons is my escort, to make sure I don't bump my head, or something."

"Is he handsome?" asked Sheyue, with a sly smile.

"Very. He is four years older than I, but treats me like an equal, not a child."

"You are not so much a child, Mengnu. I'm only two years older than you."

Kati was astounded. "I thought you were much older, perhaps eighteen, or twenty. I think Huomeng believes you are much older. His heart was pounding when he met you just now."

Sheyue's laugh was like softly tinkling bells, hidden behind her hand. "Really? He seems like a nice, intelligent man."

Man? Kati still thought of Huomeng as a somewhat arrogant boy.

"He's very intelligent, but self-centered and difficult to please. It's said he has much talent that hasn't been explored yet."

Sheyue smiled serenely, and said, "Even grown men are little boys. It is very easy for a knowledgeable woman to please them."

Oh, yes, thought Kati, but first there must be knowledge.

She changed her robe from yellow to red, and wore Juimoshu's pendant on the outside of it. Sheyue gave her an appraising look, and said, "Mengnu, please allow me to give you a gift for your birthday."

Sheyue took a black comb from her hair. It was crusted with tiny gems in green, red and blue. She put it in Kati's short, straight hair to the left of her forehead and looked at her again.

"There. It gives color to your hair."

Kati thanked her, and when they arrived back in Weimeng's suite, they were walking hand-in-hand.

Throughout the meal, Kati watched Sheyue from her place of honor at the head of the table. She watched the slow, smooth motions of sticks and silver utensils, the dainty bites chewed slowly, mouth closed, the frequent use of finger-bowl and moist towel, the smile and lowering of the eyelashes when accepting a new dish. All the adults were oblivious to it, but Huomeng also watched Sheyue constantly, and when the girl caught him looking at her, she would blink slowly, with a hint of a smile, and then avert his gaze. By the end of the meal, Huomeng had eaten little, and was sitting there in a kind of hypnotic state, looking confused.

For some reason, the sight of him that way made Kati a little angry.

✦   ✦   ✦

Her life seemed defined for her, and today there was another new thing, but again it was something she'd asked for.

Kati sat uncomfortably on the hard bench, the sword across her lap, and nervously awaited the call from Master Yung. Mengmoshu had suggested she wear her leathers, without the tunic, but still she was warm inside her light, woolen shirt. There was sweat on her forehead, though she'd pulled her hair away from it, and tied it in a little tail behind her head.

She drummed her boot-heels on the floor, fingered the sword, and sighed. Finally, the door beside her opened with a click. A little man in a plain, white robe stepped outside, and made a short bow to her. He was quite old: wrinkled face, white, wispy hair, a few long hairs on his chin. He looked at her with small, twinkling eyes, and said, "You may come in, now."

The room was small, perhaps ten meters on a side, with floor to ceiling mirrors covering two sides. The floor was ebonite, polished to a gleam, the ceiling yellow, with four light panels brightly lighting the room. The third wall was built-in storage, with drawers and cabinets floor-to-ceiling, but it was the fourth wall that first caught her eye. There was an altar, with a little shrine of lit candles, and a brass urn from which smoke rose in a helical path, and around the urn were offerings of various vegetables and fruits.

Above it, on a wall painted red, were two long, curving swords, blades crossed and gleaming.

The old man shuffled to the shrine, and came back with a bunch of grapes in his hand. The air moved with him, bringing the odor of sweet incense to Kati. He offered the grapes to her.

"No thank you, sir. I'm not hungry. I've come for a lesson with Master Yung. Will he be here soon?"

The old man popped a grape into his mouth. "Just as soon as he's finished his lunch," he said, smiling.

Kati's face flushed with shame. "I'm very sorry, Master; I've never seen you before now."

"It's nothing. I'm a deceptive man. That's how I've come to be so old." He put several grapes in his mouth at once, chewed vigorously, then beckoned to her to follow him to the center of the room. She did so, holding her sword in the crook of an arm.

When he turned to face her, close, their eyes were at the same level. "So, you come to learn the art of the sword. Now, tell me why you wish to learn it. What is your motive?"

Kati hadn't really thought about it. "I wish to learn everything," she said.

Yung shook his head. "No. You must be specific. You could learn to cook, or sew, or how to be charming. Why do you seek the ancient arts of war?"

Kati flushed again, but an answer was coming to her. "Do you know who I am, Master?"

"Of course. Mengmoshu has told me everything about you, and how you came to be here, but I know that even Tumatsin women use weapons only in ceremony. They do not practice with them."

"Mandughai did. Our Emerald Empress led her soldiers against the Emperor in ancient times. When I was little, there was a tapestry above my bed which showed the scene of her attack. And she carried a sword like those above the shrine in this room. When I was little, I dreamed of being like Mandughai—and I still do!"

Yung chewed the last of his grapes reflectively, and then there was a long moment of silence as he studied her. He moved a step to her left.

"Hold out your sword. Aim its blade at the point of intersection of the swords on the wall, and keep it there."

Kati obeyed. Yung put his hands on her arm, stretching

it out until she felt pressure in her elbow. He fiddled with her fingers, pushing and pulling. "Squeeze firmly with these two, thumb on top, gently with these two. Hold it there."

He stepped back. "The use of the sword requires concentration, quickness and balance, but a minimum of strength is also necessary. Do not move the sword. Keep it exactly as it is. I will know if you move it. I will return."

Yung shuffled over to the door—and left the room.

It seemed an hour passed before he returned. Kati was in agony, the sword shaking wildly in her numb hand. He took one look at her, and said, "Now turn, and use the other hand."

She could not speak, but did as he asked. Her right arm hung uselessly at her side. Again, he adjusted her arm, her fingers. "Remember the position of your hand and fingers. Burn it into your mind."

Again, he left the room.

Again, she endured.

When he returned, sweat had poured into her eyes, and tears were running down both cheeks, but she didn't make a sound.

"Good," he said, taking the sword from her, "the lesson is over. Each day, you will do this exercise with each hand. Start with ten minutes each, and do not go beyond fifteen. I will test you next week, and when you're ready, there will be something new."

He handed the sword back to her. She moved slowly, clutching it with two hands across her stomach, both shoulders screaming in agony. At the door, she bowed to Master Yung and he returned it, and then she left the room to find a young boy waiting on the bench outside. He had a plastic sword in his lap, and two troopers sat with him on the bench. She could hardly see them through the tears, but when the boy saw her he looked stricken with terror.

She didn't care, and turned away. She made the short, but painful walk back to her own quarters where she discovered she'd been with Master Yung for less than half an hour. She plopped the sword carelessly on the floor, and collapsed on her bed.

Half an hour later, Huomeng was pounding on her door to check her progress with the learning machine.

Weimeng looked at her with concern. "Mengnu! Your eyes are closed again, and you've hardly touched your food. What is the matter?"

Kati jerked awake and saw noodles still dangling from the sticks she had just begun raising to her mouth. "I was thinking about something," she said quickly. She blinked hard, then imitated Sheyue's slow movement with the sticks when eating.

Weimeng didn't believe her, and neither did Sheyue, who sat right across from her. "I think Mengnu has had a very strenuous day," said the girl.

"They're working you too hard. I will speak to Mengmoshu about this. I want you and Sheyue to have time together for womanly things, and men are never concerned about this. We will make a schedule to be sure such time is available in the future; otherwise, they will fill up your entire waking day."

Kati did not protest, and managed to finish the meal without dozing off again while Weimeng talked about art and showed them some of her drawings. The woman was a fine artist, but it was a thing Kati had no desire to do, and she already had learned that where there is a desire to do something there is also a talent for it, however small. Her talents lay in other areas, and they were still growing.

Most importantly, Mandughai was now involved with her training. They talked often now, and always in that place of deep shimmering purple. The conversations were brief and always initiated by Kati. They always occurred just as she was ready to drift off into sleep. And there were times when they did not occur, even when Kati wanted them to, times when Kati could not see the purple light and go to it. Mandughai no longer met her in the place of twinkling stars where she talked to the Moshuguang. She waited for her in the gong-shi-jie, the place of light, and it was there Kati had to go, the place where the Moshuguang were left behind.

Kati understood that her powers had gone beyond those of the Moshuguang and it was only hard work that was necessary to use them fully. She could move flame at will, heat or cool a room with a thought, and see the deepest secrets in an unshielded human mind. Her own shield was now absolute, when she remembered to use it. Her teachers were never satisfied —there was always something else to explore—and she wondered why. For what purpose?

Sheyue broke her reverie. "Madam, there has been little private time for Mengnu and me. May we spend the night together?"

"Oh, I would like that!" Kati said quickly.

Weimeng considered it for an instant. "Of course. You need time alone, and I'd forgotten it. Will you host Sheyue?"

"Yes!" said Kati, now excited again.

And so, after the meal was finished, Sheyue came to Kati's rooms, carrying a change of clothes and a bag filled with her toiletries.

They talked and talked, and it became late, but Weimeng did not come in, leaving them to themselves. They talked about Huomeng and Lui-Pang, and Kati told stories about her tutor's moods. Sheyue seemed interested in him. But she lowered her eyelashes and smiled when Kati talked about Lui-Pang: his face, square shoulders, the way he sat a horse, the musky scent of him.

"You like him," said Sheyue. "You think about him a lot."

"Yes," said Kati, a little embarrassed. "We ride tomorrow, and already I'm thinking about it."

"This is natural, I think," said Sheyue sagely. "Girls develop so much faster than boys. In another year or so, my body will be ready to produce children, and you are not far behind me in age."

Kati was startled. It seemed that little time had passed since she'd come to the city. But now she was ten, and in three, perhaps four years, she would be a woman. And for a Tumatsin woman, that was a time of great changes.

The fact that Sheyue was approaching womanhood was only enforced when they took a bath together that night. They bathed in the great, sunken tub, and as usual the water was too hot for Kati's taste. She had gone to the bath in her robe while Sheyue was undressing in the bedroom. She turned on the exhaust fan, and dabbled her foot in the water, calling up the feeling she wanted there, then willing it to be there, drawing energy from water to air. Clouds of steam erupted from the bath, the fan sucking them from the room, and the feeling on her foot was soon satisfactory.

She took off her robe, and eased herself into the water, relaxing in the warmth of it. And then Sheyue came in, dressed in a white robe, her hair pulled up into a single bun that made her look inches taller than usual. She slid off the robe in a slow, sensual way, and Kati saw the coloring around her nipples, the buds of young breasts there. Everywhere her skin was like milk. She stepped into the tub and sank languidly into steam. She sighed, and smiled with pleasure, while Kati kept her own body hidden by the water.

They remained that way for a while, and then Sheyue stood, waded two steps and sat down beside Kati, their shoulders touching. "You seem tired, Mengnu, and Lady Weimeng says I am also here to instruct you. Here, turn your back to me, and I will show you a woman's art I've learned from my mother."

Kati turned her back to Sheyue, and leaned against the side of the tub. Sheyue's hands were first on her neck, rubbing softly, then harder. Long fingers kneaded knots of tissue there, then moved to the shoulders, down the arms, across the back and up again in long, sensual strokes. Small knots of tension received further attention, small, firm, circular strokes with two fingers. The process was repeated, over and over, until Kati thought she might sink beneath the water. At the same time, she was tingling all over, and her breathing was quicker than normal.

"Now it is your turn to practice," said Sheyue. She turned her back to Kati, and waited.

Kati hesitated. She had never put her hands on a girl in this manner, and was suddenly shy. Still another thing to learn. She willed her hands to move, and followed Sheyue's example, beginning with the neck. Sheyue corrected her when she rubbed too hard, for Kati's hands were stronger than hers, but it seemed to go well. Sheyue's muscles were long, and quite soft compared to Kati's, but her skin was incredibly smooth, without flaws. She decided it was not such a difficult thing to learn, and Sheyue seemed to enjoy it. When Kati was finished, the girl turned and smiled.

"When a woman does that to a man, he becomes her slave. My mother has told me this, and my father has verified it."

Her laugh was a tinkle as she stood up and stepped from the tub. Her skin was a pink glow after she toweled herself, Kati watching silently.

Kati waited until Sheyue put on her robe and left the room before she dared to get out of the water.

That night, they slept together in Kati's bed, wearing robes of light polymer that breathed to cool them. In a moment, Sheyue was asleep, her breathing deep and regular, but Kati found herself wide awake. Her muscles were telling her she was tired, but her mind felt otherwise.

She closed her eyes and the twinkling stars were there, beyond them the shimmering curtain in purple, and immediately she was rushing towards it, the stars flashing past her. The matrix of purple lights was upon her in an instant, and she dove into it without selecting a point of entrance to blindly enter the gong-shi-jie, the world of light, the world of Mandughai.

Mandughai was waiting for her.

This time, her emerald eyes filled the field of view as if Kati had entered the mind of the Empress.

You've traveled boldly, child. I see an improvement in your self-confidence since I showed you the way back.

I couldn't sleep, Mandughai. There was too much excitement for me today. Have you seen it?

I see everything that happens to you, dear. You know that. But there is a question that is new in your mind, and you must ask it.

Around her swirled purple clouds without organization, yet Mandughai had told her they represented only a tiny portion of the light energy there, the rest of it hot beyond belief and beyond even her visibility.

All that has happened to me, then being brought here, the death of my mother, then Weimeng and all my teachers, now Sheyue, it is all a whirl. I see no purpose in it. I've always thought it was because of my abilities to do what the Moshuguang can do, but now I've gone beyond that and they seem to expect more. I wonder about what they expect of me, and I've asked, but even Mengmoshu won't tell me anything. He just says they need to make further tests. My days are filled with tests of one kind or another, and I'm given no reason for them.

The emerald eyes blazed forth, never blinking.

The limits of their tests have been reached, Kati. What they do now is only to satisfy their curiosity. Your real testing is here with me, in this place. The Moshuguang cannot come here with their eyes, minds, or instruments. In the entire history of Shanji, only one person has come to me in this place. And that person is you.

It was something Kati had suspected, since the time Mengmoshu told her she'd gone beyond where he could go.

But why am I so special? Why me?

It is a matter of breeding, dear. You have read a little about genetics, and know what it is. You are descended from two of my sons, through your mother and father. Not one son, but two. The Moshuguang come from one son. That has been the difference. You are something unique, Kati. A person like you has never existed before.

But there is you, Mandughai! Your powers are infinite!

No, child. I am a person, not a god. I am real and physical, just like you.

But I've never seen you! When we meet, I only see the eyes of a giant!

The eyes blazed steadily, but there was a long, silent pause. It seemed to go on forever, and Kati was suddenly frightened.

Mandughai! Did I say something wrong?

No, dear, I was just thinking. I will give you an image, but it is a false one. It is an image for you to see during my teaching, and perhaps it will help your confidence during the difficult tasks ahead of us.

The great eyes slowly closed, and Kati was engulfed in clouds of deep purple. There was a moment of panic, and she was tempted to turn and run back to the swirling vortex that would lead her to the stars. But then an image formed, small at first, then larger, the figure of a woman, floating towards her through the clouds of creation. She was tall and slender, hands folded beneath her breasts, and her robe was royal gold.

It was the most beautiful face Kati had ever seen.

It was the face of a Tumatsin woman.

A Changeling. The face was long, nose arched and prominent, and her eyes were blazing green. Her domed forehead tapered gently at the temples, and when she opened her mouth to speak in unison with words heard only in the mind, large canine teeth gave her appearance a touch of danger and warning.

Mandughai, you are so beautiful.

The apparition smiled, with full lips. *I also like it. Now follow me, and I will show you something new.*

Mandughai turned away and pointed with a long hand, and it seemed the swirling clouds were rushing past them, though there was no other sense of motion. And then she stopped, still pointing at something before her.

Do you see it? Do you see the point of entrance?

Kati looked hard. *I only see boiling, purple mist, Mandughai.*

The Empress nodded. *It is as I thought. For now, I will guide you, but soon the chemistry of your body will change; you will make this journey and many others by yourself. Now follow me.*

Kati followed her into thick mist, a fog of purple, and then it was as if a door had opened and the light of a yellow star beat down on them from a black sky. Mandughai turned again and Kati followed her outstretched arm.

A great blue planet filled half their view, and above it, floating like a moon, was a spherical ball of gleaming metal encrusted with fine projections like crystals. On one side, four mammoth conical protrusions grew from the surface, showing black maws like tunnels to a cave.

The planet below is where you now rest in your bed. The great metal ball you see is the ship that brought your ancestors to this planet. It is the mother ship, Kati, long neglected by those who have ruled Shanji. The day is coming when the ship must be used again, for the people of Shanji must take their place among my other worlds. I will have it no other way. And they must take their place as one people, not several. In the years to come, you will see all of Shanji, and then you'll understand what I'm saying. The Moshuguang will see to this.

Kati felt a kind of euphoria, for it was possible that an important question had just been answered. *Am I to take part in this? You told me once that there was a thing you would have me do. Is this the thing?*

That, and many more. Kati, you are being prepared for many tasks. Some may be too much for you, but it's too early for us to know. All who will teach you are now present in your life, and all you must know will be made available to you. But in the end, you will make choices, and your destiny will depend on those choices. I will be here to guide you, and test your preparation. The rest is up to you.

Kati was suddenly content. *Thank you, Mandughai, for showing me a purpose in my life. I think it will be easier for me to work now. Some days have been difficult for me.*

Mandughai smiled. *Some future days will be even more so, but now you must truly rest. This is enough for tonight.*

Mist swirled around them, the great metal ball was gone, and they were once again in the gong-shi-jie, the world of light. Mandughai pointed behind Kati, and said, *you know the way. Come to me when you are ready, and I will show you many other things you must see. I will be waiting.*

Mandughai faded before her eyes, and was gone. The vortex was near, as if it had followed her. She dropped into it with a purple flash, the stars still there, growing smaller, then the matrix, then darkness.

There was the odor of scented soap, and warmth at her back, coming from the girl asleep beside her.

Kati slept.

CHAPTER NINE
HUOMENG

Huomeng showed Kati the world of Shanji, but Sheyue and Lui-Pang showed her how to love.

It was a difficult and confusing time, for shortly after her thirteenth birthday a new chemistry awoke in her body, and she was suddenly a woman.

Her body was lithe and strong from the years of riding and the many hours with Master Yung. Her legs had shot forth like those of a colt, and were firmly muscled. She was now taller than Sheyue by nearly a head, growing like a wild plant, her legs aching at night as if being stretched while she slept.

Most important to her was the budding of her breasts, and the way her hips were suddenly well defined. When Sheyue wasn't with her, Kati would remove her clothes and check the progress of her body in a mirror, admiring the new changes.

The changes in her face concerned her. It had suddenly grown thinner and long, and the little nub of a nose had disappeared, replaced by one prominent and arched, with a little break in it that made it seem to her like the beak of a bird. At first she didn't like the nose, but then she decided that it made her look older, and that was good.

She had allowed her hair to grow, but argued with Weimeng about how to wear it, refusing the tight buns of the nobles' coiffure and allowing it to fall as a horse's tail down her back, tied near the scalp with a band of gold given to her by Juimoshu, who always gave her jewelry. It made her feel free and wild, unlike the other women around her. Most importantly, Lui-Pang liked it that way, and often said so.

The day finally came when he kissed her.

They were riding in the morning, for Huomeng had a full day planned for her. Over the years, their rides had taken them further and further from the city, and Mengmoshu had finally allowed them to use the mountain trail so that Lui-Pang would become familiar with the territory to the west. The time of his induction as a trooper was rapidly approaching.

They rode on the plateau by the three peaks, and in getting there had passed the site of Kati's *ordu*. It was a painful experience, for nothing was left, no sign of life ever having existed there. The *gerts*, the fences, corrals, everything was gone, the site now overgrown with grass and brush. Kati had been silent as they passed it, and had felt Lui-Pang's eyes on her. But now they trotted on the plateau in a gentle breeze, and Kati was feeling better. She looked up at the three peaks, and said, "As a child, I had a secret place up there. Would you like to see it?"

"It's very steep," said Lui-Pang. "Can we take the horses up there?"

"There's a trail. I'll show you," she said, smiling. "We can see the city from there."

Lui-Pang nodded, and followed behind her. She quickly found the trail, for it hadn't changed over the years; they followed it up an arroyo, then out onto the slopes, criss-crossing them in an ascent to the rock massifs of the peaks and up the edge of a short scree-fall to the little meadow nestled there within the summit crags.

Lui-Pang was already thinking like a military man. His

first reaction was to say, "What a tremendous observing post! You can see for miles in every direction here!"

The grass was long and aromatic. They left their horses to graze and stepped up to the edge of the meadow facing east, a terrifying drop-off of five hundred paces near where they stood. The city glowed in the distance, a single, golden point there that was the palace dome. Lui-Pang was standing behind her, so close she could feel his warmth.

"When I was a child, I came here to look at the city. I never dreamed that someday I would be living there," she said wistfully.

She felt his hands on her shoulders, lightly, then moving down her arms and back up again, resting there.

"Mengnu," he murmured, very close to her ear, and then he nuzzled her, and his lips found her neck. She leaned back against him, letting it happen. "Oh, Kati," he whispered, and then he turned her around, took her face in his hands, and kissed her.

His lips were soft, and full. Kati's arms went around his waist, pulling him to her. She felt his tongue exploring her lips, but kept her teeth clenched at first. His hands moved over her back, and she opened her mouth to him, their tongues caressing wetly. But when a hand passed lightly over a breast, the nipple there was suddenly hard as a stone, and Kati caught her breath. She pulled back, breathing hard, and held his face with her hands. "Wait," she said. "Wait."

She kissed him lightly on the mouth, and turned her back to him.

"I'm sorry," he said. "I had no right."

She looked at him and smiled. "I've wanted that kiss since I was ten years old. I've been waiting for it." She held out her hand when she saw his eyes brighten. "What took you so long?"

She sat down in the long grass, pulling him down beside

her. He said in a troubled voice: "You are a noble, and I'm the son of a soldier. Mengmoshu would skin me alive if he knew I even touched you."

Kati twisted him around, wrestled him down so his head was in her lap. "He is not my father, though there are times he acts like it. You needn't fear him, but me. I'm more fierce." She pulled his ears, and growled.

Lui-Pang reached up to trace her jaw with his finger. "Who are you?" he whispered. "Mengnu? The graceful, mannered lady of the palace? Or Kati, the rider of newly broken horses and one of Master Yung's better students? Your lessons aren't so private, you know. I have spies."

"I am both," said Kati, snapping at his finger as it passed her mouth. "I am all of it. And I am more than you know," she teased.

"Maybe you are. Your eyes—in the morning light—they're amber. You're beautiful, Kati."

She leaned over, kissed him softly, and long. They lay down in the grass awhile, cuddling. But there was little time for them; they had to go back to the city, however reluctantly. And on the way back, Lui-Pang said something that bothered her at a subconscious level.

As they neared the city gate, he looked at her and said, "Yes, it was the morning light. Now your eyes are brown again."

She barely had time to change her clothes before Huomeng was there rapping on her door. He asked her to wear the plain, white uniform of the general populace, so as not to distinguish herself, and thus she had to change again.

"Why is that?" she asked.

"People will behave more ordinary if they don't know who you are. They are used to me, and think of me as a scholar and scientist. You will seem like my student and be free to ask questions."

"But I *am* your student."

"Yes, but I'm only one of your teachers. You're really First Mother's student now, and I'm your guide. Think carefully about all you see, and ask yourself what problems exist on Shanji. There will be many excursions, and this is only the first. Mengmoshu himself will accompany you on others. This is important, Kati. We follow the will of First Mother."

And so she followed him, and that first day Huomeng took her onto the mountain on whose flank the city rested, and there he showed her a world she did not previously know.

They took the monorail up the mountain until they were far above the palace, just inside the great, clear dome enclosing the city. The car stopped, and there was a high fence of wire patrolled by many troopers. Beyond it lay a vast, flat area that was the landing field for flyers. They were parked in rows too numerous to count, and one lifted off as she watched, straight up to the dome opening a hundred meters above them, then outside for its daily patrol.

The guards let them pass through a gate, and they went to an open car on rails that ran along the edge of the landing field towards the maw of a huge tunnel leading into the mountain. The summit was still two hundred meters above them. Just the two of them got into the car. Huomeng's hands moved over a panel there. A whirring sound, and the car moved forward.

"Magnetic lifters," instructed Huomeng. "We're floating three millimeters above the rails. With these cars, we could have a public transportation system going anywhere on Shanji. But it is not traditional, and thus not allowed for the people."

The tunnel was cool and very monstrously big, lined with dim lights along the floor and walls. They seemed to float along it, and cool, moist wind whipped her hair.

The air grew warm as they came to a station, a platform with benches before a high, transparent wall, and beyond it a brightly lit cavern. Huomeng turned to her, and said, "The people know none of this. The workers here are chosen by the Moshuguang for their intelligence and skills, and they live in apartments high on the other side of the mountain. Everything you see today is kept secret from the people."

He took her into the cavern, and there she saw three different types of delta-winged aircraft being assembled by a swarm of workers. One of the craft seemed large enough to carry hundreds of people. "I've never seen one of these flying," she said. "Where are they used?"

"They are *not* used. These are all prototypes, and the Emperor will not allow flight testing for fear the people will see them. He allows the Moshuguang to play with technology without application of it. With these planes, we could live anywhere on Shanji, with rapid transport of people and goods."

They went back to the car and proceeded on, past smaller caverns filled with people, only a few of them Moshuguang. There were laboratories for chemistry and metallurgy, and one that specialized in the bioengineering of new plants for agriculture. Kati said she'd heard of none of the plants he'd named, and Huomeng laughed at her.

"You eat them all the time: rice, fruits, even grains for your noodles. None of these could survive here in their original forms. All have been bioengineered for Shanji, and all are grown on the eastern plains. The little barley and wheat fields near the city are nothing. They only contribute to the Emperor's illusion of a small, feudal kingdom."

"Those little fields were taken from my people, and you make them sound unimportant," Kati said angrily.

"The Tumatsin have the sea, and the land near it. It is

more than adequate for their needs. Kati, you also have an illusion. To you, Shanji is the city, the western mountains and the sea, yet you know it is a very large globe, and your familiar world is only a tiny part of it. To you, the people who live here are those in the city, and your own. I must tell you that the Tumatsin and the city people together are like a drop in that garden pool you used to wade in. But now I want to show you the thing that is most important to me. I have my own little world, too."

They went around a gradual curve for a long time, and Kati guessed they were now in the eastern side of the mountain on a great, looping route through it. The car slowed as they came to another cavern, the tracks bisecting it, and on either side, floor to ceiling, were massive walls of grey metal. They stopped there, and Huomeng took her to a door by a glassed-in booth, inside of which a trooper sat, eyeing them. Huomeng showed him a card, and inserted it in a slot by the door. The door clicked open and they entered a short, bare hallway to another door. Huomeng paused there, grinning. "This is my world," he said dramatically, and opened the door. A rush of hot air surprised her, and there was sudden, hot light from panels in a curved ceiling far above them.

It was the biggest cavern she'd seen: tiers of walkways circumscribing it horizontally, people walking there, going in and out of doorways. A pair of tracks, each two-and-half meters in diameter, came from the wall and branched into two other pairs of equal size. And sitting on those tracks, in the center of the cavern, were two huge wedge-shaped ships of gleaming metal. Kati's mouth hung open, and she stared.

"First Mother showed you the great ship in orbit around Shanji," said Huomeng. "That one brought our ancestors here from Tengri-Nayon. The ships you see here are the ones that brought us down to the surface of the planet.

They have no fuel left, but we will get some some day soon. They have been waiting here for an eternity of years for someone to use them again, and I'm going to be the one to do it."

His voice was soft, reverent, and there was a light in his eyes she'd never seen before. The emotion in him was deep and roiling, and he made no effort to mask it from her. She was surprised to see he could feel such emotion, and was somehow drawn to him because of it. "They're so *large*," was all she could say.

"Magnetic lifters, and fusion drive. They each hold two hundred people comfortably. That's how many there were in the beginning, Kati; only four hundred people, and nobody was left on the mother ship in the end. She's been up there nearly two thousand years, quietly taking care of herself, waiting for our return."

"You would fly one of these to the mother ship? And then what?"

Huomeng's eyes were those of a zealot. "I would fly between the stars, and find new worlds. I would not be confined to a single planet, especially this one. If I could, I would see all the universe there is to see. But even with the mother ship it isn't possible. This is one of the reasons I envy you so much. I was not born special, like you."

"Me?"

"Yes. You go to First Mother in the gong-shi-jie. I cannot do this. None of us can. You are special. You can travel anywhere in an instant. Time has no meaning for you; every star, every world is within your reach."

"I've only seen the mother ship," Kati protested, for she keenly felt his envy, now.

"There will be more. First Mother will show you. The way your abilities are growing you might even find a way to take me with you someday. In the meantime, I will dream my dreams."

"Does Mengmoshu know about your dreams?"

"Yes. We've talked a lot about this, and he's encouraged me. When I'm not with you I'm here, by his assignment. I have a little office up there on the third level." He pointed towards it. "There's not much to see. For the past two years, I've been learning all the systems on the mother ship. In another two, I should have them all down. The shuttles you see here were easy to learn, and I could fly one now. We could make the fuel. But the Moshuguang bides its time. It waits patiently, but I do not."

"Waiting for *what*?" asked Kati.

Huomeng spoke in a near whisper, though nobody was near them. "I think there are things Mengmoshu does not tell me. There are plans being made; they involve me, and they involve you. No other people are being trained so intensely as you and I. I can understand it in your case. Your abilities are unique, and First Mother has claimed you as a student. But why me?"

"I've heard Mengmoshu speak highly of you," said Kati. "He says your analytical skills are far advanced, and your memory cannot be matched."

"I know that," said Huomeng, without arrogance. "Your own memory and logic is considerable. So why have I been assigned as your tutor since the first day you arrived here? The learning machine has been enough for you."

"You've answered some questions and directed my studies, Huomeng. I've learned faster with your help."

That pleased him, and she felt it. "Perhaps. But there's more to it than that. I think the Moshuguang has deliberately put us together for a purpose. You said First Mother wants her people back. We are somehow involved with that. Somehow, our skills are to be combined."

"For what? To take the people back to Mandughai—First Mother? To leave Shanji? The Emperor will not stand idly by and let this happen!"

"No, he won't, but something is coming, and as for

the Emperor he is already old and his son is a sickly boy with effeminate ways. I see no future for his throne." Huomeng nodded his head sagely. "A change is coming, Kati. I know it."

"It is speculation," said Kati, and then she surprised herself by reaching out and taking hold of his hand for just a moment. "Huomeng, who are the Moshuguang? Where do they come from? In some ways we're alike, you and I."

"Yes," said Huomeng, giving her a wry smile. "There's no written history of us, but a story has been passed down. It's said that within three generations after First Mother's invasion of Shanji She sought to change the people by sending Her two eldest sons to selectively breed with them. Even their names are unknown, but the result was two new peoples on Shanji. The one is now called Moshuguang." He paused.

"And the other?"

Huomeng squeezed her hand. "It's said that your people, the Tumatsin, are cousins to the Moshuguang. This is why they've been so closely watched by us over the years."

Kati felt suddenly excited. "Mandughai has told me I come from two of Her sons, not one. What can this mean?"

Huomeng shook his head. "There must be Moshuguang blood somewhere in your ancestry. It's possible. Only the Emperor forbids relations between our people. There are no biological problems I'm aware of."

Kati felt satisfied by his answer, and smiled, but then Huomeng tried to release her hand and she held on.

"Huomeng—thank you for telling me about your dreams. I think I understand you a lot better, now."

Huomeng was not startled by her persistent touch. He smiled, and squeezed her hand gently before releasing it.

"I thank you for listening to them. We'd better move on, now. There's one more important thing I want you to see today."

They returned to the car and drove on in silence for minutes along a tunnel now featureless, staring at the lights. The car slowed as they came to an intersection with another tunnel, and Kati saw a car flash by, then another. Suddenly there were moving walkways filled with people, many of them women and children on both sides of the tunnel. The walls were solid with brightly lit windows of shops and stores with colorful, luminous signs advertising their wares. People crowded in the shops, and the air was filled with the odors of rice, vegetables and meat cooking in sweet and sour spices. The noise was a din, and Kati felt suddenly crowded in, a little claustrophobic.

"The workers' village!" Huomeng shouted at her. "Their apartments are off to our left!"

Cars were darting in and out of traffic from several tunnels on her left, people chatting amiably in them while the cars seemed to move according to their own minds. Kati grasped the arm rest on her seat, and hung on.

And then the village was suddenly behind them. It was quiet again, and only one car was ahead of them. The car veered into a tunnel to the left; Huomeng touched something on his control panel and they also veered left to follow it. The tunnel followed the arc of a circle to a platform with cutouts in which cars were parked before a brightly lit window, and a sign advertising tea and honeycakes. They parked there, and went inside.

Odors of tea, and honey. Many tables, mostly empty, a handful of people here and there, drinking tea and eating cakes, some reading, others watching them as they came inside. The furniture was black, tables covered with red cloth, and colorful lamps hung on long, bronze chains from a red ceiling. A mural on one wall showed a vast plain, with mountains beyond it, and birds flying. The room was quiet, and restful.

A woman came up to Huomeng, and bowed. "We'd like a table outside," he said.

They followed her to a door, and suddenly the light of Tengri-Khan was in her eyes, making her blink rapidly. They went out onto a stone patio, several tables there with red umbrellas to shield them. Kati squinted, eyes slowly adjusting to the light as they went to a table and were seated there, a transparent wall the height of a man to their left.

And then she saw what was there.

Huomeng pointed, and said, "*This* is Shanji."

They were perched on the side of the mountain only a negligible distance beneath the summit, and the rock sloped steeply below them for thousands of meters to a plain stretching towards the horizon in every direction; in the far distance was a faint silhouette of mountain peaks. To the north, spires rose from the plain, belching smoke, and near the mountain's base was a solid, packed mass of buildings with streets between them, people moving there like armies of ants. Beyond the tall buildings were clusters of smaller structures, and beyond that the plain was broken into squares of green and gold and glittering blue, as if painted by an artist's giant brush, as far as the eye could see.

"A city!" she gasped.

"It is called Wanchou," said Huomeng. There was sadness in his voice. "It is the only true city on Shanji. And the Emperor, in his palace, does not bother to speak of it. Kati, how many Tumatsin do you suppose live in all the *ordu*s you know of?"

"Oh, thousands. There were many people at Festival when we came together."

Huomeng chuckled wryly. "Actually, it's closer to a hundred thousand, so I guess a lot of Tumatsin don't go to Festival. And in the Emperor's city, with the royalty, nobility, the Moshuguang, troopers and their families, we count around twice that number. That is three hundred thousand people, Kati, which seems like many until you realize that in that city you see below you, in all those buildings and smaller houses, there now live nine *million* people. And in thousands of hamlets, on farms, zones around the smoking factories, even beyond where we can see from here there are another six million. They go about their daily lives, raising their children in ways used by the ancestors of our ancestors, before the time of First Mother. *This* is Shanji, Kati. *This* is where the people are."

There was a passion in his voice, an anger when he spoke.

"I didn't realize—" she began, stunned.

A woman came to take their order and left quickly. People at other tables were watching them. All were Hansui. Huomeng pointed behind her. "*Our* workers live there, by the village we passed."

Kati turned around, saw buildings sprouting like black crystals from the face of the rock, several tiers of them slightly lower than where she was sitting.

"The workers here have it much easier than those in Wanchou, and far better than the country people. Their rooms are cooled and heated, they have the finest medicine we can provide, and machines make their work faster and easier. The people below, the *real* people of Shanji, have none of this. Simple diseases like influenza have killed hundreds of thousands of them in past epidemics. They have adjusted to it by breeding like rabbits, unchecked, for they know that only two children in four will survive to adulthood. The nobles own their land, their homes, all the stores that provide them with goods. The people own nothing, not even themselves."

"They are like the Tumatsin," said Kati.

"No, they are not."

"And why not? The Emperor takes our land, kills those who resist, forces us to the sea. We are under His control, not ours."

"Suddenly you are Tumatsin," said Huomeng softly. "There is a parallel, of course, but it is not the same for the people below us. There is no noble class within the Tumatsin, and that is the difference. A Tumatsin farmer produces a bushel of grain, and uses it to barter for his needs. The grain is his. But here, everything belongs to the nobles, who barter with each other and the Emperor to provide themselves with luxuries far beyond those of the people. The people have nothing to call their own. They receive scrip for their labors and buy goods from shops owned by the nobles. The goods are limited, priced high, and no private enterprise by the people is allowed. There is no competition for the nobles.

"If the people are unhappy, then why don't they do something about it?" asked Kati, perplexed.

"They *aren't* unhappy. They take each day as it comes. They have a place to live, and those who work have full stomachs. They have no idea how the nobles live, and they have never seen the Emperor's city. They are content through ignorance. Their lives could be much better, but they don't see it.

"But they are happy," said Kati. "I was happy living in the *ordu*. I lived outdoors with the freedom to ride in the mountains, and I was never hungry. But I see your point. What we produced was ours. Our anger came from the Emperor pushing us around like we were cattle. We *thought* the lands were ours, but they weren't."

"Exactly. There's another problem that bothers me even more. The farms and factories continue to produce excesses. There are great stocks of copper, bronze and steel filling warehouses near the factories, and food stored in bins on every farm. We produce more than we need, and it's useless, yet there is much unemployment for unskilled people. We do not expand, and the Emperor isolates us from other worlds we could trade with. We have become stagnant on Shanji. We do not progress, but our population grows."

Their tea and cakes had arrived. Kati munched sweet honey, and said, "Mandughai told me she would have Shanji join the rest of her worlds. Could this be the plan of the Moshuguang?"

"I think so," said Huomeng. "Why else would Mengmoshu have me spending my days learning about the shuttles and the mother ship? He clearly intends to use them."

"But what is *my* part in this? I play mind games, moving energy from place to place, and talk to Mandughai in Her gong-shi-jie, and She tells me there's something I must do. So what is it?"

"Ask Her," Huomeng said, sipping tea. "Ask Mengmoshu. Maybe they don't know the answer yet. You're still changing, Kati. Don't you feel it?"

"What do you mean?"

"You're thirteen, and a Tumatsin. There are changes in your chemistry as you reach womanhood. Haven't you felt anything? Haven't you noticed people staring at us for the last few minutes?"

"No!" said Kati, suddenly uncomfortable.

Huomeng leaned over, and put a hand on hers, whispering, "Kati, the color of your eyes has changed four times since we sat down here. They were brown, then amber, even red for a moment, then brown. Now, they're red again."

Kati's face flushed.

"Even redder," said Huomeng. "Fascinating."

"Why didn't you tell me?" she whispered angrily.

"What for? It's natural. Your eyes reflect your emotions, and I think they're pretty. You're Kati, not Mengnu. You're a Changeling, and that's not a bad thing to be. You have the blood of First Mother in you."

People *were* staring, she now noticed. She wanted to close her eyes, or cover them, but Huomeng held onto her hand. "Be calm. Relax, and be yourself. I think First Mother has waited for these changes in you. Maybe these are necessary before you can do what she wants. It's all part of a bigger picture, Kati. We're both involved in it."

The words calmed her, and she closed her eyes a moment, breathing deeply. When she opened them again, Huomeng smiled, and released her hand. "Brown again," he said.

They finished their cakes in silence, and then went back to the car. In minutes, they were out of the mountain to where the flyers were, and were taking the monorail down to the palace, Kati looking out at the mountains in silence. She thought of Lui-Pang, and suddenly knew he'd seen her eyes change color that morning. Had *he* thought her eyes pretty then? Other changes would soon come. How would he react?

"You are very quiet," said Huomeng.

"My mind is a blur from what I've seen today," she said, and that seemed to satisfy him.

As they neared Kati's rooms, Sheyue came floating down the hallway towards them, and Huomeng saw her first. Kati felt the stir of emotion in him at the same time she felt Sheyue's desire.

Sheyue bowed to Huomeng, and smiled beautifully at him. "Honored teacher," she said.

"My work is finished for the day," said Huomeng, ignoring Kati. "Would you join me in the garden for a little while before mealtime? There are some new fish in the pool."

Sheyue looked at Kati. "Do you have need of me, Mengnu?"

Kati shook her head. "I need to rest before eating,

and have a lot of things to think about. I'll see you at mealtime."

As she entered her rooms, they were walking away from her, and Kati saw Huomeng's arm slide around the girl's waist.

She changed into an orange robe, looked into a mirror and saw that her eyes were their normal brown, a sight that somehow comforted her. And then she lay down on her bed, relaxing, closing her eyes.

Mengmoshu. Can we talk a moment?

I'm here, Kati. What is it?

Huomeng showed me the big ships in the mountain today, and also where all the people are living.

I know. We felt it was time.

There are other things.

Kati told him about their conversations, including Huomeng's dreams. *He says there is a plan being made by the Moshuguang, and that he and I are a part of it. I want to know what I'm being prepared for. What am I to do?*

There was a long pause, Mengmoshu masking himself from her.

Mengmoshu! Tell me something!

There is a plan, yes, but we're not certain of it yet. Your part in it will be determined by First Mother, but I ask you to do something now. Think about what you've seen and heard today. Ask yourself what is good for Shanji, and what isn't. Then decide what you would do to make things right. Soon, I will take you into the valley to meet the people and see their everyday lives. What Huomeng tells you comes from me. Remember that, Kati. Now tell me about the other new thing that disturbs you.

Kati knew instantly what he meant, for he could see everything she thought about at the moment.

The changes in my body have begun. My eyes started changing colors today.

She felt a strange elation coming from him, even happiness.

So, you are becoming a woman. That is wonderful, Kati. I will tell First Mother, and you must tell Her, too. Now, do what I ask you to do. Some people have just arrived in my office and I must leave you. We will spend much time together in the near future, and I look forward to it. You're dear to me, child.

And he was gone. Kati was left shaken by the burst of emotion, the sudden feeling of love that had just poured out of him. Suddenly, she was crying, remembering her own father bending over her in the dim light of the *ger*, that same feeling coming from him as he stroked her forehead and called her his little empress. Where was he now? Did he miss her? Think her dead? And little Baber, with his charging horse-dolls; what did he look like now?

She wondered if she would ever see them again, and if she did, if they would accept her for what she'd become: a kept, pampered girl living in the Emperor's palace, a Tumatsin, living in the ways of the Hansui nobility.

Kati was suddenly afraid.

They ate dinner in Kati's rooms, the food brought to them by Tanchun. And afterwards, they bathed together again, as they often did. Now taller than Sheyue, Kati was no longer ashamed of her body in the girl's presence, for their figures were quite similar. Kati enjoyed these times with Sheyue, for it was then when they shared their secrets, and were most like sisters. They slid languidly into the water, sitting silently across the tub from each other until Kati spoke.

"Lui-Pang kissed me today," she said softly.

Sheyue did not squeal with excitement like a little girl, but had a twinkle in her eyes as she rubbed water on her white shoulders. "Were his lips soft, Mengnu? Is he a gentle lover?"

"It was just a kiss," said Kati, but then she told Sheyue everything: the feel of his probing tongue, the hardness of a nipple when his hand touched her breast, the tingling in her groin when he pressed against her. "I felt his desire there, but did not let it go further than that. He honored my wishes."

"Then he is a gentleman," said Sheyue, leaning her head back on the edge of the tub. "Do you want more from him, Mengnu? Do you want to feel him inside you?" Sheyue's hand dipped beneath the water, and Kati saw she was touching herself between her legs.

"I suppose I do," said Kati. "I felt desire for him, deep down, but also caution. It was my first kiss, Sheyue." As she spoke, Kati also touched herself, imitating the girl. Immediately, there was a tingling sensation where her finger touched the tender place beneath her mound.

Sheyue was now stroking herself, eyes closed. "Huomeng was also hesitant at first, thinking I was too delicate until I guided him into me. He is so gentle, so caring. The first time, there were tears in his eyes at his release. When I cried out with pleasure, he thought he'd hurt me."

Kati was shocked, yet somehow not surprised. "You've lain with my *teacher*? Where?"

"In the garden, and once in my rooms. Several times, all of them wonderful."

"You will get pregnant by him!" warned Kati. "Be careful, Sheyue. His mate must be chosen by the Moshuguang. You could make trouble for yourself."

"I have the tea my mother sent with me," said Sheyue, still stroking herself, breath quickening. "I drink it every day, and there will be—no—child. Mmmm . . ." She sighed. "I feel him in me now."

Kati's own finger was rubbing softly, and the tingling was spreading throughout her groin and lower back. She took her hand away, but the feeling was still there.

Sheyue opened her eyes, and looked at Kati. Her eyes

widened, and she smiled. Her body seemed to glow, a golden, shimmering cloud enveloping her. She waded across the tub on her knees, and put her arms around Kati's neck.

"Mengnu—you are so beautiful."

Sheyue kissed Kati on the mouth with soft, full lips.

"Love your man," she murmured, then stood up and stepped from the tub, the golden cloud moving with her.

Kati followed, rubbing herself dry with a soft towel that only enhanced the pleasureful feeling within her. She went into the dimly lit bedroom and saw a golden glow that was Sheyue climbing into bed. She put on a light robe, and turned to a mirror to put up her hair.

What she saw there both pleased and astounded her.

Her own body was surrounded by a halo of gold, a layer of blue at skin's surface, fans of red, yellow and orange radiating from her head. This pleased her, this first sight of her own aura, and that of Sheyue's. It verified her womanhood.

It was the sight of her face that astounded her, for her eyes were blazing like beacons in the night, and their color was emerald-green.

eyelashes w[...]

the boy, [...]

[...]

CHAPTER TEN
SHAN-LAN

It was the first time Kati had seen The Son of Heaven
in over eight years. And when she saw him, one look at
his aura told her he was extremely ill. Just above his groin
the colors were gone, replaced by a grey fog in the energy
field, a parasitic mass growing there and slowly draining
him. Her first thought was to use her hands on him,
funneling purple energy from the gong-shi-jie itself to
destroy the mass and prolong his life. But the thought
quickly passed, for He was the Emperor, the man
responsible for the death of her true mother. She would
not help him.

She was sitting on her usual bench, the practice sword
in her lap when the Emperor appeared. He followed a
phalanx of four troopers, all armed with rifles, and walking
beside him was a young boy dressed in a simple black
robe, a polymer sword held casually across his chest.

The boy was beautiful: tall, slender, with extraordinarily
fine features for a Hansui, giving him a feminine look.
His hair hung in two pigtails and he walked proudly erect,
knowing she had seen him. She felt his apprehension as
she stood and bowed deeply to the Emperor.

"Son of Heaven," she said simply, lowering her eyelashes
as she bowed.

The guards stood around them in a semi-circle. "So

you are Mengnu," said the Emperor. "The last time I saw you, you were a child. It appears that palace life has been satisfactory for you."

"I'm in your debt for the kind treatment I've received," said Kati, nodding her head and again lowering her eyelashes with the serene smile of a Sheyue.

"This is my son, Shan-lan, who will join you in exercises with Master Yung. I'm told you are a superior student."

"I'm honored, Prince of Shanji," said Kati, bowing to the boy. "I strive to do my best in all things."

Shan-lan was staring at her, transfixed. There was a delicacy about him, a gentleness, and Kati liked him before he spoke a single word.

"You are somewhat more advanced than I," said Shan-lan, "and I hope to learn from you." His voice was soft, like that of a young girl.

The door beside them opened, and Master Yung appeared in his usual white robe. He bowed stiffly to the Emperor, then motioned his two students inside without speaking a word. He closed the door, took them to the center of the room and had them stand facing each other. Shan-lan's aura was golden but dim, a lovely, red fan surrounding his head. A creative person, an artist or a poet, perhaps, but certainly not a warrior. His energy field was weak, as if he hadn't eaten for several hours.

"There is no rank or class here," said Master Yung. "In this room, you are students and nothing more. You will not hold back on any exercise. You will not fear for hurting the other, for if you do, I will work you until the fear is gone. Do you understand?"

"Yes, Master," they said together, then bowing stiffly to each other.

"Very well. Come to sword length."

They stretched forth their swords so that the points were touching.

"First *dong*! Zhumbei!"

They crouched, arms bent, each blade pointed at the opponent's chest.

"Strike!"

Slash, slash, slash, each aimed at the head, and blocked.

"Second *dong*! Zhumbei!"

Again, as before. Kati felt his apprehension and fear, yet Shan-lan had done the first exercise well.

"Strike!"

Slash, thrust, disengage, slash, towards head and body. Shan-lan was quick, the disengagement delicate. So why was he afraid?

By the time they finished the tenth *dong*, the reason was apparent. Shan-lan's energy was draining rapidly. He had no stamina, and on the fourth beat she could have easily disemboweled him with a single thrust-cut, for he was a half-beat behind her.

There was no time for rest in the presence of Master Yung. He handed them the wire-mesh masks for combat-play, and they put them on.

"First *dong*! Zhumbei!" They moved closer to each other, now.

"Strike!"

Kati struck Shan-lan hard on the mask with her third beat, and felt his surprise.

"Second *dong*! Zhumbei!"

"Strike!"

Kati slapped his sword hard on the disengagement, and punched him sharply in the chest. The gold in his aura had faded, the red fan about his head now gone, replaced by blue spikes. Shan-lan was exhausted, but hanging on with raw courage.

By the time they reached the seventh *dong*, Shan-lan was wincing with each blow from her sword, and there was nothing left in him: no apprehension or fear, only shame.

And so she hesitated at beat three to let him catch

up. He barely parried her blade, but finished the exercise without being struck by her.

"Again!" said Master Yung.

This time she hesitated on first beat, letting him get a jump on her.

Master Yung stepped up, and put his face right up to her mask.

"AGAIN!"

Now it was Kati who felt shame, and anger, for Master Yung's instructions had been clear and she was not respecting them. A little growl escaped her throat and her face was hot. She crouched, and struck hard at Yung's command, and by the end of the tenth *dong* her own mind was in agony from the pain caused by all the blows she'd rained down upon the son of the Emperor.

But Master Yung seemed satisfied. "Leave your masks on, but put down your swords, and stand as you are."

Shan-lan was breathing heavily. Blue jets emanated from his knees, his right shoulder and elbow. His strength was gone. But for the moment, Kati could not feel for him. She had shamed herself before Master Yung, and would not do it again, even for this delicate, gentle boy.

Yung went to his shrine, and removed the two crossed swords from the wall there. He handed a sword to each of them. "You have practiced with toys long enough. Now it is time for these, but only at sword's length. Get the feel of them first."

The curved steel blade seemed like a natural extension to her arm, the balance and weight familiar, but the wire-wrapped hilt giving her a firmer grip than with the practice weapon. She held it out, made a few practice slashes with it, and the blade flashed in the light. Not a toy, but like the sword carried by her mother at a Festival in the distant past of another life. The feel of it charged her with energy and excitement. This was a weapon of war, not play. She lost all thought of Shan-lan, as Yung gave his command.

"At sword length. First *dong*! Zhumbei!"

"Strike!"

She slashed furiously; the flash of gleaming blades, the sound of steel ringing with the shock of impact surged through her like electric current, and she nearly knocked the sword from Shan-lan's grip.

By the third *dong*, the sword was barely in his hand and his technique was gone, the blade waving wildly to meet hers in pure defense. Suddenly, his point dipped to the floor, and he sank to his knees, head bowed. "I cannot go on," he gasped. "I have no strength left."

Kati could only stand there and feel his shame. But she discovered there was kindness in Master Yung. He helped Shan-lan to his feet and took the sword from him. He put a hand on the boy's shoulder as the mask was removed. Shan-lan looked down at the floor, gasping, his face glistening with sweat.

"You're improving, young Prince, and you will continue to improve. Dedicate yourself to the art, and your father will be proud of you. Please, now, wait outside for your escort. I need to have a word with your opponent here."

Shan-lan bowed to Yung, and to Kati, then walked wearily to the door and closed it behind him.

Kati thought Master Yung might compliment her, but it was not so. He jerked the sword from her hand, his face close before she could even remove her mask.

"If you *ever* hesitate again, I will have you standing with two swords outstretched for half an hour! Do you hear me?"

"Yes, Master. I'm sorry. I will not do it again."

"You are not here to play, but to prepare yourself, by order of the Moshuguang! I will not accept less than full effort from you! To hesitate in battle is to die!"

"Yes, Master. I will give you everything I have, and

more, and I'm shamed by what I did today. I have no excuses for it."

Now his face softened. "You fight well with anger in you. For several moments, I saw a fierceness that is necessary in battle."

"I was not angry, Master."

Yung reached up, pulled the mask from her head, and looked at her with a smile. "Your eye color betrays you. Anger is good, to a certain point, for it gives energy and quickness. Too much of it clouds the judgment. There is a fine line between too little and too much. This you will have to find for yourself. Now go. Your progress is excellent, but you will achieve much more with continued dedication."

Kati left the room as Master Yung returned the swords to their position on the wall. Shan-lan was sitting on the bench, leaning his head against the wall. His face still glistened with sweat, and his eyes were filled with tears he made no effort to hide from her as she sat down beside him.

Kati dared to put a hand on his shoulder. "Master Yung does not lie. You are quite good in your technique, but I think you lack energy. Do you eat before coming to practice?"

"I have little appetite," said Shan-lan. "Food doesn't interest me, and besides, I don't even want to be here."

"So why are you here?"

"My father. I must learn the sword, the bow. I must ride with the guards to impress them with my skills, and stand in court all day to hear the whining of the nobles. I'm interested in none of it."

"But you'll be Emperor someday. You *must* learn these things."

Shan-lan ignored what she'd said. "Do you know the pagoda above the garden, the one called Stork Nest?"

"Yes. I've been there once."

"I go there as often as I can with paper, inks, paints and brushes. I go there to paint and to write."

"You are an artist," said Kati, not surprised.

"Yes. But there is little time for it. My father prepares me for a throne I do not want or care about. My life is what I do in Stork Nest. It's all I desire."

"I don't have artistic skills," said Kati, "but I admire art, and I read about many things. What do you write?"

Shan-lan looked at her, finally noticing her interest. "Mostly poetry, but now I'm working on a story about a noble family involved in the intrigues of the court."

"You draw upon your own experience?"

"Some things I've seen and heard, yes, but the family is fictional."

"I know that a good artist must experience life," said Kati. "It gives authenticity to their work. Are you aware that Wang Quing-li, our third Emperor, was also a fine artist?"

"Yes. I see his paintings everywhere."

"He was an artist *and* an Emperor. It was Quing-li who engineered the dome over our city. He assumed his duties, yet continued to pursue the real passion of his life. There are many hours in the day, Shan-lan. You can do both things."

"And what about you?" asked Shan-lan. "The troopers comment about the way you ride, and I've just seen and felt what you can do with a sword. You are Moshuguang. What do they prepare you for?"

It was the first time she'd been called that, and somehow she could not deny it at the moment. She thought quickly, and said, "My purpose is not yet defined, so my preparation is broad. Perhaps I will take Juimoshu's place when she's gone. Someday, I might be serving you, Shan-lan."

He smiled. "I will remember a dream for you to interpret sometime, Mengnu. Do you display art in your quarters?"

"Yes. That is how I know about Quing-li. Lady Weimeng is also an artist, and I have some of her work."

"Would you accept a small painting from me?"

"Oh, yes. I would be honored." The movement of her eyelashes was automatic.

"I will bring something to class for you," he said. Kati felt his emotion, then, a gentle, loving feeling from a gentle person suddenly in her life.

She recovered herself by changing the subject. "Do you like honey cakes?"

"Yes."

"I have a suggestion. Eat three of them just before you come to class each week. If you do this, I think you'll have much more energy for practice. Promise me you'll do this!"

His aura was still weak, but now the red fans had returned. He took her hand from his shoulder, and kissed it, looking into her eyes. Kati was shocked, her heart fluttering.

"You are beautiful and wise, Mengnu. I will do as you say. Ah, my escort returns to take me away to court."

Three troopers were coming towards them. Kati stood up, her hand sliding from his warm grasp. She bowed deeply to Shan-lan, and turned away.

"Mengnu," he said softly, and she turned back to him.

He looked up at her with velvet, brown eyes. "Thank you for being my friend."

Kati smiled, then walked away, trying not to appear rushed. Her heart was still fluttering when she reached her rooms to find Huomeng talking to Sheyue there, waiting for still another tutoring session with the learning machine.

And in the weeks to follow, the honey cakes did their work for Shan-lan, and he gave her three beautiful paintings with pagodas, mountains, and birds.

The love poems came later.

❖   ❖   ❖

Mengmoshu met with Mengyao and Juimoshu over a lunch of rice and vegetables served in his office. They discussed the new tunnel to the eastern slope of the mountain, now half-finished, and the security measures to assure access only to the nobles and mountain personnel. And then the topic changed to their Tumatsin ward.

"First Mother was correct in saying further progress awaited the chemical changes in Kati. She now sees the aural mappings in the gong-shi-jie and is able to locate large masses beyond," said Mengmoshu.

"How far has she gone?" asked Mengyao.

Mengmoshu put down his sticks, and wiped his mouth with a moist towel. "First Mother never leaves her side, of course, but Kati has penetrated real space out to the gaseous giants. The next step is Tengri-Nayon itself. We are now only six years from closest approach."

"Yes, but has she tried any energy or mass transfer yet?"

"Not yet. First, she must find her way around."

"But couldn't we perform some short-range tests right here on Shanji? We could give her a small object to move from here to, say, the western plateau she's familiar with, a place by the three peaks."

"I've suggested such a test to First Mother. She tells me that within the gong-shi-jie the aural signature of a large mass has no resolution within itself. One point on a planet, even a small one, cannot be distinguished from another. Kati might transfer mass from this office, but it could end up anywhere on Shanji."

Mengyao shook his head. "Yet Kati returns to herself each time, at a small point in space."

Mengmoshu chuckled. "Even First Mother does not understand the process in herself. Kati goes nowhere in the gong-shi-jie. It is a projection of herself; there is no organ responsible for the phenomena. It is hereditary,

Mengyao, from the line of First Mother. A mutation, if you will, somehow related to the tangle of neural networks in these heads of ours."

Mengmoshu put a hand on his own domed forehead and carefully masked his mind. "We are descended from one of First Mother's sons. Kati is somehow descended from both of them. She has the total genetic line of First Mother, but mixed in a new way. She has the powers of First Mother. The only question is, can she go one step further?"

"*That* is a serious question," said Juimoshu, "and I hope for success, of course. But what if we find that Kati can *not* transfer even a pebble at infinite speed within the gong-shi-jie? Then we are as isolated as ever, and the problems on our own planet remain. It seems to me we should be talking about Kati's primary task and not something that relies on abilities she might lack. When do you take her to the eastern plains? When do you show her to the people? We only have six years left, Mengmoshu!"

"Within the year," said Mengmoshu. "Kati nags me constantly about it, so her desire is there. But the changes within her are still occurring, and I would like her to mature a bit further before we go everywhere. I'll also be taking her to the Tumatsin, and they must see her as one of their own. She's not yet complete as a Changeling; the fierce countenance of an aroused Tumatsin woman has not appeared on her face."

"She's fifteen, nearly sixteen. It should have happened by now," said Juimoshu.

Mengmoshu shrugged his shoulders. "We must wait for it. But I will take her to Wanchou before then. She is ready to make an impression on the people there. Her healing power could be useful, if she follows her instincts. The people have never met a Tumatsin before, and will see such power as extraordinary."

"They must see her as an emissary from First Mother," said Juimoshu. "They must see her as *Empress*," said Mengyao, turning to Juimoshu. "How goes the health of The Son of Heaven?"

"The mass within him grows slowly, at his age," said Juimoshu. "Any treatment would kill him, and the doctors have agreed to keep him from the truth. I give him their medicines to keep up his strength, and there is no pain yet. He could last a year, or five. I cannot predict."

"No matter," said Mengyao. "We can control the boy in the interim. The troopers are in our camp, and many of the nobles as well. They all see the decay of the throne, and will support anything new."

Mengmoshu waved a hand in warning. "I don't agree with you, Mengyao. The nobles will support anyone who gives them all they want. They control commerce, and can shut it down in an instant if they're not satisfied. Kati listens to us, but she has her own mind. She is young, and what she sees in Wanchou will be disturbing to her. If Kati is to be Empress, any reforms she makes must also consider the ambitions and desires of the nobles. When the time for change nears, the noble families must also meet her and hear her views. They will be biased by her age, and I worry more about this confrontation than any other."

"I think we're getting way ahead of ourselves," said Juimoshu. "The people come first, and then the nobles. She must unite the people, and this is the will of First Mother."

Mengmoshu chuckled. "You have a way of getting back to the basics," he said. "In the meantime, Kati's theoretical preparation continues at a rapid pace. Her mind is nearly as quick as Huomeng's, and he pushes her hard."

"How are they getting along, personally, I mean?" asked Juimoshu.

"They've become friends," said Mengmoshu, "and have

mutual respect for each other. The adversarial times seemed to have passed."

"Nothing more?" asked Juimoshu, a faint smile showing on her wrinkled face.

"You mean romance? I think not. Kati dreams only about Lui-Pang, and Huomeng has become a man with Sheyue. Both girls are on contraceptives, though Kati doesn't know it. Sheyue and Weimeng make sure it's in her tea each day. They are young, and full of hormones, and if things progress too far we can always restrict their time together."

"Spoken like a man," said Juimoshu. "Keeping them apart will only make matters worse. It is better to allow things to take their natural course. Sheyue is lovely, but somewhat empty-headed. Lui-Pang is handsome, but simple. I believe in natural selection, the mating of the best with the best. It will happen, if we don't interfere."

"Huomeng and Kati?" asked Mengyao, grinning.

"That is my hope," Juimoshu said. "Huomeng is the greatest talent to come along since you, Mengmoshu. I wish his father could have lived to see it."

"He was a great scientist," said Mengmoshu. "We owe the flyers and the mag-rails to him."

"Huomeng and Kati," said Mengyao. "I think they would argue each other into an early grave."

"Better to think of the child they might produce," said Juimoshu.

Weimeng was writing at the desk when Kati came into her chambers. Kati walked up behind the woman, and put her arms around her neck, their cheeks touching. "I came to say goodnight, mother."

"So early?" Weimeng put down her pen, and touched Kati's face.

"Yes. Mandughai waits for me."

"Poor dear. They give you barely enough time for sleep. And I wanted so much for you to attend my party. All the best families will be here, and with their sons, I might add. Everyone wants to meet you."

"Another time. I will be in Wanchou with Mengmoshu for at least a week, mother."

Weimeng turned her head, and kissed Kati's cheek. "How I love that word. Do you remember when you first called me that?"

"Yes. I remember both of us crying about it."

Weimeng laughed, and squeezed Kati's arms tightly to her.

There had been a dream, with fire. She was back in the *ordu*, and her *ger* was in flames, her family trapped inside. Da and Baber were screaming for help, but the canvas was too heavy, the flames too hot, and she was little again. She threw dirt on the fire, but it did nothing, and the screams of Da and Baber were growing fainter and fainter, until . . .

She must have been screaming in her sleep, and suddenly Weimeng was there, holding her tightly, rocking her like a little child, saying, "Wake up, Mengnu, wake up. It's only a dream. Hush now. Mother is here."

Kati had clung to her, half-awake, said something about the dream, and then, "Oh, mother, I miss them! I miss them so much!"

Weimeng had cried with her for a long time. The word had come out so naturally, for Weimeng *was* her mother in every way except by blood, loving her, caring for her. Since that night, Kati had not been able to call Weimeng anything but mother, and had felt content with it.

"There will be other parties," said Weimeng, standing up and hugging her, "and many young men to meet. It's not too early to think about suitors, dear. You attract their eyes wherever you go."

"I understand, mother. I will charm them until they cannot eat. I think I charmed Shan-lan after class, today. He kissed my hand."

Weimeng laughed. "Naughty girl. Now, go to First Mother, and I will complete my invitation list."

They kissed, and Kati went back to her rooms to perform the ritual for deliberate, planned contact with Mandughai. She no longer lay on her bed for it, but used a simple shrine. A short, square block of black basalt was always against the wall opposite the foot of her bed. She placed a cushion before it, went to a closet and took out the stone dish, candles, dried sweet grass and incense. She placed the dish on the pedestal, added the grass and incense. The stub candles went on three sides of the dish. She waved her hand slowly over the shrine, drawing energy from only the room, feeling it cool. Candles, grass and incense ignited with a single pass of her hand, the exercise bringing her to a focus deep within herself. She sat down on the cushion, legs crossed, hands folded loosely in her lap. Only after several minutes of staring at the candle-flames did she finally close her eyes.

And was with Mandughai again.

There were no twinkling stars, or purple shimmering curtain, only a flash and Mandughai was there, waiting serenely for her to arrive.

You are prompt.

Yes. You said this was important.

We will be together longer than usual. Today we travel far.

At first, the gong-shi-jie had been only a featureless, purple fog to her, but now it was much more. Everywhere she looked were the signatures of planets and stars, the little vortices of color from blue to red stretching as far as she could see in all directions. Everything seemed compressed in the gong-shi-jie, for Kati knew from her reading that the real-space distances between these objects extended to limits beyond imagination, a great wheel of stars and dust across which light itself crawled at a snail's pace. Even at her position, the boundary of the wheel was not visible in the gong-shi-jie, though she was half-way out from the center of it.

The stars were easiest to locate, their vortices large and colored green to deep red. The planets were most difficult, their signatures small, but Kati was slowly learning to distinguish the different shades of purple and blue that identified them by mass.

Mandughai beckoned to her and she followed, looking back to orient herself on the green vortex of Tengri-Khan, the light purple dimples that were the gaseous giants of its planetary system. Her own vortex burned brightly in deep purple, the way back to the sleeping body awaiting her return.

One alignment was sufficient, for they would only travel for minutes in real time.

But Mandughai first took her to the edge of the wheel.

Do not try to memorize the patterns. Just look, and trust me. I have gone this way many times.

Kati felt relief, for she was quickly confused by the pattern of vortices rushing by her, and so she concentrated on Mandughai's tutorial as they moved.

There. The yellow signature. A race of sentient birds lives there on a world covered with water. The sea provides their needs, and they have no technology to interest us. There are many such worlds.

The faint vortex, deep red; stay away from its center. The mass there is so great that light emitted by the star is red beyond red, and cannot be seen in real space.

Is it dangerous?

Only near the center. The gong-shi-jie is so distorted there you might not be able to return from real space. I have never dared to attempt it.

They drifted. Ahead of them, the pattern of vortices was gradually fading until there was only the gong-shi-jie, but far beyond them were bright specks of light like distant stars. Mandughai pointed to them.

This is the edge of our universe. There's only dust and gas here, but out there are other universes. I've only been to the nearest one, and it's similar to ours. Perhaps there's life there. Each speck of light is a universe; they seem to go on forever. But it will take you a lifetime to explore the one we live in, and that is enough.

Mandughai. What is a lifetime?

It is relative, child. You might live a hundred years, or less. Mandughai has lived three thousand.

Then you aren't human, but a goddess.

I've told you I'm human, Kati, but my image is an illusion in your mind. I show you my ideal of a beautiful Empress. In a few years, you will see me as I am. I'll be returning to Shanji for a short time.

My people have been waiting for you thousands of years! They will be happy to be rid of the Emperor!

Mandughai's lovely face was suddenly serious. *They will not be so happy about my return, but there will be a new ruler on Shanji. These things will be revealed to you later, Kati. Now we must go back.*

They moved even faster, now, vortices rushing by in a blur. It would take many lifetimes to learn all the patterns here, thought Kati. Mandughai has learned them all. How could she do that and still be human?

It seemed only seconds before they stopped at a vortex that was the green of Mandughai's eyes.

There is life here. Follow me closely, just to the right of center in the vortex.

They dipped into the swirling thing, Mandughai's image close. There was the usual flash as they entered real-space, and behind them the vortex was a small, whirling disk of green.

A monstrous, orange flame rushed through the place she occupied as an ethereal apparition. She looked down, and saw they were close to the surface of an orange star, so close that one of its prominences had just reached out to where they were. The surface of the star roiled with turbulence: swirling storms, protuberances spouting like boiling mud, fans of fire reaching out everywhere from the surface. But it was the jets of matter being ejected from the poles of the star that brought back the memory of a lesson from the learning machine.

The star was Tengri-Nayon.

It's young, and still unpredictable. Life has been an adventure for my people here, but it gets better, and more stable.

Another flame passed through them, carrying dust with it. There was no sense of heat, for there was no body with which to touch or feel.

It is the home star of your people, Kati. Would you like to take a little piece of it with you?

The idea seemed absurd. Even Mandughai was smiling when she said it.

I will hold the sight of it in my mind.

But your mind is here, Kati. It's as if you're in your room, and there are lit candles before you. You can make the flames move, Kati. You can make the flames come to you.

I extend my aura, and the flames come to it, Mandughai. I have no aura here.

Then you must imagine it. Think of it as a gloved hand. When a prominence comes by, reach out, grab a piece of it, and hold on. A piece of Tengri-Nayon to take back with you, even if it is only grains of dust. Try it.

Mandughai was still smiling. A game of imagination? Or a test? So many previous tests had seemed like games at the time. Still, Mandughai had made a request and Kati would honor it as usual. She imagined her own, golden aura surrounding her position and it was there, like a thing seen in a dream. She extended it outwards in a sheet, like a robe billowing in wind, and waited only seconds, for another flame was rushing towards them. She imagined the flame striking her aura, thinking them together as a person thinks a thrown ball going into the hand, and then it was there, a small globe of flame with particles of dust struggling within an aural prison that was only imagination.

I caught it!

Mandughai laughed, and clapped her hands without sound. She was delighted.

Hold tight! We're leaving, now. Keep your focus!

Another flash, and they were in the gong-shi-jie. But the aura was gone, and with it the little ball of gas and dust that was a piece of Tengri-Nayon.

Kati was painfully disappointed. *It's gone! It didn't come through with me!*

Mandughai smiled. *No matter. It was only a game, and we will try it again. Perhaps the transition from real space broke your concentration. But you had it, Kati! It was within your grasp!*

Yes, but I lost it. I'm sorry, Mandughai.

The lesson you've learned is most important, dear. You see that your aura is truly with you wherever you go, even without the presence of your body. It is simply not visible to you.

So it *had* been a test, and that was the lesson to be learned. The use of her aura extended to *all* of real space, not just to Shanji. And for a brief moment, she had held a piece of a star.

Now the pattern was familiar again: Tengri-Khan, the gaseous giants, the purple vortex leading to herself. The image of Mandughai hovered near it, pointing the way back.

Before you go, there is one more thing.

Yes, Mandughai.

You will go to Wanchou, and the people will ask who you are, and you will tell them you come from me, Kati. You are my emissary to them, for I care about all my people.

I will tell them, Mandughai.

There is more. Your skills are well developed, but now you must apply them. There is harshness in the lives of the people. Wherever you go, I ask you to rely on your instincts for goodness and compassion, and use your skills without inhibition to ease the life of the people. Mengmoshu knows my wishes and will support all that you do.

What am I to do?

You will see it, dear. Now go, with my love. I still think of you as my own daughter.

And you are my First Mother. Goodbye, Mandughai.

Sweet grass, incense, and the flickering flames of three candles; she was back in her rooms, and her back hurt. Her legs were cramped, and when she checked the time she discovered why. She'd been locked stiffly in meditative position for nearly half an hour while traveling the diameter of a galaxy.

She slept restlessly that night, awakened once by pain, and a dream she could not remember. The pain was in her mouth. She licked her lips, and tasted blood, then probed with her tongue around a sore spot inside her lower lip.

Sometime during the night, she'd bitten herself. And there was an unusually large hole there, still bleeding.

CHAPTER ELEVEN
THE PEOPLE

Mengmoshu took Kati to meet Shanji's people only two months after her sixteenth birthday. For a week and a half, they were constantly together, and he grew close to her as a father to a daughter.

She was in the hands of First Mother, and her education and social training were the privilege of Huomeng, Lady Weimeng, and Sheyue. His only participation in her upbringing had been those few precious times she'd come to his mind with a sorrow, concern or question, and he'd done what he could for her.

It was not enough. He wanted to do more. He was her father, watching others do for her what he should be doing. She did not even know who he was. And during the last few years, she had become a beautiful young woman without his fatherly presence beside her.

He had agreed with First Mother's decision not to tell the Moshuguang about his relationship to Kati, but taking her to Wanchou was a logical act for the Chancellor of the Moshuguang.

It was early morning when he met Kati at the monorail station by the landing field. She was sitting on a bench and stood up as he stepped from the car, a small valise at her feet. Her eyes changed from brown to amber when she saw him and smiled.

His own carrying case was heavy; within it his own change of clothes, recording devices, and the robe he would have her wear for the people. He plopped the case heavily before her. "How are you?" he asked.

"Excited. I thought we were never going to do this."

Her presence was striking: the long, chiseled face, finely arched nose, the magical eyes that seemed to be constantly changing color. A guard came to carry their luggage and they followed him through the gate to the mag-rail car awaiting them.

Mengmoshu punched in the second exit within the workers' city as their destination and put the car on auto-control as they entered the tunnel. Kati wanted to know the operation of the car, the route they were taking, the stops, everything. She was nervous, and apprehensive. Mengmoshu put an arm around her shoulders, squeezed gently, and that seemed to calm her. To use mental control on her was a waste of effort. They came to the smells and din of the workers' village, and took the first exit left. "Can we look in the shops on the way back?" asked Kati.

"Yes," said Mengmoshu, knowing that after her time in Wanchou the things she saw in those shops would clearly show her the relative ease of life for those who worked within the mountain.

The tracks looped towards the right, but they turned left to a platform with cutouts for parking. Two armed guards, escorts, were waiting there, a flight of stairs behind them brightly lit.

As they stepped from the car, the guards bowed stiffly to them, took their luggage and preceded them up the stairs to a long, empty hallway. They walked its length to the doors of an elevator which opened as they arrived. The guards entered with them and the elevator descended for several seconds before the doors opened again. Kati looked at him, her eyes now red; he felt the anxiety building within her.

The doors opened to a lavish suite with bare, red walls and thick carpet, bronze chandeliers, and a huge black table in the center. The guards went to two closed doors on one wall, beyond which were bedrooms. They placed Kati's valise in one, Mengmoshu's in the other, then returned silently to stand by the elevator. "We will change clothes here," he said, for Kati was looking horribly confused by this stop.

"Change?"

"I have something for you to wear, Kati. This visit to Wanchou is a formal thing and we have to dress for it." He went into his room to open his carrying case, and Kati followed him inside. "I thought we were just going to travel around and see how the people live."

"We are, but not just to look. You'll be meeting people and talking to them. Our guides are people of influence in Wanchou and they feel honored by this visit. They are entertaining the emissary of First Mother, something that has never happened before now."

"They *know* about me?"

"They know an emissary comes. I want you to wear this. You may wear your hair long, or in buns if you like." He withdrew a robe in deep purple from his case and handed it over to Kati.

"It's beautiful," she said, fondling the heavy cloth.

"The color is symbolic of the gong-shi-jie, where only you and First Mother travel. You are Her emissary and you must act the part for the people to see it."

She seemed to accept that, and nodded. "It will take me a while," she said, then left the room talking to herself under her breath, her mind masked from him.

Mengmoshu changed from his black robe into full, military armor, without sidearm, the red *shizi* emblem over his heart. He closed up his case and found it mercifully lighter, then carried it back to the elevator and waited there with the guards.

And waited. Time passed, and the guards began to shift uneasily from foot to foot. It seemed forever before Kati finally appeared at the doorway.

Even Mengmoshu was struck dumb by the sight of her. One guard rushed to take the valise from her hand before she could even take a step. She followed him back as if floating.

She had formed her hair into two tails held together by gold rings near the head, and they fell across her breasts, nearly to the waist. Lips rouged red, she'd also added a blush to cheekbones normally prominent, giving her face a triangular shape, and there were traces of purple sparkles around her eyes. She was happy about her appearance, for her always changing eyes were nearly leaf-green now, and she had enhanced the thickness of her long lashes. She carried a small gold fan in one hand, and when she reached him she snapped it open to cool herself delicately with it while coyly lowering her eyelashes.

"Well? Will I make an impression?"

Mengmoshu could not restrain a chuckle. "You are the vision of an Empress, Madam, and I'm honored as your escort. Please."

He offered an arm and she put her hand on it as they entered the elevator, the guards stumbling around with the luggage, trying hard not to look at her. "I tried to look like the image Mandughai shows me in the gong-shi-jie and it took me awhile to get it," she said. "I'm glad you like it."

She squeezed his arm and smiled, and Mengmoshu masked fiercely so she would not see the pride and love in him, or know why it was there.

They rode the elevator down for several seconds and stepped out into cool morning air within a cavern opening to the outside. A man in white uniform was there beside a small, windowed car hanging on two cables going out of the cavern opening, and down from it. The man took one look at Kati and bowed deeply to her, ignoring Mengmoshu.

"We will take two cable cars to Wanchou. This is the first, which goes to a checkpoint. There is heavy security on the mountain," he said, and helped her into the car.

"Huomeng told me. The people are not allowed to see what's here." Kati's eyes were now amber.

The car moved out and down at a forty-five degree angle along the rocky face of the mountain. Above them, the workers' village sprouted from rock, but Kati looked downwards to the sprawl of Wanchou far below. Soon, a road was drawing near, cut horizontally across the mountain with regularly spaced stone huts behind a high fence of wire, and armed troopers were pacing the road, watching their descent. They came to a platform with a large hut, and their luggage was taken without inspection to a gate, beyond which a second car awaited them. They followed, past guards stiffly at attention, whose eyes shifted slightly to follow Kati's passage past them.

The nearness of Wanchou was an illusion of size and they were on the second car half an hour before reaching the final cable towers and another compound swarming with troopers. The nearest buildings of Wanchou loomed beyond a high fence, and there was a paved road leading into a tunnel beneath it. A simple, unadorned spring wagon pulled by two horses sat there, surrounded by an escort of eight guards on horseback. Mengmoshu offered an arm to Kati, led her stately to the wagon and held her hand as she stepped into it. *More ceremony. You're doing fine.*

Mengmoshu took the reins and drove the wagon through the tunnel, guards on both sides. *Remember who you are, and rely on your instincts.* They came out in a garden of short trees, bushes with flowers, and butterflies. A hemisphere of wire mesh covered the whole thing and there was still another gate, with a guardhouse. All around them, faces were pressed to the wire from the outside, hundreds of them, young and old, even children. He stopped the wagon at the guardhouse. Troopers scurried to take their luggage through the gate as he helped Kati down. "Go to the gate," he whispered. "I will walk behind you for a moment."

Kati nodded, eyes amber, and she walked slowly ahead of him. The crowds outside were shuffling around, pressing towards the gate, but several guards were there to press them back with their rifles. A small thin man awaited them, dressed in brown canvas. He bowed deeply as Kati came out of the gate, her eyes apparently on him. She seemed oblivious to the crowd straining to get a look at her. "I am Jin-yao," said the man. "Welcome to our city." His voice shook nervously.

Kati extended her hand. Jin-yao seemed surprised, but shook her hand gently and bowed again.

"I am Mengnu. I bring you greetings from First Mother, and fulfill her desire that I visit Her people."

"We are honored, Lady Mengnu," said Jin-yao.

They went to another wagon of polished wood, two seats, drawn by two horses with well brushed manes and tails. Kati put out her hand to Jin-yao for balance as she climbed up, and stood until Mengmoshu was seated. The crowd was murmuring, pressing in tighter for a closer look, but suddenly the sound of shuffling feet stopped, and there was silence.

Kati was turning slowly, looking in all directions, her left hand out as if pointing to something near the wagon. The perceived power of her thought was huge for Mengmoshu, though he doubted the people could consciously sense it.

Peace. First Mother is always with you.

It could only be the sight, not the thought, that made the silence, for when Kati turned to face him he saw that her eyes were emerald green.

❖   ❖   ❖

She sat down beside Mengmoshu. Jin-yao took the reins, sitting on a seat in front of them and the crowd parted as the wagon moved. Mengmoshu was amazed. There were no shouts, no cheers, only silence, thousands of faces looking up at the emerald eyes. Kati looked from side to side, repeating her mental greeting over and over. A focus to keep the color of her eyes? Or were the people hearing it?

They hear me. You don't need to think up a new test to prove it.

Mengmoshu chuckled, then spoke aloud. "Jin-yao is the Comptroller for Wanchou, My Lady. He's responsible for all commerce within the city limits, but also deals with the flow of goods from factories and farms."

"A great responsibility," said Kati.

"I'm not worthy of the position," said Jin-yao, "but I work very hard."

Kati questioned him all the way to the first buildings of Wanchou, wanting to know who he dealt with: factory and store managers, city planners, transportation officials, all in the employ of the nobles. Jin-yao answered happily, pleased by her interest. There was little traffic on the road leading to the base of the mountain, few people to stare as they passed by, but as they reached the first buildings, the cobblestone street was suddenly packed with little carts drawn by animals and people, and others walking, stooped over beneath heavy burdens. Tengri-Khan was blocked out by tall buildings a step from either side of the street, buildings forty stories high, hundreds of windows with awnings and racks from which clothing was hanging in open air. The buildings were constructed of inferior, brownish concrete; absorbed water had created a myriad of cracks and peeling slabs of faded green, grey and yellow paint.

The stench of urine and animal droppings made their eyes water, but it was soon overpowered by something even worse.

The crowd parted for them, people scurrying to get out of the way, and Kati's greeting was again booming in his head. *I come from First Mother, and bring you Her greetings.*

The people who gawked at her had weathered and wrinkled faces burned brown by sunlight. All were slender, their clothes clean but worn-looking. The people stared, made way for them, and finally they stopped before a building like all the others. Jin-yao got out of the cart. "There will be a reception for you, Lady Mengnu, but I wish to show you a dwelling for our people if you're willing to climb a flight of stairs."

"Of course," said Kati. *What is that horrible odor?*

Raw sewage. It runs in conduits just beneath the street to settling ponds outside the city. A million forms of bacteria are breeding right beneath us.

They went into the building and up a flight of stairs. There were no elevators to be seen, and no lighting. Jin-yao knocked on a door and a tiny Hansui woman opened it, beaming at them and bowing, over and over again.

Jin-yao showed them two rooms while the woman and five children, two boys and three girls ranging in age from five to fifteen, stood shyly to one side. The total floor space in their dwelling might be forty square meters, thought Mengmoshu. One window, family pictures on one wall, children's drawings displayed on the other, the rooms were dimly lit by two small ceiling panels turned on in their honor. The only furniture was a table and six chairs in one room, a few cushions lining the edges of the wooden floor in the other. A small, alcohol-fueled stove was near the table.

"I'm honored to have such an apartment," said Jin-yao. And then he introduced them to his family. Kati's eyes were now amber. The woman and children hesitated to shake her hand when it was offered, but did so, and Kati held each hand a little longer than necessary.

"Greetings from First Mother," she said, each time.

The woman and children did not speak, but suddenly the woman held up a greenstone amulet, pointing to herself and smiling brightly. The gesture seemed to embarrass Jin-yao. He scowled at his wife, and quickly hurried his guests from the rooms without a word. An old woman came up the stairs and passed by them without looking up, hunched over beneath a heavy pack on her back, continuing her upward climb and breathing hard.

"She is a widow, and cannot work," explained Jin-yao, "so she has a single, small room on the forty-second floor. There is a special store for those who cannot work, and she receives her food there.

Kati's eyes blazed red.

Seven people in that tiny place! My bedroom is larger!

It is the best they have, Kati.

And that stench is everywhere!

She struggled briefly to renew her serene smile, eyes quickly amber again.

They got back into the cart and drove three blocks to a low, white building, Kati's fan in constant motion as they went. Four men met them in a white room with bare walls, a table, and chairs. The windows were opaque from dust and soot. Jin-yao introduced the men as ministers: Li-ban, the mayor, Ling-de, of transportation, Lan-tsui, of housing, and Huan-bei, a secretary to Li-ban. For half an hour they talked informally of the weather, population, the growing concern about the breeding habits of the people. Kati listened silently, nodding her head at appropriate times.

When they sat down at the table, Mengmoshu was on Kati's right, the mayor on her left. All others sat across the table from them. All wore the suits of brown canvas, like many people in the streets. They were served tea by one woman, followed by a bowl of rice with some vegetables sprinkled with tiny pieces of beef.

*It is a lavish meal. What little beef they produce here
is sent to the nobles for their consumption.*

Kati ate with the delicacy and elegance of the court,
but when she put down her sticks, Mengmoshu held his
breath, for her eyes were now the yellow of Tengri-Khan.
Perhaps she'd seen what he'd seen in the minds of the
men around her. All thought she was a spy from the
Emperor's court.

She began to quiz those who sat across from her. She
asked about production and transport rates in per-capita
terms, and they refereed her to managers in the field.
She asked about per-capita protein consumption, and
again they could not answer. They fidgeted uneasily in
their chairs.

Careful! We're not here to threaten, but to learn.

*These people are functionaries! They know nothing!
Huomeng has taught me more in a year than they've
learned in a lifetime!*

*Yes, but do not show the impatience of your teacher.
You will meet the people who can answer your questions
soon enough.*

Kati sighed, and changed the subject, asking about the
lengths of their working weeks, the size of their staffs.
The hours were long, staff inadequate, but all men were
dedicated to their work and humbly honored by their
positions. They relaxed again.

Mengmoshu was grateful when the meal was over, and
they were ready to leave. Kati shook each hand, and said,
"I will tell First Mother about your hardships, and the
vigor with which you pursue your responsibilities."

All hosts were smiling when the meeting ended.

They are puppets of the nobles. Is Jin-yao this inept?

*He coordinates them as best he can. You see what he
has to work with. The nobles choose their ministers
without consulting him, and prefer intellects that will
not be too independent.*

Puppets!

Kati's mental murmurings continued for the next few minutes, but outwardly she was calm and somehow kept her eyes amber. They toured shops where staples of flour and rice were dispensed to long lines of women and children in exchange for chits given to their men for labor. There was no hard currency in copper, silver or gold, only the chits for exchange in the stores of the nobles. Outwardly, the people seemed fed, and their simple clothing of brown canvas was not tattered. They did not have the look of people who owned nothing of their own.

As evening drew near there was another place Mengmoshu had to show her, a place unknown to the nobles. Their puppet ministers knew about it, but said nothing to their absentee masters and so Jin-yao took them there, an unmarked building without windows on a dark side street in the center of the city.

Kati was tired from the day and stifled a yawn as he whispered, "This will not be pleasant for you."

It was a hospital.

The place had been a warehouse, but now the floor was covered with beds of straw in many rows, a sea of beds dimly lit by rows of lanterns beneath a high ceiling with wooden rafters. The stench of burning oil, alcohol, and diseased flesh struck like a hammer as the door closed behind them. Mengmoshu breathed through his mouth.

Kati's composure wavered. She gasped at the sight, eyes wide, and hid a retching cough with her fan.

This is one of three hospitals in the city, and there are several smaller clinics for lesser problems. None of them are sanctioned by the nobles or the Emperor, and the physicians here could be imprisoned for their work.

There are Moshuguang here!

Several white-frocked doctors walked the isles, checking on their patients. All were Moshuguang, with high-domed foreheads.

They are the only doctors we have so far, but there will be more. We train city people first as nurses, then as doctors. It is a slow process, because the people are not prepared.

Was she listening? Kati started down one isle, looking right and left, pausing at each bed. What was she seeing? The sight of auras was a power of First Mother, a gift passed only to Tumatsin women and not through the lineage of her second son, from whom the Moshuguang had come. Kati had tried to explain it to him once, but he could only imagine a pattern of colors in the human energy field, a pattern that changed with mood, or physical condition. She was looking at that pattern now, at every bed.

Disorders of the stomach and bowels, and I see many skin infections here. You have medicines to cure these conditions.

Yes, but not enough. Our pharmaceutical production is higher than we report to the Emperor and much of it is used here, but it is still inadequate. We cannot keep up with the population growth.

A young woman lay on a bed, eyes closed, and Kati knelt down, passing a hand over the woman's groin. *She has a tumor, and it's growing rapidly.*

We only have two surgeons. She will have to wait.

She cannot wait. She could die within days.

A doctor was walking towards Kati, looking concerned, but Mengmoshu stopped him with a wave of his hand. *She comes from First Mother, and brings Her power to us. Do not interfere.*

Kati looked at him, and her eyes were emerald green. *I can shrink it now, but the residual must be removed as soon as possible if we don't return here.*

Then do what you can now.

Kati moved her hand over the woman's groin, not touching it, a circular motion, then rising, falling again and finally touching. The woman's eyes snapped open, and she gasped, her hands reaching to Kati's, then sliding away. She looked at Kati's face, and lay there staring while the hand pressed firmly on her groin for several minutes. Kati's mind was totally masked from him, in a place he could not go, her eyes closed.

Finally, Kati raised her hand, and opened her eyes. For an instant, there was a flash of green light that illuminated the sickened woman on her bed. The woman gasped again, and rubbed her groin tenderly, as if knowing that something important had just happened there.

Kati smiled beautifully. *I have drawn upon the gong-shi-jie. The tumor is shriveled, but I need two more treatments to kill it. She should have surgery within a month.*

The doctor nodded, then shook his head in wonderment. Kati put her hand on the woman's forehead. *You will be well again.*

The woman closed her eyes, and slept.

There was no meal for any of them that evening. Kati refused to leave, despite his protests which diminished as he saw what she did for the people. Her eyes remained emerald green the entire time she was with the ill, and he suddenly realized that the color was a manifestation of the love and compassion within her. As he watched her work, tears came to his eyes. He could not dare a prayer to First Mother, for Kati would hear it.

Why must I continue to hide from my own daughter?

What were her limits? She had already surpassed the powers of First Mother. Had he fathered The One: Mei-lai-gong, the Goddess of Light they had sought to breed for over a thousand years?

Now she walked as if floating between the beds, kneeling, healing, a cluster of doctors and nurses following her. She burst boils, healed burned flesh and removed a constriction in a bowel with a few short waves of her hand, and always there was a hand on the forehead of the patient. *You will be well again.*

It was well after midnight when she was finally finished. Kati was delighted, her face radiant when she came to him, this sixteen-year-old who could pass for thirty, and they went outside to awaken Jin-yao, who was sleeping in the wagon. Jin-yao drove a few blocks to a building where a room had been prepared for them, and carried their luggage inside before hurrying home, for he would pick them up again early the next day.

There were two beds with thick mattresses of straw, a screen behind which they changed clothes for sleeping. A bowl of fruit left on a table for them was quickly consumed. As he was ready for bed and about to collapse into it, Kati came up to him, eyes green, and said, "Now I know what Mandughai wants me to do. I have never felt so content or satisfied in all my life. Oh, Mengmoshu, *thank* you for bringing me here!"

She threw her arms around him, her cheek against his chest, and he hugged her to him for a long time.

"What you did tonight is a marvel, but there is much more to see, and perhaps First Mother has even greater tasks for you."

"What could be greater than healing?" she asked, looking at him.

Mengmoshu smiled. "We shall see." He released her then, and crawled into bed. And as sleep neared, he was aware of Kati still pacing the room in excitement, thinking she had discovered the purpose of her life at last.

There were three more days and nights for them in Wanchou. There were visits to countless stores, where Kati's questions were answered frankly and honestly by those who faced the people each day, those who took the brunt of their anger during the frequent shortages.

It was not a problem of production, but transportation and accounting, they told her.

Two more hospitals hosted them, but Mengmoshu made sure the visits were scheduled after a meal, for once inside Kati would not leave until she'd done what she could for everyone. She healed, and diagnosed, the doctors following her everywhere, wondering at her and often feeling helpless. But even Kati could not bring back life. The internal bleeding of a child had proceeded too far before Kati reached her, and the child, aged three, died in her arms. Her grief was horrible for Mengmoshu and the other Moshuguang present, for she held nothing back, crying, rocking the child's dead body until a doctor took it from her. Mengmoshu wanted her to sleep, but she would not, and they had an appointment with a Moshuguang social worker named Xie. When they met him outside the hospital, the workers had gone home to their families and the streets were dark, but people were there, quiet, shadowy creatures who looked fearfully at them as they passed by. Some scrubbed the streets clean of garbage and dung with stiff brooms, while others searched refuse containers for something of use.

"The night people," explained Xie. "Many have come in from the countryside after layoffs in the factories. Most are unskilled, some physically or mentally ill. All the human refuse of Shanji comes here. I try to find them a room and give them chits for food, but they sicken and starve faster than I can get to them."

They followed Xie on his rounds, down cobblestone side streets, alleys rank with garbage and open sewers to visit the basement warrens of the city, rooms with up to twenty people, beds stacked like cordwood, no stoves, no heat. Many were small children with huge, staring eyes, faces emaciated. Xie gave the adults chits for food, and the names of doctors to see, and the people stared only at Kati. Her eyes glowed green as she went from person to person with a word, a touch, a caress of a tiny face, a child's hands grabbing softly at her robe.

Mengmoshu bit his lip to hold back the tears, for he felt his daughter's loving compassion at the sight of such misery. "How many like these?" Kati croaked.

"Perhaps a million," said Xie, giving his last chit to a father of two. "They come in faster than I can find them."

In two hours the chits were gone, and they were mercifully back on the streets, but people followed them, begging for food, chits, anything, and they had nothing to give except Kati's warm touch and the sight of her glowing eyes, which amazed them to the point of reverence.

When Mengmoshu finally got her to bed, Kati was exhausted and stricken with sorrow. He tried to comfort her, reminding her she was not a God, but an exceptional person who could not magically change a world of such misery without the help of many who shared her compassion. That night, she sobbed in her sleep.

The final day in Wanchou lightened Kati's mood, but only a little. All of it was spent touring three of the schools established secretly by the Moshuguang, the students chosen for their intelligence and drive through a slow and exhausting interview process run by the young apprentices in charge. It was then that Mengmoshu told her about Huomeng, and what he'd accomplished in the city.

"Huomeng started this school a year ago for the select few who had progressed far enough to learn mathematics and physics. Now he teaches them mechanical engineering during the winter months."

"Huomeng? He's been here?" asked Kati.

The room was small, and smelled like sewage. A young Moshuguang instructor had used chalk to fill a blackboard with equations and was pointing to them as he talked.

Behind a long table sat six students, all males in their late teens. Each had a small computer before him, scrolling through a lesson as the instructor talked.

"Many months, and even more hours," said Mengmoshu. "He set up all the advanced classes here, and a class in reading for gifted young children. He's quite dedicated to the people."

Kati seemed surprised. "He showed me where his office is. I thought his dream was to fly in space."

"It is," he said, "but he also makes the time for this. He has dreams, Kati, but spends most of his time helping others to make their lives better. When you see past his impatient mind there is an honorable and unselfish person there."

Kati nodded. "Now I understand the passion in his voice when he talks about the people. He has lived with them."

"Yes. Come, now, it's time to leave."

They slipped unobtrusively out the door to where Jin-yao waited with his wagon, but found a crowd silently surrounding it. There were a few men, but mostly women and children. The jostling crowd made a path for them to the wagon, some bowing, a few kneeling and reaching out to touch Kati's robe. People murmured as Kati got into the wagon, and around her many hands were raised to show small, green stones dangling from leather thongs.

"They know you are leaving. The stones are a sign of belief in First Mother. The few who believe are mostly women," said Jin-yao.

The silence was broken by a woman pressing through the crowd, shouting, holding a crying baby over her head.

"We should leave," said Jin-yao.

"No! Wait a moment!"

The woman reached the wagon, and held up her child. "He is sick, with a fever. Please, Lady; heal my son."

The child screamed, drawing up his knees when Kati

took him. She held him close, passed a hand over his face and body, and the screams instantly stopped. She handed the baby back to his mother, and said, "He is well, with the blessings of First Mother. Take him home, and feed him milk fresh from the stores."

There were smiles now, and tearful faces in the crowd, amulets waving. The wagon moved, and the people followed them, some crying out, and falling down prostrate. Kati waved serenely, but nervously, then turned to Mengmoshu.

She fed him spoiled milk! He was cramped!

There is no refrigeration. Food poisoning is common here.

"How did she know to come to me?"

Jin-yao turned around. "Relatives of those in the hospitals. Word travels fast here." He paused, then said, "My Lady, you heal in the name of First Mother."

"Yes. All that I do comes from Her."

"The word in the streets is different, My Lady. The unbelievers call you a magician, but the others—the believers—they say that First Mother has come to them in person. They say *you* are First Mother."

I didn't intend this!

"I only represent her, Jin-yao. You must tell them that."

"I will, My Lady." He slapped the horses with the reins, and the cart jerked forward.

What will She think?

Don't worry. I've never seen those amulets displayed so openly before now, and I think there will be many new believers within the city because of the time you've spent here. She will be pleased.

They thought I performed miracles?

The people hope a Goddess will come to ease their lives, but they are wrong. Change will come when a new person sits on the throne of Shanji.

Shan-lan?

No.

Who, then?

We shall see—and don't probe me so hard. There's nothing more I can tell you at this point. Stop trying!

She didn't, but he resisted her efforts, and she finally gave up when they reached the edge of the city and saw the men and horses waiting there to take them to the factories.

They traveled four days in order to spend two with the people. Along the way they saw many travelers, hand carts loaded with families and meager possessions, headed towards an uncertain future in the city. Kati was now cautious about her actions and asked not to visit the small clinic in the unnamed town built around the smelting plants. Being thought of as First Mother had shaken and confused her badly. Her serene smile had disappeared, and there was now a stern expression when she asked her questions. The plant managers saw her as a spy for the nobles. But they were quick to learn how to judge her reactions to their answers by noting the color of her eyes, and after a few false starts were honest with her.

Production was erratic and inefficient, workers often idle, or laid off, the furnaces continually turned off and on again because of unpredictable delivery schedules of ores from the mines in the north only two hundred kilometers distant. She wanted to visit the mines, but it was not on their itinerary, and Mengmoshu personally felt her anger for that.

Hydroelectric power production by the river called Dahe was enormous, enough to power the plants, the town, Wanchou and more. She asked why a line hadn't been run to Wanchou, and was told the nobles had decided it was unnecessary.

She asked why the workers' apartments had lighting and electric stoves, but no heating or cooling systems.

The nobles had decided it was unnecessary.

Electric vehicles? Mag-rails?

Unnecessary, and expensive. Horse and cart were sufficient for the needs of Shanji and kept the people busy. Only the sick and the very old were unemployed, and they were cared for by the system. Kati saw their lies. She asked why ingots of copper, zinc, tin, lead and all manner of steels were piling up in several warehouses around the plants.

The nobles had no immediate use for them, but you never could tell when there might be a need.

Kati was frustrated, tired, and discouraged. Their last evening within sight of the tall stacks belching steam was spent briefly on the bank of the river Dahe, Shanji's largest. Water crashed past them over rocks and sprayed them with mist as they sat on a carpet of moss, momentarily mesmerized by sound.

This is impossible. The nobles control everything and do nothing to make improvements. First Mother says there will be a new Emperor, and you say it is not Shan-lan. I say whoever it is makes no difference. What we need is not a new Emperor, but a new system, a new way of doing things.

And what is that new system?

I don't know.

That's not helpful, Kati.

I don't know! I've just seen these things.

Then talk it over with Huomeng. Tell him the problems you see. Ask his advice. Share your ideas.

He'll only be critical.

Good! A worthwhile idea must withstand criticism. Work out a reformation plan with him. I will tell Huomeng I've assigned it to you as an exercise.

You won't!

I will. It's done. Now get some sleep. We get up early in the morning.

You sound like a father! I will go to sleep when I'm ready!

She was on her feet, glaring redly at him before he could move. And then she tossed her head angrily, hitched up her robe, and stomped away from him. *I am getting tired of dealing with MEN!*

Minutes after she was gone, Mengmoshu dared to wonder what it would be like to deal with an Empress who had temper tantrums, especially an Empress with the powers of First Mother.

Their final stop was a farming community east of the factories, and they followed their guide in silence the entire day. The land changed from rock-covered sand to grass, then suddenly there were lines of *yar*, their prickly branches shading meandering streams from shallow aquifers at higher elevations to the north. Beyond the streams the land was suddenly green with bean fields and rice paddies, and their destination appeared, a circular cluster of huts made from red clay. The roofs were thatched with tied bundles of dried grass, and people were cooking outside over small fires, sitting together in little groups to eat. Mengmoshu smelled meat cooking, and it was wonderful.

Kati was still in her purple robe, a bit soiled and rumpled, and Mengmoshu had changed back to his black one for the occasion. The first time he'd ridden into such a village in full military armor, the people had thrown stones at him, thinking he'd come to take away the land they regarded as theirs. These were independent people and keepers of the land. Their belief in First Mother was devout.

When they saw Kati, her rumpled robe and face glistening with sweat, they arose from where they were sitting, and bowed directly to her as if Mengmoshu were not present.

Two men hurried to help her dismount. A woman came with a basin of water and bathed her face and hands with a moist cloth. Everyone was stoic and silent, until Kati spoke.

"I bring you greetings from First Mother."

"You are welcome here," said the woman who had bathed her. "We have a place ready for you in our circle. This way."

The woman led Kati to a circle of older people. A saddle had been placed there and covered with a blanket. Kati looked expectantly over her shoulder at Mengmoshu.

"Your servant will be fed," said the woman, and Kati smiled.

I love that!

We both play our parts.

"I'd prefer that he sit with me. He's an old, and trusted advisor," Kati said smugly.

The woman motioned to Mengmoshu, and he joined them at the circle, sitting on a square of cowhide to her right while she perched on her throne. Everyone sat down, and another woman served them *ayrog* in clay mugs. There were no introductions; everyone sat silently, watching Kati.

Her eyes were amber. She took a sip from her mug, and the others did likewise. "*Ayrog!*" she exclaimed. "I haven't tasted this since I was a child!"

"You're not Hansui," said the woman who'd bathed her, and seemed to be a village elder of some kind.

"No, I'm Tumatsin."

"The hill people. How is it that you come to be in the employ of the Emperor?"

Kati's eyes glowed red in an instant. "I do *not* come from the Emperor, or the nobles. I've been sent here by First Mother. She chose me as Her servant when I was a child."

Eyes widened around the circle, but the woman who'd

questioned her showed no reaction. "Why do you come here?"

"To learn about your lives; to see what can be done to make them better."

The woman shrugged. "First Mother is good to us. We have the land, the rains, and many children. We're never hungry, and have shelter. What more could we want?"

"You have no sickness?"

"Oh yes. Many of our children die, but First Mother sends more. People become ill, and often die, but we isolate them before the disease can spread. There have been no plagues of disease here."

"First Mother would have you all live to an old age. There are medicines for treating many illnesses."

"She has given medicines to the Emperor and his nobles, and the land to us. If that is Her will, we are content with it. Please say our thanks to First Mother for all Her gifts. Maybe She feels our prayers have not been enough."

"I will," said Kati, eyes amber again.

Food was served: beans, and strips of beef over a mound of rice, all in great quantity. Mengmoshu stuffed himself, and even Kati ate more quickly than usual.

They see no problems.

Yes, but disease is rampant here. Only a fourth of their children reach adulthood. All the water is polluted by the human waste they use as fertilizer in the fields, and they don't boil it properly. Their deaths are often horrible.

They ate silently, because Kati was silent. The people would only respond if she said something, yet Mengmoshu knew they chatted constantly among themselves when left alone. They would not even exchange names with people they regarded as strangers.

Kati put down her empty bowl. "Are there any sick people among you now?"

"Only a child. He'll soon be with First Mother."

"Please take me to the child, and I'll show you Her will for him."

That's a big risk, Kati!

I have to do something! The people are too accepting about their lives! They think everything is the will of Mandughai! They live blindly!

Tengri-Khan was touching the horizon when the woman took them to a hut where a lantern had been lit. The clay walls were bare, the floor earthen. The room was five paces on a side, without furniture, some shelves of wood separated by stones holding a few meager possessions of clothing and hand-tools. Two straw mattresses were on the floor; a boy, perhaps four years old, lay on one of them, eyes closed. In the dim light, his face was ashen. A woman sat beside him, holding his hand, her face a mask of sorrow and resignation.

Kati knelt by the boy and moved her hands over him. She turned him on one side, and explored his back, looking at that thing Mengmoshu could not see.

Pneumonia, and a weak immunogenic system. No fever. His lungs are filling up.

The elderwoman winced when Kati looked at her with blazing green eyes, and said, "It's First Mother's will that this child should live. Do you have a shrine here?"

"Of course," said the woman.

"Please take me there."

The shrine was an altar of field stones in a neighboring hut. A single, fist-sized greenstone sat on the altar, surrounded by six flickering candles. Mengmoshu and the elderwoman stood in the door as Kati went to the altar, bowed, and stood silently for several seconds, eyes closed. Then she stretched out her hands towards the altar, raising them slowly, the candle flames lengthening in response, and in seconds the candles were puddles on stone.

The elderwoman put a hand to her mouth, and stared.
How am I doing?
Just fine. She's impressed.
They went back to the boy in the hut, and Kati knelt
again, touching his mother's hand, and taking it from
the boy's. "Don't be afraid. This will be difficult for him,
but he will be healed."

Kati moved her hands over him, pressed down on his
back and closed her eyes. In an instant, her eyelids seemed
to glow green. The boy stirred, mumbled something and
tried to roll away, but Kati held him firmly by his back.
Sweat burst from the child's face, and he cried out as
his mother covered her face with her hands, sobbing.
The mattress was soon drenched with sweat coming from
every pore in the boy's body, and he writhed frantically
to escape Kati's grip. A sound came from him, a horrible
gurgling sound, and Kati jerked him upright, bending
him forward and pressing on his back. There was a bright
green flash as her eyes opened, and she said, "Cough!
Cough it up!"

The boy made a sound like gravel sprinkled on metal,
and coughed up a horrible mess of mucus and blood all
over himself, Kati, and the mattress. It went on for
minutes, retching after retching, until finally the child
took a deep, clear breath, and opened his eyes, his face
flushed red.

"Ma?" he asked, and the woman who was his mother
burst into tears.

Kati stood up, and came to the elderwoman, and it
seemed her eyes still glowed, though faintly. "*This* is the
will of First Mother," she said, and the elderwoman bowed
deeply before her.

The villagers agreed to accept the services of any doctors
sent to them in the name of First Mother, but Kati felt
it was her only accomplishment with them. The people

had no problem with the stores of grain and beans rotting in their bins. They met their production quotas, and if it wasn't picked up, well, that was someone else's problem. Yes, they could raise more beef on the neighboring grasslands, but if the nobles saw no need for additional animals, the land was better off in its natural state. Besides, there was plenty of meat in the village.

They had traveled two days by horse and cart to return from the village, but Kati was now awake and alert. Mengmoshu was exhausted and drowsy as the cable car came down for them. Jin-yao had brought them through Wanchou before dawn, when the streets were empty, and Kati had slept with her head on Mengmoshu's shoulder the whole way. He wondered if she'd felt his kiss on her head as he held her.

They were back in white uniforms. The beautiful purple robe had been burned along the way for security reasons, and also because there was no way to clean up the mess that had saturated it. Mengmoshu's black robe was too hot, and he had changed clothes out of sight of the village.

The car arrived, guards loaded their luggage and Kati settled herself in a seat opposite him, seemingly lost in thought. Half-way up the mountain, she suddenly said, "Land."

"What?"

"Land! All lands are the property of the Emperor, and he favors the nobles by allowing their use of it."

"Yes. That is the system," he said.

"The more favor they receive, the richer they become."

"This is true," he said sleepily, stifling a yawn.

"But only a single percent of the land is occupied, or used! If we expand, especially to the northeast, there are many resources to exploit there. More land for favor and profit."

"And?" Now he was barely awake.

"Build new population centers, and expand. Use land

as favors that must be paid for by investments in the system: transportation systems, a power network, medical care, training, better housing conditions, all the problems we've seen. The Emperor *gives* them new lands according to their investments, and each worker is given a piece to call his own." Kati's eyes were again bright with excitement.

"Hmmm. You might try expanding on that idea with Huomeng," he mumbled.

"I will," she said.

And she did, quite soon, because Huomeng was waiting for them at the cable car station, and he seemed particularly happy to see Kati again.

PART III

CHANGELING

CHAPTER TWELVE
CHANGELING

Kati's final transition to Tumatsin womanhood occurred when she was seventeen. In Tumatsin society, the day of her flowering to womanhood would have been an occasion for joy. But Kati was not with her people now, and the day she became a Changeling ended in great sorrow for her.

She had been practicing with the young troopers for six months, and had gained a degree of respect from them despite being a girl. Master Yung had insisted that both she and Shan-lan practice with bow and sword on horseback and in simulated combat, and so he'd brought them into his classes for the young men newly commissioned as troopers.

At first the men resented her presence, but quietly, because she was Moshuguang. It took them only one day to discover her skill with the sword, and she left bruises on several of them. After that, they did not defer to her; their egos wouldn't allow it, and Kati spent many evenings using her hands to heal the bruises all over her body.

She had to learn the bow from scratch. For three miserable months, while the others rode, she stood alone on the archery range outside the dome, sending arrows at man-sized targets fifty meters away. Lui-Pang spent time with her in the evenings, correcting her mistakes in form, and the extra time they had together made the work seem worthwhile.

She wondered if she was in love with Lui-Pang, and if he was in love with her. She thought about him constantly when they were apart, but it was always the physical things she thought of. Outside of horses and weapons, they had little to talk about, but when they were together, those times when his hand was on her breast and his tongue explored her mouth and body, she had twice been on the edge of giving herself completely to him. Today would be another test of her will, for they rode together after class.

They stood in two lines, waiting for Master Yung to arrive. Lui-Pang looked back at her and smiled briefly. Their relationship was still secret, and Kati respected him for that. She'd probed all his friends and found nothing to indicate they knew what happened during those long rides. He was discreet, something difficult for a young man to do.

Shan-lan also smiled at her, undoubtedly wondering if she'd read the most recent poem he'd sent to her:

The flower has a thorn
from which my blood drips.
The finger heals.
The flower has a beauty
I yearn to hold.
My heart aches with longing.
Thorn protects beauty.

Tanchun had brought it to her the night before, a small parchment with the poem and a painting of a flower protected by large thorns—unsigned. The poems were now frequent, and Kati wondered how she would tell the Emperor's son they were only dear friends and nothing more.

Master Yung arrived with their masks and ordered the

two lines of them to face each other. They came to sword length without masks and went through the ten *dongs*, changing opponents each time by moving to their left. Kati struck hard and fast. Shan-lan did well, and Lui-Pang grinned when she gave his blade an extra hard slap after a disengagement. But when she got to the tenth *dong*, she found herself facing Xue-she, a malevolent young man who had bruised her badly on several occasions while enjoying every second of her pain. He gave her a smirk, knowing they would be paired off for ten *dongs* of masked, close combat.

On tenth *dong*, their blades flashed, but his did not touch her.

They put on their masks, and came within sword length. The fact that their practice blades were dulled by grinding was not a comfort. A hard slash to leather armor still left a long bruise on flesh, and a heavy blow to the mask could render her unconscious. Xue-she would be trying for both effects in every move he made.

Xue-she beat at her furiously in the first two *dongs*, forcing her to be purely defensive in holding him off. He chuckled, and said, "I can slow down, if the Lady wishes it."

Kati growled, and her face flushed. Sweat seemed to burst from every pore.

On the third *dong*, Xue-she slipped her blade and drove his point into her mask at forehead level, snapping her head back and pinching her neck. She rotated her head to ease the pain, and Xue-she chuckled again.

Kati ground her teeth together, and her jaws hurt as if someone were squeezing them. "Zhumbei!" she snarled.

On fourth *dong*, she touched him lightly on the chest, but not before he'd smacked her hard on the point of the right shoulder. Numbness ran down her arm, loosening her grip on the sword, and on fifth *dong* he slapped it from her grasp. The entire class had to wait while she retrieved her weapon and got back into line.

She felt furious and humiliated, and again Xue-she chuckled at her. "Perhaps you'd like to rest?" he said.

Her jaws and gums ached, and when she closed her mouth there was pressure on her lower lip, something hard and sharp there. The sound that came from her was deep and guttural. "Ahhh," she said.

Her fingers blanched white on the sword's hilt, and the muscles of her forearm felt squeezed by her leathers. Her body seemed on fire as she struck on sixth *dong*, and she hit Xue-she twice on mask and shoulder, making him wince.

"You'll pay for that," he snarled. "I'll no longer hold back because you're a girl."

Kati growled, and raised her sword. Two teeth pressed hard on her lower lip, and then Xue-she jumped Master Yung's command and poked her hard in the chest before she could react. She lashed back furiously, and dented his mask across the nose. Each breath was a growl. She suddenly realized she wanted to kill him.

When he came at her on eighth *dong* she was ready, striking him four times, once hard in the stomach. He struck back as the exercise ended, and Kati rained blow after blow on his head. "Yiiiaa!" she screamed, and with one vicious slash cleaved the blade of his sword in half. The piece of broken steel spun into the air, and landed several paces behind Xue-she.

"Enough!" shouted Master Yung. "Stop it! The *dong* is finished!"

Xue-she panted for breath, his mask close to hers. "What *are* you?" he asked.

Her voice seemed strangely deep to her. "I'm a woman who has shattered your sword," she said calmly.

Xue-she jerked off his mask as Master Yung came up to them. There was a gash across his forehead where Kati's dull blade had penetrated the mask, and blood was flowing down into his right eye. Master Yung pulled him away from her.

"Attend to your wound and retrieve your weapon! I will take your place here! *Ninth* dong!" he shouted. Everyone in class was watching them.

Xue-she stumbled away from them, panting hard, a hand to his face.

"Strike!"

Kati struck hard, though Yung faced her without a mask. The fury within her had suddenly dissipated. Her mouth was not so full of her own teeth, the leather not so tight on her forearm. Still, on ninth and tenth *dong*, she made two hits that would have been severe in battle, and Yung was pleased. He stepped close to her when it was over.

"Leave your mask on for a moment, and calm yourself. Remember your fury; let it happen when you fight for your life. It's the fury of your ancestors, a thing I cannot teach to the others. Be proud of it!"

He walked away, and all the others, even Lui-Pang, were staring at her. She turned from them, walked a few paces, and breathed deeply to calm herself before taking off her mask. A breeze cooled her face. Her hand and forearm ached, and the right arm felt heavy. She sheathed her sword, and walked back to the others, still breathing deeply. Lui-Pang came up to her.

"What *happened* to you?" he asked.

"He made me angry," she said.

"Remind me to leave our swords behind when we go riding."

Kati smiled. "I have no defense against you."

Lui-Pang grinned, raised an eyebrow, and walked away from her.

Master Yung allowed them to rest a few minutes, and then they went to their horses. The animals were a mixed breed with thick shoulders and short, muscular legs giving them tremendous accelerating power. Their muzzles were short, mane and tails sparse, always reminding Kati of her beloved Sushua. They had been bred for speed over short distances, and strength for collision of horse against horse in battle, following a genetic line going back thousands of years before the ancestors of Tengri-Nayon.

Kati was assigned a white mare who stomped and snorted as she vaulted into the saddle. She joined the line of men following Master Yung a kilometer beyond the dome to a large area fenced with logs. Straw bales holding man-sized dummies of wood and wool wrapped with cloth formed a spiral within the enclosure. They lined up at a gate for mounted drill with bow and sword, going in one at a time on an inward spiral and exiting at another gate to get back in line.

Bow drill was six arrows, one left, one right on each loop of the spiral at full speed. Yung graded them on time and accuracy, and gave a bronze ring to the overall winner. Xue-she had several rings displayed openly on a leather necklace, but he'd not re-appeared after sword drill. Kati kept her three rings in a box in her rooms; the three necklaces she wore beneath her tunic were enough.

Kati had a good day, though not perfect. She missed getting the bronze ring by three points, but her disappointment was eased by the fact that Shan-lan was the winner, and it was his first. She thought he might cry when Master Yung presented it to him, and his eyes were moist when she joined the others in giving him a hug of congratulations. "You are an artist *and* a warrior," she whispered to him, then wished she hadn't said it when he hugged her longer and closer than necessary.

Final drill was always exciting, though mostly a test of horses, and there was no grading. They formed two lines facing each other at fifty meters, and put on their masks again. When they drew their swords, blades flashing, Kati was excited. When Yung raised his arms, she thumped hard with her knees and the mare leaped forward with the others, as everyone screamed.

"SHANJI!"

The charge took seconds, animals shrieking and snapping at each other on impact while their riders slashed furiously left and right at their nearest opponent. Kati took a hit on her mask as her blade whacked satisfyingly across a chest. Satisfyingly, but she went back to regroup knowing that in battle her face would now be in two pieces.

Four rounds, four charges, the horses growing more furious each time. Each time she was hit at least once, and wondered how *anyone* could survive such a charge. The fury that had been with her had not returned, though she was boiling inside. The fury of her ancestors, Yung had said. She had felt it. Yung had seen it, even through her mask. For one moment there, she'd been a Changeling! How could she bring it back? And what would her comrades think if they saw it?

Master Yung seemed pleased, declared the class finished for the day, and there would be another week for their bruises to heal. They dropped their masks into a cart and followed it back to the dome where boys took the horses away to be rubbed down. Her classmates returned to their barracks, and Shan-lan was showing his bronze ring to the two troopers who's arrived to escort him back to the palace. She felt his pride, his excitement about showing the prize to his father, but there was another feeling there. Wistful? No, something sadder.

Lui-Pang was returning, leading two horses for their ride. Shan-lan saw him, turned, and gave Kati a faint smile.

Envy—and jealousy; that was the feeling. Shan-lan turned his head, and followed his escort back to the monorail station.

"Are you ready?" asked Lui-Pang.

"Yes," she said, smiling. The day was hot, and he'd removed his leather tunic, exposing the sleeveless shirt he wore beneath it. Kati looked admiringly at his bronzed, well-muscled arms, and said, "Good idea. It's hot."

She took off her own tunic, and put it in a roll back of her saddle. She wore a long-sleeved, yellow shirt beneath the tunic, and rolled the sleeves up to her elbows before mounting up. Lui-Pang mounted his horse, and his eyes flashed mischievously at her. "The knoll by the Emperor's thumb; first one there wins a prize. Ready?"

Kati kicked her horse, but Lui-Pang was right with her. Guards stumbled to get out of the way as they thundered out of the gate and down the torch-lined road, neck-to-neck in a turn sharply left to the sloping grass fields south.

The wind whipped her face and hair as she bent low over the animal's neck, the throb of the gallop surging in legs and knees. Lui-Pang rode like a demon, and his horse was a little stronger than hers. By the time they reached the knoll he was two lengths ahead of her, assuring his victory by swinging from the saddle before coming to a stop. His feet hit the ground, and he fell, tumbling over and over into the tall grass on the knoll, coming to a stop on his back and thrusting both arms into the air.

"I win! I win!" he shouted, like a little boy.

"You cheated!" she shouted, vaulting from her horse, and rushing to throw herself on top of him so hard that he grunted when catching her. They rolled over and over in the grass, ending up with Kati on top. She grabbed his hands and pressed them to the grass, leaning over close.

"So, what is your prize for winning the race?"

"A kiss from your lovely lips!" he declared.

She gave it to him, long and hard, their mouths twisting against each other. She released his hands and his arms encircled her, the kiss becoming softer, and deep, and then their cheeks were pressed together. "Hmmm," she murmured. "The loser also receives a prize."

Lui-Pang rolled her over onto her back, traced her jaw, nose and cheekbones with a finger. "You were wonderful today. What you did to Xui-she is long overdue. He's too arrogant for his own good."

"He's cruel, and enjoys the pain he gives," she said. "He made me angry."

"I'll say he did." Lui-Pang traced her chin, her jawline, down her neck. His hand found her breast, thumb moving over the nipple, which was instantly hard. "Ohhh," he murmured, and kissed lightly, licking her lower lip. "The taste of a warrior."

Kati's hands moved over his back and along his arms, squeezing the hard muscles there, and suddenly she wanted him as badly as she knew he wanted her. Love, or lust, it made no difference, for now it seemed her body, not her mind, was telling her what to do. For the moment, at least, she adored him, and she let him see it in her eyes. He seemed startled, and there was even some fear there, which surprised her.

"Mengnu—your eyes—they're green!" He sat up, straddling her, and her hands caressed his chest. She pulled up her shirt, and guided his hands beneath it, sighing at his touch.

"Mengnu," he murmured. "I want you—so badly."

"Then take me," she whispered, and in one motion pulled the shirt off over her head to toss it aside and reach up to his face.

He sat gazing at her for one instant before something exploded in both of them, and they were tumbling around in the grass, scattering clothes while the horses watched nervously and stomped the ground, snorting. When they came together, it was gentle, with a long, deep kiss, their hands exploring everywhere, and Kati felt wetness between her legs. The kiss did not stop, and her hand found his organ, smooth and hard. She guided him into her, and felt pleasure at his first thrust, slowly at first, then spreading deep within her. She breathed hard through her nose, opening her mouth wider to him, grabbing his buttocks tightly and pulling. Her pleasure seemed to block thought, and her mind spun blankly. There was only that feeling, groping clear to her spine, and Lui-Pang's muffled grunts as he thrust into her.

Suddenly he winced, and seemed to pull back, but she held on, her pelvis rocking furiously, eyes closed tightly. Her head felt ready to explode.

Lui-Pang winced again, and moaned. His hands pushed against her shoulders as she reached climax; she lost his mouth at that instant, and what came from her was not a woman's cry of pleasure, but a deep, rumbling growl that went on and on.

She opened her eyes as the growl subsided, and Lui-Pang was still straddling her, eyes wide and staring. His organ was limp within her, and his chin was covered with blood from a wound in his lip.

"What have I done?" he said, looking terrified. "What was I thinking of? I should have known, I should have— oh, I can't! I just *can't* do this! We are not—alike!"

"Lui-Pang! What's wrong?" Kati reached out to touch his chin, but he jumped to his feet, and began picking up his clothes as fast as he could.

"Lui-Pang!"

"It's not your fault, Mengnu. I knew about you. But I'd—never seen it. I can't—not with a Changeling. It's— It's unclean!"

Kati jumped up, and grabbed her pants, struggling into them as Lui-Pang vaulted into his saddle. "Don't leave me here like this!" she shrieked, and it was the scream of a *shizi*.

Lui-Pang jerked hard on the reins, and galloped away.

Kati pulled on her pants, found the shirt. "DON'T LEAVE ME HERE!" she screamed.

Her own horse reared when she ran to it. Its eyes rolled white and wild with fear. She grabbed the reins tightly in a fist, and growled.

Stay still! Don't you even MOVE!

The horse was stunned and looked at her dumbly, legs quivering. She dropped the reins long enough to pull on her shirt and boots, then leaped into the saddle. The animal just stood there. She leaned over his neck, and growled again. "Run, or I'll tear out your *throat*!"

The horse leaped, nearly throwing her, and she got a claw into his mane, muscles on her forearm thick and veined. "Yiiii!" she screamed, and the animal ran as if a *shizi* were on its back.

Lui-Pang was nearly out of sight, riding like the wind, but she drove her animal hard up the grassy slopes to the flats, and then to the road. She approached the dome's gate at a full gallop, riding with fury, her eyes filled with tears, but clear enough to see guards blocking the entrance, rifles raised. She didn't care, and charged at them, without thought of danger.

"Don't *shoot*! It's *Mengnu*! Let her *pass*!"

It was Master Yung, running towards the gate from the troopers' barracks, waving his arms.

She charged past the astonished guards, leaping from the saddle, but her horse kept right on running. Yung grabbed her as she started to fall, and she carried him several paces before he stopped her. "Lui-Pang! Where are you?" she shrieked, struggling against Yung's hold on her.

"*Stop* it!" cried Yung. "He's gone—back to the barracks. He came by here like a demon was chasing him, and now I see why. What has he *done* to you?"

"Lui-Pang!" she cried pitifully.

"Back to the palace! We'll get to the bottom of this!"

Yung pulled her away from the gate, the guards looking at her with wide eyes and stepping back as she passed them. Yung's arm was tight around her shoulders, and now she was crying, deep racking sobs and moans. He got her to the monorail station, where three people waiting on benches leaped up and shied away from her. When the car came, six people got out, and a woman gasped when she saw Kati. Nobody got on the car with them, and Yung hugged her to him all the way up the steep slope as she cried.

It was no better at the top; groups of startled people, a child clinging to its mother's legs, all with eyes wide and staring, full of fear at the sight of her. Yung hustled her up stairs, and an elevator, twice shouting at guards who might have shot her, and then they were in the hallway leading to her rooms and Huomeng was standing there, knocking on her door. When she saw him she moaned, and covered her face with her hands.

"What happened?" he asked. "Kati, what's wrong?"

She broke from Yung's grasp, pushed Huomeng aside, and slammed the door behind her, locking it.

"Kati!"

"Go *away*! Leave me *alone*!"

She ran to her bedroom and looked into the mirror to see what she knew would be there. Tears streaked her face, and her eyes were two, red suns. Her lips were curled back in a snarl, and canine teeth curved down to her lower lip. She was a monster, a demon. She was a Changeling.

Kati breathed deeply, but her face did not change. She clawed at her face with her fingers, drawing blood. "It won't go away! IT WON'T GO AWAY!" she shrieked.

There was a rattling at her door, and then it opened. Tanchun peered inside, then jumped back. Huomeng came inside, followed by Master Yung—and Weimeng.

Kati screamed, "I said stay *away* from me!"

Weimeng cried out in horror, covered her face with her hands and bolted from the room.

"I'll handle this," said Huomeng. "Thank you for bringing her here."

Master Yung nodded silently, and left. Huomeng closed the door, and locked it again, then turned towards her.

Kati's hands covered her face. "Don't come near me," she said.

Huomeng ignored her command. He walked slowly towards her, his eyes narrowed to slits, and it was anger she saw there, not fear. "What did Lui-Pang do to you? *Tell* me! I'll probe you in your *sleep* if you don't!"

"*Nothing*! Don't you *dare* do anything to hurt him!"

"Nothing? Lui-Pang returns as if riding for his life, and you come back hysterical, and you tell me *nothing* happened between you two? Do you think I'm stupid?"

"No."

He was a step away from her, coming within reach. "Put down your hands. I want to see you."

"NO!" She took a step backwards, but it was too late. His hands were on her shoulders, and his face was close.

"Take your hands away, Kati. I want to see the Tumatsin woman you've become."

No fear, yet he was close enough for his throat to be torn out with one bite. She let her hands move aside, and closed her eyes, tears gushing. Her voice trembled. "There. Are you satisfied?"

His hand touched her chin, tilting her head up, his other hand still on her shoulder. "I've never seen the Changeling form, but Mengmoshu has described it to me. He was quite accurate, I must say." His fingers traced her cheek, passed over the point of a tooth, then across the curled upper lip while she kept her eyes tightly closed.

She was shocked when he took her in his arms, and held her close, her mouth up against his neck as he murmured.

"This is long overdue. We'd begun to wonder if it would *ever* happen. Judging by your reaction, I think you've been suppressing it. Is it because of Lui-Pang? What he might think of you? Tell me, Kati. Tell me what happened today. If it's too painful for words, then *show* me. I want to help."

His embrace was tight, and warm. Her arms had been stiffly at her sides, but now they moved around his waist, her sobs muffled by his neck and shoulder. She moaned, and opened herself to him, and showed him everything that had happened on the knoll that day.

Huomeng only held her more tightly. "Do you love him?"

"I don't know. I thought I did, but it makes no difference now. I've lost him. He'll have nothing to do with a Changeling. I'm unclean to him."

"That doesn't *make* you unclean. Kati, look at me. Open your eyes."

He held her at arm's length as she opened her eyes. He was smiling, and his eyes weren't the angry slits of moments before. "Kati, you're beautiful as you are. Look at yourself again, without the fury, without the anger."

He turned her around to face the mirror, and stood behind her, his arms encircling her chest beneath the breasts. She saw her eyes were amber now, the lips no longer curled back to expose the gums, but the canines were still there, protruding slightly over the lower lip when she closed her mouth.

"I see a monster," she said, leaning her head back against him.

Huomeng laughed. "Look again. You've seen that face before. You've described it to me many times, how serene and beautiful you thought it was, with the long, flowing robe and emerald eyes guiding you to places I can only imagine."

"Mandughai's image?" She looked harder. The face *was*

familiar, but here it was streaked with tears, and the hair was a tousled mess.

"Yes. She shows you Her vision of a beautiful Empress. It's *your* face, Kati. That's the way She sees you, not as Mengnu, the ward of the palace, but as yourself, a Tumatsin woman."

"An Empress?" She put her hands over his, on her chest.

"Over yourself, and the hearts of others," he said, then squeezed her gently. "Kati, I'm sorry about your loss of a love. I know the feeling, and it will pass in time. Slowly, but it passes, even when the hurt is deep."

"You haven't experienced it," she said, looking at him in the mirror.

He smiled wanly. "Oh, yes I have, quite recently. While you were gone—at Weimeng's party—Sheyue met someone, one of the noble's sons. She says she's in love. Hasn't she said anything to you?"

"No! Not a word!"

"Well—it's finished. I suppose you knew about us."

"Yes. I wondered what you had to talk about." Kati watched her face. The tips of the canines were slowly drawing back inside her mouth.

"There was little talk, and I also wondered about you and Lui-Pang on all those long rides. Something has ended for both of us."

Kati twisted around in his arms, and hugged him. "I'm sorry, Huomeng. My hurt is so awful, I didn't even feel yours."

"Your masking is as good as mine, and we haven't shared such things before. I feel better just telling it to you."

"I do, too." She hugged him harder.

"Let's skip the exercise today. You need to relax."

"No! I don't want to! The work will take my mind away from what's happened, even for a little while."

"You're sure?"

"Yes, but first I want to take a bath."

He released her, then, and waited a long time while she bathed and put up her hair. There was little time left for their discussion on economic reform, or the arguments to be used with the nobles, but there would be other times. This time, his tone of voice was not so argumentative, but more encouraging, and he looked at her more often now when she was making a point. By the end of the session, she realized that something had changed between them. They were no longer teacher and student, perhaps because they had shared a deep, personal pain with each other. Or was it that they had touched each other physically in a wonderfully comforting way?

She was back to normal when Weimeng rapped tearfully on her door to apologize for fleeing the room: She'd never seen a Changeling face before.

"I still think of you as my own child, my Mengnu, and the sight of you that way reminded me you're a gift from First Mother, a gift brought to me from another people. I love you with all my heart. Can you forgive me for fleeing from you?"

Kati embraced her. "I can forgive my mother for anything," she said, and there were more tears.

Weimeng insisted they have a meal together in her suite, and they talked about the events of the day, from her first transformation during sword drill to the second on the knoll with Lui-Pang. Kati gave her every detail, including the pleasure she'd felt until that last, horrible moment.

Weimeng listened with fascination, then suddenly giggled like a little girl. "He must have been very surprised," she said. "Some women I know would like to see the same reaction from their husbands."

The image of Lui-Pang leaping up from her in terror was suddenly comical, and even Kati had to laugh.

"There will be many men to pursue you," said Weimeng, "and they will be from good families."

They will flee from me as well.

"The Moshuguang assures me you'll be free to attend my next party. Sheyue met a wonderful young man at the one you missed, and now she's walking around in a dream."

"So I hear from Huomeng, who was seeing her until recently."

Weimeng looked surprised. "Really? I would think he'd be interested in a girl with more intellect than beauty."

"That was his error," said Kati, "and mine as well."

"You need a man with gentle breeding, not the son of a trooper. There will be many to choose from. You'll see, Mengnu. Men will be standing in line to meet you."

Not after what happened today, thought Kati.

As she left Weimeng's suite, Kati saw Sheyue coming down the hallway, serene and lovely as usual. Sheyue frowned at her when she came close, and touched Kati's face.

"Mengnu! You've cut yourself!" she said, alarmed.

"Sword practice," said Kati. "I hear that you have a new love. You didn't tell me about him, Sheyue."

Sheyue lowered her eyelashes coyly. "I was going to when we had more time. Oh, Mengnu, I'm truly in love for the first time! My heart is aching!" She clasped both hands over her heart, and sighed.

Kati glared at her. "It's unfortunate that someone as beautiful as you is also so silly and foolish," she said.

Sheyue gasped as Kati walked away from her. "Mengnu! What is wrong? Mengnu!"

Kati slammed the door behind her and smiled, feeling pleased with herself. She got ready for bed, and her mind replayed the day in the quiet of the room. She was sad again, but there were no tears this time.

Mengmoshu! Are you there? He was the only person important in her life who hadn't arrived to comfort her, and she wondered why.

No answer. She fell on the bed, exhausted, and closed her eyes. The purple cloud rushed towards her with no conscious effort on her part, and she was in the gong-shi-jie.

Mandughai was not there.

Mandughai, I cannot do anything tonight. This has been the most horrible day of my life.

Silence. She was alone in the purple light, the auras of planets and stars scattered before her. *Mandughai?*

The auras and shimmering purple were somehow comforting. She felt at home in this place of creation beyond real space. It was her place, too, and the purple light was at her command when she wanted it. She felt no fear, and moved through it to a green vortex, letting herself drop into it near its center—

And coming out into real space well above the boiling surface of Tengri-Nayon. *Mandughai? Can you hear me? This is the first time I've come and you haven't been waiting. Are you here?*

The star spewed flame and dust at her. She extended her aura out several kilometers, watched hot gas flow around it, cupped a piece of it tightly for a moment and watched it swirl in her grasp before releasing it like a child playing with a toy. And then she found the green tip of the vortex, the flash, and she was surrounded by swirls of purple light.

Mandughai was waiting for her.

That was good. You only needed to see you can do it by yourself, even in your sorrow.

Kati was thrilled to see Her, and the image she saw was now quite familiar. Mandughai smiled.

You recognize me?

Yes. I'm looking at myself as a woman.

A beautiful woman, Kati. Your transition is complete, and the lessons are over.

Today was terrible, and you didn't come to me!

There was no need, Kati. You were surrounded by people who love you, who accept you as you are. Today was difficult, but the days ahead will be even more so. These people will help you find your way. It's time for you to take your place on Shanji, and the day is coming when you'll see me as an adversary, even an enemy. When that day comes, I ask you to remember that I love you, and that everything I do has a purpose.

They drifted together towards the purple vortex that was Kati. Mandughai was so beautiful, yet serious-looking now. How could Kati think of her as an enemy?

Am I doing what you want, Mandughai? Have I served you?

In every way, child. And you will do much more. Look at me again, and tell me what you see.

I see myself. The vortex was tugging, pulling her back to herself.

No, Kati. You see an Empress—

And she was back on her bed, eyes closed.

An Empress?

Sleep overtook her before she could pursue the thought further.

But she remembered it in the morning.

CHAPTER THIRTEEN
EMPRESS

Mengmoshu and Mengyao arrived at the throne room near midnight, both wondering why they'd been called at such a late hour. The Son of Heaven sat alone, slouching on the throne, and his face was jaundiced by the progression of his disease. He beckoned them to come forward, and cleared his throat with a deep, rattling sound before he spoke.

"I know the hour is late, so I won't keep you long. I have some concerns to share with you."

"What is it, Son of Heaven?" asked Mengmoshu. He probed the Emperor's mind, but saw nothing.

"I will tell you in words, if you don't mind. My many hours with Juimoshu have taught me how to conceal what I think around her."

The tone of voice was angry, and hostile.

"Some find it easier to communicate without words, and it's late. I was only trying to help you, My Emperor."

Wang-shan-shi-jie chuckled. "Indeed. I have some concerns, Chancellor. Perhaps you can ease my mind."

"I'm here, Son of Heaven, at your service."

"Good. I will begin with rumors I hear about a resurgence of religion in Wanchou. The people say there has been a visitation by First Mother, and have built a shrine to Her. Everyone is talking about Her return, saying

She will heal the sick, and prevent death. What do you know about this?"

"I've heard nothing. First Mother would tell me if She did such a thing, and She hasn't—"

"Please do not preach mythology to me, Chancellor. I'm *not* a believer, nor is any sane, educated person outside of the Moshuguang. I allow you your beliefs as long as they don't interfere with what you do for me, and so far I've been satisfied with that decision. In some way, your beliefs have now spread to the people. They shirk their work to build a shrine to a mythical goddess, and I will not have it!"

"The people have always believed, from the beginning of time. I've heard many reports of shrines in the countryside, even when I was an apprentice."

"But *not* in Wanchou! Someone claiming to be First Mother has visited them, and caused this turmoil. Who *is* it?"

He's furious, and very frightened, Mengmoshu. This is dangerous.

"How can I know? The Moshuguang has no business in Wanchou. Perhaps it's a charlatan within the city. Where have you heard such rumors?"

The Emperor leaned forward, and glared at them. "My sources are reliable. I've sent troopers to Wanchou! They have found, *and* destroyed, a shrine placed along the road leading east from the city! A flyer had to be brought in when a mob threw stones at them! People have been *killed*!"

"I would not have advised such harsh action, Son of Heaven. You must be seen as protector of the people, not their enemy. They devote their lives to your service."

"They will know who rules their lives, and that is enough!"

"But your anger should be directed against the woman who pretends to be First Mother! She has committed *blasphemy*!" shouted Mengmoshu.

The outburst startled the Emperor, and seemed to soften him.

"We will find her. A search is underway, and the people are being questioned."

They say nothing, or haven't been questioned. He couldn't hide that, Mengmoshu, but he knows a trooper was with her. Nothing about Jin-yao. A spy in the factory zone?

I think so. They had never seen a trooper or Moshuguang there before. It has to be a plant manager, who later went into Wanchou and saw the shrine.

"You will require our service in the questioning, Son of Heaven. My people are at your disposal right away, and Mengyao here is my best."

"I would be most honored to aid in capturing a person who blasphemes our First Mother, Son of Heaven," said Mengyao, bowing.

The Emperor leaned back, tapping his fingers thoughtfully on the arm-rests of the throne. "Yes, that could be useful. The people do not know the Moshuguang, and should be transparent to you. Very well, I will honor your request. I'll make arrangements for you to join the interrogation team by tomorrow morning. Please be ready by then."

It'll be the first interrogation team going out! What luck!

He's heard the news from one of the nobles. They will go first to the source of the report.

He won't know his own name when I'm finished with him!

"You said there were other concerns, My Emperor?" asked Mengmoshu.

"A secondary thing, but a concern. It's about the training of Mengnu. Isn't it complete yet? Juimoshu seems to be failing with age; I've recently noticed her dozing during important discussions in court. When will Mengnu be ready to take her place?"

"Two years, or less. Her abilities continue to grow. I remind you that Juimoshu didn't do her best work until she was well into her twenties. It will be sooner with Mengnu. She's an outstanding talent."

The Emperor nodded sagely. "So I was correct in sparing her life. She's certainly a lovely girl, and I'm gratified by the happiness she's brought to Weimeng. My son talks often about her as a friend. Her encouragement has changed his whole attitude about the duties he must assume when I'm gone."

"You will live many years, Son of Heaven."

The Emperor chuckled, leaned back tiredly on the throne. "I think not, Mengmoshu. I'm much older than you. Tell me, why all the military training for Mengnu, when you wish to train her mind?"

"She is Tumatsin, and a Changeling, and the mental training drains her young body. She needs much physical exercise, My Emperor. It keeps her healthy, and focused."

"That's all? She fights as well, and as fiercely as the best in her class. She is a warrior in the old tradition, Mengmoshu."

"Mengnu excels in all that she does, Son of Heaven. She is exceptional."

The Emperor looked exhausted, and his eyelids were heavy. "Did you know that Shan-lan has won two prizes from Master Yung?"

"Yes. Mengnu has told me he has the respect of all the students in his class. You must be proud of him," said Mengmoshu.

"I am," said the Emperor. "Shan-lan is the future of Shanji, and I am the past. I'll rest easily, knowing that he's here." Eyes closed, he patted the arm rests of the throne with his hands, and sighed. "If only he could have come from Weimeng. . . . Well, that is past."

His eyes opened, and he waved a hand in dismissal. "You may go now, I have nothing more."

Mengmoshu and Mengyao bowed and backed out of the room. As the door closed, the Son of Heaven remained slouched on the throne, staring at something far away.

"How long can he last?" asked Mengyao.

"Long enough to see the armies of First Mother," said Mengmoshu.

They discussed Mengyao's new assignment, and it was early morning before they finally slept.

Mengmoshu was apprehensive about the meeting, and resentful about discussing things First Mother could have dealt with during her time with Kati. The Emerald Empress's logic was simple. Kati revered Her as she would a goddess, a super-being. He was a man, and Kati would not fear arguing with him. But would she believe what he said?

He intended to begin the conversation lightly, but even that got a bit out of hand.

Kati arrived on-time, dressed in white uniform. She was no longer a child, but a woman. She'd grown into her face: oval, with prominent cheekbones, and the highly arched nose, the first, faint network of veins on her forehead feeding the neural network making her Moshuguang and much more. Her eyes were green when she saw him and smiled. She sat down in a chair, and crossed her legs.

"How are you?" he asked.

"I'm fine," she said. "Lui-Pang finally had the nerve to look at me in class yesterday, and I smiled back. I think we can at least be friends."

"He's lucky to *be* in the class," said Mengmoshu.

Kati laughed. "You were so *angry*, like a father whose little girl has been violated. I'm not a little girl anymore, Mengmoshu. I knew what I was doing, and I learned from it."

She said it with a smile, but there was a hardness around her eyes that hadn't been there two months before.

"And what did you learn?"

"I learned never to allow someone to make me feel bad about myself, or to think I'm something other than I am."

"I hear Huomeng talking," said Mengmoshu.

"We've discussed it quite a bit. He *is* a friend, you know."

Mengmoshu leaned back in his chair. "I only wish I could have been there when you were so distraught."

"You can't always be there for me, but it's nice that you want to."

Always the probing, but his mask was firm. It was a game between them, and her eyes were twinkling with amusement while they played it.

"Mengmoshu, you didn't call me here to talk about my sexual discoveries. What is it?"

Mengmoshu steepled his hands before his face.

"Oh, this looks serious," Kati said.

"First Mother has asked me to tell you some things before we visit your people. There's some history you need to know, so you can understand why First Mother brings an invading force against Tumatsin as well as the Emperor."

Mengmoshu held his breath, amazed at his own directness.

"What?" said Kati, and her eyes went from green to red in an instant. She uncrossed her legs, and leaned forward in her chair.

"Tengri-Nayon is nearing closest approach. First Mother will soon return to Shanji, and She brings a fighting force with Her. She comes as an invader, Kati, a foreign threat to Shanji."

"Against the Emperor, as in ancient times," said Kati, her stare intense.

"No. She also moves against the Tumatsin, and you need to understand why."

Kati sat back, and steepled her own hands, imitating him. "She *did* say I might see Her as an enemy, and that Her return would not be a joyous thing for the people. I remember that. She talks around things like you do, Mengmoshu. Why is She doing this? What you say makes no *sense* to me."

"She also told you the people must be united, and they are not. First Mother feels they can be brought together to meet a foreign attack."

"Foreign? My people have been waiting two thousand years for Mandughai to return and destroy the Emperor! They don't see Her as a foreigner! She is *Mandughai*, the mother of us all! How can she bring herself to move against people who've prayed for Her return for *two thousand years*!"

Thank you, First Mother, for this cheerful task.

"I heard that!"

"Good! Now hear *this*! The divisions between our people are extreme. The Emperors, through the years, have seen to that. Your knowledge now, Kati, includes every relevant factor; ask yourself if you, or anyone else, could unite the people through negotiation with the present ruling system."

"Of course not. The Emperor wouldn't allow it."

"Then replace him. Would the Tumatsin follow a more benevolent Emperor?"

"No. They want the Emperor destroyed."

"And the nobles with him?"

"I suppose. What are you *getting* at, Mengmoshu? You're talking around things again."

"Will you agree that the people who actually decide things on Shanji are the nobles?"

"*And* the Moshuguang, yes. The Emperor barely knows what goes on around him. A good Emperor would interact with the people, and correct the problems he sees."

"Working with the nobles."

"Yes. The Tumatsin don't realize it, and I don't like it, but I've come to see that one person can't do what needs to be done. Get *on* with it, Mengmoshu. You're confusing me."

"In the very beginning, at first planetfall, there *were* no nobles. There was only the male Emperor, self-proclaimed, and his family, and hard-working people who sought a new life among Tengri-Khan's planets—on Shanji. They fled from the system of Tengri-Nayon, where they lived in cities floating in the atmosphere of a great, gaseous planet.

"Ordinarily, the ship would not have been able to reach as far as Tengri-Khan within the lifetimes of those aboard. But the two stars were unusually near each other . . . as they will be again, very soon. They fled to escape the harsh rule of an Empress who lived on an inner world, close to a violent sun. Life on *that* planet was extremely severe. The people there had to be bioengineered to adapt to it. Their Empress ruled all Her planets with an iron fist. She was Mandughai."

Kati was struck dumb. She stared at him in shock, and he pressed his advantage before she could shout at him.

"Mandughai pursued the escapees with an army in another ship. She was old, and half-crazy, and She wanted death for all the people who'd fled Her. She thought our people would feel safe from Her, and be caught by surprise, but they weren't. Our ship orbiting us had been armed and was manned when She arrived with only a ground force."

"She honored the traditionalist ways!" said Kati.

Mengmoshu nodded. "In some ways, perhaps. She thought there was no danger from the air. Our ship was supposedly abandoned or at least unarmed; the rebels, in Her view, were incompetent malcontents. Her target was little more than a fledgling settlement on an unoccupied world."

Angry-voiced, Kati said: "Our people had been put out of the city because of a mixture of blood! She came to destroy the Emperor because of it!"

"There *was* no city, or mixture of blood, before Mandughai came. They had only been down on this world a short time—industries were just getting started. Oh, there was something they called a palace—a wooden structure—and a few other buildings, but certainly no dome, and the people who'd done well by their own initiative and intelligence lived in wooden cottages where the barley fields are.

"They felt her full wrath. She landed her forces on the plateau beyond Three Peaks, and was on them before people could react sufficiently to protect themselves. Her soldiers murdered—and raped—in the valley, fierce men with the fangs of a *shizi*; bio-engineered, remember. They had already set fire to the palace, and were only a hundred meters from over-running everything when our orbiting ship came over and shot them to pieces with laser weapons. The few survivors fled to their landers, and back to their home planet. Our ship was not in a position to destroy those remnants, but it seemed to hardly matter . . . not for many, many generations."

Kati's eyes were red and moist. "You're telling me that everything I was taught as a child is a *lie*! How can you tell me such a thing, and pretend to care about me?" She twisted her hands together in her lap, and the hurt look on her face made him ache inside.

"Part truth, part errors that grew in the telling. When the children of Mandughai's soldiers began to appear, there was outrage and, yes, an ethnic cleansing by the Emperor. He was supported by the bulk of the people. They would not allow the mixed blood of those soldiers to remain among them. The families with children of mixed blood faced death or banishment, and they chose the latter. They fled to the mountains, a new race of people. They are your ancestors, Kati."

Kati's eyes narrowed in anger. "I've been told by you, Huomeng and even Mandughai that my people came from one of Her sons. Someone is lying to me."

Mengmoshu's face flushed. "Yes; that last thing I said was incomplete. The children of Mandughai's soldiers were the *precursors* of your Tumatsin people. The true Tumatsin lineage began two generations after that, when the star systems again approached each other and Her grand-daughter sent two sons to us. The idea was to incorporate Her genetic line to produce someone like Her, or beyond Her. She wasn't the same woman who led the attack, Kati. Mandughai is a *title*, not a person's name. There have been thirty-five Mandughais in our history, and I don't know the true name of even one of them. They were just women, though extraordinary, and though you still think of Her as a *God!*"

Her probing was always there, and he allowed her one peek behind the mask. It was enough.

"You really believe this," she said.

"First Mother—this Mandughai—will verify it if you ask Her. She is a far different person from Her distant predecessor."

"You can be sure that I will. She could have told me in the first place. Why instead is it you?"

"Because she's a woman, Kati, not a goddess, and She knows you still don't accept that. She's a woman dealing with a historic tragedy, and a confrontation She sees as inevitable. Lives will be lost, and one of them could be yours. The Tumatsin must be joined with us if Shanji is to move ahead after the Emperor is gone. She doesn't think they'll do that without having to meet a threat by foreigners they now see as saviors. She will deliberately take the part of villain in order to unite our people and pave the way for a new ruler. The person who must bring us together with the Tumatsin is you, Kati. You're one of them."

"So I can talk to them. If Mandughai brings a new ruler my people can trust, there shouldn't be need for a war with anyone except the Emperor. And I still don't see why my people are so important in all of this."

He followed the unmasked churning of her thoughts, and knew she was approaching an important truth about her life. "The nobles are all related to the Emperor. Like him, through the generations they have grown soft, and stagnant. Your Tumatsin people are practical and intelligent. All their lives, they've known hardship. Everything they have, they've had to work for. They've had to develop a strict moral code and depend on each other. They have few comforting illusions. They will relate to all the people, and work for reforms if given the power to do so. Their leadership must be mixed with that of the nobles if there's to be any progress on Shanji."

"They hate the very idea of an Emperor," said Kati.

"They will not hate the one who replaces him." Mengmoshu's eyes were locked on hers, and they sat silently for a long moment.

Kati looked at him from behind her steepled hands, and sighed. "You want me to be the Empress of Shanji."

"Yes."

"Mandughai said as much."

"It's Her decision, Kati, and the Moshuguang supports it. We're doing all we can to prepare you for the responsibility."

"My first one is to recruit my people to fight a war for the Emperor, a war I don't see as necessary. Mandughai has chosen me as Her enemy."

"No! The invasion is a trial, and dangerous, but the main purpose is to rid the Tumatsin of their myths about an Empress they take as a goddess. The fact is that She was a woman who was considered evil in the history of

Her own people on Tengri-Nayon. The invasion is to bring us back together again. If we oppose Her, She will withdraw."

"And if we don't?"

Mengmoshu took a deep breath, and said, "She will kill everyone west of the mountain, and start all over again. Those are Her words."

"So you and I are both Her enemies in this?" Kati seemed calm, her eyes amber in thought. He sensed no anger in her, and thought it strange.

"We *will* oppose Her, you and I. We have our own fighting force in the Moshuguang, and we can certainly count on the Emperor to oppose Her. The important thing is to bring the Tumatsin into it. Her forces will attack *ordus* to encourage their participation, but your people must also fight to protect the rest of us. That is your task, Kati. It begins when we visit your people."

"So I'm supposed to tell my people I'll be Empress, and everything will be wonderful for them, but first they must help me fight the woman they've prayed to for centuries, fight to prevent the thing they've prayed for. She comes to place me on the throne, but first I have to fight Her. Listen to yourself, Mengmoshu! There's no logic in what you say. It makes no sense to me; it will make no sense to my people." *Now what are you leaving out?*

Mengmoshu sighed. "All right, there are other circumstances, other forces behind First Mother's decision. She will have to tell you these things. I cannot. But the decision has been made. A war must be fought to save Shanji from destruction, and we need the Tumatsin with us to fight it."

Kati's eyes were glowing rubies, her voice deep as a growl. "I'll talk to Her very soon. If you won't tell me everything, She will."

"Perhaps," said Mengmoshu, "perhaps not. Her agendum is much larger than yours, Kati. She has more than one world to rule, and many difficult people to deal with. You could be facing the same problems someday."

"If I live to be Empress, that is. I'm not Mandughai; I'll not sit idly on horseback and watch my people fight a war."

"We'll talk about that another time," said Mengmoshu. His daughter's eyes had changed color again, and now glinted like polished amber.

"It won't change anything," she said, then, "If I assume we're really going to fight this war, how much time do you think we have to prepare for it?"

She seemed strangely calm, now, but coldly so. No emotions were there, only a terrible hardness around her eyes.

"No more than three years. We'll have plenty of warning. She will not surprise us. I'm taking you to the coast in a few weeks. Your work will begin there."

"Let's talk about that," said Kati. She was breathing deeply, trying to calm herself. "Will you tell them I'm to be Empress?"

"They will hear it indirectly before our visit, but they must see it from your own actions, Kati. Does the idea of being Empress seem overwhelming to you?"

Kati shook her head slowly. "I think I've known it for some time without admitting it to myself, especially since our visit to Wanchou. Mandughai told me I must apply my powers, and now I know what She meant."

What she said bothered Mengmoshu deeply, and her mind was totally masked from him. She seemed to sense his concern, and quickly said, "I *don't* see myself as a figure on a throne, Mengmoshu. Huomeng and I have a good plan for reform, and we believe in it. I see the role of Empress as an overseer, working in a cooperative way with the people. If I'm to be Empress, the system will be changed. Will the Moshuguang support that kind of change?"

Mengmoshu relaxed a bit, and chuckled. He had just told her, and already she was assuming the role. "We'll support any change that will move Shanji ahead," he said.

"Good," said Kati. "May I tell Huomeng about what I'm to be?"

Now Mengmoshu smiled. "He's known about it for several days. First Mother wasn't certain Herself until recently. Will you meet with Her soon?"

"This evening. I'll wait until I'm not so angry as I am now."

"She works with you, Kati, to help Her people. She's not your enemy."

"Mandughai brings Her forces against us. That makes Her my enemy."

Her eyes were very hard, now, and it worried him.

"I will talk to Her," Kati added. "I need to see Shan-lan, now. After this talk, I'm in a terrible mood for it, but it must be done anyway."

"Shan-lan? What do you have to say to him?"

"Certainly nothing about *this* conversation. He's been sending me poems, declaring his love for me. I have to make him understand we're only friends, but without hurting him, and now my mood is bad."

"You can delay the meeting."

"No, it must be done now. My head is swirling, Mengmoshu, but I'll talk to Huomeng. He always helps me sort things out, and then I'll see Mandughai again."

She stood up, and frowned. "I'm sorry you had to tell me these things."

"I've had more difficult tasks," he said. But not many.

His daughter turned and marched out of the room without another word. Mengmoshu buried his face in his hands. *First Mother, please forgive my stumbling way with words. I fear I've made a shambles of this.*

✦   ✦   ✦

Shan-lan tried hard to focus on his painting of the three peaks, but his mind wouldn't obey. Mengnu's face had been so solemn when she'd asked him to meet with her, and now he was filled with apprehension.

He sat on the outer porch of the second level in Stork's Nest, facing west. His pens and brushes were arranged neatly on the little table he'd brought from inside the tower, and he sat on a bench, hunched over the nearly completed painting. It showed a young couple, backs turned, holding hands, and facing west towards the wall with Three Peaks beyond. He'd left a space for a new poem for her, not yet composed.

He didn't even know she was there until she called out from behind him."

"Shan-lan! Are you here?"

"Outside!"

He smelled her fragrance when she came up behind him to look down over his shoulder. "It's beautiful," she said. "Peaceful."

"The way I feel when I'm with you," he said softly.

She sat down on the bench, dressed in her white uniform, and leaned warmly against him to look closer at the painting. "Is that us standing there?"

"Yes."

"Two friends, looking at the mountains," she murmured.

"They are much more than that to each other," he said. "They are lovers." His heart had begun pounding as he said it.

Mengnu said nothing, but put an arm through his, and rested her head on his shoulder. His heart was now aching, not from physical desire, but just from her presence so close to him.

"Yes, I see that, but it's a love between two friends who care deeply about each other, and are sharing a private moment. It's like the moment we share now, Shan-lan. I love you as a friend."

clenched his teeth so
...lings for you are much

...I know. I see it in your
...ve given to me. I treasure
...them forever."

...cause his hand was shaking,
...Mengnu squeezed his arm even harder.

"What can I say to my heart?" he said, his voice breaking
...ke shattered glass.

"Tell it you're the only man I love, Shan-lan. Tell it I
care about you as I would for the brother I've lost, and
that I would die for you if it were necessary. Tell it that,
Shan-lan."

Tears filled his eyes. "I would also die for you, Mengnu,"
he croaked.

She reached over, and wiped a tear from his face, then
kissed him softly on the cheek. "I love you," she said.

And then she walked away from him.

*I'm grateful for you waiting to come here until your
anger was softened.* Mandughai's voice was calm. She
had confirmed Mengmoshu's story. *You listened to
everything I said without once shouting at me.*

Kati cried: *But I need to know what other forces are
behind your decision to bring war to people who love
and revere you!*

They looked out at blackness beyond the edge of a
dust cloud at the rim of their universe. Each point of
light glimmering faintly out there was another universe
like their own, and now Kati wondered if she and
Mandughai would ever journey there together.

*I have reasons for not telling you everything now.
My hope is still for a limited war, perhaps even a show
of force, but there are those around me who have
different plans for Shanji on this pass, and they are*

people of influence and politics. T
only understand power. You must s
Kati, and use it if necessary. You
destroy my armies, and even me

Mandughai! I cannot!

You must do it. There could be r
In the time remaining for us t
creation I want you to think on a grander
you move energy. You can destroy a planet or a star if
you will it.

I don't want to kill, Mandughai. I just want to help
my people.

I know. Your powers are tempered by a great compassion
I'm also grateful for. But in war, there is no compassion
when the killing starts. You must be strong. Kati? KATI!
There's more we must talk about! DON'T LEAVE ME
NOW!

Kati opened her eyes, saw the candles flickering on
her shrine and remembered the sorrowful look on
Mandughai's face the instant before she'd left her behind
in the gong-shi-jie. She stood up, looked in her mirror,
and again saw the face of the Emerald Empress.

She was crying.

Kati, but she's difficult and has influence with my military people.

I've deliberately kept her from you to avoid any conflicts of personalities. She can be harsh and abrasive, and is jealous of the training I've given you. I do not trust her to move freely in the gong-shi-jie, and have only guided her here a few times. In many ways, she's different from you, and I think it's best that you first meet her on the field of battle. Her powers are less than mine, and she cannot move mass or energy. Your abilities concern her, Kati, because soon after you're Empress you will be dealing with her, not me. My reign is coming to an end, and the two of you must work together for the good of our people.

First we must fight each other. It seems a poor way to begin. Kati drifted closer to her own image. At least I now see who my true enemy is. It is your daughter.

No! I am Mandughai, and I am Empress here, not my daughter. We disagree only on the agenda for Shanji and the scale of the war, and you must be prepared for the very worst! Tumatsin and Hansui must come together against us if they're to survive my daughter's plans. But I am also involved. I still see no other way to persuade the Tumatsin they must not separate themselves from the rest of the people by believing in myths. A foreign threat by me is the only way. Do not hesitate to threaten them with my coming, Kati. Do not use my daughter to excuse my actions. This is important. I don't think they'll believe you, anyway. Their belief will come when the first ordus burn. They will fight to protect themselves, but it's your task to make them fight for all of Shanji. Lead them, Kati. Lead them as Empress!

I will do my best, but it's like fighting a war with my own mother, Mandughai. I feel badly about this.

So do I. I would feel blessed if you were my own daughter. We must come together as Mandughai, a foreign

Empress, and Mengnu, the future Empress of Shanji. If we survive, you will know my true name, and that of my daughter. It's now time for us to be apart. I'll miss you, Kati. This must be our last meeting before I come to Shanji.

Mandughai! You said you'd always be with me!

The time will pass quickly, but it's necessary for us to distance ourselves from each other before the conflict. We are much too close to each other to do what will be necessary.

But what about our work here, in the place of creation?

It will wait. You're ready to work on your own, and I encourage you to do it, but your focus should now be on Shanji. Get your people ready, Kati. You'll be warned again about my coming — and it will be soon. Goodbye until then, dear. I love you.

The tearful image of Mandughai drifted away from her to the green vortex that was Tengri-Nayon. A flash, and She was gone, and Kati was alone in the gong-shi-jie. It wasn't sudden fear that she felt in this familiar place, but a terrible sense of loneliness. In the past, Mandughai had always been watching her, even when it seemed She wasn't there, but now She was truly gone.

Her own vortex seemed to be tugging at her, urging her back to the body sitting before the shrine in her room, but she resisted it. This place had become as much hers as Mandughai's. She traveled for a while, but not far, dipping in and out of real space to play with a prominence on Tengri-Nayon, a vortex of cooler material on the surface of Tengri-Khan, grasping, then releasing the hot gases with her aura. The third time in transition, she found herself near the great ship in orbit above Shanji, and resisted the temptation to push on it. Perhaps, one day, Huomeng would be on that ship, and she could help to hurry him along to wherever he wanted to go. Another dream, achievable only if she survived a war.

She gazed down at wispy clouds, the blue of the great sea, the mottled colors of land in the light of Tengri-Khan.

A beautiful world. Her world, and her people were *there*.

Shanji.

CHAPTER FIFTEEN
HOMECOMING

There was no sleep for Kati the night before Mengmoshu came to take her to her people. Her mind would not cease its whirling with fear and apprehension about the trip, and Huomeng's visit, while comforting, had only added to the confusion of her thoughts.

He'd stayed quite late while they talked in her sitting room. He'd pulled up a chair, and they'd sat knee to knee in quiet conversation for nearly two hours when she could have been trying to sleep. They'd talked about the visit, and what she could say to a people she'd been absent from for twelve years. They would surely see her as a Tumatsin; her physical presence was enough for that. There was Da and Baber and many others who had known her as a child, but now she was coming to them after many years as a ward of the Moshuguang, and accompanied by a Searcher. Wouldn't they see her as a spy for the Emperor? She could not hide her own mental probe from them for long and then they would see she was also a Searcher, somehow transformed by those they despised.

"But you *are* Moshuguang, Kati," said Huomeng. "It's a part of your being, and you can't deny it. And while your powers are beyond those of the Tumatsin, you're still one of them. They must see your special gifts as the reason First Mother has chosen you to lead them. You must show them these gifts, Kati, even if they feel threatened by them. And they must know that you care about their welfare."

Huomeng had leaned close and taken her hands in his, startling her. "This will be a difficult time for you. You've waited so long to see your father and brother again, and I wish I could tell you what their reaction will be in seeing you, but I cannot. It might not be pleasant, Kati, and I don't want your expectations for a joyful reunion to be too high. I don't want you to be hurt."

He'd held her hands tightly and looked straight into her eyes, and the feelings coming from him were warm and wonderful, so much so that Kati's thumbs stroked his knuckles in return and they sat for a moment, just looking at each other.

"If there is pain for you, remember who you are," he whispered. "You are to be Empress over all the people, not just the Tumatsin. Your world is much bigger now, and there is loneliness in leadership, a terrible loneliness when difficult things must be done. Your own people might reject you, but still you must lead them if they're to survive. Follow your instincts, and do what an Empress must do. This is the task First Mother has chosen you for, and now it's time to do it."

Kati nodded. "I know."

Huomeng raised her hands to his mouth, and kissed them. "I'll be waiting," he said, and his look was so intense that she felt her cheeks flush. He seemed suddenly embarrassed, releasing her hands and standing up abruptly.

Kati stood up with him, and without a thought put an arm around him to rest her head against his shoulder. She felt his arms go around her, his cheek on top of her head. Suddenly, she wanted him to kiss her, but he did not. They stayed that way for only a moment, and then he gave her a little squeeze and released her, hurrying away, leaving her trembling.

Sleep did not come that night.

Mengmoshu came for her before dawn, and she was waiting for him dressed in her riding leathers, the three precious amulets hanging from her neck, the artifacts of her two worlds that Mandughai had decreed must be made one. Mengmoshu wore the full armor of a trooper and gave her a hooded robe to wear over her leathers. They were the only two passengers in the monorail car driven by a Moshuguang trooper to the flyer field above the palace.

The guard at the gate was also a Searcher, and he led them to a flyer set apart from the others. The field was quiet and all the troopers she saw had the prominent foreheads of the Moshuguang. Not a word was spoken by anyone as they reached the flyer, and Kati saw that Mengyao was its pilot.

The field commander is a friend of the Moshuguang. The Emperor will not hear about our leaving.

Kati had never been in a flyer, and was nervous as she climbed into the open cockpit of the craft and strapped herself in.

Relax. I fly even better than I ride a horse. I didn't drop you on the way to the city, and I won't drop you now.

Where do we go, Mengmoshu?

To the border. We'll take horses from there to the ordu Manlee was last reported to reside in. Since the fences went up, we haven't kept good track of Tumatsin movements, so we might have to search for her. Mengyao will fly cover for us at all times. The Tumatsin have come to think of themselves as an independent nation since the border was established, but they have granted our request for this visit. They are expecting to see the future Empress of Shanji.

You told them that?

I told them the truth. What comes from this visit is up to you.

And they will see their Empress to be a nineteen-year-old girl dressed in riding leathers.

Their future Empress is a Tumatsin. Tighten your lap belt. We're taking off, now.

The flyer jerked upwards as she reached for her belt to pull it tightly across her thighs and chest. Mengyao looked back and grinned at her terror. The craft rose straight up, humming loudly, and she clutched at the belt, heart pounding, eyes fixed at the nape of Mengyao's neck. Above her, the dome glowed dimly and a dark patch suddenly grew there, showing stars beyond. She fixed her eyes on the stars, not daring to look down as they lifted, her stomach sinking.

The square opening in the dome rumbled, already beginning to close as they passed through it. Straight above them was the intensely orange Tengri-Nayon, now the brightest star in the night sky. Less than two years to closest approach, thought Kati, and Mandughai was readying Her army for the coming confrontation. Would the people believe? Believe that the goddess they thought would deliver them from the Emperor came to destroy them as well as him? Suddenly, Kati was filled with doubt about any success of her mission, and in her own abilities to lead a people socially divided by so many centuries of archaic rule.

"You're missing a good view," said Mengmoshu. "Look to your right."

She did so as the craft leveled, and saw the city sprawled up the side of the mountain like a crust of fluorescent crystals, illuminating the dome in a soft blue. Mengyao made a slow turn north before the city, then another turn west, passing over the cliffs and then the plateau, the summits of the three peaks a hundred meters below them. It was too dark to see the little meadow there, the place where Lui-Pang had first kissed her. The plateau glowed in starlight and she thought of her rides on Sushua and the trek to Festival with Da on black Kaidu. The trip of days on horseback rushed beneath her as Mengyao held a steady course westward. Kati began to relax and dared to look over the edge of the open cockpit, pressing her nose to the plastic windshield rising a meter above her head. She saw the rolling hills criss-crossed with trails, then the black gash that was the canyon leading to the Festival area, then more hills. It seemed only minutes before a line of orange lights appeared ahead of them, a long line snaking north to south, and suddenly the whine of the flyer lowered in pitch. They were losing altitude and Kati's stomach was rising again.

As they came close to the ground, Kati saw the wire fence with yellow lights spaced far apart, marking the boundary of Tumatsin lands. They were coming up on a stone building with a thatched roof, and people were there with horses, the area brightly lit by a circle of lights mounted on tall poles. Mengyao slowed the flyer to hover over the area, then settled it slowly to the ground as four troopers armed with laser rifles came forward to meet them. All four were Moshuguang. All four bowed to Kati, then to Mengmoshu and Mengyao as they exited the craft.

"They are waiting by the fence," said one trooper to Mengmoshu. "They've been here for over an hour."

Mengyao remained standing by the flyer, and Mengmoshu motioned Kati ahead of him to follow the troopers. Four guards standing before the stone building came rigidly to attention as Kati passed by them, and ahead was a gate in the fence, beyond it several people on horseback with two riderless horses awaiting them in yellow light. The guards opened the gate and passed through it ahead of them. They stood at attention on both sides of Kati as she came close to the riders and stopped, looking up at them.

There were six men, and one woman.

The woman was Goldani.

Kati smiled, and started to speak, but then Mengmoshu pushed past her and bowed to the riders before gesturing back at her.

"This is Mengnu, the one chosen by First Mother. We thank you for coming to escort us at such an early hour."

Seven Tumatsin faces were unreadable masks, but Kati felt their wary interest in her. Goldani looked her up and down, and said, "We came mainly to satisfy our curiosity, Searcher. She is very young, and we weren't aware that Shanji requires a new leader. Has something happened to the Emperor?"

"No," said Mengmoshu. "He's quite ill, however, and the one you call Mandughai has decided the time has come for major changes in the leadership of Shanji. She will soon return with her armies to enforce these changes and place Mengnu on the throne as Empress."

"Indeed," said Goldani. "Mandughai has not informed me of these developments."

"Perhaps she has spoken to Manlee about it. It's Manlee we wish to visit with first," said Mengmoshu.

Goldani stiffened, still looking at Kati. "Manlee has been dead for nearly two years, and I have been chosen to take her place as intermediary to Mandughai. You all see the truth of my words, including this young woman. I feel her probing my mind."

"I have the abilities of a Searcher," said Kati, "but I'm searching for your memory of a little girl carried away by the Emperor's troopers after the *ordu* with no name was destroyed twelve years ago. I didn't know you were still alive, Goldani. I thought you might have died with my mother."

Goldani seemed to catch her breath, and leaned forward to look at Kati more closely. "I see that you're Tumatsin in appearance. Am I supposed to know you?"

"You rode with my mother in Festival procession when I received my first horse. Her name was Toregene, and she could make her eyes green, Goldani. I am her daughter, Kati, and I've come to see my people again. I've waited many years for this moment."

Goldani's face was still expressionless, but now she dismounted, and walked towards Kati. The guards moved to block her, but Mengmoshu waved them away. The woman stopped within reach, and Kati saw the red of her eyes. Suddenly, her heart was aching, and she felt the sting of tears.

"I've been a ward of the Moshuguang, the Searchers, for twelve years. They always promised me the day would come when I could see my people again, and now it's arrived. You're as I remember you, Goldani. It's good to see a familiar face again."

Goldani put out a hand to finger the necklaces hanging from Kati's neck, her lips pressed tightly together.

"Ma gave me the Eye of Tengri when I went to Festival. The shells came from Edi, a little girl who also received her first horse when I did. The other is from Juimoshu, a woman of the Moshuguang. It is the eye of Mandughai, whom the Moshuguang call First Mother. We are all related to Her, Goldani, both the Tumatsin and the Moshuguang, from two different sons of Her body. She has called me to be Empress of Shanji, and unite all our people. That is why I'm here."

Goldani reached up and touched a tear on Kati's cheek, while the guards nervously shuffled their feet. "I've never seen such green in the eyes of a Tumatsin woman," she said softly.

"The green color comes when I'm happy. I've missed being with my own kind."

Kati grabbed the woman in a hug, felt her stiffen, then relax, one hand resting softly on Kati's back. Kati whispered, "I've missed Da and Baber, and the others in my *ordu*. I don't even know who's alive! Can you take me to them?"

Goldani stiffened again, and held Kati at arm's length. "This will come, but first I must know you better. I see a woman, not a little girl I remember, and your reason for coming here is extraordinary. While we ride, you must tell me everything that has happened to you since the day Toregene was killed."

"You're not certain of me, but you want to believe," said Kati.

"Yes—I want to believe. We have an hour's ride for you to tell me everything."

"Mengmoshu, here, has been my teacher in many things. You'll have questions he can answer."

"Then we'll ride together," said Goldani.

They mounted up, and the three of them rode ahead of the others along a broad trail heading west as the sky began to lighten. The ride went quickly with conversation. Mengmoshu talked about the Moshuguang's discovery of a gifted Tumatsin child, and the near-tragedy of their mission to save that child from death when the Emperor ordered a threatening *ordu* destroyed. He talked about Kati's natural abilities, her training, the intervention of First Mother in pushing those abilities to their limits.

Kati told her about the times with Mandughai in the gong-shi-jie, what she'd learned to do there, and how the Empress of Tengri-Nayon had been like a mother to her. She recited the history of the Tumatsin and the truth of the long line of Empresses, some good, some evil, all known as Mandughai.

Goldani seemed wistful. "You speak to Her as we speak now? You've seen Her?"

"When I was a child," said Kati, "I would see emerald eyes and hear a voice in my head, but later, in the gong-shi-jie, She showed me an image of a young Empress when we talked. It was years before I realized She was showing me an image of myself as a woman."

"But you hear her words?"

"Yes."

Goldani sighed. "It has never been so with me. It is more like an instinct, an intuition from something said in a dream. It was also like that with Manlee. You see what I think, so I will say it. Based on my own experience, I'm skeptical about what you tell me. You're saying that only you have direct contact with Mandughai."

"I also have it," said Mengmoshu, "but not in the gong-shi-jie. Only Kati, or Mengnu, as we call her among our people, has the ability to go there. First Mother speaks directly to me and others in the Moshuguang, but only in the way Kati experienced as a child. I've told you her gifts are exceptional and unique. First Mother has chosen her for this reason alone. Kati's abilities exceed even Hers."

"There are Tumatsin who will consider that statement a blasphemy."

"I understand," said Mengmoshu, "but it is truth. First Mother is one of many persons in history, not a god. Her daughter will soon take Her place, and as a final accomplishment of Her reign she wants Tumatsin and Hansui reunited for the betterment of Shanji. She has chosen Kati as an Empress who will bring change in the way we do things, and improve everyone's life, including those millions who live beyond the mountains."

"I've never heard of such people," said Goldani.

Millions, indeed. I see Toregene in this child, but what is she now? Why is she here?

To show you Mandughai's will, Goldani. I must unite Tumatsin and Hansui as one people.

Goldani sucked in a breath, turning to see Kati regarding her calmly with emerald green eyes. The sky was bright, now, and ahead of them the great sea spread to the horizon. Clusters of *gerts* were scattered north and south along a sloping plain leading to beaches and rocky cliffs, and several boats dotted the water near the shore.

"You have not heard of the people in the east because the Emperor has forced your isolation, and the time for that is coming to an end. Tumatsin and Hansui must work together if things are to change," said Kati.

"And if we do not?"

"Then Mandughai will force it, or kill us all," said Kati. "In less than two years, She returns with Her armies. She doesn't come as a savior of the Tumatsin, but as a foreign aggressor. If we don't oppose Her together, She will destroy us all, and start all over again. Her main concern is for the millions who live difficult lives beyond the mountains."

"The Tumatsin will not believe this. At Festival next year they will celebrate Her coming. They've awaited it thousands of years."

"I understand," said Kati. "I've come to tell you the truth and give you a warning. I expect your skepticism, your disbelief. My hope is that when the time comes, and Mandughai's armies are burning your *ordus*, you will join us in fighting Her. We will be ready to help you."

"We?"

"The fighting force of the Moshuguang is moderate in size, but well trained," said Mengmoshu. "We also have considerable numbers of friends in the Emperor's army who will join us. If we can formulate a mutual-defense pact, I can guarantee the use of these forces to defend your *ordus* if you will join us in defending the city."

Goldani chuckled. "The Emperor himself once made such a promise, but our only defense is a few troopers and a fence he has built to keep us within our own territory. Your proposal cannot be taken seriously by us, but you are welcome to make it."

"May we speak to the *ordu* leaders as a group?" asked Kati.

"They are all here. Word of your visit arrived weeks ago, and every *ordu* is represented."

"When we're finished, I want to see my father and brother. Do you know where they are?"

"They are also here," said Goldani, but suddenly her mind was closed off from Kati, the familiar blackness when someone resisted a probe.

"What's wrong?" asked Kati.

"You will first meet Baber. He will take you to see your father. We didn't know who this person Mengnu was, only that she was Tumatsin. I'm sorry."

Still the blackness in the woman's mind, hiding something from her. "Is it far?"

"No. We come to the *ordu* now. We shall have time for more talk later, when I've assembled the others. First, there will be food and drink for you."

The trail ended at the edge of the *ordu*, a cluster of *gerts* set in three concentric circles, a large, permanent building of logs with a turf roof in the center that was the traditional meeting place for a large *ordu*. People ran towards them from all directions for a look at the strangers, and there were many children of all ages. Several men sat on horseback, scowling as they passed by. Kati looked for a familiar face, but there were none there. The odor of barley cakes and cheese was in the air, mingled with the scent of horses and goats and burning wood.

The scents of the Tumatsin.

Kati turned, and smiled at Mengmoshu. *I feel like I'm coming home.*

Yes, but it isn't home. Your world has become much larger than this one.

Goldani led them to the log building and dismounted. They went through a doorway with a flap of hide. There were no windows, the only light coming from a partially opened vent made from some translucent animal membrane in the ceiling. In the center of the dirt floor was a stone hearth with freshly set wood beneath a black kettle filled with water for ceremonial tea. Benches lined the walls of the single, large room, and the air smelled like incense and burned wood.

"Our meeting will be here," said Goldani, "and we'll bring bedding for you to sleep on as long as you wish to stay. How long will that be?"

"No more than two nights," said Mengmoshu.

No more? I haven't seen Da and Baber for twelve years! We must go back before the Emperor discovers we've left the city. But you can return whenever you think it's safe.

"Food will be brought here for you. Tomorrow, I invite you to join me for meals in my *ger*," said Goldani. "We'll discuss the results of the meeting, then. Our food is simple. I hope you will find it satisfactory."

"I'm sure we will," said Kati, "and I'm happy to see that Tumatsin hospitality hasn't changed while I've been away."

My people are fond of understatement. To say their food is simple means they will serve us their very best.

Goldani nodded, cold and formal, but her eyes were constantly on Kati now. She stepped up close, and said, "I've heard enough to believe you're the little girl we thought was dead so many years ago. I loved your mother, Kati, and I still mourn her. It's her place I've taken, after the death of Manlee, and now her daughter returns to tell me she is to be Empress over all of Shanji. This is difficult for me. I still remember the little girl who would rather ride than eat, but now she's a woman standing before me with the greenest eyes I've ever seen, probing my mind like a Searcher. You are Tumatsin, Kati, yet different. Your aura fills this room in gold and red, always moving, dynamic and powerful. The others will notice this. They will still wonder who or what you really are. They will not believe Mandughai comes to harm us, and will question your motives for telling such a story."

"I'm sent by Mandughai to fulfill Her wishes, Goldani, and all my gifts come from Her. Please tell that to the others before the meeting. Whatever else I am, or will be, I am Tumatsin. This is my first home, and I haven't forgotten it."

"I'll tell them that. Rest now. Food will be brought soon. Our meeting will be after the noon meal."

"When can I see my father and brother?"

"Baber will come for you after the meeting," said Goldani, finally showing a faint smile. "Your brother has become a handsome young man you might not even recognize. You might find him shy at first. I think he will be awed by the beauty of his sister."

Goldani put a hand on Kati's shoulder, and her own eyes were light green. "I'm so happy to see you're alive," she said, then turned, pushed her way past the door flap, and was gone.

Kati was excited, yet worried. "She's hiding something, Mengmoshu. I couldn't penetrate her mind."

"Nor could I. She has excellent control," said Mengmoshu, "but if hostility were there I would have sensed it, and I didn't."

"She remembers me."

"The others will not. Goldani was from your *ordu*, and she is leader here. She anticipates a difficult meeting and has given us extra time to speak to her alone. We need to take advantage of that."

"Some might remember me from Festival, when I got my first horse."

"This will not help them believe you come as future Empress, or that you're chosen by First Mother. You must give them a sign, Kati. Use your powers when there's an opportunity."

They sat down on a bench and waited only a few minutes before food and drink arrived, verifying what Kati had said about Tumatsin understatement. A line of women, girls, and young boys entered the room, carrying bowls, plates and jugs which they arranged on a hide by the hearth, then two cushions of soft hide stuffed with wool for them to sit on. There were barley cakes and fruit, small potatoes and slabs of lamb steamed with herbs, and a small bowl of honeycomb to finish the meal over tea and *ayrog*.

Both of them ate greedily, for they hadn't had anything in their stomachs since the previous evening. The silence was interrupted only by people coming in to retrieve empty dishes, and finally to give them moist cloths to clean their hands and mouths. The people did not speak or look at them, even when they voiced their pleasure with the meal.

"It's the Tumatsin way," explained Kati, when Mengmoshu seemed worried about the people not responding to a compliment. "We're treated as honored guests, and what we say or do during our meal is considered private, as if nobody else were present."

They finished everything and sat on the benches, dozing after the early start of the day. All too soon, Goldani was standing in the doorway, and light was pouring in from outside.

"I have the others with me. Are you ready?"

"Of course," said Kati. "Please come in."

Ten women filed solemnly in behind Goldani, and seated themselves along the benches on the other side of the hearth. All eyes were on Kati and Mengmoshu. All eyes were red with wariness, and Kati breathed slowly, deeply, to calm herself.

These are my people. I love and care about them.

She knew her eyes were green, for she saw some eyebrows raised, and a few women looked at each other as if to verify what they saw. Or was her aura the thing that intrigued them? Their own auras were heavily laced with blue, and close to their bodies, while Goldani's seemed normal, extending outwards an arm's length in yellows and red hues.

"I bring you greetings from Mandughai," said Kati. "and I come at Her request to bring you important news about Her coming to Shanji. I'm called Mengnu in the Emperor's city, but my birth name is Kati, given to me by my parents Toregene and Temujin. I was born in the *ordu* without a name that the Emperor destroyed, and taken—"

"I have given them your history, Kati. All of us knew your mother, and some remember you as a child," said Goldani. "We welcome you as a Tumatsin, but need to hear from your own mouth about your relationship to Mandughai, and the reason you are here."

Don't speak for me, Goldani. She's a Searcher, altered to look like one of us. One of the women interjected the thought, harsh and peremptory.

Kati stiffened. "Very well," she said. For several minutes, she gave them a running account of her contact with Mandughai, beginning as a child, and then her later training with the Moshuguang, the times in the gong-shi-jie, the things she'd been taught by the Empress of Tengri-Nayon herself. Mengmoshu broke in once to explain why Kati had been saved from death, how the Moshuguang had seen her special gifts even when she was a tiny child.

The women listened politely until she was finished, and then voices came from the gloom on the other side of the hearth.

"You come here with a Searcher. They've been our enemies for a thousand years."

You are spy for the Emperor. Mandughai will destroy all of you if She comes again.

"They searched out truth when the Tumatsin were in rebellion against the Emperor," said Kati. "Their influence prevented the Emperor from destroying all of us! They understand the importance of the Tumatsin on Shanji. You have your own lands because of them. There are millions of people on Shanji who have nothing, and the Moshuguang, or the Searchers, as you call them, work to change that. They are not your enemies. The *Emperor* is your enemy, and his reign is coming to an end. Shanji is stagnant. It will not move ahead unless there is fairness and justice for *all* people."

That same voice again, and now Kati saw a brightening aura from a woman three places away from Goldani.

"We're told that Mandughai has proclaimed you Empress when the Emperor is gone, yet you must fight Her army for this to happen. I, for one, do not believe this. It makes no sense, and seems convenient if Mandughai is really coming with Her armies. She will rid us of the Emperor, and establish Her own rule. I think you're attempting to usurp this by getting us to help you fight Her, and then take power for yourself! You're barely a woman. How can we believe what you say without direct verification from Mandughai, The One who is always with us?"

Careful! She sees Mandughai as a goddess!

"One moment," said Goldani. "Mamai has arrived to light our fire for tea. Please come in."

A boy entered with a bag of tinder and lighted candle, kneeling at the hearth to perform his duties while everyone sat in silence. He lit the tinder at strategic places within the tent of wood beneath the water pot, and hurried out of the room.

"I will answer you with a question," said Kati. "Suppose you suddenly heard the voice of a woman proclaiming herself to be Mandughai, and the woman told you you must give up your isolation to work and live with the other people on Shanji, move from your land if necessary to be in harmony with the Hansui. Would you do it?"

Bright, blue spikes appeared in the woman's aura. "I—I would obey the will of Mandughai."

"Even though it's against *your* will? I can see it in your aura, and hear it in your thoughts! You *despise* the Hansui! Yet you would live and work with them if Mandughai ordered it?"

"Yes—if I knew it was Mandughai who ordered it. You have entered my mind without—"

"Your permission, yes. I *also* have the powers of a Searcher, you see, but any woman in this room can see the truth in your aura. Now, tell me how you could be sure it was Mandughai ordering you to do something you didn't want to do. It could be anyone's voice: a Searcher, perhaps, or other impostor. How could you know it was truly Mandughai speaking?"

"I would know," said the woman stubbornly.

The fire in the hearth had caught, but burned slowly, and smoke circled the room.

Now is a good time to show them something.

"By faith? Or by a sign of her power?" Kati pointed a hand at the fire. "For example, I may direct my aura—so."

The entire wood pile on the hearth burst into a column of flame reaching half-way to the ceiling, and was consumed in seconds. The women gasped at the sight and the abrupt, almost unbearable heat, and pressed their backs against the wall.

"Or, I may open a path to the gong-shi-jie, the place of creation, and draw a piece of its infinite energy to heat our water for tea. Watch, now."

Kati's aura snaked to the water kettle, flattening into a dish-shape just above it. She kept her eyes open, let them see the blaze of emerald green as she made the connection to the world of purple light, drawing out a trickle of radiation, and directing it into the kettle. In one second, the water was at a roiling boil. The room glowed green with the light from her eyes, then subsided.

"Would this be enough? Must I heat this room to the scalding point, or burn down an entire *ordu* with the light you've just seen? Are these the signs you look for? I show you signs, yet I do not claim to be Mandughai, but I tell you She has sent me here to proclaim Her will. Goldani has given you Her message, and I need not repeat it for you. In less than two years Mandughai comes as a foreign aggressor to force Tumatsin and Hansui together in opposition to Her.

"She is a woman, like you or me, a good woman determined to see Shanji advance and expand to join the rest of Her worlds. She has chosen me to lead this change, and to make a better life for *all* the people, but I must first unite Tumatsin and Hansui. Her armies come to enforce this, or to destroy us all. We can work together now, and agree to meet the confrontation in a united way, or wait until Her soldiers are burning your *ordu*s. The choice is yours."

"You speak blasphemy!" snarled a woman.

"A trick, with one of the Hansui light weapons!" said another.

"Nonsense. We all saw her aura. The source of power was right in this room," said still another. "But what can we do now, when the Emperor is in power, and our border is fenced and guarded?"

"We can agree to mutually defend each other against foreign aggression," said Kati. "We can come together as equals to plan a better life for the people on Shanji. But you must understand that the greatest need for change lies beyond the mountains where most of Shanji's people live. It means giving up your isolation."

"The Emperor has imposed this on us!"

"It will not be so when he's gone."

"We only have your word for that!"

"This is true," said Kati. "Trust is necessary for what we do together."

The women were now whispering to each other, and Goldani said, "Kati, suppose we cannot agree to what you say, and when Mandughai's army arrives they attack our *ordus*, and we see you have spoken the truth. What happens to us then?"

The women were suddenly silent.

"If I hear you're being attacked, I will come with Moshuguang soldiers to help defend you."

"Even if we will not help you defend the city?"

"Yes. You are my people. I will fight shoulder to shoulder with the Moshuguang to defend you, and if I survive I will defend the city as well, without your help. Mandughai expects nothing less of me. I'm committed to Her will."

There was a long silence until Goldani said, "It seems there are no more questions for now. The council will meet in my *ger* this evening for further discussion, and now, since the water in our kettle seems nicely hot, I suggest we have tea, and some informal talk with our guests."

Goldani herself served the tea in small ceramic cups. The women remained on their benches, whispering to each other as they sipped, Kati and Mengmoshu sitting alone across from them. The minds of the women were now tightly masked. Goldani talked among them for several minutes, and several of them stood up, looking nervously over at Kati, eyes red.

You did well, but I heard that business again about you fighting with the troops.

I meant it. I've been trained, and I will fight.

We will talk about that later.

Goldani was coming towards them, two women straggling behind her. She stopped, leaned over, and said, "They're impressed by your powers, but what you ask is difficult after thousands of years of animosity between Hansui and Tumatsin. I'll do my best to persuade them, but surely you can see their lack of belief in what you've told them."

Kati sighed, but smiled as the two other women came up to her. Both were Goldani's age. There were no introductions.

"We remember your mother," said one. "She's buried near here, and your brother will take you there if you wish. Despite what you've heard from us, we're happy to see that Toregene's daughter is still alive. But you've surprised us in many ways."

She would visit Ma's grave. Kati felt an ache in her throat. "I understand," she said. "Thank you."

"We cannot decide everything while you're here," said the other woman. "We must also speak to the men, and they will have their own opinions."

"Of course," said Kati. "I hope for continued communication between us, regardless of your decisions."

"Festival will be held this time next year," said the woman. "As a Tumatsin, you are welcome there." She lowered her eyes, and walked away to join the other women filing out of the room. The redness of suspicion and anger was in many eyes.

Goldani smiled. "It's another opportunity, especially with the men. We're finished for the moment. Wait here, and I'll bring Baber to you."

Then she and Mengmoshu were alone again, and Kati's heart was pounding. "What will he think of me?" she asked.

"He's your brother," he said.

"We've been raised in different worlds. And why isn't Da coming with him? Doesn't he want to see me?"

"I don't know, Kati. You'll find out soon enough. Your

little display here seemed so easy, no natural for you.
I'm wondering just how far First Mother has pushed
the limits of your abilities."

"I'm too excited to think about that now, Mengmoshu.
It's been twelve years since I've seen them!"

"I know. Do you wish to be alone with them?"

"No! Stay with me! I want them to meet you!" Kati
grabbed his arm with both hands, and he smiled.

Suddenly, Goldani was at the doorway. "Kati? There's
someone here to see you. May we come in?"

"Yes!" Kati squeezed Mengmoshu's arm, a shiver
running through her.

Goldani held the doorflap aside, and a young man
ducked his head to enter the room. He was tall and
square-shouldered, wearing riding leathers, hair tied into
a tail reaching below the nape of his neck. He came at
Goldani's side to stand before Kati, a frown on his face,
hands clenched at his sides.

Kati looked into brown eyes set in a square, chiseled
face, and the sight brought tears to her eyes. "Baber,"
she said softly. "You look just like Da. Do you recognize
me after such a long time?"

Baber swallowed hard, and pointed to her necklaces.
"I remember those."

"From Festival, when I got Sushua, and you rode back
with Da on Kaidu. You were so proud!"

"Kati? We—we thought you were dead, and buried,
or burned up. Father looked everywhere, and—"

"I'm here, and alive! Oh, *Baber*!" Kati grabbed him
in a fierce hug, her face against his chest, for he was
even taller than she. "I've missed you so much, and Da,
too. Please take me to him! We have two days to talk
about what has happened to us, and I don't want to waste
a minute of it!"

Baber's hands rested lightly on her back, and his mind

was a blank to her. "It's not far. Will the Searcher come
with us?"

"Yes. This is Mengmoshu. He's been my teacher for
many years." *Like a father to me, in many ways.*

Baber nodded to Mengmoshu. "Follow me, then."

They left the building, and walked south away from
the concentric circles of the *ordu*, past the stares of
women and children, and out onto a sandy plain ending
at shear cliffs dropping to the sea. Kati looked around,
and saw no *gerts* beyond the *ordu*. "You said it was near?"
she asked.

"A little way further," said Baber.

Something was wrong. There were no dwellings out
here, not even a horse or a goat, only sand and wind
and the pounding of the sea below them.

They came to a wide shelf jutting out from the cliff
face, and someone had built a commemorative cairn of
stones there, a small altar placed on a rectangular bed
of pebbles. Baber went to it, took a green stone from
his pocket, and placed it on the altar. He took out another
green stone, and handed it to Kati.

"Ma is buried here," he said solemnly. "Some of the
survivors of the Emperor's attack risked their lives to
go back for her and bring her here."

Sea air beating at her face did not dry the tears that
came. Kati choked back a sob, fingered the stone, then
placed it on the altar beside Baber's offering. "It's a
beautiful place," she said. "You can see to the horizon.
Ma would have loved the view."

"Yes. I remember her wanting to see the ocean up
close," said Baber.

Kati knelt on the bed of colorful pebbles around the
altar, Baber and Mengmoshu standing behind her. Her
sadness was tempered by the memory of her mother's
face. She shared it mentally again with Mengmoshu, then
ran the palm of her hand over the smooth stones.

"This place has been kept neatly. Does Da come here often to see her?"

Baber made a choking sound, and then his mind was open to her, and she knew the horrible truth before his words came.

"He's there with her, Kati, and Kaidu is buried beneath where I stand."

Oh, Kati, I'm sorry. We didn't know.

She was stunned for a moment, kneeling there with her hands at her side. She wanted to disbelieve, but couldn't, for she saw the truth in Baber's mind. She'd waited twelve years for this day, a day of joyful reunion, and suddenly all those dreams were shattered. Her breath seemed to have left her, and she gasped.

"When? How did it happen?" The horror of loss made a knot in her stomach, tendrils reaching upwards towards her chest, and into the heart.

"Only two months after Ma was killed; it was before the fences went up. When they brought Ma back, he went a little crazy. You hadn't been found. Nobody saw them take you away, and they set fire to everything. When he went back to the *ordu* there were only piles of ashes. I remember him saying how clever you were, that you'd probably escaped and were hiding somewhere. He spent weeks searching for you, with Kuchlug, but it was very dangerous. The flyers were everywhere, and there were patrols all over the plateau. Then, one morning, he went out alone, and didn't come back. After a day, Kuchlug and three men went looking for him. They found him high on the slopes of Three Peaks. His neck was broken, and he was dead. Kaidu's legs were broken, and Kuchlug ended his misery. We buried them together."

"He knew my place on the summit of Three Peaks," said Kati. "If I'd escaped, I *would* have gone there. Oh, Da!" The horror had reached her throat. She bent over, forehead touching the pebbles, and her body shook.

"It was bad for me, Kati. I'd lost everyone, including you. Manlee took me in for a few years, but then she got sick. Goldani has raised me since I was nine. She's been good to me."

Kati wept without restraint, and Mengmoshu joined her without words.

Don't let me go. Let me feel it with you, Kati. You're not alone. Not now. I never guessed your dreams would end this way. I should have checked things out and prepared you for it. I'm sorry.

Baber's hand was on her shoulder, and he was kneeling beside her. "I thought I'd lost everyone, but I hadn't. My sister is still alive, Kati. We still have each other."

Kati embraced him, clinging hard, and sobbing into his shoulder. She looked up at Mengmoshu, and he was standing there with glistening eyes. She had felt his grief for her, but suddenly his mind was as dark as a cave. She wiped her eyes with a hand, and stood up with her brother. They looked at the grave in silence for a moment, arms around each other's waists, then walked back to the *ordu*, Mengmoshu following them.

She made no effort to hide her tears from the Tumatsin, for they had already known what she now knew, and they watched her sorrowfully as she passed by them, clinging to her brother. They went directly to the log building and Mengmoshu left them there alone to talk. They sat by the hearth in gloom, and Kati told Baber every detail of what had happened to her during their separation, all the things she'd seen and learned and the tasks that Mandughai had called upon her to do.

Baber shared his simple but mostly happy life as the orphaned child of an honored woman. Manlee had been like a grandmother, and then Goldani, childless, a husband drowned in a storm at sea. He was learning the life of a fisherman, working the nets on the outrigger boats and cultivating the shellfish in the shallows. Riding was not so important here, but he had a horse named Shuel, presented to him by the *ordu* at Festival when he was twelve. There was a girl named Chilan who'd captured his affections. Kati asked if he'd kissed her, and he said yes, and she laughed. His guard was down, and she'd seen that they did more than kiss.

It was late when Mengmoshu returned, followed by two women with food for them. They ate together, then Baber excused himself, for he arose early to work the nets three days a week.

"I'll be back late tomorrow. Will you be here?" he asked anxiously.

"One more night, then we must leave," said Kati. "We can talk more tomorrow night."

Baber smiled, and left the room. Mengmoshu looked at her, concerned.

"Are you feeling better?"

"Yes. He's had a good life. At least I still have my brother. I wanted so much to see Da again, to let him know what's happened to me."

"I know," said Mengmoshu softly.

A thought brought tears to her eyes again. "He always called me his little Empress. Isn't that funny?"

"No," said Mengmoshu. Suddenly, he sat down beside her at the hearth, and put an arm around her. She buried her face in his shoulder and cried again, and his hand stroked her hair. "He would be proud of you, Kati. Any father would be proud of you," he murmured.

Mengmoshu was struggling for control of his mind, holding back something from her. She'd felt it many times before, and now it was there again, very close. She looked up at his face: mouth set grimly, silent tears on his cheeks, staring at the hearth.

"Mengmoshu, is there something you want to tell me? I feel a terrible struggle within you."

Mengmoshu stroked her hair, and held her close.

"I'm proud of you like a father," he said.

Kati nuzzled his shoulder. "There's more. You're hiding things again. I don't hide things from you, Mengmoshu. Tell me."

"I need to think some more. Aren't you ready to sleep?"

"I think so."

"Some men want to meet with you tomorrow. Talk about today's meeting has spread fast, and these men are in charge of a kind of home guard. They have no religious feelings to deal with; they'll ask practical questions about the size of our forces and our commitment to Tumatsin defense. Goldani has allowed the meeting. I think she supports us."

"When?"

"Late morning. Now get some rest."

Their bedding had been brought in with the food: straw mattresses bound in softened hides, pillows, and wool blankets. They slept in their clothing, Kati's eyelids already fluttering as her head hit the pillow. As she drifted towards sleep, she saw Mengmoshu's eyes glittering near her, still watching, as if he were ready to say something.

She slept without dreaming.

The morning meeting went quickly, and it seemed the men had mainly wanted to see her face-to-face. Mengmoshu coached her without words as she answered their questions, and it was quickly apparent the men had little belief in Mandughai or Her coming. Yes, the Moshuguang could provide an elite fighting force of two thousand within a day's notice, but only a few flyers were available to them. They had no idea of the size of Mandughai's forces, or their strategy for invasion. Kati's commitment to Tumatsin defense did not depend on *their* commitment to help defend the city, but Mandughai required it if an extensive war was to be won. Once Hansui and Tumatsin were united against

Her, Mandughai had promised to cease Her attack, and bring Kati to the throne. *If Her daughter will allow it*, thought Kati, bothered by the partial truth of her words.

At one point, a man asked for a demonstration of her powers. Kati stood in the center of the room, an arm stretched out from her side, palm up, and suddenly a ball of sizzling blue plasma was floating above her hand. She asked the man to flip his dagger at it, and he did so. There was a faint popping sound and the blade was gone; the hilt dropped to the floor, blade ionized.

The men stared, and were frightened by her, but still they did not believe in Mandughai, or in Her coming. Now they believed in Kati, seeing her as a possible threat, and she saw it all in their minds.

Mandughai had been correct. The people would not see the truth until it happened to them.

In the afternoon, she returned alone to the gravesite of her parents, and sat there for two hours to watch the sea. The water was dotted near and far with semicircles of small boats with outriggers to work the nets taking life from sea to Tumatsin *gerts*. She imagined herself with Baber on one of the boats, pulling on those nets full of struggling fish, the salty wind in her face. Their life was good here, and simple. It was no wonder they protected their isolation from a people who at one time had thrown them away because of an ethnic impurity.

Goldani served them an early meal as the men were returning from the sea. Her news was mostly bad.

"They are convinced there is a threat against us, but think it might come from you. They fear your power. Some believe it comes from Mandughai, but others feel you're in rebellion against Her and seek to establish your own rule against Her will. Out of fear they're motivated to strengthen our home guard, and intensify training, but they will make no commitment of any kind to you.

Not now. They *do* ask that I stay in communication with you. They allow the possibility of future discussions."

"The border post we came through is entirely manned by Moshuguang forces," said Mengmoshu. "Any messages you leave there will be immediately relayed to us over closed channels. The Emperor must hear nothing. Say nothing to anyone who's not Moshuguang."

"I understand," said Goldani. "I hope you're not too disappointed. It was the best I could do. Another thing, Kati; the women want to see you at Festival next year. If you are not, they will say you are no longer Tumatsin, but have become a foreigner."

"I'll be there," said Kati.

"Alone," said Goldani. "No escort, and no flyers like the one that's been hovering around since you arrived here. You must come alone."

"I'll ride the route I remember as a child," said Kati, "and I'll be armed with sword and bow."

Goldani nodded, and smiled. "Baber will be here soon, and tomorrow morning we'll escort you back to the border. I'm sorry Baber had to tell you about your father, Kati. I simply couldn't force myself to do it. He's a fine young man, and I love him. He's the child I never had, and now he has his sister back. I'm happy for both of you."

"Thank you for caring for him," said Kati, and they embraced warmly, holding each other for a long moment.

"Baber will meet you at your sleeping quarters, and we're finished here," said Goldani. "I wish you well, Kati. You're one of us, and if Mandughai has called on you to be Empress of Shanji, I hope it will come to pass. You have your mother's heart, and she was a loving and fair person. I think we can work together, if there is fairness and justice in the rule of our world."

"It's what I want, too, Goldani. In less than two years it will be decided. Please communicate with us at anytime."

"We will."

Goldani released her, and Mengmoshu said, "I'll stay here awhile."

Kati went back to the log house, and Baber arrived within an hour, bringing with him a beautiful shell glistening in a rainbow of colors. "We cultivate them in the shallows," he explained. "The meat is sweet, and rich. Even a grown man can only eat two of them."

He gave her the shell. "It makes a good dish. Take it with you."

"I've nothing to give in return; I'll send something," she said.

"It's no matter. Knowing I still have a sister is enough."

He seemed so serious, so adult as they sat down by the hearth. "The men were all talking about you. They say you have great powers and might be Empress of Shanji. They asked about your childhood, and I could only remember how well you rode a horse. Were there other things?"

"I could probe minds and hear thoughts like the Searchers. That's how they discovered me."

"I didn't know," said Baber.

"Ma did. It frightened her, and she made me keep it secret, but there were times we talked without words. I think she felt the Searchers would kill me if they discovered my abilities."

"I wonder what she would think of you now."

"I think she'd be happy for me, and support me like Goldani is doing. We've been lucky, Baber. We've both had good people in our lives, people who care about us. Not everyone has that."

"What now?" asked Baber. "Did you get what you came for?"

"No, but it's what Mandughai told me to expect. We'll have to fight Her armies, and it could be very bad."

"I'll be involved, then. All boys over fifteen are in the

home guard. I'm a bowman." He paused, sober. "My arrows are no match for laser weapons."

"She might not use them. We'll have to wait and see. We'll both be in danger, brother. I'll fight with the Moshuguang. They've trained me for battle, and I'll use that training, but Mengmoshu will try to prevent it. He worries over me too much."

"He's a good man?"

"Yes. Formal, and stern, but lonely inside. I'm very fond of him."

"A Searcher."

"A Moshuguang, Baber, and I'm one of them."

"But how? No other Tumatsin has the mind of a Searcher."

"I don't know. Perhaps Mandughai made it happen. I am what I am. I don't question it. I'm still your sister, Baber. I'm still Kati."

Their shoulders touched. "I know," said Baber, "and I'll fight by your side when the time comes."

Kati hugged him, felt the hard muscle in his arms, shoulders and back, and they sat that way, silently, until Mengmoshu arrived.

Baber left, and it was growing dark. They would leave early in the morning, and Kati went to bed early. Mengmoshu sat on his bed next to hers.

"We did as well as could be expected," he said reflectively, "perhaps even better, if they strengthen their home guard. We still need to talk about you fighting along with the troopers."

"Not now, Mengmoshu, I'm tired."

"It makes no sense for an Empress to be killed in battle. The risk isn't necessary."

"I'm trained as well as any trooper. You worry too much."

"Yes—I worry."

He was still sitting there, watching her as her eyes

closed. His face was solemn, and there was a roiling within
him, something left unsaid as she drifted into sleep.

It was only a short time before the dream came, a dream
that brought her fully awake with a moan. It began with
Ma's face smiling at her, and then another scene. Ma
was on her back, naked, and a man was on top of her,
rocking to and fro, copulating with her. Ma looked very
frightened; she scratched at the man, but he held her
hands down, rocking harder, and then there was his
release, and he turned his head, gasping.

The man was Mengmoshu.

Kati sat up on the bed with a moan, her breath coming
in short gasps. Torchlight from outside leaked past the
doorflap, and the air was cold, making her shiver. She
pulled the blanket up to her chin, and turned to see if
she'd awakened Mengmoshu.

He was still sitting there, as he'd been when she'd fallen
asleep, watching her with glistening eyes.

"Mengmoshu!" she gasped. "I—I had a dream—it
disturbed me—"

"It was not a dream," said Mengmoshu softly, "but a
vision from the past. I cannot wait any longer to tell you."

"What? What I saw was—"

"What you saw was something that happened to a young
Moshuguang captain when a Tumatsin spy was captured
near the cliffs twenty years ago. His men would have
raped the spy, then killed her, but she was young, and
beautiful, and he wished to spare her life. He used his
rank to rape the woman in place of the men, and
pretended to kill her, temporarily paralyzing her with
his own mind. He forced himself into her, using her
lustfully, and rationalizing his disgraceful act by saying
he was saving the woman's life and doing First Mother's
work by spreading the seed of the Moshuguang."

"It was *Ma* I saw in my—"

"A child was conceived, and the woman's husband didn't

know it was by another man. The captain rose in the ranks of the Moshuguang, and then one day an exceptional Tumatsin child was standing before him, showing him the images of the woman he'd disgraced, and he knew— he knew—"

Mengmoshu's voice cracked, and broke, and now he was sobbing. He held his head in his hands, body heaving with sobs. Kati reached out to touch him, but he jerked away, his voice a strangled whisper.

"I am your *father*! It was *I* who disgraced your mother that night, and then you were there, and all the guilt came back, and yet there you were, so exceptional, and somehow it was good. I—I confessed to First Mother, but she already knew, and said the secret must be kept. And then—when I felt your grief yesterday—I couldn't— I couldn't—"

Mengmoshu buried his face in his hands, and sobbed again. Kati just sat there, stunned, clutching the blanket to her. What was she feeling? Anger? No, strangely not. Surprise, yes, and relief, for now so many questions she'd had about herself were suddenly answered: the source of her childhood powers, Ma's fear and anger when discovering them, then Mandughai saying she had the blood of two sons, not one, all the little things unanswered till now.

"Mengmoshu," she said, reaching out to touch his shoulder. This time, he didn't move away from her, but kept his head bowed.

"I've loved you since you came to us, but I could say nothing. I could only be your teacher, watch you grow, feel your pain, your happiness, and be proud of my daughter in secret. It's been tearing at me for years, and then yesterday —your sense of loss—I couldn't hold back any longer. If you hate me, I accept it. I deserve it."

Kati pressed her hand on his shoulder. "I cannot hate you. How many times have I accused you of acting like

my father? And now I finally know why. I know why I'm
so different, Mengmoshu. That's important to me."

Mengmoshu took her hand in his, and held it tightly.
Tears were streaming down his rugged face.

"You are *unique*, Kati. Juimoshu came from a liaison
between a Tumatsin man and an adventuresome Hansui
girl, but there has never been someone like you. First
Mother has forgiven me because of you, but can *you*
forgive me for what I've done? Your mother's face, it's
been in my dreams for years. If only it could have been
different, the way we met, I could have—"

Kati dropped her blanket, put her arms around his
neck and hugged him. "I wouldn't be here if it weren't
for you. You're my father."

She was amazed how comfortable she felt saying it,
how natural it seemed. Suddenly she was totally centered
and at peace with herself, all her questions answered.
Mengmoshu put his arms around her, his cheek wet
against her face.

"I think of the coming battle. I don't want to lose you,
not now."

"We do what Mandughai directs us to do. The task is
much bigger than the two of us, and everything that can
be done has been done to prepare me for it. Your daughter
is a woman, Mengmoshu. I'm also chosen to serve
Mandughai, and now you must let me do it. I'm not
Mandughai. I'm Kati. I'll join the battle, and not stand
idly by as a symbol."

"If you're killed, First Mother will choose another for
the throne. Shan-lan can't do it; the nobles will lead him
by the nose."

"I intend to be alive," said Kati. "You're underestimating
my abilities again, Mengmoshu, or should I call you
father?"

"No. Never. The secret must be kept, even from the
Moshuguang."

"Have you been sitting up all night?"

"Yes."

"If you don't sleep, I'll have to pick you up when you fall out of the saddle."

Mengmoshu leaned back from her, and smiled. "The Empress orders me to sleep?"

"I do." Kati helped him slide beneath the blanket. For the moment, he seemed very old, but she felt his relief from sharing a thing that had happened long ago, a release of guilt as he looked at her. He reached up, and touched her cheek.

"I obey the Empress—and my daughter."

He closed his eyes. Kati leaned over, and kissed his forehead, then got back into her own bed, and listened to his breathing slow. She had a sudden urge to contact Mandughai, but knew she couldn't, not now. Mandughai would not be there for her. But her true father was there, close by, snoring now softly.

She closed her eyes, and sleep came quickly.

No further dreams disturbed it.

CHAPTER SIXTEEN
YESUGEN

Weimeng had never been so fussy with her, while meters away an entire roomful of people waited patiently for the appearance of the ward of the Moshuguang.

Kati had argued for braids, but Weimeng insisted on buns and finally had her way, doing them up herself. The golden robe with red dragons was also her choice. "There is enough red in it to avoid offending the Emperor," she explained, "but gold is the best color for you. I think Shan-lan will be pleased."

"Shan-lan is *here*?"

"Of course, dear. I always invite the Emperor's family to my parties. It has been His choice not to attend, but Shan-lan seemed eager to come. He says you're a close friend."

"We are," said Kati, "but I haven't seen him lately. He hasn't been attending Master Yung's classes." Kati's head bobbed as Weimeng worked the buns of her hair.

"He spends his time in court, now. The nobles are constantly at him about things they sought with his father, poor boy, and he's a bit overwhelmed by them."

"The Emperor is very ill, then."

"Yes. His energy is gone, but he's still alert. He called for me the other night, you know. I sat with him until morning."

There was a tenderness in Weimeng's voice.

"How could you, mother, after what he's done to you?"

Weimeng put her hands softly on Kati's shoulders. "He's done nothing to me, Mengnu. He needed an heir to the throne, and I couldn't give it to him. He's given me a place of honor, every comfort I could desire, and he's allowed me to care for you as my own. What more could I ask for?"

"A place in court," said Kati, firmly.

"That's only protocol. He's often sought my advice, but in private. He's not a bad man, Mengnu, only rigid. Our concern for each other has never diminished. The shame I've felt is because I couldn't give him a son. It's my own shame, not his. There, I think it's ready."

Kati looked at herself in the mirror. "I look older," she said, and Weimeng giggled behind her.

"They will stumble over themselves to meet you," she said. "Let's not keep them waiting any longer."

They went to Weimeng's suite, and Tanchun opened the doors for their grand entrance. There was barely room for standing, people shoulder-to-shoulder in conversation, but the din of their voices stopped abruptly as Kati entered the room.

Shan-lan was the first to reach her. He bowed, and kissed her hand.

"You're beautiful. I feel another poem coming to me."

Kati smiled, and lowered her eyelashes coyly for him.

Sheyue came up to introduce Kati to her betrothed, a handsome young man whose family controlled metal production on Shanji. Kati heard his name and quickly forgot it, thinking instead about the mess she'd seen at the factories.

Kati looked around for Huomeng, but didn't see him at first. Her father, Mengyao and Juimoshu were there, all in formal black. Weimeng guided her through the crowd, stopping here and there to introduce her to nobles and to those of their sons she deemed suitable for her Mengnu. Kati fluttered her eyelashes, charming them all. Two of the young men were struck dumb by her presence, and the few who attempted to engage her in conversation prattled on about the weather and her appearance and wondered how such a delicate woman could bring herself to practice the arts of war with the sons of commoners.

She forgot them all, continued looking for Huomeng and finally spotted him talking to a group of older men in a corner of the room. She steered Weimeng towards them until she caught Huomeng's eye, and he beckoned to her.

"There are some men I must speak to with Huomeng," she said.

"Don't be too long," said Weimeng. "There are four young men following us at this very moment, working up their courage to speak with you."

"Just a few minutes, mother," said Kati, and Weimeng released her arm. She went to Huomeng, and the three men with him turned to give her frankly appraising looks as he made their introductions. Older men, all nobles and ministers, they seemed eager to meet her and began asking questions immediately.

"Huomeng has told us about your plan for economic expansion," said one.

"It's *our* plan," said Kati. "We've worked on it for over a year."

"How can you proceed with such a plan when the Emperor discourages expansion? He says our needs are met by what we have now."

"He doesn't consider the needs of the people who produce the goods, and it seems you don't tell him about them."

The men were startled, and Huomeng chuckled. "I warned you about her directness."

"Our managers are responsible for the workers' needs when they relate to productivity, nothing more. How people live is their own choice."

"I don't agree. People live as they're forced to live. You enjoy privileged lives by the grace of the Emperor, and have responsibilities like his, the well-being of Shanji and all its people. A man of truly noble character cares about those who serve him. You're responsible for the basics: adequate housing, food, sanitary facilities, and health care."

"We provide that."

"That's not what I hear," said Kati. "I think you provide a certain sum to your managers and trust them to spend it wisely without your checking on how they do it. The results are in the production figures both you and the Moshuguang receive each month, figures we've spent weeks studying. What we see is chaos: sporadic production, frequent layoffs, excesses and shortages, no organization whatsoever."

Without telling them she'd seen it in person, she recited the problems in Wanchou, the factories, the farms with bins of unclaimed, rotting foodstuffs. Suddenly the rhythm of her speech was quick, as in her exchanges with Huomeng when they were working on a problem. "Considerable investment is needed to solve such problems, and the market for the goods you produce even now is too small. You should disperse the population of workers, build new cities, each specialized in particular industry and connected by fast transportation."

"That's impossible. The Emperor pays us in gold for the needs of His city, nothing more. We cannot make such an investment."

"Not with the Emperor as your only customer. He sets prices, takes his taxes before you're paid, and controls all lands. I say put the lands in the hands of the nobles, according to their investments, and let them set the prices.

Let them expand at their own initiative, and deal competitively with each other in a free market, paying taxes only on net profits. New cities will provide the markets you need for centuries as the standard of living increases. Expansion is the only way to move Shanji ahead, and eventually there should be trade with other worlds. A space program will create industries you haven't even considered. The ruler of Shanji must support this. Talk to Shan-lan about it. He's here, in this room. Get his opinion."

"He's a boy, a poet, not a ruler," said one man. "He runs to his dying father for advice, and nothing changes."

"Careful," said another. "The Emperor has ears in this room."

"Give him a chance," said Kati. "At least talk to him about it. We're friends, and he'll listen to me. I'll support any plan for expansion, but the people's needs must be met. When they're happy, and healthy, they'll produce more for you."

"Yes, we hear you'd give them land of their own."

The way he'd said that bothered her. "As bonuses for hard work and productivity. Land, and finer homes, goods to make their lives comfortable, yes. They will produce more if it benefits them. It's a small price to pay for the increased profits you can realize. Huomeng will have to continue. Weimeng is glaring at me, and I must meet some new, potential suitors she's gathered."

Sober-faced, the men bowed. "Your ideas are interesting," one said. "Perhaps we can talk again?"

"I hope so," she answered. "Please excuse me now." She turned deliberately to give Huomeng's arm an affectionate squeeze, which pleased him, then went back to Weimeng and the three young men who stood nervously awaiting her.

For nearly an hour she endured their prattle, responding coyly, laughing at their little jokes, eyes darting occasionally to Huomeng, who remained talking to the men the rest of the evening. Mengmoshu, Mengyao and Juimoshu never spoke to her, but remained on the sidelines of the party all evening to watch her every move.

To please Weimeng, she accepted the invitations of five young men to call on her in the future, but by the end of the evening she couldn't remember their names. She stood at the door with her foster mother to bid goodnight to each guest, ending with her Moshuguang friends and her own father, whose hand she gave an extra squeeze. Weimeng followed them down the hall to the outer door, and Kati turned, thinking she was alone.

Huomeng was still there, smiling at her.

Kati held out a hand to him. "Walk with me," she said.

Huomeng walked the short distance with her to her own rooms, and followed her inside.

"The ministers are wavering," he said, after the door was closed. "They're interested in our ideas, but still think small. With support from the court, though, I think they would move ahead. It's much better than I expected, Kati."

They sat down on either end of a couch in her sitting room. "One man kept asking if 'I' would do this or that. Do they know about me?"

"I don't see how they could. But they know about your training, and see you as someone pushed by the Moshuguang into a position of possible influence. Your friendship with Shan-lan is no secret, you know. The most important thing is their respect for your ideas. They see the benefit to them, and will remember that when we bring you forth as Empress."

"Assuming we survive a war," said Kati, standing up to pace the room reflectively. "What will happen to Shan-lan?"

"That's up to you. It's clear to me the nobles will not accept him as Emperor when his father's gone. They've reached the end of their patience, and there will be no better time for change. Mengmoshu tells me you intend to fight alongside the troops. He's worried, and so am I. If something happens to you, we have no Empress, and First Mother is sure to establish Her own rule without choices by us. It's a terrible risk you don't have to take. Even your own Mandughai, in ancient history, guided Her army's movement from a hilltop. She didn't risk her life in battle."

"I'm not Mandughai," said Kati. She sat down again, so close their shoulders touched, and he looked at her curiously when she did it. "You fear for me, Huomeng?"

"Yes."

"You fear losing an Empress?" Kati put a hand on his arm.

"Not just that. You could be hurt, even killed."

Kati rubbed his arm up and down. "Would you miss me if I were killed, Huomeng?"

"I'd miss our arguments," he said lightly, but his smile faded when he looked at her. Her face was close, and now she gripped his arm.

"Something has changed between us. Do you feel it?" she asked.

Her eyes were green, and mesmerizing. He said nothing, but nodded in agreement. Kati leaned her head against his shoulder, but his hands remained clasped together in his lap.

"We aren't student and teacher anymore," she said.

"I have nothing more to teach you."

"But you come here every day, and we talk for hours."

"We make plans for Shanji when you're Empress."

"More than that, Huomeng. We share dreams, ambitions, feelings. The masks we put on our minds don't work well when we're together. Have you noticed that?" Her hand moved across his chest, and he lifted his own hand to hold it there.

"Your heart is pounding," she said, pressing on his arm so that he turned towards her. Her face was right there, her breath sweet, chin tilted upwards. Her full lips parted. "Huomeng," she murmured.

Their lips came together softly, then harder, the kiss deepening as his arms went around her. She moaned when their tongues met, and her breath quickened. He kissed her nose, cheeks and neck, and then their cheeks were together as they clung to each other, and she was murmuring into his ear.

"When did it change, Huomeng? Do you know?"

"A gradual thing," he whispered. "We'd been together so much, and suddenly you were a woman. I began to see you differently, Kati. Now you'll be an Empress, and I'm only Moshuguang, not yet in middle ranks. I can't expect you to see me as anything but a—"

"Lover? Friend? Husband? I see all those things, Huomeng. I think I'm in love with you."

He held her tightly, and kissed her neck again, shivering.

"You feel the same. You can't hide it from me."

"I managed to for awhile," he said, then they both laughed.

"It's less than two years," she said. "It'll all be decided then."

"I don't want to think about it. I just want to hold you."

They went no further with their desire for each other, but cuddled together on the couch until Weimeng knocked on the door to find out what her Mengnu thought about the potential suitors she'd met that night.

Juimoshu met Mengmoshu at the door to the Emperor's chambers. "His strength comes and goes," she said. "One day he's in court, and then three in bed. A simple argument exhausts him and I have no idea why he's called us here."

"How long do you think he has to live?"

"Less than a year, but it's difficult to say. He's still alert and his will is strong. I've made every effort to prolong his life, Mengmoshu. Without the drugs I give him his life could have been finished a year ago, but the mass is now reaching close to his heart."

"It would be best if he were still alive when First Mother arrives with Her forces. A transition period with Shan-lan on the throne would be quite awkward."

"We might have to deal with that," said Juimoshu. "I don't think he can last so long."

The door was opened by Yang Xifeng, second wife to the Son of Heaven and mother of the heir to his throne. Mengmoshu had rarely seen her, even in court, and remembered her as a lovely, graceful young woman with the neck of a swan. Now she was well into her thirties, and looked much older: ashen face, the wrinkles of worry under her eyes and on her forehead. She gestured for them to enter.

"Please don't allow him to talk for long. He refuses to acknowledge his condition, and pushes himself too hard."

"We understand," said Mengmoshu.

They went through a reception room and sitting room with red walls and black stone floors in near darkness to two doors which spilled forth light when Yang Xifeng opened them. "They are here," she said softly.

"Ah, good," came the Emperor's voice.

They entered, and found themselves in a bedroom with golden walls and ceiling, and a thick, red carpet. Mirrors lined the walls, and one was on the ceiling above a huge bed upon which the Emperor leaned back against several pillows, a small book in his hands. The room was brightly lit by three chandeliers of brass and crystal, the only other furniture a desk and chair across from the bed.

Yang Xifeng closed the doors behind them. The Emperor smiled, and beckoned them to come closer.

"I've been reading the ancient histories of Shou-tze,

particularly during the time of Wang Chen-Ma, our founder. It was he who repelled the invading hoard from Tengri-Nayon, and although I consider the possibility remote, I might be soon called upon to do the same."

"There's been no invasion for two thousand years, My Emperor, but the closest approach of Tengri-Nayon *is* two years away. Do you think First Mother will attack Shanji? Have you heard something?"

Mengmoshu's expression was one of genuine concern and sudden anxiety.

The Emperor smiled. "Surely you would hear it first, being as close as you are to First Mother." His eyes fixed on Mengmoshu's face, looking for a reaction, but Mengmoshu only shrugged his shoulders, as if ignorant.

"She would surely warn us, Son of Heaven."

The Emperor chuckled, eyes bright in an otherwise haggard face. "If she even existed," he said with disdain. "I don't concern myself with mythology, but the fact is the Tengri-Nayon system is nearing us, and if there *is* to be an attack it will be in the near future. I intend to be prepared for it, and there is precedent for an attack. Those who are educated will expect me to be ready. They know their history."

"Of course, Son of Heaven. What can we do for you?"

"I need a feeling for our present forces. How much can we provide for our defense?"

"Including the trainees, your army stands at around three thousand cavalry, and twice that in infantry if we bring in all the troopers from our border outposts."

"What about the Moshuguang you keep hidden in the mountain?" the Emperor said loudly.

"Barely a thousand, but trained to fight on foot or horseback with both lasers and traditional weapons. The flyers are also equipped with lasers."

"How many?"

"Fifty—perhaps sixty. I'm not sure."

"Hmmm." The Emperor rubbed his chin, then thumped the little book in his hand with a finger. "Shou-tze says only that the first horde of invaders numbered in the thousands, and their armament was bow and sword. Despite a sneak attack which brought them to the gates of the city, our flyers had no difficulty in dispersing them."

"The mother ship, Son of Heaven, not the flyers. That was two thousand years ago. If they've left the traditional ways to develop a fully technological society, their weapons could now be quite advanced over ours. They might attack from space and not even land an army. We have no way to meet them there."

"The ship that brought us from Tengri-Nayon is still here."

"It was manned at the time of the invasion, coming so shortly after our landing. Your predecessors ordered it abandoned, and you have kept that tradition. We monitor its instruments from our facilities in the mountain. It can still serve as an early warning system for us. If invading ships arrive in orbit around Shanji, we will see them. But we cannot operate the mother ship's weapons systems from here."

The Emperor shook his head. "We have the smaller ships from our landing. You could fly these to the mother ship and occupy it again."

Mengmoshu automatically masked his mind, keeping even a partial truth from Juimoshu. "The hydrogen fuel for the landing ships has boiled away centuries ago. Even if we had fuel, there are no trained pilots to fly them. Spaceflight has not been part of our traditions for nearly two thousand years, Son of Heaven. The Moshuguang honors the traditions."

The Emperor scowled. "Then we are limited to a ground defense, with cover by the flyers and an army without battle experience."

"Perhaps we can recruit the Tumatsin to support us?" asked Mengmoshu.

"They have no fighting force. I've forbidden it. The Changelings are not involved with this."

"You've promised to defend them against aggression, My Emperor. They have thousands of men who could be trained quickly."

"I said nothing about defense against foreigners. If the Tumatsin are attacked, they must protect themselves. My only concern is this city."

Mengmoshu wasn't surprised. "As you wish, My Emperor. We must wait, then, and be ready with the forces we have. As you say, there's a good chance no invasion will take place. Is there anything else?"

The Emperor closed his book, and leaned tiredly back against the pillows. "A dream—for Juimoshu."

"What is it, Son of Heaven?" she asked.

Wang-Shan-shi-jie closed his eyes. "I saw my son in battle. He was on horseback in full armor, and was shouting to someone. His sword was raised, and blood covered his face. I awoke with a terrible foreboding about him and couldn't sleep again. Earlier this evening I had the same dream, only this time his horse was surrounded by soldiers with fierce faces and the teeth of the *shizi*. I awoke shaking, Juimoshu. I fear for my son. What is the meaning of such a dream?"

"You think about war," said Juimoshu, "and mix those thoughts with your concerns for the future of Shanji. Your son is trained as a soldier, and will be Emperor after you. The blood you saw is a metaphor for the sacrifices he will make to lead the people in the ways of his father. He will be a fine Emperor, Son of Heaven. He will honor you with his life."

The Emperor sighed, eyes still closed. "I'd hoped for such a meaning, but the dream frightened me. Shanlan is so gentle as a human being I've feared for his ability

316   *James C. Glass*

to rule, but he works hard and does all he can to please me. He's brought me pride. I only wish—he could have come—from Weimeng. . . . "

The words faded away, and the Emperor was asleep. Mengmoshu and Juimoshu left the room quietly, and closed the doors behind them.

"Despite the misguided rule of the man, I cannot despise him," said Juimoshu.

"Nor can I," Mengmoshu said.

During the time of anxious waiting, Kati trained with the troopers, and there were two more bronze rings from Master Yung, another two for Shan-lan, now beginning to excel with the sword. She still met him occasionally in Stork Tower, still accepted his poems and paintings of loving friendship. His mind, however, was increasingly occupied with the proceedings at court. He followed his father's views on matters, not asking for her advice, but she'd had opportunity to express her ideas for expansion and economic reform. He listened politely, seemed interested and receptive and genuinely concerned about the physical needs of the people. This saddened her. In time, he might be a fair and just Emperor, but there was no time. He would not be Emperor of Shanji; Mandughai would not allow it. She would place another on the throne, perhaps Kati, perhaps not, in little more than a year. Her star was now dazzlingly bright in the night sky.

Huomeng came to her rooms nearly every day now, and they cuddled on the couch to talk. They talked about Shanji, Huomeng's dreams of flying in space, Kati's continued work alone in the gong-shi-jie, and their own relationship, the love that had blossomed for a long while without their notice. Huomeng feared for her, feared her decision to fight, but didn't try to dissuade her from it. He yielded to her right of personal choice, even at risk of losing her, and she loved him for it.

Several times, she thought of inviting him to her bed, but always stopped herself. Strong emotion, especially passion, brought The Change upon her, and she still remembered the terror on Lui-Pang's face. How could she expect Huomeng to react differently? How could they *ever* consummate their love in a physical way, when even the touch of his lips aroused her so?

More and more, Kati spent her time alone in the gong-shi-jie and in real space reaching out to the gaseous giants. Alone, undistracted, she explored her powers, often playing like a child. The transition from real space to the place of creation remained a flash to her: As much as she calmed herself, she could not slow it down. Time and time again she tried and failed to transfer mass into the gong-shi-jie. One evening she re-entered real space at the same point after such a trial, and found the mass still there, a hot tongue of ionized gas now cooled to a cloud of frozen molecules. She could bring energy with her in either direction, but in the form of light. The mass would not follow her.

She was limited, then, and must work within those limits. Light had energy without end in the gong-shi-jie, and was accessible to her for more than just magic tricks to impress people. She had to think on a grander scale. Energy from the gong-shi-jie could push a light-sail craft anywhere in real space as long as she were there to direct it, a thing she could do without transition. Huomeng could travel anywhere and she could be with him, but the task was delicate. One slip on her part, one lapse of concentration, and the light-sail could be a cinder along with the man she loved.

She practiced with dust, blowing it around with light pressure, then moved to larger pieces of debris left over from planetary formation. The delicacy of her ambitions became apparent when she turned a small asteroid the size of Shanji's mother ship into glass, and vaporized a two-kilometer wide world of ice and frozen methane. But it was a matter of practice, and her confidence grew.

There were alternatives. Huomeng had talked about ram-jets used by the ancestors, and powered by hydrogen gas sucked in by mammoth electromagnetic scoops. If the gas were plentiful, and extremely hot, little fuel was necessary on board the spacecraft itself, and even that fuel could be obtained on the gaseous giants nearby. A similar system had been used to power the mother ship.

During an evening only weeks before Festival, Kati was examining this possibility. She went to Shanji's gaseous neighbor with its tiny, icy moons, and drew out a dense cloud of gas from its atmosphere in several steps, cooling it in transition after transition until she had a ball of frozen gas a kilometer in diameter whirling above the moons of ice. A fueling station. The spacecraft could be fueled here, but how to bring it from Shanji, or the fuel to it? That question remained unanswered. If she pushed the ball closer to her planet, the light of Tengri-Khan would work against her, and she would have to continually remove heat from the fuel. Still possible, but much time would be necessary to prod the fuel-ball close to her planet.

Once fueled, there should be little difficulty in getting the ship as far as Tengri-Nayon. Nayon and Khan had been formed together, and much gas had been blown from the younger one. There was a plentiful supply between the two stars, and she could move ahead of Huomeng to heat it for his electromagnetic scoops.

She tried it with the ball of frozen gas she'd formed, opening a concentric shell of space around it to the gong-shi-jie, flashing it to vapor, then molecules, then ions which quickly ran away from each other. She concluded the spacecraft needed to be close when the ions were formed, or she would have to somehow move those ions in a directed way.

Kati was still thinking about the problem when she returned to the gong-shi-jie and the swirling clouds of purple that always brought her a feeling of privacy and tranquillity. The auric signatures of planets and stars stretched in every direction, and the purple exit to herself was nearby. But something now bothered her, a presence, not here, with her, but in her mind, and that was nearly the same thing. Someone was participating in her experience here.

Mandughai? Are you here?

Silence, and swirling light. She drifted towards the vortex leading to her body. The space near it shimmered, the pattern of purple light changing there.

Someone is here; I can feel it. Why do you hide from me? If it's you, Mandughai, have you come to warn me of your arrival? I've been expecting it.

The shimmering space began to take form, the image of a Tumatsin woman in leather pants and white, sleeveless blouse. Her hair was black, a long, hard chiseled face with full lips curled in an arrogant smile around sharp, protruding canines. Her arms were well muscled, and she slouched on a throne of black stone, one leg draped carelessly over an arm rest.

I'm not Mandughai, but I do come to give you a warning.

Kati's recognition came in an instant. *You're Her daughter. Where is Mandughai?*

She sleeps. I've given Her something to encourage it so we can meet alone here. My dealings are with you, not my mother.

Kati felt dark hostility and aggression coming from the woman. *So, we're here, and I see your image.*

And I see yours. You show yourself as an Empress, which you're not. I show you a soldier, which I am, so you'll recognize me when we come together.

I'm also a soldier. I look forward to demonstrating that

for you. If there was to be posturing, she would participate in it.

The woman chuckled. *That will be soon. We're now in transit to Shanji, and I estimate another eleven months until our arrival. We'll make no effort to hide ourselves, though we're capable of it.*

You can't hide from me. I'll see your ships long before they arrive.

I'm aware of your abilities. I come here often to watch your little games. Even mother hasn't been aware of my presence. I am self-taught, you see. I have not enjoyed the favor of my mother's teachings.

So why do you come to me now?

To be honest with you. To let you know the kind of war you're really facing. The woman's eyes were suddenly red, her upper lip curled up in a toothy display.

Mandughai said I should prepare for the worst. I will do that.

The woman tilted her head back, and laughed. *You have nothing to prepare with. I dare you to show me one soldier with battle experience on Shanji. All of my people have tasted blood, and number ten times what you can put together. My mother has comforted you with her desire for a limited war, but that is a decision only I can make, with the support of my field commanders. It is a military, not a political issue, and we have plans for Shanji that don't include you.*

Then make your decision. We'll be ready for you.

Brave words supporting a false hope. My forces can crush yours in a single day.

And I can destroy yours with a wave of my hand.

The woman's bravado disappeared. She rested her chin on a fist and looked warily at Kati. *You? The one with a compassion for people that has captured my mother's love? Do you really think you can bring yourself to kill a living thing with the energy that surrounds us here?*

I'll use all power necessary to defend my people. When the time comes, I'll demonstrate that for you.

Now the woman scowled. *Very well, then, let us discuss the terms of battle in light of your abilities. My mother would have a limited campaign with ground forces in the traditional way to honor our ancestors, but there are many of us who would do otherwise. Our weapons could destroy all life on your planet, from space. It would be my method, but she's my mother, and for the moment I allow her to hold me back.*

Wisely so. If you attack my people with weapons from space, I'll vaporize your ships from the gong-shi-jie. More posturing, but with effect. Kati now felt the woman's uncertainty.

It's my mother's intent to bring change to Shanji, not destroy it, and a devastated planet is of no use to me. There must be restraint from both sides if any of our missions are to be accomplished. The tone was now more conciliatory.

So what do you propose?

Ground action only, without the use of airpower or weapons from space, including your use of the gong-shi-jie.

I can't guarantee that. I have no control over the Emperor of Shanji. He has armed flyers and will use them against you. I can't prevent it.

Then we will shoot them down from space!

And I'll retaliate in kind, as I've said! Kati said it with conviction, an anger and determination within her that hadn't been there a moment before.

The woman slouched on her throne, and smiled. *Now you show me your true face. We're more alike than I thought. Perhaps we can reach a compromise.*

How large is your force?

I won't tell you that. It's more than sufficient for us to overwhelm you.

Then I must use every advantage possible for Shanji. Perhaps I should just move against you by myself. Kati was thinking fast. How could she compromise her own powers, when she could destroy an invading force before they even landed?

The woman seemed to hear her thought, and was no longer arrogant, or scowling. *My mother insists the battle be traditional, hand-to-hand between our people. I'll not tolerate the use of armed flyers, and they will be shot down. I'll agree not to use my weapons in space on any other targets except the flyers.*

Very well. I'll still use the gong-shi-jie, but agree not to direct its energy to destroy your ships. If I see a single violation of our agreement, your ships will be dust and hot gas! And any forces far outnumbering our own will suffer the same fate. We will fight with equal forces!

Agreed. The woman's leg bobbed up and down over the armrest of her throne. *Our troops carry laser weapons like yours, with three-hundred-burst power-packs. They bring sword and bow for close combat.*

That's not an issue. We're trained with all these weapons.

We? Do you intend to wield a sword in battle? The woman raised an eyebrow.

I do. And I'd like to know the name of my adversary before our swords come together.

I am Yesugen, and I'm not so foolish as you. Our swords will not meet, but I'll watch you from a safe place. I'll live to be Empress of many worlds. You will not. There will be new rule on Shanji, but it will not be by your hand.

You say that because you don't know me. Are we finished here?

Yes—for now. This meeting has been interesting, and we'll meet again soon enough. I look forward to it.

So do I. The purple vortex was now pulling at her. *Until then.*

She opened her eyes, and felt cold sweat on her forehead. The odor of incense was sweet, and the little candles on her shrine had burned down to nubbins on waxy puddles of red. Her face felt taut, and drawn. She stood up, and looked in her mirror to see a Changeling face, eyes blazing green, the canines protruding well over her lower lip.

It was not just emotion or passion that brought the emerald green to her eyes, or the changes in her face.

It was the thought of war.

CHAPTER SEVENTEEN
FESTIVAL

The women were waiting on the knoll above the mouth of the canyon when Kati came to Festival. She'd ridden through a day and night, using several stops to heal and energize her animal with the purple light from her hands. The horse was tiring again when Kati saw the women, and she urged it to a trot; it responded, but was near exhaustion, for it was not a mountain horse.

Goldani was there to greet her, and the other *ordu* leaders nodded politely. Kati was in her leathers, quiver and bow across her back, a sharpened sword in the saddle scabbard. The women had already changed into their colorful robes and sat quietly on horseback, thinking private thoughts to bring on The Change in their faces for the procession. Goldani had achieved it, her canines glimmering, eyes light green like Manlee's and Ma's had been.

Goldani reached over to hold Kati's hand warmly in hers for a moment. "You're punctual, but we would have waited for you. I ride in the place that should have been your mother's. I'd be honored if you'd ride with me. Do you remember the rituals?"

"Yes, Goldani. Thank you for inviting me."

"This is your place among us. Are we ready?"

The other women nodded, eyes red, with faces of the *shizi*.

They formed a column and descended the knoll to the
sandy trail into the canyon: high, orange walls of sandstone
with seams of black coal, the walls closing ahead beneath
an arch. She had come this way before, sitting on Kaidu,
Da's chest against her back. Her little Empress, he'd
thought, and then died without knowing the truth. Now
she'd returned as a woman, a Tumatsin, riding in a place
of leadership because of Goldani's graciousness.

It was a lie. She was not Tumatsin, or Moshuguang,
but a unique blend of the two, trying to somehow bring
them together with a common cause.

The din of a thousand voices came to her from beneath
the arch. The trip through the canyon seemed so short
this time, and the people were there, just ahead, waiting
to see the woman who said she would be Empress of
Shanji. Kati was suddenly apprehensive.

Goldani drew out her sword, and Kati did likewise,
placing its pommel on her knee, curving blade upright.
The blade was scratched and pitted from countless blows
aimed at her face and body, while Goldani's was pristine
and ornamental. *My blade is not for ritual*, Kati thought.
It is for killing.

Kati thought of war, and felt The Change come upon
her, as if an invisible hand gripped her face to pull it
downwards. The canines pressed hard on her lower lip.
She opened her mouth slightly, and allowed a soft growl
to escape with her breath.

Goldani looked over at her, and smiled.

Voices, sudden shouts, and the sound of rushing water
as they passed beneath the arch and out onto soft sand.
The waterfall, the pool, all was as she remembered it,
but now there was a sea of faces, all looking at her, and
the only sound was the splash of water. She growled again,
opening her mouth wider in display, and her upper gums
were aching from the pressure of distended teeth. The
blade of her sword was now tinted green in the light of

her eyes, and people ogled her, drawing back a step as she passed by.

They went to the pool, and stood in a line before it. A few tents were up, but mostly there were heaps of possessions, tightly packed together on the sand, the people sitting on top of them. Near the front of the crowd, a young woman smiled up at Kati with an expression of delight, pointed at her, then whispered to a man sitting next to her with their two children.

Goldani waved her hand, and the waterfall ceased flowing behind them. Kati remembered thinking it magic, but Ma had explained that a man simply closed a gate at the top of the waterfall, diverting the stream that fed it, and giving them the silence to hear the hot breath from the Eye of Tengri-Nayon.

And it was there, the sound from deep inside the ground, coming down the hanging canyon to her left. All those assembled listened to it for a moment, and then Goldani raised her arms.

"We're gathered for a special Festival in the Eye of Tengri-Nayon, and in the presence of the living Empress Mandughai, who watches over us all! She comes soon to free us, and has sent an emissary to tell us what we must do! She has chosen one of our own as emissary, a Tumatsin woman taken from us in tragedy and returned in triumph. That woman sits beside me. She is Kati, daughter of Toregene and Temujin. The leaders of your *ordu*s have told you the story of Kati's life and how she came to be chosen by Mandughai. There are those of us who have seen a sampling of her powers. But she comes with a warning about our liberation by Mandughai, for it is not to happen in the way we've believed! Many of you have doubts. You must hear that warning directly from the mouth of The One our Empress sends to us."

The people were silent, all expressions serious; their eyes were on Kati.

"Tell them," said Goldani, "exactly as you told it to me."

Kati took a deep breath, cheeks flushed, and her voice came forth as a hoarse, throaty growl that surprised her audience.

"I bring greetings from Mandughai, who has sent me here and made me all that I am! She arrives in only a few months with a great army to rid you of the Emperor and bring freedom for *all* the people of Shanji, of which you're only a part. She brings freedom to Tumatsin and Hansui alike, but especially to the millions living in poor conditions to the east of the mountains, people you've never seen who live in filth and poverty while slaving for nobles who do not care about them. Your lives are good, by comparison. There is much misery in our world, and Mandughai will not have it remain any longer! She will rid Shanji of poverty, and requires all the people, Tumatsin and Hansui, to work towards that goal! We must come together, work together. We are all one people, with one Empress. The division between us must come to an end when the Emperor is gone!"

The expression of many men had turned to scowls, and they were whispering among each other. Kati glared at each of them until the whispering stopped.

"Your hatred for the Hansui runs deep, and has reason. I also have reason to hate them; they killed my mother, and burned the *ordu* of my childhood. But I've learned there are many good people among the Hansui, people who care about every living being, and work for justice and equality, all the things you expect Mandughai to give you. She will give you *nothing*! She expects *you* to do it, by working together as one people."

The men were whispering again. This time, she didn't stop them.

"I know your doubts! I *hear* them in your minds, for Mandughai has also made me Moshuguang, a Searcher.

She also hears your doubts, and has told me you'll only unite with the Hansui to fight a common threat. I didn't accept that, at first, but now I do. Her army will move against *all* of us, Tumatsin and Hansui alike. We'll unite in fighting Her army, or be destroyed, and leave Her to begin again. I'm committed to your defense, even if you will not aid me in defending the Hansui. I ride with my soldiers! I do not watch from afar! I'll give up my life to defend *all* the people of Shanji, not just the Tumatsin. And I ask you to join me in defending our world."

"You proclaim yourself Empress!" shouted a man.

"You're rude!" cried Goldani. "Quiet!"

"No! Let him speak. It's the men who risk their lives in war, and they must believe in the reason for such risk. Mandughai has chosen me, not I. She's taught me, extended my powers, all of it in preparation to bring change to Shanji, and a better life for all the people. You've all been told of my plans for reform."

"So give us a sign of your powers!" shouted the same man.

"I'll do that tonight—by this pool. I'll expect to see you here. But I fear you'll only believe when your *ordus* are burning. And when that time comes, I *will* be there to defend you!"

Goldani interrupted before Kati could take a breath.

"You hear her words! She has given her warning, and you must think about it. We can be destroyed, or we can follow the will of Mandughai, and do what has been told to us. Our long wait is over. Our prayers have been answered, though not in the way we've expected. There will be new rule on Shanji! There will be justice, and a better life for all of us if we choose it. Now, let us go to the fields to eat, and to celebrate the fulfillment of our prayers!"

The children jumped to their feet, excited, though the adults were still serious looking and quiet. One exception was the young woman who'd been smiling at Kati. She was beaming now, and rushed to Kati's side as the women were just turning their horses.

"Kati! It *is* you! You're still wearing the necklace of shells I gave you when we got our horses!"

"Edi? Is it you? I would never have guessed!" Kati reached down to take the woman's offered hand. "I saw you there, You have *children*!"

"Two," said Edi. "Do you remember the little wooden knife you gave me?"

"Yes."

"You see, on the belt of my son Tuli. I've passed your gift on to my son."

"We must go," said Goldani.

"I want to talk more," said Kati. "After our meal?"

"I want to hear everything," said Edi, and released Kati's hand.

The column of women on horseback started up the hanging canyon, and the people formed a long line behind them, those in front pressing in closely to keep watching Kati as best they could. Hot air and a sharp odor swirled between the rock walls towering above them, the roar of Tengri's Eye drowning out any conversation as they neared it.

"I wish to make a small demonstration," said Kati, as they reached The Eye. She stopped by it, and the other women went on. Kati held up a hand to the people and shouted.

"I came here as a child, and The Eye burns as it did then. I will make it burn brighter to celebrate the fulfillment of our prayers! Stay to your left, so you'll not be burned by it!"

Kati held out a hand towards The Eye of Tengri, and the burning coal seam deep within, a column of organic vapors rising from it. The gesture was only ritual, her aura entering the hot cavern and drawing heat from it like a cosmic bellows. The fire hurried to follow her, intensifying. A column of hot gas and flame erupted from the cavern, searing rock to a glaze, and startling Kati's horse into rearing.

Stay. She froze the animal in place, enveloping the two of them in a blue auric shield she knew would be seen by the women. The column of flame rushed upwards, and past her within two arms' length as she sat there calmly, hand outstretched. The people shielded their eyes, pressing to the rock wall to slide past her as quickly as they could.

It was half an hour before all the people had filed past in a tumble, and then they stopped to look back at her.

"Now sleep!" said Kati. She lowered her hand, and the column of flame disappeared as if sucked on by a great inhalation from deep within The Eye.

There was fear on the faces of the people, and yet she saw faint smiles from some of the women. The terror of such wonderment, such power, was somehow muted by the fact she was one of them. Kati followed them up the canyon, but they kept looking back, as if expecting a new wonder.

Then they reached the plateau, with the colorful *gerts*, the smells of meat cooking, the big field roped off for games, all as she remembered.

With the reversal of her change, her face relaxed and the tension left her mouth; she was the familiar Kati, or Mengnu, again, a daughter of the Tumatsin—and the Moshuguang.

When the people saw her on the plateau, now smiling as she looked around to recall memories, they also seemed to relax. Children ran past her with honeycakes, and young boys trotted their horses on the game field, sitting erect and looking around to see who was watching them. The adults were lined up for food, the men shouting as they heard the pop of an ayrog skin being opened.

Goldani came up to her on foot, and Kati dismounted, tethering her horse at the edge of the game field. They waited in line with the others, and stuffed themselves with lamb, potatoes, cheese and barleycakes, even drank cups of ayrog offered to them by the men. Kati noticed the way the men looked at her, a few cups of ayrog now in their bellies, and it was different than it had been before. For the moment, at least, they saw her face, not her power, and she was able to relax even more. For the moment, she was simply one of them.

Edi came by to sit with her while they ate their meal before a *ger*. She talked about her husband, a herder of sheep for the Kereit *ordu* well down the coast. She'd discovered him at Festival, and now there were children, a boy and a girl, their first horses yet to come.

They stood together at the edge of the game field, and Kati's eyes filled with tears as they watched three boys and two girls receive first horses from their fathers: the squeals of joy, the hugs, fathers at first leading the animals, then releasing the children to ride round and around the field.

Edi saw the tears in Kati's eyes, and hugged her arm. "We rode around and around, until it was dark, and they had to come out to get us off our horses."

"Yes," said Kati, but she wasn't thinking about dear Sushua. She thought again about Da, and his loss. Her loss.

Forgive me, Mengmoshu, but he was the only father I knew as a child.

These children were no different than she and Edi. They rode until nightfall, and the fathers had to go out and pull their protesting children from the horses.

With a brilliant Tengri-Nayon overhead, they left the plateau to walk down the canyon, passing the glow of The Eye. Goldani offered her tent to share with Kati, for Baber had not come with her. It was a disappointment to Kati, but Goldani pointed out he was a fisherman now, and none of them were there. The fish did not come to Festival. As a child, it had seemed to Kati that *all* Tumatsin were at Festival, but now she saw it was only a small portion of them, only those who could make time for fun, or the few who truly believed in Mandughai or Her coming. They'd prayed for two thousand years, and nothing had happened. Now it was happening, and they didn't believe.

She saw the man who'd shouted at her when she'd spoken earlier. He was drinking ayrog before his *ger*, and a woman sitting with him nudged him with an elbow as Kati approached.

"You wanted a sign?" she asked.

"I saw what you did with The Eye," the man said, lowering his eyes.

"I'll do something more useful, now."

Kati walked back to the edge of the pool, heard whispers and the shuffling of feet behind her. She stood at pool-edge, waiting until it was quiet, then stretched her arms out over the water. She pushed her aura out over the pool, flattening it to a disk, then closed her eyes, and breathed deeply. All ritual, the aura a point of focus for her mind, for Kati did not yet understand how she brought the light from the gong-shi-jie, It was simply there when she wanted it, streaming through openings small beyond imagination, and now it was coming again, a purple shower like rain, falling from aura to pool.

The people behind her gasped as fog appeared above the water, then steam and bubbles as the pool came to a roiling boil in only seconds.

Kati turned around, and smiled, as if amused. "The night is cold, and now we can all have a warm bath," she said, and sat down to remove her boots.

People scrambled to their *gerts* to change clothes, and Goldani laughed. "I will get you a robe," she said to Kati.

The little children bathed nude, the men in their underclothes, the women in robes. The pool was quickly filled, but the water was so hot that people willingly gave up their places after only a few minutes. Kati went in three times, finally emerging for sleep, drowsy and wobbly. Goldani helped her into bed, the sound of happy bathers still coming from outside.

Goldani smiled. "I think you'll be a very practical Empress," she said.

The people saw them as games, but not Kati. Tests, yes, but not games, not with a war so close in their future.

She watched the men shoot their arrows at fifty paces to man-sized, straw targets, and asked if she could join them, an unheard-of request by a Tumatsin woman. The men allowed it out of curiosity more than anything else. Then they seemed surprised by her accuracy and speed with the bow. Still, there were men more accurate than she, even better than the troops she'd practiced with for years.

It was with the sword, even on horseback, that they lacked training. The sword was a symbol of a Tumatsin past, when the first Mandughai's army had come. The women carried it in ceremony, the men used it in games on horseback, striking at straw targets with great force, but little technique, and a trained soldier on foot would disembowel them in an instant. On foot, they knew nothing of the blade's art. On foot, man-to-man, they were helpless.

Kati asked to join them again, and again they were curious about what she could do in a man's game. They loaned her a grey mountain horse, a young mare with thick shoulders and good spirit. Her own horse from the city still limped slightly on a sore foot. When she felt the animal bunching its muscles in excitement beneath her, she knew it would be a mountain horse she rode

into battle, both for stamina and quickness. There were
none better; even the Hansui knew it.

She rode with the men, and felt The Change come
upon her as she charged around the field in pattern after
pattern, growling, then shrieking as she struck each target,
not just slashing wildly, but using deft jabs with single,
double, even triple feints, her blade a blur to the eye. It
was like practice with the troopers, and she was quickly
focused on it, oblivious to anything else around. She didn't
hear the quieting of the crowd around the field, or notice
the men ride to its edges to watch her.

She completed another round, and finally noticed she
was alone on the game field. It was embarrassing to her,
all the people watching, the men just sitting on their
horses. Kati walked her horse to them as she sheathed
her sword. "I'm sorry. I didn't notice you'd finished with
the game."

"You didn't learn to do that when you were a child,"
said a man, smiling. All the men studied her alertly, and
she was relieved. They did not seem offended by her
display.

"No. I've studied with a sword master, and trained with
the Emperor's troopers for several years."

"They are as skilled as you?" asked the same man.

"Some better, but I've held my own with them. When
The Change is upon me, not one of them has defeated
me. My Tumatsin blood gives me an advantage they don't
have."

"The advantage of a woman," said the man, and she
knew what he was thinking. The skill she'd displayed
was superior to theirs. The skill of the Emperor's troopers
was superior to theirs. They'd played games, while others
prepared for war. They were vulnerable to attack.

"Do you practice hand-to-hand with the sword?" she
asked.

"No." The men looked grim, now.

"I can give you some exercises to practice, if you're willing. You only have a few months to practice, but it's enough to make a difference. I can show you now, if you wish, but you'll have to teach others. I'll not be able to return before Mandughai comes with Her army."

"Then show us," said the man, dismounting, and drawing his sword.

The others followed him, and Kati took them to a far corner of the field, forming them into two lines facing each other. For one hour, and another hour later in the afternoon, she taught them the ten *dong*s of Master Yung, and had them practice at sword's length. A first lesson, but there was no more time. Still, they learned quickly, and she was able to correct the most glaring errors they made. A small skill was better than nothing. It would not be much against Mandughai's troops. Kati's people would not be prepared for war.

Kati did what she could, and the crowd around the field was amused by the sight of the men hacking away at each other. Goldani finally came out to the field to halt their practice. "Get to your horses. It's time for the ceremony of Mandughai's charge against the Emperor."

The men left, talking among themselves, and Goldani turned to Kati. "When you were a child, it was Toregene, your mother, who led the charge. I would like you to do it with me, in her place."

Kati was moved to tears. "I thank you for such an honor, Goldani. Your kindness is more than I expected. I'll join you to honor my mother."

She went back to her horse, and rode over to join the ceremonial warriors assembled at the end of the field. Goldani was again in her robe, eyes light green. The Change was upon her, and a group of perhaps fifty men were jostling their horses behind her. As a child, it had seemed there were thousands participating in the ritual charge, but now she saw how few there were. They were farmers, herders, craftsmen, not soldiers. They played games, and acted out war, based on a memory that was false. The first Mandughai had come with fierce, bioengineered troops to destroy them all, not to save them from the Emperor. Her soldiers had the faces of *shizi*, and battle was the purpose of their lives. How many would come? Thousands? Tens of thousands? And now, here was Kati, leading a charge of fifty untrained men to entertain the crowd watching them.

The Change was fully upon her as the men formed two lines behind them. "There's a ritual we use with the Emperor's troopers before a charge," she growled to Goldani. "Will you trust me to use it here?"

Goldani nodded, and Kati turned her horse towards the men.

"Hold out your swords!" she shouted with a hoarse voice.

They did so, blades gleaming. Kati withdrew her own, battered sword, and shrieked at them, "This is not play! It is real! The next time you do this, a hoard of invaders will be coming at you to murder your families and burn your *ordus*! You're all that stand in their way! You are the only defense of your people!"

The men looked at her, astonished. Kati kicked her horse, and rode back and forth along the two lines of men, slapping each blade hard with her own, and screaming, "You defend your families! You defend your *ordus*! You defend *Shanji*! Now let the enemy hear you coming!"

The men were screaming before she made the last turn back towards Goldani. The woman saw her coming, and kicked her horse, but then Kati was past her, blood boiling, her blade outstretched as she screamed.

"SHANJIIII!"

They covered the length of the field in seconds, the crowd trilling and screaming with them. They formed

up again, horses snorting, banging hard against each other
in their excitement.

"Again!" shouted Goldani.

"SHANJIII!" a chorus of bass screams as they crossed
the field a second time to the cheers of the crowd.

Now everyone was laughing, dismounting, the swords
again in their scabbards. "It was a good charge," said
Goldani. "They have the spirit."

"Yes," said Kati, frowning at her, "but they do not
understand."

There was nothing more she could do. Kati felt
frustration, and some despair. Even the trained troops
of the Moshuguang had never known true battle with a
skilled army. And battle would come, forced on her by
a woman she loved, and another who craved only power.
How many would die before Mandughai was satisfied
with their opposition? Or would it be all of them? All
her loud threats to Yesugen were suddenly silly. Destroy
all her ships indeed. She didn't even know if she could
bring herself to use the light of the gong-shi-jie against
a human life. If she could not, then Shanji was doomed,
for Yesugen would bring a superior force for conquest,
and only Kati's powers could stop her.

The joy of Festival was suddenly gone from her. She
went back to a *ger* to sit grimly before it while the people
ate and visited with friends. The little children came out
again to ride their first horses. Some were already leaving
the field to pack their belongings for treks back to the
more southerly *ordu*s.

Goldani brought her a plate of food, and sat beside
her to eat, "You're not happy," she said.

"I'm afraid," said Kati. "I'm afraid about what will
happen to them when Mandughai's army comes. They
don't even believe it."

"I believe, and there are others. Many are not here."

"It won't be enough. I'll do what I can, Goldani. I'll

bring as many troopers as I can, but I'm still afraid for them all. It's coming so *soon!*"

Goldani put a hand on her shoulder, then went back to her eating, chewing slowly.

"How can you be so calm?" asked Kati.

Goldani smiled serenely. "I take you at your word. You've said Mandughai hopes to break off Her attack at the first sign of unified opposition from us. That is my hope."

"Those were Her words," said Kati. She'd said nothing about Yesugen, and would not do it now.

"You don't believe Her?"

"I want to."

"But you have doubts."

"Yes." Kati thought again of the *real* leader of the invasion: Yesugen, the cold, imperious one from the gong-shi-jie, the one who had drugged her own mother to enable a private meeting with her adversary. She might have killed her mother in such a way. What else was she capable of?

"Don't underestimate your own people, Kati. We live simple lives in isolation, but we've not survived all these years by being foolish. We're practical people, capable of making decisions we'd rather not make. I think we'll demonstrate that when the time comes. Things will be decided by Mandughai's mercy, not by how well we do in battle. We must trust Her."

"Your belief is strong, Goldani, though you've never seen Her, or talked to Her as I have. I admire your faith."

"I also have faith in the Tumatsin woman who will be Empress of Shanji," said Goldani, "and I have faith in the people."

Kati leaned against her, and Goldani put an arm around her shoulders.

"So soon," said Kati. "So soon."

She worked with the men a final time in the afternoon,

and then Festival was over, and everyone was leaving. She found Edi again, and they talked while the horses were packed, and then they were gone. The people were gone, and the sand was empty by the pool, the only sound that of the breath from The Eye of Tengri-Nayon, and she was standing alone with Goldani as the waterfall began to splash again. Everything was completed, and the people were still not together.

There would be war soon.

She rode through the canyon with Goldani, and they parted at the intersection of trails heading west, east, and south. Goldani leaned over, and kissed her on the cheek.

"Have faith in Mandughai," she said, "and in yourself."

Goldani turned her horse, and rode away towards the glimmering sea. Kati watched her until she was a speck, then turned her horse east. The animal seemed rested. She walked it for several hours, breaking into an occasional trot as the sky darkened, and Tengri-Nayon was glaring down at her. The following afternoon, when she saw the silhouette of Three Peaks, not far ahead, she went to a slow gallop, holding it much of the way back to the Emperor's city—and Huomeng.

She wondered how much time they were destined to have together.

PART IV

MEI-LAI-GONG

CHAPTER EIGHTEEN
MEI-LAI-GONG

The warning was quite late, and arrived from three different sources.

Kati was sleeping, and suddenly the emerald eyes were there as they'd been years before, the times before her travel in the gong-shi-jie.

Kati!

She awoke with a start, and kept her eyes closed.

Mandughai! Is it you?

Yes, dear. I would have come sooner, but hesitated because I knew you'd been warned of our transit.

I've talked to your daughter, Mandughai. It wasn't a pleasant meeting. Her agenda is clearly the conquest of Shanji, and I will not allow it. This war will be fought with more than sword and bow.

I know. I wasn't so soundly asleep as she thought. I've said nothing to her; you know something about her, now, and I did warn you that she's different from you. She fears your powers, Kati, but will never admit it. I fear them also, but only because I want minimal loss of life in our engagement. My purpose is change, not killing. You were angry when you spoke to Yesugen, and your threats were clear. Do you still feel the same way?

You're like my mother, Mandughai, but you've forced me into a war I don't want. My people aren't prepared

*to meet trained soldiers in battle, and I'll do anything I
have to in defending them. Yesugen and I have discussed
the terms of battle.*

There was a long pause. Kati sat up in bed, eyes tightly
close, fists clenched in her lap.

*I understand, Kati. I can only ask you to control your
anger, and remember my intent to break off the attack
when I see a unified force against us. I still have some
control over that, and if you show willingness to use your
powers my hope is that Yesugen and her supporters will
see the futility of attempting a conquest of Shanji. The
details of strategy are up to Yesugen, but I'll tell you she
plans a two-pronged attack: one division coming up your
northern valley, and another moving south along the sea
before heading east towards the city.*

When?

*We're coming into orbit within a day. My guess is two
to three days until we land. I can tell you nothing more.*

*And there's nothing more I can do to prepare for war,
Mandughai. I'll fight alongside my soldiers to meet your
attack.*

*I've always expected it, dear. It's a risk I'm willing to
make in light of your abilities, but my heart's desire is
to see you alive and well when this is over. Remember
that.*

I will.

The emerald eyes were gone with a blink. Kati jumped
from her bed, and began to dress in her leathers.

Mengmoshu! Are you there?

No answer.

FATHER! Answer me!

Nothing.

She dressed without care for her appearance, and
rushed from her rooms, taking the elevator to her father's
floor and hurrying past an astonished guard to pound
on his door.

The door opened, and he was there in a robe, hair disheveled. "Stop shouting, and come in! I had to talk to First Mother, and now you and Huomeng are screaming at me! One at a time, please!"

Kati followed him into the small office he kept in his suite and saw Huomeng's face on a console screen there. "Kati, are you there? I heard a voice—"

"I'm here!" she said as Mengmoshu sat down at his desk again.

Instrument panels glowed behind Huomeng. "We saw them over an hour ago, but our resolution's so terrible I thought it might be an asteroid. In an hour they're nearly on top of us, and braking hard. I can see the glows of ionic drag on every ship, and they're *huge*! The ships must be several times the size of our mother ship, and there's over a dozen of them. I can't be sure yet, with this lousy resolution we've—"

"Keep watch; get the exact number, and size of each ship if you can," said Mengmoshu. "I have to inform the Emperor right away. First Mother has talked to Kati, and me. We have a good idea about what to expect, but an estimate of force strength would be useful."

"As soon as I can," said Huomeng. "Kati, are you all right?"

"I'm ready," she said.

"Good, because I'm not. I'm stuck in this mountain, and I want to see you again."

"There will be time," she said softly.

"But not *now*!" growled Mengmoshu. "Keep an eye on those ships! I'm going to the Emperor!"

It was her father who broke the connection with Huomeng, and she scowled at him.

"Later!" he said, and went into his bedroom to dress while Kati waited by his desk.

"I have to warn Goldani!" she called out. "One prong of the attack will be coming their way!"

"I'll take care of it! Stay here until I get back. I have to convince the Son of Heaven an attack is coming, and he's barely aware of his surroundings. I might be dealing with Shan-lan tonight."

"What can I do?"

"Nothing for now, except wait for me and relax, even sleep. It might be the last sleep you get for days. You're the center for all of this."

Mengmoshu came out of his room unbuttoned and rumpled. Kati fussed over him until he pulled her hands away, giving her a dark look.

"It begins, child," he said, then kissed her on the forehead and hurried out of the room.

There was no sleep that night, and little the next. Kati spent the entire time in her father's office after his return. The Emperor had been more than coherent, but Shan-lan had also been there. Officers were awakened from sleep, and troops were spilling out of their barracks well before dawn to stand on alert.

Mengmoshu made call after call, asking the return of favors given years before. Elite troops of the Moshuguang came out of the mountain tunnel and were loaded into flyers, six men at a time for shuttling to the western border. Appearances had to be kept, and only ten flyers could be used, shuttling back and forth all night and day, then night again.

Huomeng called again before dawn. "The first ships are going into orbit. I count at least twenty, now; they're coming in clusters of four, and they're all monsters, Mengmoshu. We could have ten thousand or more coming against us."

"As soon as they begin landing, Her weapons crews in space will be on alert. I can't risk using flyers for trooper movement after that," Mengmoshu warned Kati. "You should take a flyer to the border today or tonight, to

meet the attack on your people as you promised you
would."

"No! I'll stay here awhile."

"You only want to see Huomeng again! He won't be
coming here until the invaders have landed!"

"No, I said! I don't trust Yesugen. She could change
her attack plan and I'd be stuck at the border with only
a horse to get me back here. I want to see her movements
first."

It was only a partial truth, and he saw it.

But Kati was dismayed when she saw the final result
of trooper transfer. When Huomeng called in to say that
the twenty-eight ships of First Mother's force were now
in orbit and spewing forth their landing shuttles like wasps
from nests, the flyers were on their way back and fewer
than three hundred elite troops had been taken to the
border.

"Three *hundred*? I told them a *thousand*!"

"With the border guards, it's four hundred! I can't do
more! I'm grounding the flyers, at least temporarily."

"I *promised*! You were *there*!"

"Too *much*! Use what you *have*. We have to consider
our field commanders; their job is to defend the *city*!
You'll *need* them when this is over. We must have their
support for you. Quit thinking like a Tumatsin, and think
like an *Empress*!"

The rebuke hurt her to tears, for she knew he was
correct.

She could only wait, as new word came in. The eyes
of the mother ship were now on Shanji. Huomeng
reported lights glimmering from a broad peninsula jutting
into the sea only a few kilometers from the northernmost
ordus of the Tumatsin. A small river entered the sea just
south of the peninsula, and lights were also scattered
along the floodplain there. A quick march east over rolling
hills and the invaders would be in the valley leading to

the Emperor's city, totally bypassing the mountains. A sprint south along the sea could take the major *ordus* in a day, and give them access to the plateau for a pincer move against the city. A simple plan, but clear, and there was no longer time for waiting.

"I want to leave before dawn tomorrow," she said to Mengmoshu. "Can you get a good mountain horse for me?"

"Yes, but no remounts. It'll be saddled and ready by the city gate. Our men will wait for you at the border, and Goldani will be notified. Women and children are being loaded into boats and sent out to sea, and the home guard is mobilized. Everyone saw the shuttles coming down, but they're *still* waiting to see what will come. The home guards remain in the *ordus* when they should be moving north!"

"They protect their own homes, father. They've never fought as a single army before. I don't know if they can do it."

Mengmoshu embraced her hard. "Say it again—what you call me when we're alone."

"Father." Her hands caressed his back.

Mengmoshu kissed her neck. "Kati, take care of yourself. Don't get trapped by your agreement with Yesugen, or First Mother, and use your powers to the fullest. You can destroy them all with a wave of your hand!"

If she could bring herself to do it. It was no time for argument, no time to talk about the honor of an agreement, or self-doubts, or using her powers to prevent her people from doing what was required of them. She had a pact with her people, but there was also one with Yesugen— and Mandughai.

"I'll do my best," she murmured, kissing her father on the cheek. And then she left the room, without looking back at him.

✧   ✧   ✧

It was late afternoon when she returned to her rooms, planning to eat and then retire early. Weimeng wasn't there, for the Emperor had requested her presence at his bedside, and she now spent most of her time there. Tanchun brought her food, and Kati ate alone in Weimeng's suite. She went back to her own suite along the silent hallway and locked herself in. Apprehension was growing, and the food felt sour in her stomach. She took a long, hot bath and rubbed herself down until her skin glowed, then put on a light robe and sat down before her shrine to light the candles, incense and sweet grass in the little bowl there. The smoke curled upwards, and she drew it to her nostrils, closing her eyes.

Quiet, and peace. Her skin felt tingly, and warm. She breathed deep, with long, slow exhalations, hands in her lap, feeling the apprehension melting away as she repeated a phrase of self-assurance over and over to herself.

I am Kati, a person chosen by Mandughai. I am Mei-lai-gong, a ruler of Light. The light comes to me, and goes from me. I use it in the service of Mandughai, and my people.

Over and over, she repeated it, and there was only darkness before her. She was not yet in the gong-shi-jie, did not rush to it this time, but reflected on what was there: the power to create a universe, the power to destroy it. The swirling clouds of purple were only a signature of the coolest light, like the vortices of planets and stars, so immobile, so cold. But where she saw the purple, there was The Other, the light of purple beyond purple, beyond even the vision of her special mind, a light of unimaginable energy. How much she'd drawn on it in her exercises, playtime and magic tricks was a mystery to her, but what was necessary was always there. She needed only to imagine the scale, and think the thought, and it was always there.

The matrix of bright points opened at her command,

and she was surrounded by purple chaos. The vortices of green, red, and yellow leading to things were more organized, more real, with size and shape, and time. She hovered there, urging herself to probe beyond the purple light, to see what was beyond, but the sight wasn't there, only the instinct, the consciousness of The Power, waiting for her command. She called up a vision of the mother ship above Shanji, and was instantly there in real space, drifting near it, a phantom unseen by Huomeng's instruments.

There were others who saw the mother ship with her.

The ships of Mandughai's army were there, a long line of them in a single orbit higher than the mother ship's, but close to it. Round balls bristling with superstructure bearing communications, shuttle docks, ion scoops and weapon manifolds with the long cylinders of microwave lasers capable of scouring continents. There were twenty-eight, as Huomeng had said, each of them easily five times the size of the mother ship. As she watched, a shuttle detached itself from one of them; a spurt of gas aft of the wedge-shaped craft, and it was dropping into the atmosphere of Kati's planet, deploying stubby wings for a gliding descent along a helical path.

She could reach out, and let the light come; the occupants of the craft would feel warmth, then searing heat in the instant before their organs boiled and burst. She held the thought, savored it, was tempted by it. The great transit ships tempted her even more with the challenge of their size, but it would be the same. Light of purple beyond purple, energy beyond light making the particles that were the basis for all matter, all would come to her, penetrating the thick hulls and reducing everything to fundamentals with a single thought if she willed it. The thought intrigued her, excited her, and she resisted it also with great effort. She wondered if Mandughai could see the storm in her mind, the sudden anger at self-limitation, of holding back to meet a threat she'd not asked for, a threat that could, no, *would* kill people she cared for.

Kati could stand it no longer; the temptation was too great, too close to fulfillment, and again there was the flash of transition, the mindless, instantaneous flight to the gong-shi-jie, away from her enemy and to the whirlpool signature of herself, diving into it.

She opened her eyes with a growl, face drawn taut and flushed with heat, the canines pressing back on her lower lip. Her fingernails had drawn blood from the palms of her hands, and there was a pounding in her ears that went on and on, a pounding, then a voice.

"Kati! Let me in! Kati!"

The door. The pounding came from the door to her rooms, and she knew who was there. She rushed to the door, crying out hoarsely as she flung it open to see Huomeng standing there. He was startled, flinching backwards half a step, but only for an instant. He grabbed her shoulders hard with both hands, and pushed her back, kicking the door closed behind him, then crushing her to him so hard she grunted.

His hands moved over her back, her buttocks. He kissed her neck, her cheeks and forehead, murmuring, "Kati, Kati. Oh, Kati. Mengmoshu told me. It's too *soon*! Tomorrow is too *soon*!"

For one instant, she was terrified. His face was so close, his hands now on her cheeks, and here she was, looking like a—

Huomeng ran a finger over her canines, then her lower lip, rubbing the inside of it, and touching her tongue. "There's no time," he murmured. "We only have tonight."

Kati moaned as he swept her up in his arms and carried her to the bed, dumping her hard enough to bounce. She was only dressed in her robe, was quickly ahead of him and helping him to peel out of his white uniform, her breath coming in growling gasps. The muscles in her arms knotted large and hard as she clutched his waist to pull him down on top of her, opening her mouth wide to receive his.

In seconds, she noticed how deftly he avoided her teeth, wedging his lips between them, and pressing so hard she thought he might swallow her. He entered her quickly, erect and hard, to move urgently with her. He brought her to the brink once, then twice, each time closer, and her growl was a continuous thing stifled by the press of his mouth. She shrieked as they came together, and still there was no sound that could escape the doors of her room. The shock was electric, up and down her spine and throughout her groin, and suddenly her energy was gone. She felt his release, the sudden warmth within her as he shuddered again and again.

His lips left hers, and pressed to her neck. She touched his face, and his cheek was wet. His body still shook, and Kati suddenly realized he was crying softly against her neck.

"Shhhh," she whispered. "Just hold me. Love me."

"I do," he whispered. "Always, Kati. I'll always love you. There can never be another. Ever. Just you."

"Forever," she murmured. "I want you with me forever."

She realized too late it was the wrong thing to say. He was crying again, holding desperately onto her as if she might suddenly be gone.

Kati shushed him gently, kissed his face, neck and shoulder, her hands moving all over him. He was still in her, and they stayed that way for a long time, breath slowing, bodies cooling as they caressed each other without another word. Finally getting drowsy, she rolled him gently onto his side, and saw that he'd fallen asleep. She kissed the wetness on his cheeks, held him, watched him, felt the ooze of his seed from within her.

"Forever," she murmured, and then quickly fell asleep.

❖   ❖   ❖

She awoke to find Huomeng's face against her shoulder, an arm draped across her. She slid beneath it, got out of bed without disturbing him, then picked her leathers up from the floor and dressed quickly in darkness. The guards in the hallway looked especially alert, and snapped rigidly to attention as she came to the elevator. Both Moshuguang, their masks still failed them. She saw that they knew the reason for her early rising, and they feared for their own lives in the coming defense of the city.

Outside, it was cold and dark, all the city lights shut down. She walked alone down the steep, narrow street beneath the monorail, her breath making little puffs of fog as she quickened her steps. Ahead, and below, were the lights of a thousand torches around the barracks, the gate, and the fields beyond, glimmering fireflies in blackness. As she drew closer, she could see figures moving, the blue auras of men and horses, clouds of fog from their breath hanging like smoke in the torchlight.

A mountain horse stood by the gate, held there by a trooper, and she went straight to it. The trooper heard her approach, and turned.

It was Lui-Pang.

He was in leathers and armor, a helmet and faceshield, and he held another helmet in one hand.

"Master Yung saw you coming," he said. "He was just here."

"Where is he?"

"Out there, in the darkness. He left something for you—in the saddle. He wouldn't wait to talk to you."

Kati walked around the horse, prepared to sheath her sword in the saddle-scabbard there. The scabbard was already occupied. Brass gleamed in torchlight and the emerald glow of her eyes. Kati withdrew a sword with a pristine, curved blade, tested its balance, jabbed with it.

"He said to tell you the sword is a thousand years old,

and made by an ancient master. It has never been used, and it's yours. He says there is nothing more he can teach you. You're no longer his student, and you're to remember who you are when you use the sword. And then he went away."

Kati sheathed the sword, and tied her old one on the back of her saddle with the bow and quiver there. "Tell him I'm honored by his gift and his teachings. Tell him I understand what he says."

She mounted the horse, and took the reins from Lui-Pang. Their hands touched, and the light of her eyes reflected brightly from his faceshield.

"You will fight today," he said.

"Yes. I fight for Shanji."

Lui-Pang smiled, and took a step back, coming to attention. "I fight for the city, and for the Empress who will govern it. I want her to wear this helmet to protect her green eyes from a scattered laser burst, if she will accept it."

Kati took the helmet, and put it on. "You know," she said.

"The secret was leaked weeks ago," he said, then stepped forward to put a hand over hers on her knee. "I'm not alone in wanting to see you return," he said softly. "Take care of yourself, Mengnu."

"And you," she said, as he withdrew his hand.

Beyond the two of them was silence and gloom, faces dim in torchlight, perhaps a thousand, many of them her classmates, and Master Yung was among them. He would not, or could not talk to her at this moment, and so she would give him a sign. The Change had not left her since the evening before, yet Lui-Pang had touched her hand, and said gentle words. She would touch them all in another way.

They could not see her aura, their attention now held only by the twin beacons of her eyes, but the aura was there, a great fan of gold with radiating streamers in red. She only touched the gong-shi-jie, bringing forth the coolest light to outline her auric field and mingle with it; the ground for meters around her was suddenly illuminated in purple and deep blue.

A collective sigh came from those who watched her.

Kati faced the crowd of troopers, and withdrew her new sword with a sweep of her arm to hold the blade over her head.

"SHANJI!" she cried out hoarsely.

A thousand blades appeared in the light, and the chorus of male voices thrilled the soul that wandered the place of creation.

"SHANJI!" they replied.

Kati returned the sword to its scabbard, turned her horse, and walked it through the gate and along the torch-lined lane without looking back. She walked it up the steep, rocky trail in darkness to the place where an *ordu* had once stood, then into the mountains, past the peaks with a meadow near their summit, and flowers that a child's horse had been named after. When she reached the broad expanse of the plateau, it was still dark. She leaned over, and whispered into the little horse's ear as the muscles in her legs bunched hard.

"You are a mountain horse, Now, you *fly!*"

The animal obliged her, heading west towards the sea.

CHAPTER NINETEEN
WAR

The sky brightened for an instant, well before dawn.

It was a flash of blue and green, lighting the sky to the watery horizon, and many seconds later rolling thunder filled Kati's ears, startling her horse to a gallop. She reined him in and looked back toward the mountain peaks to see a shimmering green tendril of color stretching high into the sky, as if a meteor had fallen, fading rapidly until nothing was there. The eastern horizon beyond the peaks did not yet show the first red hues of morning, and the stars still twinkled, Tengri-Nayon outshining them all.

Kati urged the horse to a trot. She'd run him the entire length of the plateau, and mountain horse or not, he was now tiring. The sky was paling as she passed the trail leading down into the canyon where Festival was held, and she wondered if it would happen again; if a little Tumatsin girl would ever again receive her first horse at that place.

An hour later, there was heat on the back of her neck; the orb of Tengri-Khan had now risen above the peaks. She wanted to feel the heat on her face, and twisted in the saddle to look eastward.

And was nearly blinded by a series of three, closely spaced flashes of light coming down from the depths of space to strike beyond the mountains. The visor of her helmet darkened, so that there were only the flashes of green and blue, and Tengri-Khan was gone.

The thunder came with the return of her sight of Shanji's sun, long rolling peals of sound that seemed to surround her, and finally she understood. Weapons of light on Mandughai's orbiting ships; they'd opened fire on ground targets or flyers.

The attack had begun.

Her horse was exhausted, breathing heavily, but responded to the press of her knees and was trotting again along the broadening trail into a shallow valley of dry grass and over a hill, the sea close, now, and spreading north and south from her.

More. A little more. You're a good horse, a strong horse.

She topped a second hill and saw the border: the fence, the little buildings spaced along it, figures scurrying like ants in confusion. Much closer, a rider was heading towards her, a trooper in helmet and armor. When he came closer, she saw he was Moshuguang, one of the elite. She charged towards him and he turned around, heading west, slowing his mount until she'd caught up with him. The flanks of their horses collided as they rode close together at a slow gallop, shouting.

"They were moving before dawn! The nearest *ordu*s had been evacuated, and they burned them to the ground! The Tumatsin home guard has fallen back to a point just north of us, and we can reach them within half an hour if we ride hard! I sent most of the unit ahead!"

"Are you the commander?"

"Yes! The others are not to open fire until we reach them! Mengmoshu's orders!"

"You heard from him?"

"He tried to send out a flyer to give us air cover, but it was shot down from space! He wanted to know if you'd arrived!"

The fence was coming up fast and men were leaping to their horses, trotting them through the gate and forming up on the other side.

Kati pointed. "How many here?"

"Fifty! The rest should be getting into position now, on a hill where we can shoot down on them!"

Her horse was wheezing, and she wondered how much further she could push him. "My animal's exhausted! I need a fresh mount!"

"I'm sorry. The spare mounts went with the others! It's not far now!"

They slowed when they reached the gate, and she felt her horse falter, agonizing for rest, its sides heaving. "One minute! Give me one minute!"

She vaulted from the horse before it had stopped, and grabbed its bridle. *Good horse. Strong horse. Hold still, now.*

The animal's mouth was open, sucking air, thick tears like mucus beneath its eyes. She did not draw from the gong-shi-jie, but used the light of Tengri-Khan, energy flowing from the crown of her aura and out through hands stroking a muzzle, massaging a neck, shoulders, caressing flanks. She released the bridle, but the little horse stood firm, still panting, and groaning when he first felt the heat from her hands. She worked the legs, then the ankles, spending an extra few seconds there, then ran both hands along his belly. The horse coughed, then sneezed and whinnied, shaking his head.

A little further, and you rest, and there will be more of this for you.

She cleaned the mucus from his eyes, and held his muzzle with both hands. *You're a Tumatsin horse, now! You carry me fast!*

The horse rolled his eyes, and nickered.

Kati vaulted into the saddle. "Point the way!" she shouted, and the horses bolted together, heading north.

She sprinted to come alongside the commander. Laser rifles clattered against the chest armor of helmeted troops, but something was missing.

"Where are your bows?!" she shouted. "You have only swords and laser weapons!"

"Useless!" he shouted back. "They're sure to be armored, and arrows will be ineffective, even in close!"

It made her angry. Hadn't Mengmoshu told him *anything*? The battle was to be as traditional as possible; that was the agreement. Flyers would be met by fire from space, lasers met by lasers, leaving only the bow and the sword to honor the ancient ways. And if—

A sudden, horrible thought came to her. Lasers meet lasers. And her people, the Tumatsin, *had* them, a few stolen from the Emperor's troops when her mother was a girl, like the weapon Da had hidden beneath the stove. If the home guard had them, they would be used, and how would Mandughai's forces react? One laser burst, or four or five, to be answered by a thousand?

The Change intensified within her in an instant. Her horse seemed to sense it and ran like the wind as the first growl escaped her. They ran over undulating hills of dry grass, and in the distance was a plume of black smoke. Waves crashed on sandy beaches less than a kilometer to their left, and riders were racing along water's edge, heading north. Tumatsin riders.

How many home guardsmen can we count on?" she shouted.

The commander narrowed his eyes, noting The Change. "Less than a hundred. We've only heard from the northern *ordus*, and there aren't many. I don't know if the rest are even moving yet. They might keep their forces close to home!"

Let there be no lasers among them, she thought. She looked west, but the riders along the beach had disappeared. For some reason, that bothered her. There was a kind of presence, a tension, tugging at her mind, but she had no time to pursue the source of it.

The hill ahead of her gleamed as if covered with crystals, a long line of them just beneath the brow, and then she saw horses tethered in a great mass at the base of the hill. Troopers, hundreds of them, lay close together, sighting their rifles from the top of the hill to a target beyond it. The line stretched for a hundred meters, and a man was running down the hill towards them as they came to a halt and dismounted.

"They're coming in! The Tumatsin are just sitting there, waiting for them. They don't stand a chance!"

The troopers who'd arrived with Kati were running up the hill to find places in the line of defenders. Kati followed the commander and his subordinate, taking bow and quiver, but leaving her sword on the saddle. They climbed to the brow of the hill, and stood behind the line of prostrate troopers to look north.

Below them, by fifty meters to the left, four lines of mounted Tumatsin waited quietly at the edge of an alluvial fan formed by a small river which was now little more than a creek running into the sea. The sea was a hundred meters to their left, and the sandy beach only meters away. Soft sand, she noted, and difficult for a horse to run in.

The alluvial fan reached east to a cliff of sandstone running north from near her position, connected to it by a ridge. North of the fan was a broad, grassy slope leading up to a plateau, and if there was grass there it was now totally obscured by the wave of enemy soldiers descending it on foot and horseback, a solid mass of fighting men with gleaming armor, flowing like water. They came forward leisurely, like a crowd of invading pests bent on destroying everything in their path. It was Mandughai's horde, highly trained, bioengineered for war, and facing them were perhaps a hundred fishermen and herders of sheep, who had never known battle.

The invaders' infantry was crowded to the front, cavalry at the back, and more horses appeared at the edge of the plateau as Kati watched in horror. The cavalry moved down the slope, and laterally as the first infantry reached the soft earth of the alluvial fan. The cavalry was forming a crescent behind the wedge of infantry, reaching to the cliff, moving into position to charge the right flank of the defenders, so painfully few in number.

The Moshuguang commander ran along the line behind her, repeating his orders. "At first laser-burst—fire at will. At first laser-burst—fire at will."

He was meters from her when Kati stepped between two men, and stood on the brow of the hill in full view of the invaders. A trooper grabbed at her ankle. "Get down! They'll see you!" he whispered.

"Let them," she growled. She looked down at the mounted Tumatsin, and one of them saw her. Even at fifty meters, she saw him smile, and then he took something from a saddle scabbard, something that glinted metallically in the morning light. The other men in the front line of Tumatsin did the same. The things she saw were not swords. They were laser rifles. It was as if the sight of her had been a signal to the men. The one smiled at her, then raised his rifle, carefully aimed it, as did his comrades, and together they fired a single volley into the ranks of the invaders, now only two hundred meters away from them.

The return fire was instantaneous, and blinding, a thousand lasers aimed at the men and their horses, and they all went down in smouldering messes of burned flesh.

The rest of the Tumatsin turned their horses and fled, heading south along the beach and out of Kati's sight.

"FIRE!" screamed the Moshuguang commander behind her.

Bursts of laser fire streamed down from the hill and

into the ranks of the invaders' infantry, bursts accurately
aimed by hundreds of the Moshuguang elite. Fierce-
faced men went down, others staggered backwards against
their fellows in surprise, and the wedge of Mandughai's
infantry faltered, but only for a moment. Now there was
a chorus of howls that echoed from the cliff. The infantry
were coming on again, at a run, firing as they came, and
the line of cavalry was circling to get around them.

One burst of laser fire, met by thousands. Kati looked
down at the smoke and steam coming from what had once
been Tumatsin men, lying there now alone, abandoned
by their companions.

Kati felt rage, felt it rise in her like an animal, a cold,
killing thing. Laser fire still tore into the invaders, but
now they were moving fast and spreading out, firing as
they came. Kati had not left her exposed position and
now flashes of fire burst rock and soil, moving up the
hill towards her. Men fired from horseback, and she heard
an agonized cry from her left. There was no time for
consideration of any act, no time to debate the fairness
of it. There were only the invaders who had come to
kill her people and burn their homes.

Mandughai's infantry mass flowed towards them,
breaking into two fingers like a hand opening, one heading
towards where the surviving Tumatsin had fled, the other
charging the hill, firing wildly to provide cover for the
circling cavalry. Their howl was continuous and shrill,
like wounded *shizi*; short, stocky men with red, blazing
eyes in dark faces, canines like tusks thrust down from
their open mouths. They came on like a wave, and the
Moshuguang cut them down, but as their ranks thinned,
each man ran a zig-zag path, making a difficult target.
Now infantry were on the hill, charging up towards her
like mindless beasts. Laser fire splattered the ground
right in front of Kati, and she screamed, a horrible,
guttural thing, holding out clenched fists in front of her,

watching them turn green in the sudden blaze of light from her eyes.

And the light of creation followed those eyes.

A soldier of Mandughai raised his rifle and aimed it at her, and there was a flash like purple lightning, leaving nothing of him there. The atmosphere in front of her ignited in a wall of violet, red and green, and she felt white heat on her face, smelled singed hair, scorched leather. She pushed, and the roiling wall of gas, burning like a sun, swept down the hillside like a great wave, igniting the air as it went, rolling out onto the alluvial fan with a mind-numbing roar to drown out the screams of men and horses standing in its path. A column of burning nitrogen and oxygen rose upward with tornadic force, towering far up into a great anvil, but the sound of the lightning strokes within it could not be heard as the roiling wave moved on, scouring the fan to a fine surface of glassy pebbles mixed with the ashes of flesh and bone, and up the grassy slope beyond. The cavalry remaining there turned, and fled, but for many it was too late as the wave overtook them, reducing their bodies to elementary particles.

Kati screamed again, closing her eyes, the sparkling, purple matrix in her mind opening to receive the light.

And the wave was gone, leaving behind a fluorescent glow of green and red that lingered there for a moment, while lightning thundered in the great cloud overhead.

It began to rain, a light sprinkle at first, then a torrent, falling in sheets before her over the area of her destruction. Kati kept her eyes closed, and felt a kind of peace from the sound of the rain, but then someone called out.

"They're moving east! All cavalry! They're heading east from the plateau! They've broken off the attack!"

Kati's eyes snapped open. "They'll join the force attacking the city! Get after them! KILL THEM ALL!"

There was terror in the eyes of those who dared to look at her, and then they were all running down the hill to mount frightened horses jerking hard on their tethers, rearing and shrieking. Kati was the last to leave the hill. She'd seen a group of riders top a rise near the beach, and watched until she recognized them as Tumatsin, perhaps the same group of cowards who'd fled the action. Now she ran hard to catch up. A trooper held a fresh mountain horse for her, her saddle and swords in place. She reached it as the Tumatsin drew near, and she saw her old horse grazing contentedly nearby.

She vaulted into the saddle, knocking mounted troopers aside to ride at the Tumatsin. They halted when she screamed at them.

"*YOU*! I *saw* you down there! You ran at the first burst of fire! You left your comrades to *die*!"

One man stepped his horse forward as she reined in, her Changeling face flushed and gaunt with fury.

"NO! You don't *understand*! It was a *trap*! We were to provoke them, get them to chase us along the beach, stringing them out along the narrow strip of firm ground this side of the beach!" He pointed back towards the sea. "Short, box canyons all along there, our people hidden, waiting for them to nearly pass, then charging out to cut their ranks to pieces we could deal with! Everyone's down there, but I've called them out! They're right behind me!"

"Everyone? How many is that?"

"As many as we could muster. I've seen what you've done. As few as we are, we're all ready to fight for you! We couldn't be sure you'd come! We planned our own defense, and those who died knew the certainty of it! They knew you were *here*! They died for *you*!"

She could not speak, for her eyes had detected movement beyond these men, riders appearing at points along the last hills leading down to the sea. They came over the hills from ascents of steep canyons, riders in single file from countless points south as far as she could see. As they reached flat ground, they galloped to join lines, trickles streaming into a growing mass of cavalry until the roar of hoofbeats came to her ears, louder and louder. They streamed over the hills like an army of ants, more trickles coming from the beach to join them until the grass was covered with a black mass of riders and the ground trembled beneath her feet.

She remembered the Tumatsin propensity for understatement.

The man who'd spoken to her didn't look so afraid, now. "We're here! You tell us what to do, and we'll do it!"

The thunder of approaching horses made it necessary for her to shout. "We follow the force that attacked us, and hit it from behind, destroy it if we can, and continue on to the city! Moshuguang in front, with lasers, but after what we've been though, the weapons will soon be spent!"

She looked at the Moshuguang commander for a reaction, but he only nodded.

"The Moshuguang drop back, and we go in fast with bow and sword! We don't have heavy armor to slow us! We have to move! The enemy isn't waiting for us! *Now!*"

She turned her horse, and climbed up the hill, the Moshuguang commander going with her, his troops following, then the great mass of Tumatsin home guard riding hard to catch up. They went over the hill, and down through the lifeless area scoured by cosmic light, the towering cloud still above them, still releasing wet mist to cool earth now turned to glass. The devastation she'd wrought continued up the far slope, extending many meters out onto a small plateau and the broad valley heading southeast.

There were bodies there: men and horses, scorched black, the smell of cooked meat in the air. Kati felt sorry

for the horses. Further up the valley were a few more
bodies of fang-toothed men only partly burned, but dead
from shock, their horses gone. She rode hard, outdistancing
the Moshuguang with their heavy armor and large horses
not bred for the mountains. It wouldn't do, and then she
began noticing the curved, sparkling sheets of thin-filmed
metal scattered to either side of her, growing in number
until she suddenly stopped with the realization of what
she was seeing.

"They've taken off their armor so they can ride faster!"
she shouted, as the Moshuguang caught up to her. "Take
off your armor, and let the Tumatsin get in front! We
have to ride even *faster* now!"

They lost precious minutes in getting the Tumatsin
moved to the front, but it was a welcome rest for the
horses. Kati reared her horse.

"Now! As fast as we can ride! If we get close enough,
use your bows! For SHANJI!"

Her horse leaped forward, and the men howled behind
her. They thundered up the valley at a gallop. How long?
An hour? Four? The Tumatsin mounts were relatively
fresh, and again she was on a mountain horse. She hoped
it was like the dear one she'd ridden from the city: a
good horse, an *incredible* horse, willing to put out full
effort for her. But for how long?

There were enemy riders along the rims of hills to her
left, appearing, then disappearing in groups of four or
five. She worried about a trap, if they were being enticed
into a flank attack from above, but then she saw the dust
ahead, dust kicked up by many riders where the valley
began curving south towards the city. She waved an arm
and pointed, hoping the others would see the dust and
know they were rapidly gaining on the ones they pursued.

Riders within the dust cloud were moving at a trot,
and her force was rapidly closing in on them. The sound
of Tumatsin hoofbeats was a dull roar in Kati's ears, and

she saw a soldier of Mandughai turn in his saddle to see
them. He waved his arms wildly, shouting ahead. She
was now a hundred meters away, closing fast, and saw a
few figures visible in the cloud of dust. The enemy horses
were already tiring; their stamina was poor, perhaps due
to many weeks in transit to Shanji.

Kati turned to see the front rank of packed Tumatsin
only a horse's length behind her. She grabbed bow and
quiver, and held them overhead. "Shoot into the cloud!
As deep as you can!"

She wrapped the reins loosely around the saddle horn,
and made a knot, then nocked an arrow at full gallop,
pressing tightly with her knees. She fired her arrow in a
high arc, well into the dust cloud, and used her bow to
beckon the others to do the same.

Shouts behind her, then a long pause. She nocked
another arrow, and drew her bow as there was a
commanding shout behind her.

A yellow cloud that was a thousand arrows arched high
over her head and fell into the swirling storm of dust.

She heard horses scream, and men, and then another
cloud of arrows was on its way, and then another. Kati
fired with them as fast as she could, her arrows flying
blindly into the cloud without a target. Shower after
shower of arrows arched into the cloud, and then dust
was swirling around her, her vision suddenly limited.
Ahead, a horse had fallen, bristling with arrow shafts.
Its tusked rider charged her on foot, sword raised, and
she fired her last arrow through his throat.

Fallen horses and men were everywhere, and men
stumbling towards both sides in panic. One dared to meet
her, sword arm cocked defiantly. She rode him down,
but felt the pain of a sword-slash deflected from the saddle
to her leg as he fell beneath her. She threw down bow
and quiver, unsheathed her sword, and screamed as she
raised it.

The sound of her people thrilled her, the screams of a thousand *shizi*.

She rode into the scattered, fallen soldiers of Mandughai, slashing left and right. Most of them escaped her blade, only to be crushed by the wave of horses behind her, and then suddenly they were running on grass, and the dust was gone. She was ten meters behind the remainder of those who'd escaped her by the sea, and a last volley of arrows from her people shrieked by her head to strike them. Men went down by the dozens, but the others charged on, and now she could see why.

Far ahead, the dome of the Emperor's city glistened, and they were heading down a final slope to the broad valley of plowed earth and barley stubble now covered with horses and struggling men, black smoke belching from the ruins of three downed flyers. As far as she could see, horses were charging each other, men fighting hand-to-hand, blades flashing. She caught up to a dark man who turned to slash at her. She parried his move, then stuck him in the throat and pushed him from his horse with her foot. She was riding among Mandughai's ranks, slashing and parrying, not wondering where her terrible strength came from. Her people were piling in behind her, enveloping the invaders like an amoeba encountering a bacterium, absorbing them, cutting them down, crashing straight through with the weight of their numbers, then charging down the slope to the stubble fields, Kati waving her sword, hoarsely screaming the word that empowered them all.

"SHANJIIII!"

CHAPTER TWENTY
THE FALLEN

The moment had been electric when Mengnu shouted the name of their world. Her eyes had blazed emerald green, ivory jutting beneath her lip; the purple aura surrounding her had seemed supernatural, yet he'd not been afraid this time. In a way, he still loved her, and now it was said she would be Empress over all of them.

Lui-Pang watched her ride alone up the mountain trail until the glow that accompanied her disappeared in trees at the edge of the cliff. His courage rose. One girl, supernatural or not, was riding alone to lead a small force against an army of unknown strength, and he was left with a far greater force in defending the city.

Still, there were rumors that the enemy camp had been examined from space with the instruments on the mother ship, and that the number of invading soldiers was at least three times their own. There was also the matter of experience; none of them, young, old, even their officers, had ever known battle. What was the experience of those who would come at them from the valley to the north?

Lui-Pang pondered these things as he mounted up with the other young troopers at the rear of the long lines of cavalry reaching from the gate to far beyond the barracks where the dome intersected the mountain. Hours earlier, before Mengnu's arrival, the Moshuguang's elite guard had gone out on foot, leading their horses to dig in along the valley slopes and establish a cross-fire against approaching infantry. Each man carried an extra power pack, giving him a capability of six hundred bursts, but against a sizable force it would surely not be enough. It would serve mainly to deplete the capability of an enemy on foot or horseback to return laser fire when charged by Hansui cavalry.

He looked for Master Yung, but couldn't find him. He'd said that Mengnu was no longer his student. The student days were over. Today they would be soldiers, and veterans if they survived.

It was still dark, and two hours after Mengnu had left they all filed through the gate and out of the city, marching hundreds of meters into the fields to form their companies of three hundred in twelve blocks four wide and three deep across the valley. Somewhere in front of them, up on the slopes, the Moshuguang were dug in, lasers poised. Lui-Pang looked for a sign of them and saw nothing.

Their wait was not long. The first sign was a dull sound, like heavy breath, coming up the valley towards them. Lui-Pang's horse snorted, hooves stomping nervously. Far ahead an officer shouted, but he couldn't make out the words.

The second sign was more dramatic and nearly drove their horses into a panic. A flyer hummed behind them, lifting out of the dome and heading straight west towards the cliffs. Even at this distance, he could see it was full of men. A few troopers cheered them.

The sky was lit up by a single, blinding flash that came over their heads from the stars in the northwest, and the flyer was gone, leaving a ball of sputtering gas that settled slowly to the ground and seemed to explode there. But the sound was drowned out by the crack of a horrible thunder that shocked his ears and made his horse jump, screaming. Lui-Pang fought to control it; the closeness of their ranks was all that kept it from running.

Weapons in space. More rumors, now verified. Weapons that could destroy an army in a flash, and they were sitting there, in the open, a target much larger than the flyer.

Everyone was looking up, waiting for death to come from the sky, some still fighting to control their animals. Lui-Pang had never felt so vulnerable and watched the stars, waiting for one to suddenly brighten.

Calm returned slowly. If space weapons would be used against them, it should have happened by now, and hadn't. The flyer was the target, not men on the ground. Even his horse was settling down. Lui-Pang tried to do the same, and failed. The dull roar still came up the valley, the sound of many feet, many horses. Getting louder.

They were coming.

The sound was soon loud enough to distinguish hoofbeats from the armor-clanking steps of men, then there was a loud whine and seven flyers rose through the opening in the dome. This time, nobody cheered. Seven flyers, with laser cannon and crews of three, formed into a vee and came over their heads at low altitude, turbines screaming as they headed down the valley. Half a kilometer, then one. Lui-Pang held his breath, then cried out as the light came out of the sky from a point further east than before, seeming to come right towards him but striking only the flyers with terrible precision. Three flyers went down in fiery ruins to crash and explode, while the others were only balls of ionized gas popping and sputtering. A column of air clear out to the stars glowed eerily red and green. The thunder was as before, and again Lui-Pang fought for control of his terrified horse. With the shock and fright came a strange relief. The flyers were indeed the targets, not ground troops. The thing he had to fear was on the ground, not in space, and an hour later laser fire began coming from the valley slopes northeast of him. The Moshuguang had opened up. The enemy was within laser range.

There was shouting from the front ranks, and word was passed back. "No lasers! String your bows! Ready an arrow! They're a kilometer out, infantry coming on the run! No cavalry! First shot at two hundred meters!"

A burst went over his head, sizzling air, and there were screams from the front. An officer galloped back to stand several meters from him, and raised his sword.

"Two hundred meters! Ready! Fire at will!"

All the training, now applied, arrow nocked, bow elevated to the proper angle, the pull smooth, release, re-nock rapidly, smoothly. Laser fire was streaming from the hills and first rank in rapid bursts, was returned. Grass blazed.

His heart was pounding. Laser fire from the Moshuguang was swinging near their front ranks.

Screams, and howls, like demons coming at them, and now the first glow in the eastern sky. Lui-Pang fired again and again, until the officer screamed.

"Cease fire! Prepare for cavalry! Second and third ranks hold! First rank! At the gallop, charge!"

The ground trembled with the charge of the first rank, the oldest of the troopers. Lui-Pang couldn't see past the others, but heard the clash of blades, the howls, the screams.

"Second rank! At the gallop, charge!"

A last volley from the hills, and the laser fire ceased. The sky was paling now, and standing in his stirrups, moments later, Lui-Pang could see troopers returning, and beyond them, far out, a black mass of enemy horses moving over a slope towards the valley floor.

Riders raced south along the hillsides. Laser fire over, the Moshuguang elite now hurried to establish a final defense line for the city, less than a kilometer away.

The orb of Tengri-Khan rose above the mountain at

that moment, and it was suddenly quiet again. Lui-Pang stood in his stirrups for a better look, and saw movement far out, a flow of enemy cavalry up a slope to higher ground in the valley, where it curved northwest.

There was cheering from the front rank. An officer rode back through their formation, waving his sword. "We've mutilated their infantry, and given their cavalry a taste of our steel! They pause to give themselves courage again, so stay alert!"

Lui-Pang had doubts. First cavalry action was traditionally a probe of the enemy's skill. The infantry had been clearly sacrificed to deplete all laser fire at long range, and the next action would certainly be a charge of massed cavalry. The enemy was only preparing for it, forming their ranks. Even at this distance, he could see a wedge-shaped phalanx developing on the high ground.

They waited and waited for something to happen, and suddenly there was a low rumble, like thunder, and everyone looked up, again expecting death to come out of the sky. Nothing happened. The rumble continued for minutes, but its source was distant, somewhere to the west. Another battle was raging there. *Kati*, he thought, *be alive*.

For the next hour he sat on his horse, getting hot and impatient, and the officers told them nothing. Tengri-Khan moved higher in the sky, and they were all wet with perspiration beneath their armor. The enemy cavalry had formed a single phalanx shaped like an arrowhead, yet the defending forces remained spread out, vulnerable to penetration. Lui-Pang fidgeted in his saddle, anxiously awaiting the call to change formation. Finally it came.

"Second rank left, third rank right, form phalanx and close up, *move!*" an officer shouted.

The movement was familiar and rehearsed. They formed three wedge-shaped phalanxes, overlapping to make a single mass when seen from the front, but leaving room for independent maneuvers by three distinct units. Within each phalanx, the flanks of the horses were touching, but Lui-Pang found himself at an edge near the point of his unit, with a clear view ahead.

For hundreds of meters, the field of barley stubble was littered with the bodies of small, bare-skinned men. Most were blackened by laser fire, others bristling with arrow shafts and stained red. Some had nearly reached the Hansui ranks before being killed, and their tusked mouths were still open in a silent scream. They had the faces of demons.

The enemy phalanx remained where it was, its point halfway down the slope leading to the distant edge of the barley field. And as the horses around him quieted down, Lui-Pang again heard that dull sound, like heavy breath, coming up from the valley behind the invaders.

Many feet, many horses; it was the sound he'd heard that morning, before the enemy first appeared.

More were coming.

Everyone heard it. Troopers were now looking nervously at each other, and suddenly the enemy phalanx was moving, a great arrow aimed at them, coming down the slope at a walk, and onto flat ground. They didn't stop there, kept on coming, a mass of bare-skinned infantry following the cavalry at a walk. Where did *they* come from? *They said the infantry was cut up!*

The enemy cavalry went to a trot, and the ground shivered. An officer appeared, riding back and forth to shout at the Hansui defenders. "Draw swords!"

Horses stomped hooves nervously, and snorted.

"The ancestors watch you! You fight for your families, your Emperor, and yourselves! Long live the Emperor!"

And our Empress Mengnu, thought Lui-Pang. He raised his sword, screamed hoarsely with his comrades, and saw the great mass of cavalry now charging towards them.

"Charge!" screamed the officer.

They leaped forward with a shout, packed tightly together. Behind them was only the Moshuguang elite left to defend the city. His pride and commitment surged with his courage, and he beat his knees hard against the flanks of his horse. So soon, so soon, and yet he'd waited half a day for this moment. They were closing fast, the enemy without armor, grinning tusked faces, muscled bodies swinging back and forth and dipping beneath the necks of their animals in a show of riding expertise. Mountain horses, smaller, and lighter than his. He aimed his horse at one man, and went straight at him as the forces came together with a sound that echoed from the hills.

The man went down beneath his horse, and Lui-Pang slashed the man next to him, opening his chest. In seconds his momentum was gone, and blades were coming at him from every direction. He twirled his horse, parrying, slashing, stabbing, felt a blade skitter off his armor. Another whipped by his face and opened a gushing wound on the neck of his horse. The animal reared, and screamed, Lui-Pang stabbing into the mouth of a grinning face. He moved forward, hacking left and right, and was suddenly in an open space. The valley ahead was empty, except for the litter of bodies, but another large force was coming down the slopes, led by a single rider. He felt despair, turned back to the tangle of men and horses, and charged into it.

Blades clattered over him, and then there was searing pain in his shoulder. He slashed left, and a grinning head toppled from a man with a bloody sword. Four came at him at once from the front. He gutted one, ducked another's thrust, but the third slashed his right leg, and the fourth thrust a sword into his horse's throat.

Lui-Pang went down, one leg pinned beneath his horse. Two men rushed by, slashed down at him, and he parried their blades, pulling his leg free and staggering to his feet. They turned their horses, and came at him again. He ducked under a blade, and slashed at the ankles of a horse, tumbling its rider. Before the man could recover, he pierced him through the heart.

There was a chorus of screams, and a rumble, an astonished look on the face of a rider prepared to strike at him. Lui-Pang took his advantage, and stuck him in the chest, then turned to look back at the city, from where the sound had come.

Armored troops of the Moshuguang elite were charging in hard, led by a trooper in golden armor. They crashed into the struggling ranks, pressing towards him, and the man in golden armor went down swinging his blade in a cluster of enemy infantry.

Lui-Pang stumbled towards him, pulling one man from his horse and opening his throat, then thrusting upwards into the belly of another. The one in gold armor was on his feet, fighting alone against one on horseback, and two soldiers on foot. Lui-Pang reached them and stabbed the mounted man in the back. He pulled him from the horse, and reached for the reins, and then there was a sharp pressure at the back of his neck. He stared in amazement at the sight of a long blade issuing forth from his throat, then withdrawing. He dropped to his knees, and saw the one in gold armor go down near him under the blades of five infantrymen.

He clutched at his throat, and his palms were filled with blood. All feeling was gone. He fell on his side, saw Moshuguang soldiers dispatch those who had killed their leader, and heard the horrible sound of a thousand more warriors coming to destroy them all.

Too few. too few, he thought.

And then he thought nothing at all.

They came down the slopes like a great wave from the sea, and those ahead could not turn to fight them, could only charge ahead to aid their comrades. The last of the Tumatsin arrows flew true, and many fell from their saddles, then swords flashed as her people screamed behind her.

Kati had seen the Moshuguang charge from the east, but their timing was bad. They'd already engaged, and lost their momentum. Still, the soldiers of Mandughai were being forced back by the charge and into the path of their own people, with Kati right behind them. They turned to see what was coming, and she was gratified by the astonished looks on their faces when they saw she wasn't one of their own.

She opened her mouth wide for the enemy to see, raising her sword high and screaming again the instant before her people crashed into them.

"SHANJIII!"

They were a tidal wave breaking on soft sand. The Tumatsin sucked the enemy beneath the hooves of their horses, crashing through the remaining ranks of those they'd chased and into the ones sent against the city. The momentum of their charge carried them to within fifty meters of the ranks of the Moshuguang, and they fought towards each other. Many of the enemy fought on foot, their riderless horses screaming and running away, but even more were still mounted.

Kati's fury was mindless, her scream shrill and continual as she fought. How many she killed she would never know; her targets were only a red blur to her. She fought with a sword in each hand, using her old sword in her left when her horse's momentum was gone, and she was twirling him to slash and thrust in all directions. There was no thought, no feeling, though she knew she'd been struck several times. There were only the movements of her blades, until suddenly the grinning, tusked faces were gone, and still she was twirling, twirling in search of a target.

"Mengnu! Mengnu!"

A Moshuguang trooper rode up to her. All the other horses were still, their riders looking at her. None of them were soldiers of Mandughai.

"It's over! It's all over, and you're wounded!"

She didn't know him. Her head swirled, and she couldn't think. She panted to catch her breath, and held her swords defensively as he warily approached her.

"Mengnu! They've thrown down their swords! We have many prisoners here! We've beaten them!"

Physical feeling returned, and it was terrible pain in her left shoulder, both legs, and forehead.

"That looks serious! You need medical attention!"

Something warm was running down her face, but the trooper was pointing to her right leg. She looked down, saw blood flowing from a slash there, and growled at it. It was deep, but she could flex the leg. She moved her hand near it, and let the light come to her, a narrowly focused beam flashing blue from her palm, moving along the cut.

She screamed a horrible scream, but kept her hand in place until the flesh there was cauterized.

Pain brought awareness. She looked around, saw only Tumatsin and Hansui faces, many of them bloodied. "Enough," she growled. The wounds in her other leg, left shoulder, and forehead were small and shallow, and she allowed them to bleed. Let them see her blood, as she saw theirs.

"The prisoners are behind me, two hundred or so still standing, and many wounded that need care. Do we spare them, Mengnu? What is your wish?"

"My wish is for an end to this. I want no more death here. How many have we lost?" Kati ground her teeth in pain, and added to it by biting her lip.

"Many. We have no count, but First Mother has lost many more, perhaps six to our one. The numbers She sent against us was not as great as it seemed at first. She kept moving their ranks up and down the slopes to make us think there were more of them."

"I take no comfort in her losses," said Kati. She held a bloody sword over her head, and shouted.

"It's over! And the city has not been touched by war! The people of Shanji have defended it! They have fought together in its defense. This war is *ended*!"

Hear this, Mandughai, and now honor our agreement!

Swords were raised all around her, and the people cheered, and although the sound of a united people thrilled her, there was a terrible sadness for the life that had been lost. And then the Moshuguang trooper leaned close to her to shout over the cheers.

"There's someone you must see! He's near death and wants to see you! Over here!"

Kati followed him into the crowd, towards where the prisoners stood sullenly, surrounded by mounted Tumatsin. Someone near death, who knew her personally? Who? Her heart pounded with apprehension.

They came to a circle of Moshuguang kneeling by a prostrate man with golden armor, and she knew who it was before she even saw his face. Her face was in his mind, and she was smiling at him.

It was Shan-lan.

She dropped to her knees beside him. His pants were saturated with blood from a wound just below his armor, near the groin, and his face was grey. "Oh, Shan-lan," she murmured, and caressed his forehead. His eyes flickered open, and he smiled.

"We could do nothing, Mengnu. He acted as Emperor, and led our charge," said a trooper. "He would not remain in the palace."

"I could not," said Shan-lan. "Mengnu, you're alive!"

"Yes," she said, moving her hands over him in despair. His aura flickered dimly, the last of his life flowing out of him, and even her own powers could not reverse it now. "I came to see my poet and friend."

"I was also Emperor—for a little while," he said weakly, "but it's not my favorite job. It's better that you do it, if what I hear is true."

"I didn't ask for it," she said, stroking his head.

Shan-lan nodded, and closed his eyes. "I know how things can be forced on us, Mengnu. I would rather we sit in the tower and watch the sunset together. I feel your hand. It's cool."

Kati leaned over, and kissed him lightly on the lips. "I love you," she whispered.

"As a friend," he whispered. "I have—another poem— but —there's no time—"

He sighed, and the mental image of her that he held dearly went away with him.

Tears came to her eyes; she turned her head, and saw the face of a dead trooper lying on his side, close by, blood pooled beneath a gaping wound in his throat. Lui-Pang. His eyes were open, eyes that had once looked at her with great passion.

"Ohhh, noooo," she sobbed, and buried her face in her hands.

She knelt there, and cried, and a hand touched her shoulder. "You need rest. We'll take you back to the city when you're ready."

Kati nodded, and swallowed hard to stop the tears in the presence of fighting men. She stood up, saddened and exhausted and hurting all over, but then she saw movement from her left.

Her heart leaped when she saw who it was: Baber, waving to her and grinning from his horse where he was helping to stand guard over the prisoners. Very likely he would complain about the youngest guard members being forced to ride in the rear of the ranks and not getting in on the action before it was nearly over. She waved back to him, and felt her spirits lift a little.

For one moment she felt relief, then there was a new sound in the valley, a whine, high pitched, coming from the north. She looked towards the hills, and saw a monstrous ship, wedge-shaped, a ceramic underbelly burned by the heat of atmospheric entry, floating along the far edge of the valley and disappearing beyond the rims of the hills. As it disappeared, the rims of the hills were suddenly lined with riders as far as she could see. There were thousands of them, with sparkling armor and scattered pennants.

It was the main army of Mandughai. Untouched. Waiting to descend on them.

Men called out in dismay. Others hurried to mount up as Kati swung into the saddle. "Stay here!" she shouted. "Don't follow me!"

She rode away from them, past the bodies of her people and those bioengineered for war. When she was a kilometer away, she stopped, and looked up at the horde lining the hills. She held up her sword.

I will not fight you with this, but I will fight you! Hear me, Mandughai! My people have done what you wished. If you send more soldiers, they come against me, not my people. Not one more of my people will die, but when it's over, you'll have no army, and the ships that brought you here will be food for new stars!

The choice is yours, Mandughai. I'm here, waiting for your decision.

There was no answer. Pennants waved on the rims of the hills, and there was a high-pitched sound coming from there. It was the cries of Mandughai's horde, men bred for fighting, for dying, now awaiting a final command from their leaders.

You don't answer me, and I hear the battlecries of your soldiers. Your intention is now clear to me, but I will not wait for you to come to me. I will come to you.

Kati sat rigidly on her horse, whose neck was suddenly illuminated brightly in emerald green. A part of her was now elsewhere, physical pain forgotten, and her heartbeat slowed, all emotions drained from her. She cupped her hands, held them out to her sides and blue fog enveloped her, a thick fog that hissed and moved the hairs on the back of her neck. *Laser, sword or arrow, none can come to me now, but I will come to you.*

Her horse was shocked rigid with terror. She brought her arms forward in arcs, outlining the area her aura should cover, and the fog seemed to thin around her. Ahead of her a wall of shimmering blue and purple appeared as if drawn by the stroke of a great brush, a mammoth thing of roiling color in an arc across the valley and extending tens of meters up from the ground.

She pushed it, as she'd done by the sea, but more slowly this time, at the speed of a trotting horse. The explosions of bodies it passed over were only flashes of light, and even the smoke of destroyed barley stubble was consumed in the swirling colors.

I give you a few moments. I will not stop until I'm assured that our business here is finished, and your threat against us is gone.

Still there was no answer, only a dull roar resonating from the hills.

Riders still lined the rims of those hills.

Kati pushed harder, and sent her wall of death up the slopes to meet them there.

CHAPTER TWENTY-ONE
ABAGAI

There was panic along the rims of the hills. Pennants were dropped, and horses were rearing in fright, trying to run back from the rim but blocked by the crowd behind them. The wave of her awful energy surged ahead with a mind of its own, faster than she wished. She spread her aura over it, pulled back, but nothing happened. Now it was two hundred meters from the rims of the hills, blackened soil behind it, closing rapidly on its target.

KATI! STOP IT! We surrender! Don't let this happen! PLEASE!

Mandughai. Kati pulled again, harder, felt resistance from an energy density suddenly too great for her to handle.

Don't you understand? We GIVE UP! The war is OVER!

This time it was Yesugen. There was no time, now. Death was seconds away from the rims of the hills. Kati released her auric hold on her terrible creation, breaking the connection with the gong-shi-jie. The wall of swirling colors disappeared in a flash, leaving a shimmering image of the hills. Cool air rushed to fill the hot void; there was a sharp crack and grumble, like rolling thunder.

Tears stung her eyes, and her skin felt cold. Her horse jumped at the sound of the thunder, and she grabbed the reins tightly to control him.

Calm yourself, Kati. It's over, now. You've convinced everyone of that. All we've set out to do is finished, and there will be no more killing.

Mandughai! Why did you wait so long?

It was Yesugen and her followers who needed convincing, and the delay was theirs. You've given us all a bad fright, but that's good. Please, Kati, be calm. It's now time for us to meet, and I'm sending Yesugen to you personally to declare the end of this war and escort you here. You needn't be gentle with her. She has learned a hard lesson, and is quite terrified of you now. But she will come to you because she has courage.

Mandughai, we've done a terrible thing here today.

It may seem so, but it was necessary. We'll talk about it when you come to my ship. Remember who you are, Kati. You're Empress of Shanji. We are foreigners whose challenge you've met and turned back, and we stand on your ground. Yesugen must be reminded of that. Hurry, Kati. I've waited years for this meeting.

Yes, Mandughai. So have I. Kati sighed with relief.

A single rider had detached from the others, and was plunging rapidly down the blackened slopes, carrying a red pennant on a long staff. Kati sat where she was, but turned and gestured for her people to move back when she saw many of them moving towards her with apprehension. They were silent, still stunned by what they'd just seen.

They obeyed when the approaching rider was still a kilometer away, moving at a slow gallop, but they watched warily in close-packed ranks behind her.

Kati was also wary, now vulnerable to a laser burst from afar, or a sword thrust from the rider who approached her. She called on the light again to tinge her aura in deep blue, a reminder of the power that was only a thought away, waiting to touch a threat against her.

It was a woman, dressed in a simple black robe, and

she held a sword across her chest. She was in her late twenties or thirties, and tall in the saddle, her face gaunt, with sharp features, highly arched nose and veined, domed forehead. She slowed to a trot as she drew near and smiled, showing fine white tusks thicker but shorter than Kati's. Kati returned the smile with her own toothy display, for The Change hadn't left her since that first laser burst by the sea.

"Yesugen," she growled.

Yesugen's eyes glared red as she came hesitantly to Kati's side within arm's reach, and she jammed the shaft of her plain, red pennant into the ground. Her fear was terrible, but it was not apparent to the eye. "You're undoubtedly pleased to see me," she said. "Do I call you Kati, or Mengnu, or just Empress, now that this day is over?"

"It makes no difference, now that we're one people."

"So you hope," said Yesugen. "I think that remains to be proven."

"I intend to do that. Mandughai says you'll take me to Her now."

"Yes, but first some ceremony for the people now ready to kill me if I make a sudden move against you. It's a token of your victory, and I give it willingly."

Yesugen pulled a scabbard from her saddle, slid it slowly over the blade she held across her chest, and then, with a slight bow, handed them over to Kati. "I am the vanquished," she said, and the words seemed to catch in her throat.

Kati took the sword, and bowed in return. "I accept this in thanks for the end of the killing. The only vanquished people I see are the ones who lie dead around us, and I have no pleasure in that. I see no victory in the death of even one soldier, yours or mine."

Yesugen laughed. "We're different indeed, you and I. Our people are different. Mine are bred for war. They're bred to kill, and be killed. The names of our dead will live forever on our monuments, and their families will be honored for their losses."

"My people will bury their dead, and forever wonder if there was good reason for the loss," said Kati.

"Ah, but *you* are the reason. You'll now be Empress."

Kati growled. "I didn't choose this tragic war to achieve it. That was done for me by others. I will never again ask my people to fight. I'll meet any threat in my own way."

Yesugen's smile disappeared, and she bowed. "You showed your way by the sea today, and I'm grateful for your restraint. There are things we must talk about, but now my mother is waiting."

Yesugen sullenly turned her horse, and Kati rode with her at a walk. "I warned you I'd do what was necessary, and I had no choice in the action I took against your people by the sea today. A thousand lasers against fifty isn't my idea of equal forces."

"I'm aware of it," said Yesugen, then paused. "I'm also quite impressed by what you did with your sword. You fight hard, and with skill. It reminds me we're related by blood."

Yesugen had made no effort to mask the feeling that showed it was a compliment, not just a thing said out of fear. They rode in silence for a moment until Yesugen said, "You know I'll someday be Empress of Tengri-Nayon and its worlds."

"Yes. Mandughai told me that."

Yesugen made a snorting sound. "Has She told you about the mess She leaves me to deal with when Her generous rule is finished?" The woman's fear seemed to be dissipating.

"No."

"Of course not. She is Mandughai, who will bring all the people together, even if it means the destruction of

Her own planet. She sees unification as Her place in history, and not of the consequences I'll be left to deal with."

"Unity on Shanji is necessary for us to prosper," said Kati. "My people must work together to ease the lives of many, but of course that's not your concern."

Yesugen looked at Kati without hostility. "I speak of my own world, Meng-shi-jie, not Shanji. You'll have many problems to solve here, but a violent sun won't be one of them, or an overwhelming influx of people from a dying planet. Now is not the time, but there are things we must talk about. Our worlds are too close for us not to have a connection. We're all descended from the same people."

No condescension, only concerns, a discussion between neighboring worlds. "When? When can we talk?"

"As we have before, but after I've returned to Tengri-Nayon, perhaps much after. I'll call you from the gong-shi-jie, and we'll speak privately." *Do you hear that, Mother? Privately!* Yesugen smiled. "Enough for now. Her ship is just over this hill."

They climbed a blackened hill, and the mounted troops were still there: small, thick men on mountain horses, swords sheathed, watching them come with narrowed red eyes.

There was not one line of men along the hills, but many; a mass of soldiers numbering in the thousands. They all looked towards her, many craning their necks to see her face. A corridor appeared, horses pulled back to give them a wide passage through the ranks, and ahead was a broad plain with several shuttles there. The shuttles were twice the size of the ones she'd seen in the mountain, but similar in design, with ceramic bellies, a line of thick glass ports above open maws with loading ramps leading down to the ground. Sitting on eight landing pods, they looked like spiders ready to spring at her.

They rode to the nearest ship and up a ramp into a huge space the size of the warehouse she'd seen in the east, but broken into hundreds of cubicles separated by head-high dividers and filled with tangles of webbing for securing horses during takeoff and landing. They veered right to an open lift, and dismounted. The lift was large enough for four horses and rose slowly up into the ceiling, where monstrous fans turned lazily. Blank steel walls slid past them, and there were odors of horse, and hay, and oil. They passed two floors, passageways of metal latticework and red lights, the sounds of machinery humming, and stopped at the third. Red lights in a vaulted ceiling illuminated concentric semicircles of consoles, all attended by seated women and men with tusked faces and sharp features. All were dressed uniformly in form-fitting black uniforms. They followed Kati's blue aura with their eyes as Yesugen led her left to a short corridor ending at a door. She knocked softly on it.

"Come!"

The room seemed dark at first, indirect lighting around the edge of a low, domed ceiling. The walls were bare, and the room was filled with a single, round table surrounded by plush chairs.

One chair was occupied. A figure stood up there, a glorious aura of red and gold in the gloom, and walked around the table to where they stood. Kati's heart thumped, and her mouth was dry.

"Hello, Kati. There were moments when I thought our meeting wouldn't happen, but fortunately I was wrong."

Mandughai, the Emerald Empress of Tengri-Nayon and all its worlds, held out her hand in greeting, but suddenly Kati was stiff, arms at her sides, hands clenched.

She was a woman, and not so old as Kati had expected. She was dressed in a simple black robe like her daughter, her face more rounded beneath the domed forehead, tusks short, barely showing below her upper lip. Her skin was smooth, without wrinkles, her nose ordinary, without the high arch. It was both the Moshuguang and Tumatsin face of a woman perhaps in her early sixties, with the exception of one feature.

Her eyes. In the dim light of the room, they glowed —emerald green.

Mandughai held out her hand for a long moment. When Kati wouldn't take it, the woman frowned.

"Kati? I've spoken to you since you were a child. Don't you know me? Are you all right?" Her voice was soft.

"I have some wounds, but they'll heal," said Kati.

"Where? Yesugen, you knew she was injured? I didn't feel it!"

"The wound on her leg should leave a fine scar if she rubs salt into it," said Yesugen gruffly. "The rest are quite superficial."

Mandughai pulled out a chair, and beckoned to it. "Please sit, Kati, and rest yourself."

Kati sat down, back rigid, and clasped her hands in her lap. Mandughai sat next to her, and leaned forward so that their knees were nearly touching.

"What's wrong? Your aura is so blue, and I feel a repulsive force there. Why do you draw away from me? We've waited so long for this moment."

Kati swallowed hard. "I suppose I've changed. A year ago I was full of dreams of making the lives of my people easier, and today I'm responsible for their deaths."

Yesugen snorted behind her. "In war, there's always death. A good commander can only minimize it. You're not—"

"I understand," said Mandughai, waving a hand to silence her daughter. "What you've seen today is horrifying."

"You haven't seen what's out there," said Kati. "You haven't been there. I sat with a friend and watched him die; a gentle person, not a soldier. He was the Emperor's son."

"One less complication in your assumption of power," said Yesugen.

"He was my *friend*! Doesn't human life have any meaning for either *one* of you?"

Yesugen laughed. "What hypocrisy! I suppose you were thinking about the meaning of life when you ionized half of my southern battalion by the sea! You came close to doing the same thing to the rest of our army, and the ships that brought us here. You're certainly no pacifist; your words don't match your deeds!"

Mandughai raised an eyebrow. "She has a point, Kati. You did what you felt necessary to defend your people. I did what I felt necessary to bring them together. We've both accomplished our objectives, but not without cost. I've ruled for over forty years, and yours is just beginning. You'll see that everything you strive to do will have a cost, and you'll be constantly deciding how much you're willing to pay to meet your goals. The price can be money, human misery, death, or the loss of friendships, even loved ones. People will oppose you, undermine you, work behind your back to destroy your visions, and much of the time you'll be alone. If you're lucky, a few will be close to you, and even they will be potentially traitorous. The life of an Empress is hard and lonely, often dangerous. Examine yourself, Kati, right now, and ask whether or not you're ready for it."

Her words had been quick, and firm, like the admonition of a mother. Mandughai leaned back in her chair, waiting for an answer. Her eyes darted to Yesugen, who stood right behind Kati. Perhaps she'd been talking to both of them. Veins throbbed at her temples, and were suddenly prominent on the great dome of her forehead. She cupped her chin in one hand, and the glow of her eyes intensified.

"Well?"

Still the superior in this group of three, but only by experience, for her physical powers didn't approach Kati's. All the conversations in the gong-shi-jie, the careful training, the patience and encouragement of a mother to a daughter was clear in Kati's memory.

"There were things you said you'd have me do when I was a woman. Have I done them, Mandughai?"

"Yes, you have, and more. More than I hoped for. You call me Mandughai, the Empress, but it's *you* who are the Empress of Light, the closest thing to the Mei-lei-gong we've sought for so long. You're a miracle, Kati. I don't want to lose you, not after the sacrifices that have been made to put you on the throne here."

Kati shook her head. "There was more to it than that. My people have sacrificed their lives to solve political problems between you and Yesugen and whoever else has seen Shanji as a world to be conquered. I don't care about your political problems, Mandughai. I've done things for you, but now there are things I want to do for my people, and I want to be free to do them without threat from you or Yesugen."

Mandughai glanced at Yesugen, and smiled. "You've always been free, Kati. When you will it, it will happen. We cannot stop you, but I ask for the privilege to discuss things with you. You still have much to learn. I hope you'll listen to me and to your father, but all decisions will be yours to make."

"Mengmoshu! Does he know I'm safe?"

"Yes, dear. He's on his way here right now."

"I didn't feel him," said Kati.

"Be glad for that. He was frantic with worry over you. He wouldn't show it when there was danger, for fear of distracting you."

Kati sighed. "Then I'll bring the people together in making the necessary reforms on Shanji without fear of another war with you?"

Mandughai nodded. "Our unfortunate war is ended, and there *will* be peace between us." Her eyes again moved towards Yesugen when she said it.

"There's more, mother," said Yesugen. "Shanji cannot remain isolated as it has." She stepped over to stand behind her mother, eyes red. "There must be tangible relations between our worlds, for mutual benefit."

"What kind of relations?" asked Kati.

"Trade, exchange of technology, even people with special skills, that sort of thing."

Mandughai watched Kati for a reaction, and smiled. "We can talk later about this, but there *is* opportunity for you, Kati. With the calming of Tengri-Nayon, we're emerging from our buried cities to build on the surface. We'll have great need for building materials and new seed varieties for surface crops. You have that, but you've lost your space-faring capabilities for delivery. I intend to leave two shuttles here for you when we depart. They should give you a new start in developing interplanetary and interstellar trade. You'll find we've come a long way since the ships the Moshuguang tend in the mountain."

"That's most generous of you, Mandughai. Trade is an important part of my program." Kati tried hard not to show her excitement, but her voice betrayed it, and so did her aura.

"There are other things as well, but they can wait. I also want to talk to your father. Yesugen, could you see if our other guests are ready to come in? They have just arrived."

Yesugen frowned. "Yes, mother, but Kati and I must talk, soon."

"Of course, dear. In private."

Yesugen pressed her lips tightly together, then turned abruptly, and marched out of the room, closing the door behind her.

Mandughai seemed to listen for something for a

moment, then suddenly beamed, leaning close and taking Kati's clenched hands in her own.

"Kati," she said softly. "At last I can touch you, see you face-to-face as a person, not an image. All these years with you, and here you are, a woman, an empress of both this world and the place of creation. Who could know that by simply looking at you?"

Gently, she coaxed Kati's rigid fingers to relax, folding them out, and stroking the palm of one hand with a thumb. She looked into Kati's eyes and said, "Ah, that's what I want, not the red of wariness and suspicion, but the green that links you to our common ancestors. My blood is in you, Kati. If only you could have been my own child. You're a comfort to this old woman."

Kati's heart softened from the touch on her hand. "You're not so old," she murmured. "Your hands are soft, and smooth."

"Yours are hard, and calloused," said Mandughai, "but now we touch, and are real to each other, not phantom images or thoughts. We only have a little time, and it may be we'll never see each other in person again. Kati, I want to hold you for just a moment, if you'll let me. Please?"

Mandughai stood up, and Kati with her, wincing from a stab of pain in her leg. After sitting rigid, feet flat on the floor, her leg had begun to throb fiercely. Mandughai took a short step and put her arms around Kati, pressing against her with surprising strength, her mouth against Kati's ear, whispering to her.

"My dear little girl, my Tumatsin, I'll always be with you, until my last breath. Whenever you call, I'll be there, not as the empress of your childhood, but as the woman who holds you like her own daughter. From now on, I'm not Mandughai to you, but Abagai, the woman."

"Abagai," said Kati softly. Her hands had moved of their own will, and now rested lightly on Abagai's back.

"Call me, and seek the advice of your father as you grow in experience. He loves you with a devotion I'd not thought possible for him."

"I will, Mandu—Abagai. I'll always seek advice, and listen to it."

Abagai squeezed her gently, then released her and held her by the shoulders. "There is another you'll listen to, a man who also loves you and waits outside now with great impatience."

"Huomeng! He's here?"

Abagai laughed. "Your eyes glow wonderfully at the sound of his name, and your spirit softens with your love for him. For some moments, when you first arrived, I felt and saw a hardness in you that frightened me, but now it's gone. Don't allow your spirit to become hard, Kati. The love and compassion within you can yield a power greater than what you bring from the gong-shi-jie."

Kati nodded solemnly, for now there were tears in Abagai's eyes. Kati's heart seemed to crack, and she embraced Abagai tightly, their cheeks pressed together. "I've had three mothers in my life, not one. All have been good to me, but at times I've misunderstood them."

Abagai struggled from her grasp, eyes filled with tears as the door opened without warning, and Yesugen was standing there.

"They've arrived, mother. Should I bring them in now?"

"Yes, please," said Abagai sharply.

Yesugen gave Kati a sour look, but closed the door immediately, and went away.

Abagai put an arm around Kati, and walked her slowly towards the door. "I'll try to find more time for us before I leave, but there's something I must say while my daughter is distracted. Beware of Yesugen, Kati. For the moment, she is subdued by her fear of what you can do, but it won't last. She's also jealous of you, and I must take the blame for that. Deal cautiously with her when she comes to power. We have different agendas, and if she had her way now, she'd round up all the many emigrants from Lan-Sui, our dying inner planet, and move them here to be rid of them. She's hard inside, and militant like her late father. She believes in force, not persuasion; she will not respect your compassion, but only the power you can wield. Remember that."

"I will," said Kati. Her leg was throbbing horribly now, as if nerves there had suddenly awakened after being cut by the sword. "How long before she takes your place?"

Abagai opened the door, and Kati fought a limp as they went to the elevator.

"Some years, yet, without mischief on her part. Most of the people are still behind me. Yesugen's support has come from her field commanders, and the governor of Lan-Sui. Still, it'll be all too soon, and then there will be you and Yesugen to finish what I've tried to begin. I want *all* the people united, Kati, not just here, or on the worlds around my violent star. Our suns are a pair, Kati; they are one system. I want *all* our people united, and what you do on Shanji is only the beginning. *You* are the one to do it, not Yesugen. You or your successors; perhaps your own children."

They reached the elevator, and Abagai embraced her again. "Remember I'm ready to come to you when you want me. And remember this day, but don't dwell on it. Use love, patience and persuasion when you can, but don't forget the powers you have. Build on them, and be ready to use them as you did today, if necessary. You've seen horror today, and I hope you'll someday forgive me for forcing this war. I hope you'll forgive yourself if you ever have to do battle again. Dear Kati, I wish you well!"

Abagai hugged her fiercely as the elevator door opened. Kati kissed her softly on the cheek, and said, "You're still Mandughai to me. We will not be apart until the breath is gone from both of us."

Kati stepped into the elevator, but Abagai's back was to her as the doors closed. She felt sadness at leaving, was determined to see Abagai again before she left, and then there would always be those times in the gong-shi-jie. She felt pain, from her leg. She checked it, saw no bleeding, only burned flesh in and around the deep cut. She moved her hand over it, taking heat from the air, but it only hurt worse.

When she stepped out of the elevator she was limping and saw Mengmoshu and Juimoshu approaching, Yesugen in the lead. Juimoshu smiled, but her father looked grim. He took her by the shoulders, but did not embrace her, not in front of Yesugen. She felt him nearly bursting with the urge to do it anyway, even if it destroyed the image others had of him.

"There's blood all over you!" he said gruffly.

She smiled, reached over to touch a hand on her shoulder. "My leg is hurting badly now. I think there's dirt in the wound."

"Mengyao is with the flyer. He'll take you right back for treatment. We'll talk tonight."

Juimoshu ran a hand down Kati's arm as she passed silently by her, Yesugen waiting impatiently in the elevator, and then the doors were closed, she was hobbling alone to the loading ramp and painfully down it. She saw Mengyao standing near a flyer. Grinning, he raised a fist at her. She was filthy, bloody, and exhausted. Perhaps he found her appearance amusing.

Movement from her right, a man intercepting her at the base of the ramp. It was Huomeng, and tears came to her eyes at the sight of him.

Huomeng looked her up and down, then held out his arms.

"It looks to me as if you've had another one of your terrible days," he said.

Kati limped to him, and threw herself into his arms.

Mengyao finally came over to separate them, check Kati's wound and get them into the flyer. He lifted off gently as two more shuttles came in to land beyond the others. Soldiers of Mandughai were already loading their horses.

They circled the valley, part of the field of battle still littered with the dead, the rest scorched black by Kati's purple light. The ranks of Moshuguang, Hansui and Tumatsin now sat in clusters where they'd been when she'd left them. Mengyao flew low, wiggling the stubby wings of the craft, and Kati waved to the men through the clear canopy. Mouths opened in cheers she couldn't hear over the whine of the flyer, and a thousand swords were raised.

They lifted up, up, far above the dome of the city, and began settling down towards it. Huomeng's arm was around her, her head on his shoulder, and for a moment she could see the eastern valley, the tunnel into the mountain, the three peaks, and far beyond it the shimmering sea in the yellow light of Tengri-Khan.

Her home. Her place. Shanji.

EPILOGUE

Kati was awakened before dawn by the baby's pounding on her bladder and got out of bed. Huomeng mumbled something in his sleep and flopped over on his back, an arm draped across his face.

She put on a robe to ward off the morning chill, went out to the balcony overlooking the city from the imperial suite, and sat on the stone bench there to watch the sky brighten. Tengri-Khan was up, but still behind the mountain. The distant summits of Three Peaks were already dully illuminated in deep red, and only Tengri-Nayon was visible in the sky.

Kati sighed, and ran both hands over her distended stomach. There was further movement within her, something hard, perhaps a heel, making a little wave across her flesh. "Ooo, you are so *active* this morning! Yesui, my darling baby girl! I think you're in a hurry to be born."

She patted her stomach softly, and the movement ceased, but only for a moment. Now it felt like a hand, with little fingers exploring, a tickling feeling, and warm. Kati placed her hand at the site, and returned the warmth. She closed her eyes, and felt the child's presence in an abstract, instinctive way, like knowing that someone is in a dark room with you without seeing them. No visions, only a kind of alertness, and she knew her thoughts were received, without response.

The doctors had verified her child was a girl, but somehow she'd known it before then. Kati had named her Yesui because she liked the sound of it, and Huomeng had agreed with her. It was a sweet name for a child conceived the night before a battle that had left her mother scarred on one leg, Kati thought. It could have been no other time, for she'd spent two weeks regaining her strength, and then they'd restrained themselves from coming together until after their second wedding in the Kereit *ordu* by the sea.

Less than a year since war and death, and now the Empress of Shanji was nearly bursting to bring forth new life. The time had passed so quickly; she was just getting started in her duties, and now there would be a delay while her child was born.

The Emperor had lingered on for three months after being informed of his son's death, and Weimeng had been there for his final breath. Mengmoshu had taken over the duties of court, and continued his lobbying with the nobles until the body of Wang Shan-shi-jie was interred in a mountain vault next to his son's. A vote by the nobles had been solicited by Kati's father, and one month after the Emperor's death, Kati—formally Wang Mengnu-Shan-shi-jie—was installed as Empress in a quiet ceremony attended by nobles, Moshuguang, and Weimeng. Yang Xifeng had refused the invitation, and still remained in the private suite Kati had provided for her, mourning over the loss of husband and son. The woman had completely withdrawn, and Kati feared for her sanity, but until Yang Xifeng responded to Kati's probing there was nothing she could do to help her.

Kati caressed her stomach, and talked to her child while Three Peaks changed from red to orange. "People will think you're born too soon, or they will know the truth, but I'll not be the first noble girl to conceive before marriage. When you're older, you can tell them you're a love child, Yesui. They'll understand that." She laughed, and the baby moved inside her. Again Kati felt a relaxing warmth there.

Their civil marriage had been the signing of two papers, but Goldani would not stand for something so simple. She'd given them a great feast in the Kereit *ordu*; the hills had been covered with the *gert*s of visiting Tumatsin, and their first real night together as husband and wife had been spent in a *ger* within sight of the graves of her parents by the sea. They had placed green stones there before leaving.

So much in a short time: assembling her cabinet, the first meetings, the first arguments, requests for travel to visit her people in the east, Huomeng slaving away to understand the workings of Mandughai's gift shuttles before attempting to fly them, and now childbirth.

"I'll make them give me time for you," she said to the baby. "I'll not allow you to be cared for by a servant, and if they insist on a meeting when you're hungry, I'll suckle you right in front of them. Do you hear me, Yesui? Tickle, tickle."

Kati tickled her stomach; something pressed back, and was gone. Again, there was the feeling of a presence in her mind, a watchful, alert presence. Somehow, it made her feel wonderful. "I want to hold you in my arms right now, and show you what there is to see outside of your tight little place. I want to show you the stars, especially a big orange one that's home to a special lady I already miss. I know she'll like you. Do you see the picture of her I hold in my memory? Now, I'll put another picture beside her. See? That's me, Yesui. You're inside me, now, and my body feeds you. I'm your mother, Yesui."

The baby was now very quiet, as if listening to her.

"I wonder about what you'll be like. Will you inherit any powers from me? Will you have the intelligence and impatience of your father? I promise you will not grow

up alone. There will be a brother or sister for you to
fight with. It will keep you from being spoiled."

Kati caressed her stomach, but the baby didn't respond.
"I think you're listening, Yesui, and seeing the things I
show you. Do you see the Three Peaks out there, glowing
in morning light? That was my favorite place when I
was little. Our sun is behind me. Would you like to see
it close?"

The idea had come suddenly. Could her baby go with
her on a mental journey? Could there be harm if she tried
it? A short journey, so if Yesui were left behind, her mother's
presence would be missing for only a minute or so.

"There's a place I go to, a beautiful place with swirling
colors, and time doesn't move there. I'll show you our
star, and let you touch it if you can. It's a test, Yesui.
Watch, now. Watch for the pretty colors."

Kati breathed deeply and closed her eyes, moving
slowly, leisurely, so that Yesui might follow her steps if
she had the gifts of her mother. She didn't rush to the
matrix of purple light-points, but held it there, floating
in black void and letting the points grow steadily larger.

*We aim for one point, but any will do. We enter at
any point, and it will be marked for our return. Slowly,
now; getting closer.*

A flash, and the swirl of color was there, the purple
vortex by her, the deep red of Tengri-Khan's nearby.

*Are you here? Do you see it? The purple light? All
the universe, the stars, planets, galaxies, were made from
this light. Isn't it pretty?*

There *was* a presence with her; she could feel it, and
looked for a signature.

*Do you see me, Yesui? I show you what I look like to
your adopted grandmother in this place we call the gong-
shi-jie, the world of light, the place of creation. Do you
see my green eyes? What color are yours, Yesui? Show
me. Show me you're here!*

A wispy tendril of green extended from the vortex leading to herself, still connected there, wavering uncertainly as if fearful of moving further.

Yesui? Is that you? Come with me. We won't go far.

Kati drifted slowly towards the vortex that was Tengri-Khan, and looked back.

The green tendril was hurrying to catch up with her.

She could barely restrain her joy, and focused hard to keep from being drawn back to herself. *Oh, Mandughai! My little girl is with me in the gong-shi-jie, taking her first steps here! Come quick!*

There was no response, but now the tendril of green was with her again, close, wavering like a flame. Kati imagined her own aura reaching out to envelope it protectively.

Come with mother, dear.

The flash of transition, so fast, and she was in real space. Would she *ever* learn how to slow the transition? She concentrated hard, for in real space there were no signatures, not even visible auras, only the mental presence drawing energy from the place of light.

It was there again, but only as a feeling she hoped was not imagination. It was a feeling that she wasn't alone.

Tengri-Khan was close, and active. Three prominences issued from it, and there was a flare spouting near the equator, blowing a hole in the outer atmosphere and spewing ions through it. The flare was hot and bright, and Kati moved north of it to a cooler prominence, reaching out to touch the flame, and draw a wisp of it to her, the wisp a cloud of hot gas the size of Shanji.

Touch it, Yesui. Feel it. It cannot hurt you. Here, I'll bring it closer.

The cloud drew near, swirling madly, and cooling as it came, becoming deep red.

See how pretty? This is a piece of a star, Yesui. Your star. It keeps us warm, and gives us life on Shanji, so

*we'll leave it here to do its work for us. Follow me closely,
now. We're going back.*

Now was not the time for another attempt to bring
mass with her, and Kati didn't even consider it. She made
the transition with some apprehension, not certain that
Yesui had even been with her in real space. There was
an instant of fear, and then she saw the little, green tendril
wavering there, its tail still attached to the deep red vortex
of Tengri-Khan.

*Did you come with me? Did you see the star, or stay
here? This is enough for a first time, and Mandughai
still hasn't come to see you. Let's go back, now. Stay close.*

The tendril detached from the vortex, and followed
her back to the signature of her true self on Shanji. As
she descended into it, she looked back to be sure the
tendril was right with her, and saw a dark shape writhing
along behind them like a snake.

The flash of transition, and then a thunderous crash
that echoed all around her. She felt a wave of heat on
her face and opened her eyes, nearly blinded by a column
of light rising up from Three peaks as if there had been
an explosion there. The light dimmed rapidly and she
saw a swirling cloud of dust and glowing gas ascending
from the peaks to form a flat-topped, roiling mass high
overhead. The thunder went on and on, and her child
was kicking furiously inside her.

"Kati! Kati, where are you?" The voice was Huomeng's.

Kati gasped, and put her hands on her stomach. *What
have I done?* The pounding was terrible. "Quiet, quiet;
we're here, now, and it's safe. We're together again." She
willed calmness, and brought heat to her hands. The baby
pushed up against both of them, but still moved back
and forth, as if rocking inside her.

"There you are! What happened? What's *that*?"
Huomeng knelt at her side, pointing to the sky.

"I don't know," she said, her voice quavering.

"It looks like an explosion on the peaks! I thought we were under attack again! Are you all right?" He put an arm around her, placed a hand on her stomach, his eyes widening. "It frightened the baby, whatever it was. Doesn't that hurt?"

"Yes, it does, but it's my fault. Something happened— when we came back—I don't know."

"What?"

Kati looked at him solemnly. "I took Yesui to the gong-shi-jie. I wanted to see—I wanted her to see Tengri-Khan. I wanted—"

"She was there with you?"

"I—I think so."

Huomeng rubbed her stomach, and leaned his head against her arm. "I think she's calming down, now."

Kati reached over, and ruffled his hair. "She feels her father's hand," she said, "and her father needs to put some clothes on. Aren't you cold?"

"Not while I'm by you," he said, caressing her.

They watched the roiling cloud, Kati breathing deeply until the baby was calm again, but she could not hide her thoughts from the man she loved.

"What kind of child have we made?" he finally asked.

"We'll know soon," said Kati.

The experience had not been terrifying, but exciting to her, and now the comforting touches and sounds that made her sleepy. Yesui opened her eyes again, and saw her hands, legs and feet bathed in green light within her tiny place. She pressed against the softness around her, and felt the warmth coming, the feelings from two beings, not one, but it was one of them she'd seen in that beautiful place with all the colors. At first, there had been the pretty lights, connected by thin strands that she had to stretch aside to follow the being who'd led her so quickly to where the colors were, and then again to where she touched something that followed her on her return. That something had lost its color for awhile, then suddenly reappeared, close behind her with heat she found threatening, and so she told it to go away to a place she'd seen only moments before, and it went there.

The sound had been terrible, and her place seemed suddenly smaller, pressing in on her. She'd pushed back on it in surprise, and held it there, but now she didn't have to press so hard. The feelings were calmer, more normal, and the deep red glows of the touches had returned. She pressed her feet against them, and tickled them with her hands, feeling wonderful again.

Yesui yawned mightily in her warm, liquid place, and closed her eyes. And suddenly there were two great eyes there, glowing emerald green, and new sounds, not heard, but felt in her mind, words she didn't understand now, but would hear again later.

Yesui. Yesui—my child. I am Mandughai. I was with your mother, and your grandmother, and now I will be with you. Sleep, now, and build your strength. You have much to learn from your mother and I, and there is something I would have you do for me when you're a woman.